DUDLEY PUBLIC LIBRARIES

The loan of this book may be renewed if not required by other readers, by contacting the library from which it was borrowed.

BL33

RB55

D1313315

000003150950

Royal Weddings

Royal Weddings
A Nine-Month Surprise

ANNIE WEST

MAISEY YATES

KAT CANTRELL

MILLS & BOON

First Published in Great Britain 2022
by Mills & Boon, an imprint of HarperCollins*Publishers* Ltd,
1 London Bridge Street, London, SE1 9GF

www.harpercollins.co.uk

HarperCollins*Publishers*
Macken House, 39/40 Mayor Street Upper,
Dublin 1, D01 C9W8

ROYAL WEDDINGS: A NINE-MONTH SURPRISE
© 2022 Harlequin Enterprises ULC.

Sheikh's Royal Baby Revelation © 2019 Annie West
The Prince's Pregnant Mistress © 2016 Maisey Yates
Matched to a Prince © 2014 Kat Cantrell

ISBN: 978-0-263-31806-7

MIX
Paper | Supporting
responsible forestry
FSC™ C007454

This book is produced from independently certified FSC™ paper
to ensure responsible forest management.

For more information visit: www.harpercollins.co.uk/green

Printed and Bound in Spain using 100% Renewable electricity at
CPI Black Print, Barcelona

SHEIKH'S ROYAL BABY REVELATION

ANNIE WEST

For the late-night laughter and plotting
just when I needed it!

Thank you AA, Bron, Kandy, Shaz,
Denise, Rachel and Reeze.

CHAPTER ONE

ASHRAF WOKE TO the sound of a door slamming and the taste of blood in his mouth. Blood and dust.

He lay facedown, head and ribs burning with pain, the rest of him merely battered. Slowly he forced his eyelids open. He was in a dark room, lightened only by a spill of moonlight through a small, high window.

Then came rough voices using an obscure local dialect. Three men, he counted, walking away. He strained to hear over the merciless hammering in his head.

They'd kill him tomorrow. After Qadri arrived to enjoy the spectacle and pay them for the successful kidnap.

Ashraf gritted his jaw, ignoring the spike of pain in the back of his skull.

Of course Qadri was behind this. Who else would dare? The bandit leader had even begun to style himself as a provincial chief in the last years of Ashraf's father's rule.

The old Sheikh had moved slowly when dealing with problems in this remote province, the poorest and most backward in the country. He'd left Qadri alone as long as the bandit preyed only on his own people.

But Ashraf wasn't cut from the same cloth as his father. The old Sheikh was dead and Ashraf had introduced changes that would see Qadri dispossessed.

He could expect no mercy from his captors.

Ashraf wasn't naïve enough to believe Qadri would negotiate his release. The man would fight for his fiefdom the only way he knew: with violence.

What better way to intimidate poor villagers than to execute the new Sheikh? To prove that modernisation and the rule of law had no place in the mountains that had only known Qadri's authority for two decades?

Ashraf cursed his eagerness to see a new irrigation project, accepting the invitation to ride out with just a local guide and a single bodyguard into an area that was supposedly now completely safe.

Safe!

His belly clenched as he thought of his bodyguard, Basim, thrown from his horse by a tripwire rigged between two boulders.

Ashraf had vaulted from his horse to go to him, only to be felled by attackers. There was little satisfaction in knowing they hadn't overpowered him easily.

Was Basim alive? Ashraf's gut clenched at the thought of his faithful guard abandoned where he'd fallen.

Fury scoured his belly. But fury wouldn't help now. Only cold calculation. He had to find a way out. Or a way to convey his location to those searching for him.

His father had always said he had the devil's own luck. It had been a sneering accusation, not a fond appraisal, but for the first time Ashraf found himself hoping the old man had been right. He could do with some luck. And the energy to move.

A slight scuffling broke his train of thought.

He wasn't alone.

Ashraf refused to lie there waiting for another knockout blow.

Ignoring the pain that exploded through him at the movement, he rolled over and up onto his feet, only to stop abruptly, his right arm yanked back.

Spinning round, Ashraf discovered he was chained to a wall. Another turn, so swift his bruised head swam and pain seared his ribs. But with his back to the wall, his feet wide, he was ready to take on any assailant.

'Come on. Show yourself.'

Nothing. No movement. No sound.

Then, out of the darkness, something gleamed. Something pale that shone in the faint moonlight.

His guard was *blond*?

Ashraf blinked. It wasn't an hallucination.

Whoever it was, he wasn't local.

'Who are you?' He switched to French, then English, and heard an answering hiss of breath.

English, then.

The silence grew, ratcheting his tension higher.

'You don't know?' It was a whisper, as if the speaker feared being overheard.

Ashraf frowned. Had the blow to his head damaged his hearing? It couldn't be, yet it sounded like—

'You're a *woman*?'

'You're not one of them, then.' Her voice was flat, yet taut, as if produced by vocal cords under stress.

Stress he could understand.

'By "one of them" you mean…?'

'The men who brought me here. The men who…' Ashraf heard a shudder in her voice '…kidnapped me.'

'Definitely not one of them. They kidnapped me too.'

For which they'd pay. Ashraf had no intention of dying in what he guessed was a shepherd's hut, from the smell of livestock. Though the sturdy chain and handcuff indicated that the place was used for other, sinister purposes. He'd heard whispers that Qadri was involved in people-smuggling. That women in particular sometimes vanished without a trace, sold to unscrupulous buyers across the border.

The pale glow came closer. Ashraf saw her now. Silvery hair, pale skin and eyes that looked hollow in the shadows. She swallowed and he made out the convulsive movement of her throat. Calm overlying panic. At least she wasn't hysterical.

'Are you hurt?' he asked.

A tiny huff of amusement greeted his question. 'That's my line. You're the one who's bleeding.'

Ashraf looked down. Parting his torn shirt, he discovered a long cut, no longer bleeding. A knife wound, he guessed, but not deep.

'I'll live.'

Despite the playboy reputation Ashraf had once acquired, he'd done his time in the army. A stint which his father had ensured was tougher and more dangerous than usual. Ashraf knew enough about wounds to be sure he'd be alive when his executioner arrived tomorrow.

'How about you?'

Tori stared at him, wanting to laugh and cry at the same time.

Except tears wouldn't help. And she feared if she laughed it would turn into hysteria.

'Just scrapes and bruises.' She was lucky and she knew it. Her jaw ached where she'd been backhanded across the face but that was the worst. Despite the hungry gleam she'd seen in her captors' eyes as they'd inspected her, they hadn't touched her except to subdue her and throw her in here.

Looking at this injured man, she trembled, thinking she'd got off lightly. So far.

He'd been unconscious when they'd dumped him on the dirt floor. Either he'd put up a mighty fight or they had a grudge against him to beat him up like that.

She hadn't had time to investigate how badly he was injured. His shirt was torn and stained and his head was bloody on one side. Even so, he stood tall. His ragged shirt hung from wide, straight shoulders and his dusty trousers clung to a horseman's thighs. He looked fit and powerful despite his injuries. Under the grime he had strong-boned features that she guessed might be handsome, or at least arresting.

Would she see him in daylight or would they come for her before that? Terror shuddered down her spine and turned her knees to jelly. Panic bit her insides as she imagined what was in store for her.

'Where are we?' Like her, the stranger kept his voice low, yet something about the smooth, deep note eased a fraction of the tension pinching her.

'Somewhere in the foothills. I couldn't see from the back of the van.' She wrapped her arms around her middle, re-membering that trip, facing a grim stranger with a knife in his hand.

'There's a road?' The man before her pounced on that.

'Part of the way. I walked the last part blindfolded.' Which was why her knees were rubbed raw after she'd stumbled and fallen time and again over uneven ground.

'Is there a guard at the door?'

'I don't think so.'

She'd heard the men talking as they walked away. Even so she crept to the door, peeking through the gap between it and the wall. No one. She moved along the wall but it was surprisingly solid, with no chinks to peer through.

As if it had been used as a prison before.

Tori thought of the heavy chain that secured her com-panion and her stomach curdled.

'There's a light further away. A campfire, I think. But no one here as far as I can tell.'

Why would they bother? The door was bolted. Her com-panion was chained and she didn't have as much as a pocket knife to use as a tool.

What wouldn't she give for her geologist's hammer right now? Designed for cracking rocks, the sharp end might prise open the chain and it would make an effective weapon.

'What are you doing?' He'd turned his back on her and she heard the rattle of metal links.

'Testing this chain.' There was a grunt, then a muffled oath.

She crossed to stand behind him. 'You won't pull it out,' she whispered. 'It's fixed securely. Believe me.'

'You've checked?' His hunched shoulders straightened as he lifted his head and turned around.

Suddenly he was closer than she'd expected, towering above her. Her hissed breath cut the thick silence.

Only hours ago she'd been grabbed by strangers: big men who'd overpowered her despite her frantic struggle. Fear curdled her belly anew and adrenaline pumped hard in her blood, freezing her to the spot.

Yet as she stiffened the man stepped back towards the wall. Giving her space.

Logic said he wasn't the enemy. Her abductors had kidnapped him too.

Tori sucked in oxygen and tried to steady her breathing. In the gloom she met his eyes. It was too dark to be sure but she'd swear she read sympathy in his face. And something else. Pity?

Because the fate of a woman abducted by violent men would be truly pitiful.

Tori stiffened her knees against the images she'd tried so hard not to picture. She couldn't afford to crack up now.

'Of course I checked.' She made herself concentrate on the conversation, not her fear. 'I thought if I could pry it loose I might use it as a weapon when they came back.'

'One against three?'

Despite their desperate situation, Tori felt a throb of satisfaction at surprising him. 'I won't go down without a fight.'

'It would be safer if you don't resist.'

Tori opened her mouth to protest but he went on.

'Three to one aren't good odds. Wait till you're alone with one of them. Someone will probably transport you elsewhere tomorrow.'

'How do you know? What did they say about me?' Her voice was harsh with fear.

He shook his head, then winced. The soft whisper that followed might have been in a language she didn't know, but she knew a curse when she heard one.

'I didn't hear them mention you,' he said finally. 'But their leader arrives tomorrow. They're expecting payment for their efforts then. They'll leave us be until he arrives.'

Tori sagged, her knees giving way suddenly. She stumbled to the wall, propping herself against it. For hours she'd been on tenterhooks, expecting at any moment—

'Are you okay?' He moved closer before stopping, as if recalling her earlier recoil.

She nodded. When she opened her mouth to reply a jagged, out-of-control laugh escaped. She clapped a hand to her lips, hating the hot tears behind her eyes and the sensation that she was on the verge of collapse.

It was ridiculous to feel relief, hearing she was safe for tonight. She was still in terrible danger. Even so, her exhausted body reacted to the news by slumping abruptly.

Firm hands caught her upper arms as she sank, taking her weight and easing her descent to the floor.

His hands were big and hard, yet surprisingly gentle. Tori heard the clank of metal as he withdrew, hunkering before her.

'Sorry.' The word wobbled and she tried again. 'I just…' She looked up into dark eyes. 'What else did they say? What are they going to do with us?'

Did she imagine that his expression turned blank? In this light it was impossible to tell.

'Nothing about you.' He paused, then continued slowly. 'I have no proof, but I suspect they'll take you over the border.'

Like a smuggled commodity? Tori bit her bottom lip. She'd heard stories of the illegal slave trade, particularly in women. Nausea rose as she contemplated where she might end up.

'If that's so there might be a chance to escape. Maybe some of them will stay here.' Tori knew she was grasping at straws but it was better than giving up hope.

'I can guarantee it.' His tone grabbed her attention.

'Why? What else did you hear?'

He shrugged those wide shoulders and sank cross-legged before her. Despite the heavy chain and his injuries he looked at ease. Strange how his air of confidence reassured her.

'Their leader is my enemy. I think it fair to assume he'll be more focused on me than you.' There was a note in that deep voice that sounded almost like wry humour. Grim lines bracketed his mouth.

Suddenly Tori remembered the gesture one of their captors had made as he'd chained this man to the wall. One man had asked a question and another had laughed, a sound that had sent a chill skittering down her backbone. He'd said something sharp and dragged his finger across his throat in a gesture that crossed all languages. Death.

They were going to kill this man.

She should warn him.

Except even as she thought it she realised he knew. Tori read it in that stern face, a chiaroscuro masterpiece of male strength, and knew he wouldn't surrender to fate. Not with that pugnacious set to his jaw.

Instinctively she reached out, her hand fleetingly touching his, feeling living warmth flow into her chilled fingers. 'What can we do?'

For long seconds he surveyed her. Then gave another infinitesimal shrug. 'Check for a way out.'

'I've done that. It's *all* I've done for the last five hours or so.' That and try not to panic.

'I don't suppose you've got a hairpin?'

'For picking the lock on your handcuff?' Tori shook her head. 'I don't need hairpins with a ponytail.'

He watched the swish of her hair around her shoulders and something unexpected zipped through her. Something other than fear and despair.

Tori stilled.

'And I unfortunately didn't think to bring bolt cutters for the chain.'

She choked down a laugh. It was only mildly amusing, but in her emotional state any humour was a welcome break from constant fear.

'The windows are too small even for you.' He paused. 'The roof?'

He rose in a single fluid motion that revealed enviable core strength and left Tori gawping. A short time ago he'd been unconscious.

'Come.' He extended his hand.

She didn't know if it was the command in his tone or not, but a second later her hand was in his and he was drawing her up. They stood so close that she identified the tang of cinnamon and male, and the comforting smell of horse, before he stepped away, surveying the roof.

'Here.' He turned and beckoned.

'What do you have in mind?'

'Hands on my shoulders. I'll lift you so you can check for a way out.'

'But *you* can't get out.' Her gaze dropped to the manacle on his wrist.

'That's no reason for you not to try.'

That voice, as smooth and rich as her favourite coffee, warmed her as his gaze captured hers. Tori's racing thoughts stilled. She felt a moment of communion, as if this stranger understood the guilt that made her protest even as the idea of escape made her thrill with excitement.

'What's your name?'

The question made her pause. What would it be like to hear him ask that in different circumstances? There was something about this man…the resonance of his deep voice, his inner strength in the face of adversity, his sureness… that drew her.

Her heart beat hard against her ribs.

'Tori. And you?'

'You may call me Ash.'

Before she could wonder at his phrasing, he continued.

'If you can get onto the roof and away, there's a chance you can raise the alert before daybreak.'

He didn't have to spell out what would happen when day came. That captor's slicing gesture was vivid in her mind.

'But I don't know where I am. Or where to go.'

Long fingers folded around her hand, steadying her. 'You don't have to know. Get away from the hut and the campfire. Stay low. When you're a safe distance out, circle the camp. You'll eventually come across the trail where you entered. Keep out of sight and follow the trail.'

'And hope to find the road or a village?'

'You have a better idea?'

Tori shook her head. It was their best chance. Possibly Ash's *only* chance.

'Let's do this.' She planted her palms on his shoulders, then sucked in a breath as he bent, wrapped his big hands around her and lifted.

It was probably only fifteen minutes before they admitted defeat. To Ashraf it felt like hours.

Frustrating hours, with that cursed chain curtailing his movements. They had only been able to explore one end of the roof and it was disappointingly sturdy.

The slashing pain across his ribs had become a sear of agony. His head pounded. Stiff muscles ached from boosting his companion high, then holding her up while she strained and twisted, trying to find a weakness in the roof structure she could exploit.

Physical exertion compounded with frustration at his helplessness. But it was another sort of torture, holding Tori.

Trying to ignore her rounded breasts and buttocks. Standing solid, holding her high, his face pressed to her soft belly as she heaved and twisted, trying to force her way through the roof. Feeling the narrowness of her waist, inhaling her female essence, fresh and inviting, despite the overlay of dust and fear.

Beneath the loose trousers and long-sleeved shirt she was all woman. Firmly toned, supple and fragrantly feminine.

By the time he lowered her for the last time and sagged against the wall his body shook all over. From reaction to his wounds. From fury at himself for allowing Qadri to get the better of him.

And from arousal. Flagrant and flaming hot.

Ashraf told himself it was the adrenaline high—a response to life-or-death danger. Naturally his reactions were heightened. His need to fight his way free. His primal urge was to defy death in the same way generations had done since the dawn of time, by losing himself in the comfort of a warm, willing woman. Spilling his seed in the hope of ensuring survival, if not for himself, then for the next generation.

'Are you all right?'

She was so close her breath was a puff of warm air against his face.

'I *knew* it was too much with your wounds. We should have stopped earlier. Are you bleeding again?'

A gentle hand touched his chest just above his wound.

'Don't!' Ashraf grabbed her hand, flattening it against his chest. His eyes snapped wide and he found her staring up at him, clearly concerned. This close, he saw her eyes were pale. Blue? Grey? Maybe amber?

Realisation slammed into him.

She feels it too.

The tug of need. The connection between two people trapped and desperate. The powerful urge to find comfort in the face of impending death. For, even if she wasn't being executed in the morning, Tori's fate was dark.

'Don't fuss. I'm fine.' He pulled her palm away from his body. Yet he couldn't bring himself to relinquish her hand.

Because her touch brought unexpected comfort?

He was furious with himself for getting captured. Frustrated that, after all that had happened, maybe his life would end tomorrow and his father would have been right. The old man had said he'd never amount to anything. If Ashraf died within the first six months of his reign, with none of his changes cemented in place...

He released Tori and turned from her searching stare.

'I'm not fussing.'

She drew herself up so her head topped his chin. Her little sound of frustration reminded him of his favourite falcon, fluffing up her feathers in huffy disapproval when he didn't immediately release her for flight.

'I apologise.' He paused, surprised as the unfamiliar words escaped. 'I'm not bleeding again.' Hopefully. 'It was kind of you to be concerned.'

'Kind?' She choked on the word and it hit Ashraf that she was fighting back tears.

For him? No, she couldn't know that he faced death tomorrow. It was a reaction to her kidnap. She'd been courageous—more courageous than most men he knew—projecting a calm façade, persevering in trying to find a way out when many would have given up.

'Thoughtful,' he amended.

She shook her head and silvery hair flared out from her ponytail. Ashraf's hands curled tight. He knew an urgent desire to see that shimmering hair loose, so he could tunnel his fingers through it.

Temptation was a cruel thing. He couldn't take what he wanted. Or ask for it. Not from this proud woman who still fought panic.

'You'd better get some rest,' he murmured, his voice gruff as he ruthlessly harnessed his baser, selfish instincts. 'That's what I intend to do.'

Ashraf lowered himself to the floor. He felt every muscle, every movement. His wrist had rubbed raw against the manacle and there seemed little hope of escape.

Yet despite the pain he felt a sense of exultation. He was

still alive. He had no intention of meekly submitting to execution for Qadri's pleasure.

Ashraf had spent his life fighting for his place, proving himself, ignoring the jibes. Showing his father that his disdain meant nothing. Thumbing his nose at him by building a public profile as a pleasure-seeking playboy, delighting in scandals that he knew would rock the old man.

Now he was back in Za'daq and everything had changed. Especially given his brother's recent sacrifice. Ashraf's belly contracted at the thought of Karim.

'I'd feel better if you'd let me examine your wounds.'

Tori knelt beside him. So close he barely had to move to touch her face, her rounded breast. Too close for a man so severely tempted.

'There's nothing you can do in this light. Unless you have a torch and a first aid kit hidden somewhere?'

She pursed her lips and looked away, that silvery mane sliding over one shoulder.

Instantly he regretted his harsh response. He felt ashamed. It wasn't concern for Karim that had made him snap, but his visceral sexual response to her. He wanted things he shouldn't.

'I'm sorry.' It was the second time he'd apologised. 'That was uncalled-for. You're right, there's some pain, but it's not as bad as it looks.' What were bruises and cuts in comparison to what tomorrow held for him? 'But there's something you *could* do.'

'What's that?'

'Rest. We need to conserve our strength.' He stretched out, stifling a groan as abused muscles throbbed.

After a long silence she finally followed his example, lying down nearby.

Ashraf didn't sleep. Instead he focused on tomorrow, wondering if his security detail would find him before it was too late. Wondering if Basim was alive.

Finally a tiny sound caught his attention. Were Tori's teeth chattering? The desert night had turned chill.

'Come here, Tori. We'll be warmer together.'

She lifted her head. 'But your injuries…'

He reached out his untethered arm. 'Snuggle against this side.'

When she did Ashraf bit his tongue against a sigh of satisfaction.

'Put your head on my shoulder.' She complied and he felt the gentle whisper of her breath through his torn shirt. Soft curves cushioned his side, silky strands of hair tickled his neck and her hand rested warm at his waist.

Ashraf lifted his hand to stroke her hair. It was silken. Like the softest cushions in the royal harem, spun in the days when the Sheikhs of Za'daq had had a bevy of concubines devoted to their pleasure.

Pressed against him from shoulder to knee, she felt…

His breath clogged in his lungs and a tremor started low in his body, vibrating out.

'Am I too heavy?'

She shifted as if to move away and Ashraf rolled a little towards her, capturing her knee between his.

'Just relax. You're not hurting me.'

It wasn't strictly true. He was definitely in pain. But the ache of his wounds and the indignity of the chain were eclipsed by another sort of pain. The taut stretch of a body fighting luscious temptation.

Ashraf's mouth stretched in a mirthless smile. He'd spent years giving in to temptation. He wished he had more experience at resisting it. Perhaps that was why the tension he felt was so acute, the tug of war between honour and desire so fierce.

But honour won.

Finally he felt her breathing slow. She shifted, shimmying her hips as if to get more comfortable, and the friction was exquisite torture. But it was a torture he willingly bore.

Till she moved her arm and her hand accidentally brushed the evidence of his arousal straining against his trousers.

She froze.

Everything inside him stilled.

Ashraf swore they both stopped breathing.

Then his blood pumped again—harder, more urgent. His groin tightened. He had to force himself not to tilt his pelvis, seeking the feel of her palm against him.

'It's okay. You're safe with me, Tori.' Could she tell he spoke through gritted teeth? 'Nothing's going to happen.'

Silence. He waited for her to scurry away.

Then he knew he was hearing things when she said, 'Maybe I don't want to be safe with you.'

CHAPTER TWO

TORI HEARD THE words spill out and then Ash's swift intake of breath. But she refused to play coy. Not when this might be her last night alive.

All afternoon she'd fought not to imagine what awaited her at the mercy of her kidnappers. Pain. Forced sex. Slavery.

A few hours ago she'd have said experiencing desire in her current situation was impossible. But that was before Ash. Before they worked together. Before his matter-of-fact courage bolstered her own flagging determination to be strong. Before the touch of his hand and his understanding made her feel connected to him. Before the undeniable flare of arousal ignited in her belly and saturated her skin till she burned up with it.

She knew their excruciatingly intense circumstances created the connection. Yet it wasn't quite so simple. There was something about this man that spoke to her at a primal, instinctive level. Tori knew with a resolute certainty that defied explanation that this was more than a simple response to danger.

She'd never known such a potent link. As if they'd weathered a lifetime's emotions in a couple of hours.

Never felt such an urgent need for a man.

Never felt so reckless or so absolutely sure of what she wanted.

'Tori?'

His voice was deep and gravelly, his smooth tone banished by shock. Or, she hoped, by matching desire.

She moved her hand tentatively across his flat abdomen, resisting the urge to slip it lower and explore him more intimately. Iron-hard muscles clenched at her touch and a tremor racked his big body.

Tori's heart clenched in sympathy. He was so vibrantly, emphatically alive. She couldn't bear the thought that to-morrow—

Long fingers brushed the hair back from her face, the gesture achingly tender. Then, to her horror, he stroked his thumb across her cheek and smeared the hot track of a tear she hadn't even felt fall.

'Ah, *habibti*.'

She heard the clink of metal as he wrapped his arms around her and pulled her up against him. Soft words fell into her ears as his lips moved against her eyelids, cheeks and hair. The ribbon of words was lilting and beautiful, like the unexpected sound of a spring, bubbling up clear and life-giving in a desert.

Greedily Tori drank in the sound as she absorbed his tender caresses. Blindly she tilted her head, seeking his lips, letting her leg fall across his thighs as she sought purchase to climb up his tall body.

'You have my word, Tori. If there's a way to save—'

Opening her eyes, she pressed her hand to his lips. 'Don't.'

She breathed deep, feeling her breasts push against him. Was she too heavy? But when she made to pull back the warm steel of his embrace held her.

'Don't talk about tomorrow. Please. I only want to think about tonight.'

She was so close that even in the gloom she saw the shift of muscles as he clenched his jaw. His face was strongly made, with bold lines against which the sensuous curve of his lips seemed shockingly desirable. Through the blood and dust she thought she imagined laughter lines near his eyes, but the grooves around his mouth spoke of weighty concerns.

The man's injured. He's likely to die tomorrow. Despite

that, he's done his best to stop you falling apart. Of course he has more on his mind than gratifying your selfish desires.

Tori's heart contracted. He might be aroused, but that was a simple physical response to proximity and, perhaps, to danger. It didn't mean he wanted her. Perhaps he had a woman. A wife, even.

Choking back an exclamation of self-loathing, she pulled back, determined to put distance between them.

But his arms stopped her. She wriggled, trying to escape, but couldn't find purchase to resist his strength—not without elbowing his injured side.

'Let me go,' she whispered. 'I need to—'

'I know what you need, *habibti*. I need it too. So very badly.'

His voice ground low through her body, awakening those few dormant female nerve centres not already attuned to his closeness.

Tori felt herself quicken and soften, warmth spreading in a wave of anticipation for his big, hard body. Her legs splayed around his, her pelvis pressed needily against his hipbone.

Flame scorched her cheeks as one large hand slid down to cup her bottom and pull her closer. Thoughts splintered at the dazzle of carnal pleasure erupting through her.

'I...'

She fought to find a coherent chain of thought when her body was already immersed in an intimate conversation with his. What did she want to say? The important thing?

He tilted her chin so she looked into hooded eyes. 'Talk to me, Tori. Are you certain you want this?'

She wanted it, *him*, so badly she shook with the force of her desire.

'Are you married?' The words sounded strange, in a breathless voice she hardly recognised, but now the thought had entered her head she couldn't ignore it. 'Is there anyone—?'

'No one.' His tone was grave. 'And you?'

Tori shook her head.

She felt his chest rise beneath her on a sighing breath.

Even so, what had seemed so natural, so easy, moments before, now felt difficult. She felt gauche, unsure how to proceed. Till his mouth curved slowly into a smile that stole her breath and set her heart fluttering up in her throat.

She'd had an impression of Ash as strong, ultra-masculine and handsome in a severe way. But when he bestowed that smile on her Tori discovered he was far, far more. Attractive didn't cover it. Sexy was closer. Her befuddled brain grappled for a second to find a word that did him justice. Then she gave up and simply *felt*.

His hand rose to the back of her head, pulling her closer. She went eagerly, sinking into a kiss that was devastating for all its gentle persuasiveness. Fire sizzled and sparked from her toes to her ears. From her lips to her breasts and her womb.

Her mouth softened on his, opening automatically around his tongue. She didn't even try to prevent the mew of delight as he delved deeper, inviting her to let go on the wave of wellbeing that swept her up.

The kiss went on and on, deliberate and slow, stoking the blaze between them. Till his hand cupped her breast and Tori seized up. Not in rejection, but because the sensation of that hard hand so gentle on her was exquisite.

She pulled her head back, sucking in a dizzying draught of air, meeting eyes that gleamed like obsidian in the shadowy light.

His hand froze. Clearly he'd misinterpreted her withdrawal.

Once more Tori felt a surge of respect for this man who even now let scruples override potent need.

In another place, another time, she'd want to discover everything she could about him. But they had so little time. The thought brought a desperate sob to her throat. She swallowed it and pressed his hand to her breast, revelling in the delicious sensations.

She leaned down so her lips grazed his ear. 'I want you, Ash. But I'm afraid of hurting you.' He'd stopped bleeding, but she didn't want to reopen his wounds.

She felt a rumbling beneath her that, remarkably, she identified as laughter. 'Let me worry about that.'

While she was still catching her breath he rolled her onto her back, only to freeze mid-movement. It took her a second to realise his arm was stretched out behind him, caught by the chain.

The reminder of their dire circumstances should have splintered the brief comfort of the moment. Except Ash sounded merely rueful as he murmured, 'Not my smoothest move.'

His humour made this once more about *them*, not what lay beyond these walls, and Tori bit down a smile as together they shuffled awkwardly across the floor till Ash had the freedom to move both arms.

'Better,' he whispered, gathering her close. 'Much better.'

Broad shoulders blocked out the moonlight as he bent and kissed her hard on the lips. Then, as everything in her clamoured for more, he pulled back, propping himself on his good arm as he fumbled for the zip of her trousers.

'Let me. It will be quicker.' Excitement fizzed in her blood.

When he moved back to deal with his own trousers Tori stripped off her boots, trousers and knickers. She'd never had a one-night stand but she felt no embarrassment, just an urgency that grew with every passing moment.

'Leave your shirt.' Ash's hand on her shoulder pushed her gently down onto her back. 'It will protect you from the floor.'

His own shirt hung open to reveal a wide expanse of muscled chest. Her hungry gaze began to rove him, only to stop at the dark line across a couple of ribs. Her stomach clenched.

Suddenly it wasn't sex on her mind but the fate that awaited Ash tomorrow. The thought of what they'd do to him and what they might do to her—

'Changed your mind?'

His voice held no inflection other than curiosity—as if he had no qualms about stopping. Yet even in the gloom there was no mistaking the tension in his tall frame or the sight of his arousal straining towards her.

He wanted this, needed it, as much as she.

The sight of him made her wet between the legs, her muscles tightening in anticipation. Tori drew a shuddery breath, shoving away all thoughts of tomorrow.

Live for the moment had never held such profound meaning.

'Wouldn't it be safer if I was on top? With your injuries?'

His chuckle was liquid chocolate, or perhaps a shot of malt whisky, heating her blood. 'Probably. Call me a traditionalist, but I want to lie between your beautiful thighs and take us both to Paradise.'

His words ratcheted her level of arousal from fierce to ballistic. As did the nimble way he flicked open her shirt buttons, then made short work of her front-opening bra, pulling it wide to survey her in silence.

Tori's heart battered her ribs as she felt the cold night air drift across her puckering nipples and waited for his next move. Then he smiled. Another of those charismatic smiles that drove a spike of sharp emotion straight through her rib cage and stopped her breath.

When he spoke again it was in a language she didn't understand. A fluid ripple of sound that wrapped itself around her, caressing her as effectively as those callused hands stroking her breasts, waist and hips. Drawing her into a world of seductive urgency.

Then Ash lowered himself over her and she almost cried

out at how right it felt. Strong, hair-roughened thighs between hers. The weight of him heavy against her. The jut of his hipbones. Broad shoulders above her and heat…heat everywhere.

Tori drew her knees up above his hips and heard a grunt of masculine pleasure. Then long fingers slid low, past her abdomen, down to her hot, slick, swollen centre. She jolted as a shock of pleasure raced through her. His fingers moved again, circling and teasing.

Her hand on his wrist stopped him. 'No. Don't. I just want *you.*'

She was strung so tight, on an unbearable edge of arousal, that she feared one more touch might fling her into rapture. But she needed something more profound than the touch of his hand. She craved the ultimate connection, the intimacy of their two bodies linked as one.

Tori sighed her relief when he nodded. Even so Ash took his time, surveying her face as if memorising it. Tori *felt* his gaze cross her cheeks, lips and forehead. And when his hand brushed the hair back from her face it was a gesture that spoke of tenderness and restraint, for she felt the tiniest tremor in those long fingers.

'Your hair is like silk,' he murmured.

Tori wanted to say something profound, to offer this strong, gentle man something to match the gift of his tenderness. But there were no easy words.

Instead she lifted her own hand, cupping the stubble-roughened jaw, hard and warm. She felt his slow pounding pulse, then skimmed her hand higher into dark hair that felt thick yet soft. His eyes closed as she massaged the uninjured side of his scalp.

He positioned himself against her. Instinctively she lifted her pelvis, feeling that velvet weight nudge her. Tori held her breath as he pushed, long and slow and further, surely, than any previous possession. Her eyes widened and his grew more heavy-lidded as they held their breaths at the perfection of their joining. The moment went on and on till finally Ash was lodged deep within, vital and impossibly, lavishly male.

A quiver ran through Tori, starting at the muscles surrounding him and spreading till she trembled all over. A matching shiver rippled across his wide shoulders and muscled arms.

Then he withdrew, and the movement was so exquisitely arousing that Tori had to bite her lip to stop from crying out. Ash's lips pulled back in a grimace that looked like pain, but she knew it was a sign of pleasure and his battle for control.

The sight of him fighting for restraint and the generous pleasure of his returning thrust sent Tori spiralling over the edge.

'Please.' Her hands dug into his shoulders as she struggled to keep her voice to a whisper. 'I need you now.'

Ash's mouth covered hers, blotting out the scream rising within. Strong arms held her close as he abandoned restraint and pounded fast, hard and satisfying, filling her so that it seemed there was no longer Tori and Ash but only one being, straining after pleasure. Rapture exploded in a shuddering conflagration so powerful that the very air vibrated with it.

Together they rocked and shuddered. She was overwhelmed by sensations so intense they defied description. Except that at their heart was a delight so profound Tori half expected to die from it.

The world shook. Senses swam. Blood roared in her ears loud as a helicopter coming in to land. And through it all they stayed locked together, mouths and bodies fused.

Finally, when sanity began to creep back in, Ash rolled onto his side and then his back, taking Tori with him. Aftershocks ripped through her as overloaded pleasure receptors reacted again and again.

A rough gasp of pain reminded her of Ash's wounds. Instantly she tried to shift from his grasp. He didn't need her weight on his injuries.

'Stay.' His voice was hoarse, a rough wisp of sound that Tori found it impossible to resist.

She kissed him open-mouthed in the hot, male-scented curve where his shoulder met his neck. He shivered, hauling her closer.

Never had Tori felt this profound oneness. It was shared physical pleasure but surely something more. Something inexplicable that had swept them up and cradled them together.

Tori gave in to the protective urge to spread her arms as wide as she could around his brawny shoulders. She rested her head on his chest, absorbing the reassuring heavy thud of his heartbeat. She'd wait till she caught her breath. Then she'd try to define the change she sensed with every cell yet couldn't name.

It was her last cogent thought for hours.

'Tori.'

The luscious deep voice was warm and seductive in her ear. Ash's hands moved over her body and she stretched sinuously, arching to meet them.

She frowned, for he wasn't caressing her, he was—

'It's time to wake up.' His hands were deftly doing up her shirt buttons, right to the collar.

'Ash?' She opened her eyes to discover pale light filtering through the small windows.

He was dressed, she realised, his torn shirt buttoned and tucked into dusty trousers. Then she recalled him insisting in the night that they dress again. For warmth, he'd said.

Now she felt a chill that was only partly due to the temperature. Grey dawn light revealed a clearer view of Ash than she'd had so far. His features were starkly sculpted and compelling. His face would turn any woman's head. But now she saw clearly the blood caked in his hair. His torn clothes were liberally marked with dark stains and the chain securing him looked brutally heavy.

Tori's stomach turned as dread reality hit her full-force. Nausea rose. Her pulse accelerated to a panicky rhythm. Impossibly, in Ash's arms the peril they were in had been pushed to the back of her mind. Now realisation slammed into her.

She clutched his hands and he paused. His eyes met hers and something passed between them. Then Ash took hold of her hands. In this light she still couldn't make out the colour of his eyes, yet the warmth she read in them counteracted the chill crackling across her bones.

Slowly, as if he had all the time in the world, he raised her left hand and kissed her palm, his warm lips soft on her flesh. He repeated the gesture with her other hand, sending a squiggle of heat from her palms to her breasts and lower, arrowing to her core.

He murmured something against her palm that she couldn't catch. But his eyes as they met hers glowed with a message that made her chest clamp.

'Thank you, *habibti*.' He inclined his head, sketching a quick, graceful movement with his hand that spoke of respect and admiration. 'You did me great honour last night. Your gift is one I'll carry with me.'

Tori was about to respond when Ash's expression changed. His head whipped towards the door, his features intent, as if he heard something she couldn't.

'Quickly.' He grabbed her boots and shoved her feet into them.

'What is it?'

But she guessed the cause of his urgency. Someone was coming.

The thought of their captors made her fingers shake, and she watched Ash push her hands aside to do up the laces with swift efficiency.

'Remember what I said.' His voice was urgent and low.

'Don't fight back till you're alone with one of them. You'll stand a better chance.'

Tori looked into that stern, handsome face and nodded. She swallowed hard. 'You—?'

'I'll be fine. Now the sun's rising the search party will find it easier to locate the camp.'

Neither admitted that the search party might be too late for him.

His hands tightened on hers as they heard voices outside. Leaning in, he whispered, 'When you escape—' *when*, not *if*… Tori's heart leapt with hope '—keep low and—'

His words were cut off by the door banging open to rattle against the wall. Tori blinked against the light, realising belatedly that Ash no longer held her hands but was on his feet, facing the three men who had entered.

What came next was the stuff of nightmares. Brutal, pawing hands and leering faces. A slap that made her head ring as she struggled to free herself. But far worse was the sight of Ash, pulling one of the men off her and then being set upon by two of them. Hampered by the chain, he was eventually overwhelmed by vicious blows to his injured head and ribs.

The last she saw of him he'd crumpled to his knees and then pitched sideways, a scarlet bloom spilling from his wounds across the dirt floor.

The rusty tang of fresh blood was sharp in Tori's nostrils as she was shoved, stumbling, into the chill morning.

CHAPTER THREE

Tori stared at the data before her, wishing she could blame her lack of concentration on a post-lunch slump. Stretching, she leaned back in her chair and took in the view of Perth's Swan River, sparkling in the sunlight.

It had been tough, moving from Sydney to Western Australia. She'd had to find a new home, start a new job, create a new life, all on top of the trauma that still haunted her.

If her father had been at all supportive she'd have settled in Sydney. Family was supposed to be there for you during difficult times, after all.

Tori shuddered, remembering the last time she and her father had spoken. It was pointless wishing for the impossible—like a caring father—but his icy disapproval on top of recent events had made Tori miss her mother more than ever. She'd been warm, practical and supportive. Tori could have done with the unconditional love that had died years before, with her mother.

Yet it wasn't any of those things distracting her now. Or even last night's broken sleep. She was used now to perennial tiredness.

It was the date. Fifteen months to the day since she'd been kidnapped in Za'daq.

She'd been about to leave Assara, her geological survey complete and her companions already gone. She'd spent her final afternoon investigating an outcrop that hadn't been in her survey zone but had looked promising.

Until she'd found herself surrounded by armed men.

Fifteen months since she'd last seen Ash.

Fifteen months since the sharp rattle of gunfire had

echoed across the arid landscape, raising the hairs on her arms and neck and devastating her.

She'd never forget that sound.

Or the gloating chuckle of the leader of the small party that had left the bandit camp to make its way across the foothills.

He was the one Ash had knocked aside after the man had grabbed her, his hands insinuating themselves under her shirt. When gunfire had sounded from the camp the man had leered, slicing his hand across his throat in a violent gesture. He'd spat out words she hadn't understood but his meaning had been clear. Ash was dead.

Even now the nightmare reality was almost too much to take in.

The fruit smoothie she'd had for lunch curdled in Tori's stomach and she swallowed hard, trying to keep it down.

Traumatic memories were normal, her counsellor said. And, what with having been up half the night, it was no surprise that Tori was susceptible today to distressing flashes of memory.

They'd pass. They always did.

Meanwhile she had a report to sort out.

Breathing deep, she turned back to her computer.

She was frowning over an anomaly when a waft of pungent aftershave reached her.

'Head down, Victoria? Good to see you making the most of the time you're actually in the office.'

Tori repressed a sigh. It *would* be Steve Bates—leader of the other team on this floor. He always carped about her part-time hours, implying that she took advantage of the company instead of actually working harder than some of her full-time colleagues. And that never stopped him staring at her as if he could see through her clothes.

She needed to tackle him about his attitude. But not today, when she felt so low. Besides, she'd survived far worse than Steve could dish out.

The thought steadied her.

Tori swung around in her chair to meet his stare. Naturally it wasn't her face he was looking at. She sat straighter and his eyes lifted.

'This new survey data is intriguing. Is that why you're here? I'll have the report ready by—'

He stopped her with a dismissive wave. 'I'm not here for that.' He paused, his X-ray stare focused on her face, his gaze sharply assessing. 'You're full of surprises, aren't you?'

Tori frowned. 'Sorry?'

Steve smiled, but instead of putting her at ease his calculating expression made disquiet flicker.

'I had no idea you had such…connections. No wonder the bosses were eager to snap you up. But then it's always who you know, isn't it? Not how good your work is.'

'Now, look here!' She shot to her feet, fury rising. She had no patience for people who thought she'd got where she was through her father's influence. 'I won this job on merit. Simple as that.'

The idea of her father interfering on her behalf wasn't just wrong, it was risible. Despite what he said in public, Jack Nilsson didn't approve of her career. As for exerting himself on her behalf… Not unless it would win him positive publicity.

'If you say so.' Steve raised his hands but his knowing smirk lingered. 'Don't be so touchy and emotional.'

Tori raised one eyebrow at the typical putdown. When she spoke again she used the clear, carrying tones she'd learned when her father had insisted she take up debating at school. 'Was there a work matter you wanted to discuss? Or did you just interrupt me to shoot the breeze?'

Steve slanted a glance towards the open-plan office behind him. His expression grew ugly. 'You're wanted in the boardroom.' His tone was as hard as the diamonds the company mined. 'Immediately.'

He turned on his heel and disappeared, leaving Tori relieved and confused. She hated Steve's snarky sexism. He deserved far more than the mild rebuke she'd given him. But she had no idea who wanted to see her and why. She knew where the boardroom was, but she wasn't significant enough in the company to be invited to meetings there.

She tried to remember if she'd heard anything about an executive meeting today but nothing registered.

Tori smoothed her hair then reached for her phone, her tablet and the not yet finished survey report. Taking a deep breath, she marched across the office, feeling curious glances as she pushed the lift button for the executive level.

Minutes later she stepped into the rarefied atmosphere of extreme wealth. The company was one of the most successful of its type and the executive suite was all plush carpet, expensive artworks and bespoke wood panelling. The views up here were dizzyingly spectacular.

Tori was staring about her when a young man in a pinstriped suit approached.

'Ms Nilsson?'

His manner was friendly, but there was no mistaking his curiosity. She resisted the urge to check her hair or straighten her collar. She'd learned never to fidget in public. Her father hated it because it spoiled the perfect press shot.

'Yes. I understand I'm wanted in the boardroom?' She let her voice rise at the end of the sentence, hinting at a question. But he didn't offer an explanation.

'That's right. This way, please.'

He led the way past a beautifully appointed lounge with panoramic windows. As they approached a set of double doors Tori noticed a man in a dark suit nearby. His feet were planted wide and his hands clasped.

A bodyguard. She'd seen enough of them to recognise the demeanour.

This one met her eyes calmly, no doubt sizing her up. He looked sturdy and, despite his impassive expression, intimidating.

Tori gripped her belongings tighter. Unusual that one of the company's executives should bring a bodyguard into the building. Then she remembered Steve's snide challenge. *'It's always who you know.'*

Which meant it was her father in the boardroom. Though why he'd brought a bodyguard… And why he'd chosen to meet her at work… He hadn't mentioned coming to Western Australia and he never made paternal visits.

'Here you are, Ms Nilsson.' Her guide pushed open one of the doors.

She stepped in to find the room empty. There was no meeting. The long polished table was bare.

Tori blinked and hesitated. She was about to go out again and ask what was going on when a shadow at the far end of the room detached itself from the wall.

A man. A tall man, spine straight and shoulders wide. He was silhouetted against a wall of glass. For an instant all she had was an impression of strength and the loose-limbed saunter of an athlete as he approached. She didn't recognise the walk, but there was something familiar about him.

Tori's skin tightened as premonition swept through her. A split-second certainty that she knew him.

She opened her mouth to say hello, but then he drew close enough that she could make out his features instead of just the shape of his head.

Tori heard a hissed breath. Her hands slackened. Something hard grazed her shin as it dropped with a thud onto the carpeted floor. But her gaze was glued to the man who had stopped just an arm's length away.

Bronzed skin pulled tight over a bone structure that would have made Michelangelo weep. A sensual mouth set above a determined jaw. Eyes that even from here looked black rather than dark brown. Black eyebrows. A forceful nose that transformed his face from an ideal of masculine beauty to one of power. Black hair that Tori knew was soft to the touch.

Her nerveless hands twitched as memory flooded through her. Of channelling her fingers through hair so soft and thick it felt like a pelt. Of being careful to avoid the clotted blood of his head injury.

The twitch in her hands became a tremor. A shudder thundered through her as her heart crashed into her ribs.

Heat suffused her as she met gleaming eyes. Then a wash of icy cold as other memories battered her brain.

Kidnappers. Gunfire.

Her eyes prickled and she blinked rapidly. Tears came easily now—another thing her counsellor said was normal. Yet instinctively Tori tried to dam them.

She swayed. The floor seemed to ripple and the walls appeared to close around the man watching her so intently. Tori grabbed the back of a leather conference chair for support, fingers clawing.

There was no scarring on his face. Nothing to indicate he'd ever been brutalised or shot at. He wore a dark grey suit tailored by an expert. It rivalled anything in her father's expensive wardrobe, and on this man's rangy, powerful frame looked spectacular. A white shirt complemented his burnished skin and a perfectly knotted silk tie completed the image of urbane sophistication.

It couldn't be. It was impossible. And yet…

'I thought you were dead.'

It didn't sound like her voice, so husky and uneven. Yet he understood. His eyes widened and something passed across his face.

'Ah, that explains a lot.'

That voice! That deep, rich voice. She'd only heard him whisper before. They'd both kept their voices low so as not to attract the guards' attention. His whispers had threaded through her dreams for over a year. How often had she woken from a nightmare or the occasional erotic dream with the sound of his voice in her head?

'It *is* you?'

Tori wanted to touch him, to check for herself he was no mirage. But her limbs felt like blocks of basalt. All she could do was stand and stare.

'It's me, Tori.'

Ashraf stared down into her oval face and felt a wave of emotion tumble through him.

He'd searched for her so long, against impossible odds, when even the best investigators had advised him to give up. He recalled the moment he'd received news that she was alive. Alive and safe. Relief had been so intense, so powerful, that for a moment he'd found it difficult to breathe.

He'd been fully prepared for this meeting, and still reality was nothing like his expectation.

Seeing Tori in the flesh unsettled him profoundly.

Maybe it was her eyes. He'd wondered about their colour. Now he knew. Soft blue. The colour of the dainty yet hardy forget-me-nots that grew in Za'daq's mountain valleys. Her gaze held his and he felt the bite of need, of hunger, of regret and a hundred emotions he wasn't in the habit of feeling. Those lovely eyes shone over-bright and her lip quivered.

Deep inside something responded with an intensity that rocked him back on his heels. As if his feelings were engaged in a way that was totally unfamiliar.

He'd admired her in Za'daq. She'd been courageous and strong, hiding her fears. He'd found comfort and welcome oblivion in her lithe body.

But he hadn't expected such a visceral reaction after all this time. He'd told himself danger had heightened their responses.

Ashraf registered the thunder of his pulse and the tingling in his blood that betrayed a surge of adrenaline. He wanted to touch her. More than touch her. He wanted—

He slammed a door on such thoughts. His reason for being here was too important for distraction. Despite other unexpected urges. To comfort and assure her. To protect her as he hadn't been able to fifteen months ago.

Guilt sliced at the memory. But it was blunted by other emotions. Desire. Possessiveness, rampant and untrammelled.

Ashraf tunnelled his fists into his pockets and forced himself to stand his ground rather than close the space between them.

'You need to sit. You've had a shock.'

She blinked up, eyes round and lips open as if she couldn't get enough oxygen.

He knew the feeling. His lungs were labouring as if he were the one surprised. He hadn't expected to feel—

Ashraf leaned past her, pulling out a high-backed chair from the table, and gestured for her to sit. She did, and he saw that even in extremity there was a familiar grace about her movements. He'd thought he'd imagined that, embellished his recollections of this woman with qualities she hadn't actually possessed. He'd told himself guilt and regret had turned her in his mind into someone more remarkable than she really was.

Striving for emotional distance, he catalogued what he saw. She was the same as in the photos his investigators had sent. Yet she was *more*.

Regular features in a face that was long rather than round. Fine lips. Even finer eyes. Eyes that watched his every move with an intensity he felt as a sizzle in his veins. Even the faint shadows of tiredness didn't mar her attractiveness. The hair he'd remembered as pale was platinum-blonde, pulled back and up in a chignon that left her face clear. But why would she hide those cheekbones? She wasn't classically beautiful, yet he defied any man not to take a second look.

Even in a plain white blouse and black trousers Tori Nilsson drew the eye.

That explained his racing pulse. That and the intimate secret they shared.

For a second his attention lingered on those breasts, quickly rising and falling against her blouse. They seemed plumper than he remembered—

'Can you sit, instead of towering over me?'

Ashraf huffed back laughter. *There* was the woman he remembered. Indomitable and practical. How lucky he'd been not to be stuck with a hysterical companion that night.

He pulled out a chair and sat knee to knee with her.

'You're really real.'

Slim fingers skimmed shakily over his cheek, down his freshly shaved jaw, and two things struck him.

First, no one these days ever touched him. He'd been busy in the last two years and it had been a long time since he'd had a lover. Plus his position meant that casual touching was out of the question.

Second, her hand shook. Perhaps he'd been unfair, confronting her like this with no warning. But he hadn't known she'd believed him dead. If he'd realised…

No, even if he'd known he'd still have wanted to see her in person.

'Yes. I'm real.'

He captured her hand, feeling the quick pulse throb at her wrist. At the same time he registered a hint of scent. Something sweet and enticing, slightly citrusy. It transported him to that night they'd been captives together. He couldn't recall noticing it then, but at some subliminal level he must have. It both enticed and disturbed him, reminding him of how close they'd come to death, and how he'd allowed himself to weaken in this woman's arms.

He released her hand and brushed her cheek with his knuckles. Satiny skin trembled at his touch and made his blood fizz.

He'd assumed his physical response to Tori had been fuelled by danger, by the knowledge that he might die. Was this just a hangover from that night? That had to be it.

But he wasn't here for sex.

Ashraf dropped his hand and sat back.

'How did you get away? I heard gunfire. I thought—'

Tori bit her lip, hearing the wobble in her voice. Clearly she'd thought wrong—so why was she upset? Seeing Ash again was a miracle. One she'd never dared hope for. Her reaction had to be due to shock.

'You thought they'd shot me?' His eyebrows rose and then he nodded. 'I'm sure they wish they had. You heard security forces storming the camp. Qadri, the bandits' leader, had just arrived. He was killed in the raid with several of his followers. The rest are serving time for various offences—including kidnap.'

The words sounded matter-of-fact. Like a news report of some distant, almost unreal incident. But the sound of those guns had been brutal reality for Tori for too long. She strove to absorb Ash's news but couldn't prevent a tremor of reaction.

'I thought you were dead. I—' She searched his face, even now finding it hard to believe he was there and whole. 'What are you *doing* here? It's an incredible coincidence.'

'No coincidence, Tori. I've been looking for you.' His voice was deep and assured.

'You have?'

Ash sat straighter. 'Of course! Did you imagine I'd forget about you? That I'd leave you to the mercy of people-smugglers?'

'But it's been fifteen months!'

His dark eyes flashed. 'I'm not in the habit of forgetting my friends.'

Was that what they'd been? Friends? Allies, for sure. Lovers too. And now…?

'I regret it took so long. I'd imagined…'

He shook his head, as if his imaginings weren't important, but the grim set of his mouth told its own story. If she'd been tormented by the thought of him dead, he'd had the burden of thinking her at the mercy of men like those who'd kidnapped her.

Tori closed her hand over his fist where it rested on his thigh. 'I'm not blaming you, Ash. That wasn't a rebuke. I'm just…surprised.' Make that astounded. She'd never in her wildest dreams believed she'd see him again. 'How did you locate me?'

He shrugged. 'A team of top investigators, persistence and in the end one lucky break.'

Investigators working for fifteen months? That must have cost a fortune.

Tori's gaze skittered across that beautifully made suit. Ash wasn't ostentatiously dressed but he projected an aura of authority and wealth, like a man used to wielding power. A little like her father, except in Ash it seemed innate, less cultivated for public consumption. Her father revelled in the importance his position gave him. Ash, on the other hand, wasn't showy or obvious.

'You're a determined man.'

If there'd been an easy trail to follow he'd have found her ages ago. The fact that he'd persevered all this time spoke of a doggedness she could only admire. If she'd still been at the mercy of people-smugglers she was sure he'd have found a way to free her. The knowledge made her heart lurch.

'How did you get away? Month after month my people scoured Za'daq and the border territory for you. They found nothing.'

My people. He made it sound as if he had his own personal army.

Belatedly Tori realised she still held his hand. She forced her fingers open and sat back, folding her hands together and telling herself the throb of heat she felt had nothing to do with touching Ash.

But hearing he'd made it his quest to find her unravelled something she'd kept locked up tight since the horror of the kidnap. And looking into those dark eyes was messing with her head. She squeezed her eyes closed and drew a breath.

This was so complicated. So profoundly difficult. What on earth was she going to do?

'Tori?'

She snapped her eyes open. 'Sorry. I'm still a little stunned.'

The implications of Ash being here were only just seeping into her whirling brain. There was so much to consider. So many variables and, yes, worries. Her skin prickled with anxiety and it wasn't from reliving the past.

But for now she owed him her story.

'Three of us rode away from the camp. Me, the guard you knocked down and a boy—barely a teenager. When we heard the gunshots the older man was happy. He thought you were dead.' Tori snatched a fortifying breath, remembering the sour tang of fear and horror she'd felt at his gleeful triumph. 'But after the first couple of shots he said something to the boy and then headed back the way we'd come.'

'Probably realised there was too much gunfire for an execution.'

Slowly Tori nodded. She hadn't considered that. She'd thought the firing squad had been overly enthusiastic, or perhaps celebrating.

'The pair of us kept riding, but the boy wasn't happy. He began to look scared. Maybe he understood some English, because I told him what would happen to him when he was caught. I might have exaggerated…'

'Good for you!' Ash looked admiring and Tori was amazed at how good that felt.

'What did I have to lose? Besides, I was upset.'

An understatement for the raw rage and fear that had consumed her as they'd trekked through the wilderness. Hearing that gunfire and believing Ash dead had been a living nightmare. Even remembering that moment—

'Go on.'

Tori spread her hands. 'It wasn't really hard to get away. I realised later he let me escape.'

Ash nodded. 'He must have realised something had gone wrong and he'd be in trouble if he was found with you.'

'I ran away during a rest stop. The rope was a little loose and I eventually got it undone. I was terrified he'd come after me but I never saw him again.'

Tori flexed her hands, remembering the burn of dust against red raw flesh.

'Hours later I stumbled into the path of a four-wheel drive. A couple of foreigners were returning to their private yacht after a trip inland.'

Foreigners who had been sympathetic but, for reasons of their own, avoiding the authorities. She'd wondered if they were smuggling contraband.

'They were on their way to the Maldives and took me with them. Once there I made contact with the Australian authorities.'

'You crossed the border from Za'daq into Assara,' Ash said. 'We made enquiries in neighbouring countries, but using official channels it was a slow process with no leads. It was only recently that a witness came forward. A driver passing through on his way to a family wedding. Recently he returned to visit his village again and heard about the search for you. He remembered three foreigners boarding a yacht in a deserted cove.'

Tori digested that. 'And from something so vague you located me?' It was remarkable! She could barely imagine the resources, or sheer luck, required to find her.

'Eventually. Fortunately the yacht was distinctive, so it could be tracked. Your trail was easy from the Maldives, after I knew you'd escaped and where you were headed.' His mouth twisted ruefully. 'If we'd exchanged full names and addresses it would have saved time.'

Heat tickled Tori's throat. Despite their physical intimacy they'd never got past first names. It seemed strange now.

'Well, you found me. I'm glad.' She smiled up at him. Despite the complications she'd now have to face, it was wonderful to know he'd survived. 'It's good to see you alive.'

'And you, Tori.'

His look seared her and she shifted in her seat. It wasn't just relief she felt. Her emotions were complex and she found herself growing nervous all over again.

The longer she sat with him, the more she realised how little she knew about Ash, despite the way her body hummed with awareness. He seemed light-years away from the stoic man with whom she'd shared intimacies in the desert.

She couldn't imagine—

No, that was wrong. She *could* imagine all too easily the urge to be with him again. The realisation sent heat spiralling through her middle and surging up her throat to scald her cheeks.

Yet it wasn't sexual awareness stretching her nerves tight. It was apprehension. For she knew next to nothing about him. His life, hopes, expectations. How he'd react when faced with what she had to tell him.

For a craven moment she wondered if she could avoid that. It would be taking a giant step into the unknown. But it had to be done.

She moistened her lips, ready to speak, but he was too fast for her.

'So, Tori. Or should I call you Victoria?' He leaned closer, his black-as-night gaze pinioning her to the seat. 'Are you going to tell me about my son?'

CHAPTER FOUR

IF ASHRAF HAD had any doubts about the child being his, they were banished by Tori's reaction.

The flush colouring her face disappeared completely, leaving those high-cut cheeks blanched like porcelain. Her gasp filled the silent room.

His investigators had provided a photo—part of a slim dossier on Victoria Miranda Nilsson. A photo of a tiny child with dark hair and what might be dark eyes, though the shot had been taken from too far away to be sure.

Now he was sure. She'd had his baby.

Another surge of adrenaline shot into his blood, catapulting around his body. It took everything he had to sit there, holding her gaze, instead of erupting to his feet and pacing the length of the room.

But Ashraf had learned in childhood to control his impulses, even if later he'd made his name by giving in to them. No, that wasn't quite right. Even when he'd gone out of his way to provoke with scandal and headlines his actions hadn't been impulsive, even if they'd seemed so. They'd been carefully considered for maximum impact.

But now wasn't the time to think of his father and how they'd always been on opposing sides. Now *he* was a father.

Ashraf registered awe as the reality of it sideswiped him. As he thought of this slim, self-possessed woman fruitful with his child. How had she looked, her belly rounded with his baby? Did that explain the urge he now battled to feel her pliant body against his again? Because she'd borne his child? He wished he'd been there, seeing her body change, attending the birth. So much he'd missed out on. So much she'd had to face without him.

'I was going to tell you, Ash. I was just…' She waved her hand in a vague gesture at odds with the determined tilt of her chin.

How wrong he'd been—imagining she'd deliberately withheld the news of his son.

Satisfaction eddied in his belly that his first assessment of her appeared right after all. He'd thought her practical, brave and honest. He'd admired her, wanted to believe she'd got away. Yet when finally he'd received proof that she had, doubts had filtered in. Because she hadn't informed him about the baby.

Now he knew why.

What had she gone through, having his child alone? Without, as far as he could tell, family support? She'd believed him dead. Her shock on seeing him had been no charade. Ashraf tried to imagine how she'd felt, struggling with the effects of trauma alone when she'd most needed assistance.

'You're still in shock. You thought me dead.'

'It's true! I did.' She spoke so quickly she must have read something in his expression.

'I believe you.'

'But?'

He lifted his shoulders, spreading his hands. 'In my work I sometimes appear on the television news. It seemed likely you'd see me.' That had been one of the reasons he'd feared for her—feared that she was dead or unable to contact him.

'Do you? You must have an important job.'

When he merely shrugged she laughed, the sound short, almost gruff.

'My father is a politician. Years of being force-fed a diet of politics means I avoid the TV news.'

Cynicism threaded her soft voice. A dislike of politicians or just her father?

'Especially news from Za'daq.' Another wide gesture

with her hand. 'After what happened I've actively avoided reports from that part of the world.'

Now he saw it in her eyes. Not prevarication but a haunted look that spoke of pain and trauma. Her abduction had left scars.

His hand captured hers, reassuring. He was pleased to feel its warmth. She looked so pale he'd imagined her chilled. Yet when they touched there was a definite spark of fire.

'Besides,' she went on, 'new mothers have priorities other than TV current affairs programmes.'

The baby. *His* baby. That had been her priority.

Now it was his too.

Ashraf would do everything necessary to ensure his son had the sort of life he deserved.

'Tell me about him.'

She looked down at his hand enfolding hers, then away. 'He's the most important thing in my life.'

'As he will be in mine,' he vowed.

Startled eyes flashed to his. Ashraf felt the shock of contact, read the flare of…was that *fear*? Then Tori looked away. This time she slipped her hand back into her lap, curving her other hand protectively around it.

Tori looked into those gleaming eyes and her heart stuttered. Had she ever seen a man so intent?

Yes. The night she and Ash had made love, finding solace in each other's arms. Finding rapture.

For so long she'd wondered what it would be like if Ash hadn't died. If he'd been at her side through the pregnancy and birth, and later to care for Oliver. The thought was a secret refuge when the burdens she'd faced grew too heavy.

Now she discovered her fantasy was real—too real, given her response to him. And Tori had to remind herself that he wasn't the embodiment of her exhausted daydreams but a man with his own agenda.

A shuddery sigh began deep in her belly and travelled up through lungs that contracted hard, stealing her breath, making her turn away.

Ash had done that to her fifteen months ago—stolen her breath, her senses, her self-possession. Now he was doing it again, without trying.

She was in deep trouble. If she'd learned one thing about him, it was that he followed through. When he determined to do something he did it.

Now he'd staked a claim on his son.

Her son. Her precious Oliver.

Suddenly, as if she'd taken an unwary step and plunged off a precipice, Tori was out of her depth.

The working part of her brain told her she should be used to that by now. After her kidnap and escape. After childbirth alone and unsupported by anyone except the competent, kind midwives who'd delivered her son. After relocating to the far side of the country to build a life for her darling boy free of her father.

But this time it felt different. Perhaps because what she shared with Ash was so personal. Not merely her body and her passion, but her son.

Did he expect her to give Oliver up? She knew little of Middle Eastern culture but guessed fathers might have more authority there than mothers.

Her gaze slewed back to Ash to find him watching her with a stillness that did nothing to assuage her nerves. It was the stillness of a predator.

Tori dragged in a deep breath. She was overreacting. Ash wasn't a bully. He was...

She didn't know what he was.

'You'll want to see him.'

Even saying it sent a wobble through her middle, as if she was walking a tightrope and one misstep would send her tumbling.

He inclined his head. 'Of course.'

'That's why you came.'

Now it became clear. If he'd hired investigators to find her they would have discovered she'd travelled to Western Australia accompanied by her infant son.

Tori wrapped her arms around herself.

One dark eyebrow climbed that broad forehead. 'I was searching for *you*, Tori. And when I discovered you'd given birth to a child nine months after the night we spent together...' His straight shoulders lifted in a fluid shrug. 'Of course I wanted to come myself. To hear your explanation.'

Explanation. As if she'd done something wrong—namely deprived him of his child. Was he here to punish her for that? Perhaps by taking Oliver from her?

No, that was unfair. Nothing she'd learned about Ash that night indicated he was anything but decent and admirable. Besides, would she have liked him if he'd learned about her baby and ignored the fact? If he'd shied away from responsibility?

The nervous roiling in her stomach settled a little as the thought penetrated. She was allowing fear to build upon fear, when the little she knew about Ash should have reassured her.

The Ash she'd met last year.

This man, in his hand-stitched suit with an air of assurance in the plush executive suite, was someone she had yet to know.

'If I'd known you were alive I'd have told you about Oliver.'

'Oliver...' He said it slowly, rolling the name around his tongue as if testing it.

'Oliver Ashal Nilsson.' Fire climbed her throat and moved higher, making her ears tingle.

'Ashal?' Both eyebrows arched this time. 'That's an Arabic name.'

So his investigators hadn't got as far as checking the birth certificate. For some reason that made her feel better.

'I know. I wanted...' She dropped her gaze to her knotted hands. 'I wanted him to have something from you so I gave him your name—or as close to it as I could find. I wasn't sure if Ash was your real name.'

She looked up to see Ash staring at her as if he'd never seen her before. He swallowed and she tracked the movement of his strong throat, finding it strangely both arousing and endearing, as if it indicated he was affected by the revelation.

Perhaps her imagination worked overtime.

'I found Ashal in a list of baby names. It means light or radiance.'

'I know what it means.'

Ash's voice was so low Tori felt it trawl through her belly.

'It's a fine name.' He paused. 'It was very generous of you to give him a name that honoured my heritage.'

Tori spread her hands. 'It seemed apt. He's the light of my life.'

Awareness pulsed between them. Not sexual this time, but an unprecedented moment of understanding. The sort she imagined parents the world over shared when they discussed their beloved children. It reassured her as nothing else had.

'So what *is* your name? Is it Ash?'

'Ashraf.'

'Ashraf.' She said it slowly, liking the sound.

'It means most honourable or noble.' His mouth kicked up at the corner, lending his expression a fleetingly cynical cast. A second later the impression was gone. 'Ashraf ibn Kahul al Rashid.'

He watched her closely as if expecting a reaction. Something about the name tickled her memory but she couldn't place it.

When she merely nodded he went on, 'Sheikh of Za'daq.'

'Sheikh?' Weren't they just in books?

'Leader.' He paused. 'Prince. Ruler.'

Tori's mouth dried. She swallowed, then swiped her bottom lip with her tongue. 'You're the ruler of Za'daq? Of the whole country?'

For the second time in half an hour the world tilted around her. Hands braced on the chair's cushioned armrests, she fought sudden dizziness.

Oliver's father was a *king*?

'That explains the bodyguard.'

If she'd known what waited for her in this room, would she have entered or turned tail and run?

'Basim? He's head of my close personal protection team.'

No wonder Ash—no, Ashraf—had spoken of *his people* scouring the land, searching for her. His protection team must have been beside themselves when he was abducted.

'Do many people want to kill you?' Tori's thoughts had already veered to her tiny son and his safety.

'Not any more. Za'daq is actually a peaceful, law-abiding country. But it's customary and sensible to take precautions. Besides, it's expected that a visiting head of state will bring a security detail.'

Head of state. There it was again—that horrible slam of shock to her insides, creating a whirl of anxious nausea.

'Breathe.'

Firm hands clasped hers, anchoring them to the arms of the chair. A waft of spice and heat surrounded her, tantalising.

Tori stared up into fathomless eyes that looked like pure ebony even now as Ash… Ashraf…leaned in. Eyes so like Oliver's, and yet their impact was completely different from the feelings evoked when she looked at her son.

'I'm breathing. You can let me go.'

Even so it took one, two, three rapid beats of her heart before he released her. Was she crazy to think she saw regret in his expression?

'It's hard to believe after our abduction, I know, but you could travel in that same area unharmed today.'

'You said he was your enemy?' Tori murmured. 'That man—Qadri. In Australia, even in politics, when you speak of an enemy you don't mean someone who'd have you executed at dawn.' Even if the backstabbing and political manoeuvring in her father's world was violent in its own way.

Ashraf sat back and the tautness in her chest eased. When he'd leaned in, capturing her with his intense regard as much as his touch, she had felt ridiculously overwhelmed.

'Qadri was a relic of the past. A criminal who, because his powerbase was in a remote province, was allowed to remain untouched for too long.' Ashraf's mouth thinned. 'My father, the previous Sheikh, had no appetite for tackling intractable problems like ousting a vicious bandit who preyed on his own people. It was too far away from the capital and too hard when there were other, easier initiatives that would win him praise.'

So Ashraf and his father hadn't seen eye to eye? It was there in his voice and the slight upward tilt of his chin. Tori could relate to that.

'So you sent in your soldiers to kill Qadri?' That would explain his violent retaliation.

Ashraf's mouth curled in a small smile. 'Is that how things are done in Australia? In Za'daq the Sheikh upholds the law, rather than breaks it.'

He was laughing at her naivety, making a point about Za'daq being a country as enlightened as hers.

'But, given your experience, it's not surprising you thought otherwise. And it's true that centuries ago the Sheikh would have ridden in with his warriors and slaughtered such a man.'

'So what *did* you do?'

'Deprived him of his powerbase. Introduced schemes to bring the province out of the Dark Ages with adequate power, water and food. Began establishing schools and employment opportunities.' He shook his head. 'I'd only been Sheikh for half a year when we met, and the initiatives were in their infancy, but still they'd had a powerful effect. So had enforcing the law. I had police stationed locally to arrest Qadri's stand-over men when they tried to intimidate people. Qadri realised that soon the people wouldn't see him as the power in the region. They'd have choices and laws they could rely on.'

'So he had you kidnapped?'

'Unfortunately I made it easy, riding with only Basim and a guide into a deserted location to view a new project. The guide was in Qadri's pay.' Another twist of the lips. 'Clearly the security assessment was flawed, but no doubt some would say I was reckless.'

Tori frowned. That didn't gel with the man she knew. He was strong and astute, a strategic thinker and formidably determined.

And he was here for his son.

The reminder was a crackle of frost along her stiff spine.

'You can be assured that Za'daq is now safe to visit. As safe as your country.'

Was that code? His way of telling her that Oliver would be okay in his father's homeland? *Did* he mean to take Oliver from her?

Firming her lips, Tori beat down rising panic. She was jumping to conclusions. No one was going to take her son. There were laws about that. Hadn't Ashraf just taken time to prove he valued the law?

She wondered what the law in Za'daq said about custody of a child. Especially a male child. Was Oliver the Sheikh's heir?

It was no good. She couldn't sit here, pretending this was some polite catch-up with an old acquaintance. The rising burble of her emotions was too unsettling.

'Excuse me.' Tori shot to her feet and paced shakily to the wall of glass. She sensed rather than heard him come up behind her.

'I realise this is overwhelming.'

Tori nodded. She felt as if she'd stepped into a different reality. One where people came back from the dead and where handsome princes mingled with ordinary people.

'Imagine how I felt when I discovered you'd survived. And that you'd had my child.'

Ashraf's voice was low, a caress that tickled her flesh and tightened her nipples. Even after the reality of childbirth and six months of single motherhood, there was something seductively intimate about the way he spoke about her having his baby.

In the window she saw his reflection over her shoulder. His face was sombre, and it struck her for the first time that she wasn't the only one dealing with shock.

She turned to him. 'So where does that leave us?'

He didn't hesitate. 'I want to see Oliver. As soon as possible.'

Naturally. She looked at her watch. It was getting late. 'There's a report I have to complete today. It should only take me another hour.'

Ashraf considered her assessingly. Was he insulted because she didn't instantly jump to do his bidding? Did royal sheikhs ever have to wait for anything?

But he merely nodded. 'An hour, then.'

Two hours later Ashraf paced the sitting room of Tori's small villa, battling impatience and what felt remarkably like nerves.

After sleeping on their way home from the crèche Oliver, his son, had begun to fidget as soon as they'd entered. Ashraf had been torn between the need to reach for the child and wariness because he knew nothing about babies. Except that they were tiny, fragile and totally foreign to his world.

Oliver—the more he used the name, the more he'd get used to it—made him feel too big and clumsy to be trusted with a fragile new life.

Yet none of that had prevented the immediate visceral

connection he'd felt. He'd seen a tiny fist wave, caught the gleam of bright dark eyes, and felt emotion pound through his diaphragm strong as a knockout punch.

His son. His flesh and blood.

He'd missed seeing Tori grow big with his baby. He'd missed six months of his child's life. Precious months he could never get back. He had so much to catch up on. So much to learn and experience. And to give. Ashraf would ensure Oliver had the things he'd never had. Paternal love. Tenderness. Trust. Encouragement.

Ashraf would be involved in his son's life. In a positive way.

For a fleeting few seconds it hit him how much his own father had missed by distancing himself from his younger son. By choosing hate and distrust.

But he'd had Ashraf's other brother, Karim. Not that the old man had loved Karim either. Ashraf doubted their father had been capable of love. But he'd taken an interest, encouraged Karim and crowed over his elder son's successes.

A high-pitched grizzle cut into Ashraf's thoughts like an alarm signal resonating through his body. Was something wrong with Oliver?

Fifteen minutes ago Tori had led the way to a small white and yellow room with a cot, a rocking chair and a low bookcase littered with toy animals and little books made of boards. A mat on the floor looked like a farm, with more friendly-faced animals.

Ashraf had never felt so out of place. Especially when Tori had lifted their son high and he'd seen how tiny the mite was without his covering blanket. She'd cast a harried glance at him over her shoulder and suggested he make himself comfortable in the other room while she changed Oliver.

Reluctantly Ashraf had complied. He was curious about the boy but he knew he'd have to give Tori space. He'd thrown a live grenade into her world with his appearance today. He guessed she'd battled traumatic memories since the moment she saw him.

Ashraf frowned. Was it too much to expect her to be pleased to see him? He was used to delighted women… eager women.

For his part, he'd seen her and instantly been swamped with the need for more. The attraction between them might have started as the product of mortal danger, but it was there still, stronger by the moment.

Then he recalled her breathless reaction when he'd held her hand, the tell-tale tremble and the flutter of long lashes over soft blue eyes. She might not have wanted to feel it but she'd been attracted.

He glanced at his watch. How long did it take to change a nappy? They had things to discuss. He wanted to know his son. He'd allowed her time, even permitted her to stay at work and finish off the project she was so worried about. As if he, Ashraf al Rashid, was of negligible importance.

Ashraf strode down the corridor, knocked once and stepped into the nursery.

Wide eyes brilliant as starlight met his. Then he took in the rest of the scene. Tori in the rocking chair, the baby in her arms. His throat thickened. Her blouse was undone, hanging wide open on one side. A tiny dark head nuzzled at her bare breast.

Ashraf's gaze focused on the voluptuous curve of that breast, on his son's tiny starfish hand patting Tori's alabaster flesh, and heat drenched him from head to toe. The heat of arousal, fierce and primal. A surge of lust erupting with dizzying intensity.

Breastfeeding wasn't something he'd ever thought about. If he had it wouldn't have been in terms of eroticism. Yet, watching the woman he'd made pregnant feed his son, Ashraf had never felt such hungry possessiveness.

'We won't be long.' Tori's voice was husky as she twitched her blouse across to cover herself.

Ashraf nodded.

'He's almost finished.' She looked down, her gaze softening instantaneously on her baby.

Ashraf realised that for all the experience he'd gained in the royal court, in the rigours of army life and in the deliberate hedonism of his globetrotting playboy years, he'd never come across anything as real and fundamental as this.

His son.

His woman.

There wasn't even astonishment. Just calm acceptance. Ashraf hadn't got as far as considering a future wife. He'd been too busy cementing his role in a country that had never expected or wanted the younger, scandalous royal son to inherit.

Besides, this wasn't a matter of logic, but instinct.

He smiled as a glow of satisfaction spread out from his belly.

Tentatively Tori smiled back.

Ashraf felt that smile in places he couldn't even name. He'd never seen her smile before—not properly. He wanted to see her grin, he realised. Hear her laugh. Watch her as their bodies joined and she lost herself to ecstasy. In broad daylight. Not in the murky darkness of a desperate hovel that smelled of terror and pain.

'Ashraf...?' She frowned.

Was she picking up on the anger that simmered in his blood at the memory of what she'd suffered? Or was she frowning from embarrassment at him seeing her feed their child?

He smoothed his expression and leaned against the doorjamb, shoving his hands into his trouser pockets. Tori needed to get used to him being around.

'It's okay. There's no rush. Let him feed.'

Whether it was coincidence, or the sound of his voice, Oliver chose that moment to stop feeding. Ashraf saw a glazed pink nipple before Tori quickly drew her blouse further across. A tiny head turned, dark eyes meeting his.

Ashraf crossed the room in a couple of strides. Oliver tracked the movement. Was that usual for a six-month-old? Or was his son inordinately clever? It was nonsense to think he sensed the link between them. Of course it was.

'Would you like to hold him?' Tori's voice was different, as if she couldn't catch her breath.

'Show me how.'

She demonstrated, supporting the baby and then lifting Oliver up to her shoulder, gently rubbing his back. 'When he's hungry sometimes he gulps down air as well as milk. This helps.'

'I didn't think you'd be breastfeeding when you're working.'

Not that he knew a thing about it. Just that he'd been rooted to the spot by the sight of Tori nursing his child.

'I express milk for him to drink when I'm at work.'

Her cheeks grew pink and Ash stifled the urge to ask exactly what that meant. Time enough later.

'Here.'

She lifted Oliver towards him and suddenly, looking down at the tiny form, Ashraf wasn't so sure about holding him.

Tori read Ashraf's uncertainty and bit back a smile. It was the first time she'd seen him anything but confident. Even facing execution he'd been resolute. And there'd been no mistaking his eagerness when he'd seen Oliver.

That had simultaneously reassured and worried her. She had yet to discover what he intended to do about their son.

Now she read consternation in his bold features as well as…hunger? Her amusement died. Why should their son be any less of a wonder to Ashraf than he was to her? Gently she placed the baby in his arms, holding on longer than necessary while he grew familiar with Oliver's weight.

'Gah,' Oliver said, looking up into the dark, serious face above him. 'Gah-gah.'

'Hello to you too, Oliver Ashal.'

Ashraf's voice held a rough gravelly note that made her insides flutter. When he switched to husky Arabic Tori sank back in the rocker, spellbound by both the lilting sound and the sight of the two males staring into each other's faces.

Ashraf stood stiffly, as if wary of dropping his burden. But gradually he shifted Oliver into a more comfortable hold and Tori's chest squeezed at the contrast between the powerful man and the tiny child. The sight of them tugged at some primitive maternal instinct.

But there was more. Something to do with her feelings for Ashraf. Something that had been there from the start and which, remarkably, was growing stronger.

Tori looked away and focused on doing up her bra and shirt. There was a lot to discuss. Ashraf's appearance from the dead changed so much.

She glanced towards him, her busy hands stilling. Ashraf had Oliver tucked close, as if he'd held him since the day he was born, and the smile he gave his son made Tori's heart wobble. It was radiant.

It made her voice what she'd avoided till now. 'What do you want, Ashraf?'

'Want?'

'From me—us?'

'To be a father to my son.'

'It will take some planning since we live in Australia.' Caution told her not to push this now. But she was on tenterhooks. She needed to know his expectations.

Dark eyes meshed with hers. 'But you don't need to. You could live in Za'daq. Marry me and give our son the life he deserves.'

CHAPTER FIVE

ASHRAF LAY ON his back, staring through the gloom at the bedroom ceiling, and berated himself for his impatience. Being Sheikh often meant holding his tongue and waiting for the right moment to act, persuading people to accept his plans rather than forcing them to follow. Especially since in Za'daq his reputation as both a profligate playboy and his father's all but ignored son meant he battled prejudice and mistrust.

He was used to that. Was used to exerting patience as well as an iron will that stopped his father's old cronies from undermining him too blatantly.

But when Tori had asked what he wanted he hadn't been his usual composed self. He'd been holding his child in his arms for the first time, had felt the uprush of an emotion that nothing had prepared him for. In that moment he'd wanted never to let Oliver go. To ensure his life was better than Ashraf's had been.

Plus there'd been the sight of Tori in her plain white blouse, the buttons done up askew in her haste, tendrils of moonlight-pale hair drifting loose to frame her beguiling face. His heart had whacked his ribs in a rhythm of need, want and determination.

He'd realised his error in the split second it had taken her expression to close at the idea of marriage and Za'daq.

Now, here he lay, sleepless, seeking the winning argument to overcome her doubts and persuade her to accept what he offered. What was clearly best for their son.

Tori's refusal was a salutary lesson against complacency. He was accustomed to eager women, not women regarding him with suspicion. She probably thought marriage to a sheikh meant she'd be walled up in an old-fashioned harem.

His mouth rucked up at one side. The idea had some appeal. Tori available at his beck and call, reclining with an inviting smile on silk sheets... Heat threaded through his veins and gathered in his groin.

He shifted restlessly. Right now he could be lying in a king-sized bed in the exclusive suite that took up the top floor of Perth's most prestigious hotel. Instead he lay on the carpeted floor of Oliver's room.

Ashraf grunted and rolled onto his side. It was his fault for not treading carefully. For spooking Tori with his abrupt announcement. They'd discussed the matter through the dinner he'd had delivered to her home, and afterwards. But despite her attempt to appear calm he'd read her tension, and the fear he'd done his best to diffuse.

Finally, seeing tiredness in her slumping shoulders, he'd insisted she sleep. But he hadn't been able to leave for his luxury accommodation. It was too soon. He'd just found Oliver, and Tori, and something inside had screeched a protest at the idea of leaving them.

So he'd suggested sleeping on the sofa and Tori had eventually agreed, perhaps because she'd realised she hadn't a hope of shifting him. Apparently Oliver was teething—something Ashraf hadn't even known was a thing—and Tori had admitted broken sleep was taking its toll.

Another reason for him to remain. Tori's refusal to accept the logic of his plan was a nuisance, but seeing her exhausted had made him protective.

As soon as she'd checked on Oliver and gone to her own room Ashraf had taken the bedding she'd put on the too-short sofa and spread it on the floor beside the cot. He'd slept in worse places on army manoeuvres. Besides, this might remind him to think before he spoke.

A cry sounded from the cot and Ashraf shot to his feet.

Flicking on the lamp, he peered down to find Oliver's face screwed up and turning red.

Ashraf slipped his hand beneath his squirming son and lifted him to his chest. The baby felt almost familiar this time, his nestling warmth both comforting and a reminder of how scarily fragile he was.

Ashraf inhaled the smell of talc and baby that in a few short hours had become so satisfying. He stilled his thoughts, focusing on the moment. On the wonder of his child, flesh of his flesh. The promise of a fulfilling long life ahead. A life Ashraf was determined to share.

A couple of hours earlier he'd persuaded Oliver back to sleep with gentle words, rocking and a pain-relieving gel rubbed onto his gums. This time he suspected Oliver wouldn't be so easily settled.

Ashraf paced the room, gentling the fractious baby, murmuring soothing words in his own tongue. He wanted to win Tori a little more sleep. The sight of the smudges of tiredness beneath her eyes had made him feel wrong-footed, steaming in and demanding she upend her life to move to Za'daq.

Except that Tori marrying him, creating a family for Oliver and allowing their child to grow up in the country he'd one day rule, was the most important thing. Ashraf's experience as an unwanted child, ostracised by his own father, made him determined to ensure Oliver *belonged*. That he was accepted and given every opportunity to shine.

He'd do whatever it took to persuade Tori, for Oliver's sake.

Tori opened the door and felt her jaw drop. She'd been barely thinking as she'd pushed back the covers and climbed out of bed, blearily acting on instinct when she'd heard Oliver cry. Now she was fully awake, and staring.

Ash... Ashraf...filled the room, tall, athletically built and almost naked. His wide shoulders and bare back gleamed, a symphony of muscle overlaid with burnished satin skin.

Tori's throat closed as her gaze tracked his spine, moved down long, powerful legs, then up to navy underwear that clung to rounded buttocks. Near his feet lay the pillow and bedding she'd put on the sofa.

He'd slept on Oliver's floor.

The idea stunned her as much as the sight of Ashraf, overwhelmingly virile and masculine, in her private space.

Then there was the way he rocked from side to side, cradling Oliver against his shoulder. Ashraf's voice was a soft, deep hum as he sang a lullaby in a language she didn't understand. It didn't seem to be working on Oliver, who still fretted. But it worked on her. Tori swayed and reached for the doorjamb to prop herself up, her insides turning to mush at the combination of supercharged sexy male and breath-stealing tenderness.

For a dangerous moment she let herself imagine what it would be like if they were a real family—not as Ashraf suggested, for convenience, but because they loved—

No. She wasn't going there. She'd got this far as a single mother and knew she could manage it. Dreams were all well and good but she couldn't confuse them with reality.

'I think you'd better give him to me.'

Ashraf swung round and Tori was hit by another pulse of—okay, she'd admit it—arousal. He was a truly magnificent man, and the sight of her little son secure against that broad bare chest sent emotion curvetting through her.

Tori blamed overactive hormones. And weariness. But then she read Ashraf's expression and thoughts of herself faded. In those strong features and glittering eyes was a reflection of her own feelings when she surveyed Oliver. Wonder, love and protectiveness.

Ashraf might be new to fatherhood, but that didn't mean his feelings for Oliver were less real. Or that he had a smaller claim to parenthood.

The knowledge rushed at her like a biting wind, piercing the mental armour with which she'd shielded her fears.

She'd told herself Oliver was *hers*. That because she barely knew Ashraf, that he came from a faraway place and a time in her life best forgotten, his claim on the baby was less.

How untrue that was. This man, who ruled a country and probably slept in a gilded bed with silk sheets, surrounded by every luxury, had bunked down on the hard floor beside his son. That hadn't been done to make a point.

'Tori! Are you okay?' Ashraf stepped close in a couple of long strides, one warm hand closing around her elbow. 'You look unsteady on your feet.'

She shook her head, pushing her hair back from her face, and stood straighter. 'I'm all right.' As all right as she could be when her life had suffered a sudden seismic shift.

As if from a huge distance she saw her plans for a new life in Perth fracture. Whatever the future held, it wasn't going to be as straightforward as she'd expected.

Ashraf led her to the rocking chair, his hold supportive and expression serious. When Tori experienced another jolt of awareness she felt like a fraud. Then, when he leaned close to pass Oliver over, the warm, evocative scent of spiced cinnamon and male flesh surrounded her. Her nipples tingled, and it wasn't just reaction to Oliver's hungry cry. It was connected to the pulsing throb low in her body.

She shivered and tightened her hold on her baby.

'You're cold?'

The words trawled over her bare arms like a velvet ribbon.

No, she was burning up.

How could she react so viscerally to a man she barely knew? She wasn't by nature promiscuous. Yet with Ashraf...

She'd told herself that what had happened that night in Za'daq had happened because they'd been in mortal danger. That they'd been driven by a primal impulse to procreate and ensure the survival of another generation. What excuse did she have now?

It was as if she was wired to respond instantly and catastrophically to Ashraf.

'No, not cold. Just tired.'

'I'll get you a hot drink. You need to replace fluids.'

Then, before she could stop him, he strode out of the room.

Ashraf spent as long as he could in the kitchen. Anything to stay away from Tori and regroup.

She'd stood in the doorway, looking dazed and delicate, and he'd been torn between concern and fascination at how the hall light behind her outlined her tantalising shape through her nightdress. Pouting breasts, narrow waist, long, slender legs and gently rounded hips.

He'd wanted to grab her hard against him. Need had clawed, urgent and unstoppable.

Her hair was a messy halo, her cheeks flushed. Her lemon-yellow nightgown had a row of buttons down the front, presumably to make breastfeeding easier. Only a couple of those prim buttons had been fastened, allowing him tantalising glimpses of pearly skin.

Memories of losing himself in Tori's sweet body bombarded him, of her soft cries of encouragement and the incredible bliss of a coupling that had far transcended the brutal reality of that foul kidnappers' hut.

He frowned and moved to the kettle, filling it with water. His years of scandalous indulgence might have been designed to infuriate his father, but they hadn't been a complete sham—even if his sexual exploits *had* been exaggerated. He was used to sophisticated women well versed in seductive wiles. He was used to silk, satin and lace, or complete nudity. Not dainty cotton with embroidered flowers. Not nursing mothers.

Ashraf shook his head and straightened. Nothing about this trip was going to plan. But he was adaptable. He had no intention of leaving without his son. Or Tori.

* * *

Tori had finished feeding Oliver but Ashraf still hadn't returned. Had he thought better of spending the night there? The possibility made her feel curiously bereft. But sneaking off without declaring his intentions wasn't Ashraf's style.

'Shall we swap?'

At the sound of his low voice she swung round, hugging Oliver close.

Far from planning to leave, Ashraf hadn't even bothered to dress. Tori's skin tingled with a blush as she fought to stop her gaze going lower than the mug he held.

She'd never been particularly bashful, and until today rarely blushed. Maybe that was due to her father's demands that she accompany him to public events from an early age. Or because female geologists were still outnumbered by men. As a result she'd learned to hide anything that might be viewed as feminine weakness.

Ashraf put the steaming mug down on a chest of drawers and reached for Oliver.

'He's almost asleep.' Tori hugged him closer, as if the baby could protect her from unwanted feelings.

'Good. I'll hold him for a little, then put him down while you have your drink.'

Remembering the look on Ashraf's face as he'd watched Oliver, how could she resist? Tori passed the baby to him, supremely conscious of her nakedness under her nightie and Ashraf's bare arms brushing hers.

Not that Ashraf noticed. His attention was all on Oliver as he paced to the window, stroking the baby's head with one big hand. Something dipped hard in Tori's chest and she turned away, picking up the mug and taking a sip as she sat down.

'This is good!'

'No need to sound surprised. Even kings can boil water.'

She liked the teasing lilt in his voice too much.

'I expected tea.'

Dark eyebrows lifted as he caught her eye then turned away, rocking Oliver. 'I didn't know how you took it, and I didn't want to interrupt, so I made my own favourite.'

'Lemon, honey and...' she paused, taking another sip '... fresh ginger?' So simple yet so delicious.

He nodded, but kept his gaze on their son.

Tori drew a shaky breath and confronted the reality she'd fought from the moment Ashraf had told her his intentions.

'I've been thinking.'

'Yes?'

His head lifted, gleaming eyes pinioning her. It didn't matter that Ashraf was more than half naked and holding a sleeping baby. He looked as powerful as any sovereign in full royal regalia.

Anxiety feathered her spine but she kept her gaze on his, refusing to be intimidated.

'I can't marry you.' She watched the corners of his mouth fold in, as if he was holding back an objection. 'But I understand your desire, your *right* to be involved in Oliver's life.' Her heart pattered faster as she made herself continue. 'I'm still not sure about him being a prince, though. Surely when you eventually marry your legitimate children will inherit?'

'I told you I can legitimise Oliver. I intend to. And I have no intention of taking any other wife.'

Heat flashed through her like a channel of lava, incinerating more of her defences. It shouldn't make a difference, but when Ashraf spoke like that part of her enjoyed it—though it was ludicrous to believe he cared about her as anything other than Oliver's mother.

Of course he'd marry. Some glamorous princess who'd charm his people and give him a bevy of children.

Something sharp lodged in Tori's ribs and she had to breathe slowly to ease the spike of discomfort.

'I'm not entirely convinced becoming Crown Prince of Za'daq is what I want for him.'

Ashraf's brow corrugated and his mouth tightened. Tori

wondered what he wasn't saying. That it wasn't up to her to decide such things?

'Because you believe my country is unsafe? That's understandable, given your abduction, but believe me, that's not the case now.'

'That's part of it, but not all.'

How did she even begin to express her horror at the idea of her precious boy being thrust into such a public role with no choice? She'd spent her childhood and teenage years as a handy asset in her father's politicking. She'd hated it—especially as she'd got old enough to understand his cynical use of a good photo opportunity and his focus on self-aggrandisement rather than public service.

'I want Oliver to have the opportunity to be a child just like any other.' Not shunted around to smile for the press when the polls looked bad or family values were a hot issue for voters.

'Oliver will have that. You have my word.'

'You've said he's destined to become Sheikh. What if he doesn't want to be?'

The idea of her little baby inheriting seemed impossible. Ashraf was so vital and strong. Tori's insides squeezed at the idea of him dying. But he'd come close just last year.

'That's what you're worried about?' He shook his head and the lamplight caught indigo shadows in his inky hair. 'Most women would be thrilled at the idea of their child inheriting riches and power.'

'Most women don't have a politician for a father. Power shouldn't be an end in itself.' She paused, weighing her words. 'It can have a negative effect on a person and on those around them.'

Her father would say he did what he did for the public good. Tori knew he was driven instead by the need for acclaim and power. He was self-serving, and as a father...

'You're right. Power is an obligation.' Ashraf studied her intently as if fascinated by a new insight.

Tori wished she had more than her nightie and a hot drink to shield her from that penetrating gaze.

Conditioned by a lifetime's training, she found it hard to admit aloud her negative feelings about her father and his profession. But this was about Oliver. Nothing, not even the ingrained habit of old loyalty, took precedence.

'Yet you want to tie our child to that before he's even old enough to understand!' She wanted to grab the now sleeping baby and tuck him close. Her fingers clamped hard around the warm mug.

Ashraf's features tightened, the proud lines of nose and forehead growing more defined. 'I will give Oliver the opportunity to inherit what is his right as my son. To lead the people of Za'daq is an honour as well as a responsibility. I won't deprive him of his birthright.'

For a long, pulsing moment Ashraf's eyes bored into hers and she felt her breath clog in her lungs. He was formidable. Daunting. Yet still she felt the fizz of attraction like effervescence in her blood.

Biased by seeing her father and his cronies at close quarters, Tori had told herself she disliked powerful men. But strength was intrinsic to Ashraf and still she was drawn, fascinated, even as her saner self warned her to keep her distance.

'There's always a choice, Tori. No one will force Oliver if he truly doesn't want to become Sheikh. My brother, Karim, was heir to the throne. Yet when my father died Karim declined his inheritance. I was proclaimed Sheikh instead.'

Tori wanted to ask *why* Karim had chosen not to inherit. What he was doing now. Had Ashraf wanted the throne? But the stern set of his mouth warned against questions.

'Surely it's not too much to give our son the opportunity to learn the ways of his forebears? To have access to both cultures—Za'daqi and Australian.'

'I agree.'

'You do?' The fierce glitter in his eyes softened.

'I told you I'd been thinking.'

She swallowed, her stomach churning at what she'd decided. But she had to follow through. It would be cowardly and selfish not to.

'I have serious doubts about the Sheikh thing…' Ashraf's eyebrows rose, yet he didn't interrupt. 'But I'm willing to accept your suggestion. *Not* to marry,' she hurried to clarify, 'but to take Oliver to Za'daq for a visit.'

She read no change in Ashraf's features. No smile, no lessening in the intensity of that stare. But the next breath he drew was so deep it lifted that mighty chest like a cresting ocean wave.

'Thank you, Tori.' He stepped close, one arm effortlessly holding Oliver, the other reaching for her.

She stumbled to her feet, feeling at a disadvantage in the low rocking chair.

Ashraf took her hand, and the hard, enveloping warmth reminded her of the physical differences between them. Differences that, to her dismay, made her body hum and soften.

Instead of shaking her hand, he lifted it. 'You are generous as well as wise and beautiful.'

Tori blinked, and would have tugged free of his grasp except, still holding her gaze, he pressed his lips to the back of her hand. Instantly energy arced from the spot, shooting to her breasts, her pelvis, right down to her toes.

'There's no need to soft-soap me.'

'Soft-soap?'

For the first time Ashraf looked out of his depth. Tori enjoyed that puzzled expression. It was rather endearing. For once she didn't feel as if she were the one playing catch up.

'Flatter me,' she explained.

'I never flatter. I simply speak the truth.'

Which trashed her fleeting sense of superiority.

She stood, her hand in his, staring up into liquid dark eyes and wishing—

What? Wishing that they'd met under different circumstances? Ashraf would still be a king and therefore not the man for her. Wishing that he was someone altogether different? Some guy she'd met at a weekend barbecue? But she couldn't imagine that. Ashraf's identity was part of what made him intriguing.

But it wasn't the forceful, charismatic side of his personality that had made her change her mind. It was his genuine interest in Oliver. His determination to be a meaningful part of his son's life even if that meant waking in the night and walking the floor with a teething baby. One thing she was sure of: Ashraf wouldn't be a father who only showed up for the fun stuff. He'd be there through thick and thin.

Oliver deserved no less. Therefore Ashraf deserved more.

Belatedly she realised he still held her hand. She slipped it free. 'Don't get too excited. It will take me a while to organise. I've only recently begun this job and—'

'Getting leave from your work will be no problem.'

Tori's hackles rose. 'You haven't already asked without consulting me, have you?'

She saw him register her rising indignation. *Good.* She had no intention of being railroaded.

Ashraf shook his head. 'I know the CEO of your company. He's interested in exploring for diamonds in Za'daq.'

Tori wasn't surprised. The possibility of finding diamonds and other gems in the region was what had taken her to the survey team in neighbouring Assara. That experience was part of the reason she'd won her current position.

'He knows it was you I came to meet. I'm sure, if I indicate that his company can bid for the upcoming exploration contract, he'd believe it worthwhile to give you leave of absence.'

Tori opened her mouth, then shut it again. Of course he

would. The company would probably pay her airfare and keep her on full pay indefinitely!

She felt cornered. She'd counted on having more time before taking Oliver to Za'daq. A year, perhaps.

'I need to sort out a passport for Oliver.'

'No problem. I can expedite that.'

Tori stared up at the big man holding their son and unease slipped down her spine. She reached out and took Oliver, hugging him close before putting him in his cot. The comfort of his tiny body against hers eased her nerves. No one would steal her son. Yet she took her time, trailing her knuckle over his satiny cheek, feeling her heart lurch as he turned towards her touch.

Breathing deep, she straightened. 'You've already made enquiries, haven't you?'

Ashraf's expression confirmed it.

'You haven't got him a passport already?'

'I cannot without your consent. But my staff have checked with the Australian authorities and there's no problem.' He paused. 'I cancelled my schedule to come here but I need to return soon. We can leave tomorrow.'

'Tomorrow!' Tori crossed her arms over her body, holding in rising panic. 'That's impossible.'

He spread his hands in a gesture that might have seemed apologetic if not for the look of satisfaction on his face. 'One of the perks of being a visiting head of state…' His expression grew sombre. 'You don't appear happy to have these impediments removed. Didn't you mean it about bringing Oliver to Za'daq?'

'Of course I did.' She rubbed her hands up her arms. 'I just didn't expect things to move so fast. And…' She chewed her lip.

'And…? Something's bothering you? What is it?' His gaze probed. 'Tell me, Tori. I can't deal with the problem if I don't know what it is.'

She hitched a breath. 'I feel you're taking control. As if

I have no say. That makes me wonder how much power I'll have in Za'daq.' She angled her chin. 'Whether you'll have the power to take Oliver from me there.'

Ashraf read Tori's fear and guilt scrolled like an unwinding roll of calligraphy through his belly.

Of course she was concerned. She'd be crazy not to worry. It was true. In Za'daq, once he'd claimed Oliver as his heir, Ashraf would have the authority to keep his son permanently. Just as he'd have the ability to keep Tori within his borders or, alternatively, have her deported.

Ashraf refused to countenance Oliver living half a world away. He'd do whatever it took to have his son with him, where he belonged. Marrying Tori would ensure that. But their future together would be most successful if Tori *chose* to marry. If she *wanted* it.

Oh, she wanted him. He'd read her physical response. But persuading a woman like Tori into marriage would take patience and finesse.

Or an all-out assault on her senses.

Ashraf considered seducing her here and now. Till he remembered her concern to do the right thing by him and Oliver. He owed her more than that. Even though he was impatient for their physical union.

She spoke of a visit to his country, whereas he intended to keep Tori and Oliver with him in Za'daq. Permanently. That would require a concerted attack on Tori's doubts and defences. Showing her how much his homeland had to offer, how much *he* could offer.

'You have my word. On my family name and my country's honour I won't keep you or Oliver in Za'daq if you wish to leave.'

Ashraf's mouth curved. He looked forward to convincing her to stay.

CHAPTER SIX

TWO DAYS LATER Tori peered through the window of Ashraf's private jet, taking in tawny desert plains far below and misty blue-smudged mountains in the distance.

If it wasn't for the high ridge of mountains this might be central Australia's vast arid zone. But the tension prickling her skin belied the comparison.

This was where she'd been kidnapped.

Where those men—

Ashraf's hand covered hers where it gripped the armrest. His touch quelled the shudder ripping through her.

'Okay, Tori?'

She wasn't. She'd told herself she could do this, that it was right to do this. But at the sight of the desert she felt terrifying memories stir. Distress prickled the back of her eyes and she feared she'd lose the exquisitely prepared meal she'd just eaten.

'Of course.' She blinked, keeping her focus on the view as the shudder reduced to a rippling undercurrent of unease. 'It can't be long till we land.'

Ashraf said nothing. He must have registered her anxiety, yet instead of pulling back and following her lead in the change of subject he leaned closer, his warmth penetrating through her jacket and shirt.

Tori caught her bottom lip, stunned at how needy she felt for more. Even now, when fraught memories threatened her fragile composure.

Ashraf's breath caressed her cheek as he pointed to the mountains in the distance. 'Those foothills mark the border territory between Za'daq and Assara. You were abducted there, then brought to the encampment on this side of the border.'

Tori didn't want to think about it. Yet she craned towards the window.

'Then you crossed back into Assara. No wonder we couldn't find a trace of you. If you'd worked in Za'daq we'd at least have been able to identify you through your work visa.'

Tori wasn't interested in unmarked borders or the state of record-keeping in the neighbouring country of Assara. She stared at the sharply folded hills and her stomach swooped.

'The people there are very poor,' he went on. 'That's one of the reasons I'm considering allowing mineral exploration in the region.'

'Mining doesn't necessarily lead to money for the locals. Some are employed for minimum wages but most companies bring in their own expertise.'

She worked in the industry but that didn't mean she was blind to its flaws.

'It depends on the terms negotiated,' Ashraf responded. 'Nothing will be endorsed unless it provides decent local employment and infrastructure. Profits will be channelled into regional initiatives.'

Tori blinked. In her experience profits went to wealthy investors, making them wealthier.

'That's very admirable.'

His fingers tightened, reminding her that he still held her hand. Then he withdrew, leaving her feeling ridiculously bereft.

'You thought my interest was for personal gain?' Ashraf's lovely deep voice sounded different. Distant. Or perhaps affronted.

'No.' She swung round to meet his stare. 'I—'

'It's fine, Tori.'

Though when he said her name it wasn't with the warmth she'd become accustomed to.

'It's what many will think—that I'm looking for riches to spend on myself rather than the public good.'

No mistaking his bitterness.

'But contrary to popular opinion my focus is my people, not myself.'

She was intrigued—not only by his words but also by the hint of vulnerability she'd sensed at his withdrawal. It belied the haughty cast of his expression.

'Your people believe you're not interested in them?'

He shrugged, those wide shoulders spreading. 'Many do. Or at least...' He paused, as if choosing his words. 'I spent several years scandalising polite society with my "reckless, self-absorbed, self-indulgent lifestyle". Some find it hard to believe that's over.'

Anxiety forgotten, Tori twisted towards him. 'That sounds like a quote.'

'Sorry?' His eyebrows crinkled in confusion.

'The bit about being reckless and self-indulgent. It sounded like someone else's words.'

Ashraf's eyes widened and she read his surprise. Then his gaze became shuttered. Clearly this wasn't something he'd allow her to pursue. But whose words had made such an impression?

'You're not reckless and self-indulgent now.'

It wasn't a question. How could it be when Tori had first-hand experience of Ashraf's character? He'd tried to protect her in the desert. He'd searched for her for over a year, never giving up. He'd accepted his role as Oliver's father without question, without even hinting about the need for a paternity test. No avoidance or denial, just unflinching acceptance of the circumstances and a determination to do the best he could.

One black eyebrow rose as if he doubted her assessment.

'Well, you're not.'

It was true that he'd been notorious—as Tori had discovered when she trawled the Internet. But for the last two years he'd barely been out of Za'daq. Every photo showed a serious, almost grim man, usually surrounded by a flock of courtiers or regional leaders. News reports about him focused on social and political issues, regional trade discussions, health improvements and so on.

However, older reports revealed that the younger Ashraf had lived a lifestyle that kept the paparazzi on its toes.

Skiing at the trendiest resorts, escaping to fabled islands in the Pacific and the Caribbean, frequenting exclusive clubs, casinos and the sort of parties that fuelled the media's insatiable appetite for gossip.

She'd found photos that had made her stare. Prince Ashraf stumbling out of a casino in the early hours, accompanied by not one glamorous model but three, all looking as if they'd like to eat him for breakfast. A long-distance shot of him diving, naked, off a billionaire's yacht after a week-long party. Even the grainy quality of the shot hadn't disguised his taut, powerful frame, and Tori's pulse had tripped to a rackety beat.

'You sound very sure of my character,' he murmured, and she couldn't work out if he was annoyed, intrigued or merely making an observation.

Tori shrugged, turning to the view. This time those rugged hills didn't fill her with quite the same dread, though she still found herself clasping her hands tight.

'There's a lot I don't know about you, Ashraf, but we've shared some intense experiences. Self-absorbed isn't how I'd describe you.'

'How *would* you describe me?' he asked after a heartbeat's silence.

Tori sucked in a breath.

Magnetic. Sexy. Disturbing.

And one step ahead of her since the moment he'd confronted her in Perth. Tori felt she was playing catch-up with someone who knew the rules in a game she had yet to learn. And yet...

'Decisive. Obstinate, but with a well-developed sense of responsibility. Used to getting your own way.'

Tori heard a crack of laughter but refused to look at him. She'd seen him smile, felt the full force of his attractiveness, and wasn't ready to face it again. Not when she was so out of her depth.

'If only that were true. Being Sheikh means tempering my impatience for change so I can persuade others to see my vision for the future.'

Curious, unable to resist, she finally turned, noting the tiny lines bracketing his firm mouth. Lines that spoke of weariness and restraint.

'I thought the Sheikh of Za'daq had absolute power? Can't you just make a decree?'

'You've done your homework.'

'A little. I haven't had time to discover much.'

Again Tori experienced that plunging sensation in her stomach. Everything had happened so quickly.

'There's plenty of time to learn all you want to.' He paused, ebony eyes resting on her in a way that made the blood sizzle under her skin. 'And you're right. Technically I have the power to do as I wish. But in practice the Sheikh works with the Royal Council, which is made up of powerful provincial leaders. It would be madness to institute major change without bringing the Council on board.'

His tone was easy but Tori sensed strong emotion ruthlessly repressed. Or perhaps she was making something from nothing. Essentially he was a stranger. Surely it was crazy to believe she could read him.

Tori tugged her gaze back to the view.

'It's true, you know…'

His voice dropped, holding a low, resonant note that ran through her like warm treacle.

'The border province is peaceful now. You have nothing to fear in Za'daq. You and Oliver are safe in my country.'

Safe? Protected from marauding bandits, perhaps. But

Tori knew with a shiver of premonition that the most peril-
ous threat came from the man beside her. The man determined to raise Oliver as a Za'daqi prince. The man who'd
turned her world on its head and undermined all her cer-
tainties.

She was glad of Ashraf's supporting hand as the plane's
door was opened to reveal steps down to the Tarmac. For
as they emerged bright sunlight engulfed them, and with it
the scent of the desert.

A tremor of panic racked her, making her shake all
over, gluing her soles to the top of the steps. Rough fingers
seemed to scrabble up her nape then curl around her windpipe, crushing the flow of air.

It should be impossible to smell anything other than avi-
ation fuel and the warm cinnamon notes of Ashraf's skin
as he stood close. Yet her nostrils twitched, inhaling the
faint scents of dry earth and indefinable spice she associ-
ated with the desert.

Instead of hurrying her down the stairs Ashraf stood
unmoving, his hand firm at her elbow, giving her time to
take it all in. The airport building to one side. Cars at the
foot of the steps, where a knot of people waited. Hangars,
aircraft. And beyond that, just visible over a collection of
modern buildings, arid brown earth.

Tori inhaled sharply, fear stabbing her chest. Her arms
tightened around her sleeping son and the pulse of her blood
became a panicked flurry in her ears.

Ashraf spoke. She heard the reassuring murmur of his
voice, felt his gaze on her face, and finally managed another
breath, steadier this time.

Eventually his words began to penetrate. A gentle flow
describing the new airport building, finished last year. The
recent economic boost as Za'daq had capitalised on its location to become a regional transport hub. The businesses
clustered around the airport as a result.

Another listener would have heard a sheikh proud of his country. But Tori, catching his eye as her body finally unfroze, saw concern glimmer in those black eyes. A whump of emotion hit her. Like the invisible force-field of an explosion that would have knocked her off her feet if he hadn't held her.

He knows. He understands.

There was no impatience in those strong features. Just reassurance to counter the chill that defied the blaze of sunlight and turned her bones brittle.

Had he expected her to panic? Tori had been nervous, but nothing had prepared her for the sudden freezing dread.

She took a breath, then another. This time Ashraf's warm scent filled her nostrils, and Oliver's comforting clean baby smell. Tori licked her lips, moistening her mouth. Ashraf followed the movement and heat of another kind flared.

'So much development in such a short space of time,' she murmured, her voice husky. 'It must have taken a lot of work.'

It wasn't an insightful observation but it was the best she could do. Ashraf nodded. He appeared relaxed, yet Tori felt the tension in his tall frame, as if he was ready at any moment to gather up both her and Oliver. His eyes flickered to the baby and Tori read his unspoken question.

But with his help her panic had passed. Her knees had stopped wobbling and her hold on Oliver was firm. She inclined her head and Ashraf turned towards the steps and the group of people watching.

He led the way, taking his time as he spoke about the long-term vision to make Za'daq a centre for communications and information technology.

Neither the aircraft crew nor the people by the limousines would have guessed at Tori's sickening wave of fear. Gratitude filled her for Ashraf's support. Especially when they finally reached the Tarmac and she read the barely veiled disapproval on some of the faces turned her way.

An older man approached and bowed. The bow spoke of deference, but the dismissive glance he cast her and Oliver spoke volumes. It shored up her determination to stand tall.

Ashraf frowned as the man spoke. His voice was no longer mellifluous and reassuring as he asked the man a question, then another, in the same language.

A short time later, after a few brisk words from Ashraf, the entourage retreated to the limousines.

'I'm sorry,' he said, turning to her. 'Something has come up which requires my attention. I won't accompany you to the palace. But you'll be well looked after.' He gestured towards a slight gangly figure in a pale grey robe who, instead of retreating with the others, stepped forward. 'Bram will see you settled.'

This man also bowed to Ashraf, but then turned and bowed to her too. 'Ms Nilsson.'

He straightened and Tori looked into a pair of blue eyes, startling against swarthy skin.

'It's a pleasure to meet you.'

'And you... Bram.' Had she heard that right? She'd thought it an Irish name.

He smiled, his mouth hitching higher at one side because of a long scar cleaving his cheek. 'This way, please.'

Tori peered up at Ashraf. He was her only anchor in this foreign place. She battled the impulse to clutch him. That impulse was far too strong.

Ashraf opened his mouth to speak again but she forestalled him. 'It will be good to get Oliver settled.' Their son was awake now, waving one tiny hand. Soon he'd be demanding a feed.

The predictability of his needs helped ground her. Nothing was more important than Oliver. So, within minutes of arriving in Za'daq, she and her son were on their way to the capital while Ashraf attended to his important business.

Bram, in the front beside the driver, turned with that lopsided smile. 'There's our destination. The royal palace.'

Tori's nerves jangled as she stared. Of *course* a king would live in a palace. She'd had so much on her mind she hadn't considered that.

The palace sprawled magnificently across a hill above the city. Its acres of white stone gleamed in the sun, making it visible well beyond the city fringe.

From a distance its size and pristine colour caught the eye, and then its fairy-tale towers and gilded domes. Eventually, as the limousine climbed a road lined with public parks, Tori felt her breath catch at the palace's sheer beauty. There was carved marble, patterns of lustrous tiles worked in deep blues, greens and golds. Even the intricate ironwork of the tall fence pleased the eye.

Yet Tori's skin turned clammy. *This* was Ashraf's home? The place he wanted her and Oliver to live? This was a palace for a potentate, proclaiming wealth and power. Despite its beauty, it sent a shudder through her.

It didn't matter that they were only visiting, or that he hadn't mentioned marriage again. She suspected Ashraf wasn't a man who'd easily give up when he had his mind fixed on an idea. If they were to agree on some way of sharing Oliver this place would become a significant part of her son's life and therefore hers.

As the daughter of a senior politician she'd attended functions at luxury hotels and private venues, but never anywhere like this.

She looked down at the slate-blue trousers and jacket she'd thought so perfect for travelling and felt completely out of her depth. But how *did* one dress for a palace straight out of a fairy tale?

A bubble of panicked laughter rose as she tried to imagine herself bedecked in glittering gems or ermine or whatever it was that royals wore in places like this.

If Ashraf were here beside her it would be easier.

Even thinking that felt like a betrayal. Tori had always stood up for herself and it was especially important that she do so now. Ashraf and his managing ways had swept her back to a country where she'd never wanted to venture again.

Once more icy fingers played up her spine. Had she made the biggest mistake ever, coming here? She'd agreed to come when she'd been tired and stressed, thrown by seeing Ashraf again when she'd believed him dead.

She'd experienced a destabilising uprush of emotions on seeing him so caring of Oliver, so charismatic that her heart had fluttered in a ridiculous butterfly beat high in her throat. That toned, muscle-packed body, those incredible eyes that seemed to see more of her private self than anyone ever had. Even the thin scar along his ribs that told the story of their near-death experience made her feel close to him. As if they shared something profound.

Tori huffed a silent laugh. They did share something significant. Oliver.

Of course she'd done right in coming here. This was a first step in coming to an agreement about how their son would be raised.

Tori's gaze slewed back to the dazzling white edifice taking up the whole hilltop, her hands clenching. She needed some space after days and nights in Ashraf's company. Yet...*she missed him*.

Tori's eyes widened.

How long since Ashraf had prowled the length of the Perth boardroom and her heart had taken off like a rocket? A mere couple of days since he'd blasted her life to smithereens.

The limousine swung past the palace's monumental main gates and followed a road around the perimeter, eventually pulling in to a more utilitarian entrance.

A uniformed servant opened her door. By the time she'd picked up Oliver and stepped out Bram was urging her inside.

Out of the air-conditioned car, with Oliver warm in her

arms, she felt flushed and crumpled. But pride made her stand straight as she was introduced to the palace chamberlain, a tall man in snowy robes.

Gathering her wits, she did what she'd failed to do on meeting Bram, exchanging greetings in Arabic. She knew just enough to understand his wish that she would be comfortable during her stay and to thank him in the same language.

Was that surprise in his eyes? She didn't have time to find out, for Bram was ushering her into a cool, beautifully tiled hall.

'Your apartment is here, at the rear of the palace.'

After turning into another hallway, even more lavishly decorated, and through a courtyard filled with the scent of lilies, he opened a door and invited her to precede him.

Tori stopped dead a few paces in.

'A maid has been assigned to you, and a nanny to help—' Bram's words halted as he saw her face. 'Is the suite not suitable? If not I—'

'It's perfectly suitable, thank you.'

Tori dragged her eyes from the domed ceiling with its mosaic tiles depicting an idyllic garden filled with flowers. The glittering background tiles couldn't be real gold, she told herself. As for the elegant sofas and the beautiful, delicately carved side tables and the pots of colourful orchids… It was impossibly luxurious and gorgeous.

Tori felt simultaneously out of place and desperate to flop down on one of those pale couches and close her eyes.

The sound of water caught her ears and she turned. Tall, arched windows gave on to another courtyard where water sprayed in jets beside a long, inviting pool.

'There's a cot in the second bedroom and a range of baby supplies. If anything is missing you just need to ask the maid or pick up the phone. I can personally—'

Tori roused herself from her daze. 'I'm sure we'll have

everything we need. Thank you, Bram. You've been most kind.'

Twenty minutes later she was feeding Oliver, seated in a deeply upholstered chair so comfortable it felt as if her bones melted into it. Her luggage had been unpacked for her. At her side was a frosted glass of juice and an array of mouthwatering pastries brought by a friendly maid.

She was surrounded by luxury, by people eager to please. And yet as she surveyed her sumptuous surroundings Tori wondered if she'd walked into a trap.

A trap devised by a man intent on securing his son at any cost.

CHAPTER SEVEN

'THERE'S ALREADY CONJECTURE about Ms Nilsson.'

'So soon?' Ashraf met Bram's eyes. The rumour mill around the royal court was more efficient than any modern communication software. 'I should have expected it.' Yet he'd convinced himself they had more time.

He rolled his head from side to side, feeling the ache in his neck from too many sleepless hours. They faced a full-blown public scandal when the truth of Tori's and Oliver's identities were known. Yet he had no regrets. How could he have done anything other than bring Oliver and his mother here?

Bram spread his hands. 'Once the Minister for the Interior heard you had a female companion—'

'He manufactured a reason to meet the plane.' The Minister had been a friend of Ashraf's father. He'd absorbed the old Sheikh's disdain for Ashraf and now waited—daily, it seemed—for his new King to take a false step.

Ashraf wasn't naïve. He knew the powerful men who'd formed his father's innermost clique still harboured hopes that something would go wrong. That *he'd* go wrong and then his brother, Karim, would return to take the crown.

That would never happen.

Karim's reason for rejecting the crown was insurmountable. Karim would return to Za'daq one day, but only to visit. He'd made that clear. Only the two brothers knew the real reason for his refusal to become Sheikh, and Ashraf cared for Karim too much ever to betray that secret. Not even to squash the machinations of those trying to destabilise his rule.

He was more than capable of dealing with them. Life had

made him more resilient and determined than those waiting for him to fail. As for being underestimated…they'd learn. Ashraf wouldn't countenance failure. He'd never been good enough for his old man but he was determined to be the Sheikh his country needed, no matter what the political establishment thought.

'If it's any consolation,' Bram went on, 'we discovered who leaked the news that you had a travel companion. Someone in the palace administrative team. He's been dismissed.'

Bram paused, frowning, presumably at the knowledge that it was someone in his own unit who'd breached confidentiality.

'But this morning I offered him an alternative job, in the outer provinces, coordinating the infant immunisation campaign. It will give him a chance to put his talent for disseminating information to good use.'

Ashraf felt a smile tug his mouth. 'You think he'll do well there?' The rural location would challenge someone used to city life.

Bram spread his hands. 'I said if he did an outstanding job, meeting all our targets for immunisation over the next three years, I *might* be able to persuade you not to prosecute him for breach of privacy.'

Ashraf's smile became a grin. 'Trust you to turn a problem into an opportunity.'

His old friend was an expert at that—possibly because he'd had so much experience at picking himself up and moving on, no matter what life threw at him.

Bram shrugged. 'He's got talent. It would be a shame to waste it. As for fixing problems—that's what you pay me for.'

'We need to change your job title from Royal Secretary to Chief Troubleshooter!'

Ashraf would have sacked the palace employee and

washed his hands of the man. But then, as his father had enjoyed pointing out, Ashraf was his impulsive son.

Over the years he'd changed that, learning in the military to think strategically as well as quickly. But sometimes his desire for swift action led to complications. Like taking a too-quick security assessment at face value, riding into bandit territory and getting kidnapped...

He rubbed a palm around the back of his neck.

'The news is contained for now,' said Bram. 'No one knows the truth about Ms Nilsson or the boy. Just that they're here.'

Ashraf nodded. 'I want it to stay that way as long as possible.' And it wasn't just that he needed time to persuade Tori into marriage. 'We need to suppress the story of how we met. Permanently.'

'Of course. Admitting you were kidnapped within our borders—'

'It's not just that.' Though such news wouldn't do his standing any good. 'She'd be horribly embarrassed if all the world knew just when and where our son was conceived.'

Ashraf's time with Tori had been a pure blessing in the midst of what he'd imagined would be his final painful hours on earth. He didn't want the press or his father's cronies discovering the details and turning them into salacious gossip, so the world could picture Tori giving herself to him in that foul prison filled with the stink of past torture and brutality.

A shiver scudded down his spine and Ashraf's mouth firmed. If nothing else, he'd save her that.

'When the time comes the world can know that we met and I fathered a child. But as for anything else—' He sliced the possibility off with a swift lopping motion.

'You're shielding her?'

'Of course.'

Bram nodded, but Ashraf knew from the speculative

gleam in his eyes that he was processing his friend's protectiveness.

'We should be able to manage that. The rescue team never saw Ms Nilsson at the camp.'

'Excellent.' Ashraf looked at his watch. 'Have we finished?' He'd already been delayed for hours. He wanted to see how Tori and Oliver were settling in. Make sure she wasn't planning to get the next plane out of there.

Not that she'd succeed.

But it wasn't merely that concerning him. The look she'd sent him at the airport when he'd told her to go with Bram had revealed how much he'd asked of her. For a second she'd looked beseeching. The sight had stunned him as even her moment of panic on the plane hadn't.

Before today he'd seen Tori shocked, struggling to process the news that he was alive, and he'd seen her battling to hide terror during their kidnap. But her vulnerability in that split second when her gaze had clung had curdled his gut.

It had taken more determination than he'd imagined to watch her walk away before turning calmly to the officials awaiting him.

Ashraf had wanted to lash out at the politician whose judgemental gaze had rested so dismissively on Tori. Who'd inserted himself into the royal schedule solely, Ashraf knew, to make mischief. He'd wanted to turn his back on the high-level meeting that had been arranged in his absence.

But instead Ashraf had quashed the impulse to ignore his regal responsibility and go with Tori and Oliver—his family.

The word snagged the breath in his lungs.

Given his utterly dysfunctional family background, Ashraf had never dwelled on the idea of creating a family of his own. Now he had one. The realisation was arresting, satisfying and disturbing.

The sound of Bram clearing his throat jerked Ashraf's attention back. 'Yes? Is there something else?'

'Nothing.'

For second he could have sworn he saw amusement in his friend's eyes. But the next moment Bram was frowning at the royal schedule.

'We're finished for today, but tomorrow's timetable is packed. Suddenly half the Cabinet Ministers need to see you urgently.'

Ashraf lifted one eyebrow. 'I'm sure they do.' He shook his head, resisting the urge to massage those tight neck muscles again. 'If only they spent as much energy on public policy as they do trying to undermine me.'

'Actually, on that… It's too soon to tell, but you may have had a couple more wins. Two provincial governors have been in contact privately this week, full of enthusiasm about the results of your latest initiatives. They're hoping to meet you to discuss ideas they have for further implementation.' Bram paused. 'It could be that the tide is turning.'

Or it could be that you'll never be accepted, no matter how hard you work or how sound your policies. You're an outsider. You always have been. Nothing will change that.

The voice in Ashraf's head wasn't new. It had always been there, undercutting his early attempts to be a son his father could be proud of.

With the ease of long practice he ignored it. 'Let's hope.'

And he hoped, too, that he could win Tori over. She'd agreed to this visit but persuading her to stay, to accept his proposition, would take all his persuasive skills and more.

Tori hadn't answered his knock so he entered her suite, taking in the silence and lengthening shadows. A quick investigation revealed no sign of her or Oliver.

Ashraf frowned. Had she turned tail and left the palace? But that wasn't like Tori. Nevertheless he felt better seeing her clothes in the wardrobe.

He retraced his steps to the sitting room, then went out into the suite's private courtyard. A slow smile curved his lips and warmed his belly.

Tori lay on a sun lounger set in dappled shade beside the long pool. A portable cot where Oliver dozed was positioned beside her.

Heat thwacked Ashraf's chest as he looked at his tiny son. And as for Tori...

His gaze trailed over her silver gilt hair, enticingly loose across her narrow shoulders. Over the open shirt and slinky scarlet bikini that revealed full breasts and a narrow waist. Down lissom bare legs.

His groin stirred as desire smoked across his skin. He wanted Victoria Nilsson. Wanted her naked and eager. Wanted so much more. Everything he discovered about this woman attracted him. Plus, he wanted all that maternal love for his son.

Ashraf drew a deep breath, relieved at the reason for these unusually intense feelings. The need to provide for his son. That explained his determination to have Tori permanently. Ashraf wanted the very best for his boy. That meant Oliver's mother to love and care for their son. As Ashraf's mother hadn't been around to love and care for him.

As if she sensed his scrutiny Tori's eyelids fluttered open. For a second Ashraf read pleasure in those forget-me-not-blue eyes. Pleasure and welcome. But only for a second.

Too soon she was scrambling to sit up, hauling her shirt closed with one hand, eyes wary.

'Relax.'

Ashraf sank onto a nearby chair, looking around the courtyard. He needed to concentrate on something other than Tori. He refused to betray the urgency that sang in his blood when she was near.

Yet even with his gaze elsewhere he was aware of her. The soft hitch of her breath, the creak of her chair as she moved, her sweet, tantalising scent.

He forced himself to focus on his surroundings. He hadn't been in here before. The royal family's rooms were on the other side of the palace and he'd never investigated the guest apartments. Bram had chosen well. The courtyard was restful and private.

'Does the apartment suit you? If it's lacking anything…'

'Lacking?' Tori shook her head and that stunning hair spilled around her shoulders. 'It's beautiful. More than we need.'

Ashraf dragged his attention back to her face, to the frown lines between her brows. As if she was worried she'd been allocated something to which she wasn't entitled.

Didn't Tori realise how much more she'd be entitled to as his wife? Or was she really not concerned with wealth?

Another reminder that she wasn't like the women he'd known.

'I'm glad to see you resting. It's been a turbulent time for you.'

Ashraf congratulated himself on his tact. Far better than blurting out that she looked tired. How she'd managed those months alone with Oliver and starting a new, demanding job…

'Now, *there's* an understatement.'

A ghost of a smile curved her lips and Ashraf felt his tension lessen.

Once more he sensed a fragile understanding and acceptance between them. It was rare. He'd only experienced it before with his brother and Bram, the two men who really knew him and rather than just his reputation.

Deliberately Ashraf settled back and let his eyes rove the tranquil garden. Sweet blossom perfumed the air and from nearby came the chitter of a bird.

How long since he'd taken an evening off?

His gaze turned to the small table beside Tori. A newspaper lay there, and a book. He tilted his head to read the title.

'You're learning my language?' Satisfaction glowed. This was a good sign.

Tori made a deprecating gesture. 'Trying. A little. It seemed like a good idea.'

'It's an excellent idea.' He beamed and watched her eyes widen. 'But you don't need to use a book. I'll arrange a tutor.'

Instead of thanking him, she frowned. 'That's not necessary. I'm only here on a visit.'

So much for seeing this as an indication that she'd decided to stay. Ashraf schooled his features not to reveal emotion, but that didn't stop the bite of disappointment.

'You can't *really* expect marriage, Ashraf,' she said when he didn't respond.

Her voice was low but he heard the echo of the arguments she'd put up before. Arguments she thought were reasonable but which meant nothing in the face of his all-consuming need to protect his child.

Impatience grated. How did he make her understand? Make her see the damage that threatened little Oliver if they didn't work together to protect him?

Ashraf knew Tori's relationship with her father wasn't close now, but surely she'd grown up with a mother and father, a sense of belonging. She'd been nurtured and, he guessed, loved.

Oliver would survive with the love of both his parents even if those parents weren't together. Yet that wasn't enough for Ashraf. Not when he knew first-hand the isolation of being different. The poisonous rumours. The continual battle to be accepted.

Ashraf would do anything to ensure his son didn't face that. He didn't want Oliver merely to survive. He wanted him to thrive.

Ashraf expelled a slow breath, realising there was only one way to convince Tori. He'd planned to seduce her into agreement. But, while that might help, Tori was a woman who thought things through. Who weighed up options and responsibilities. Sexual pleasure wouldn't be enough. She needed concrete reasons.

The thought of baring those reasons filled him with cold

nausea. Even with Bram and Karim the past was a territory he didn't visit.

'Family is very important,' he began.

'Of course. But Oliver can have that without us marrying.'

'Not the sort of family he'll need.'

'Sorry?'

'Za'daq is a modern country but it still has traditional
roots. Traditional values.'

'You're saying we should marry because you're worried
about what people will *think*?' Her mouth tightened. 'You
believe public opinion is worth an unhappy marriage?'

'You assume it will be unhappy?'

Tori spread her hands. 'We don't know each other. We
probably don't have anything in common—'

'We have Oliver.' That made her pause. 'And we have
more too. Respect.' Ashraf held her eyes. 'Liking. Attraction.'

White-hot desire was a better description, but he sensed
she'd baulk at such straight talking. He'd seen her nervous
reaction to the craving they both felt.

'That's not enough.'

'You want romantic love?' He searched her face, watching her gaze skitter away.

'It's usually the basis of marriage.'

'In your country, but not mine. Here love often comes
with time, with respect, with liking and shared experience.
All of which we have.'

'We shared one night of captivity!'

'An intense experience. You can't deny the connection
between us is strong because of it. Far stronger than if we'd
met on an online site and begun dating.'

Tori pursed her lips but said nothing.

'We have what it takes to make a good marriage. For
Oliver's sake we need to try.'

Ashraf paused but she refused to admit his point. He ignored the churning in his belly and plunged on.

'I want our son to have what I didn't. Two parents who care for him. Who are there for him every day.' He watched her brow knot. 'Every child deserves a supportive environment. Without that life can be tough.' His lips curled as a sour tang filled his mouth. 'I don't want that for Oliver.'

'I didn't know your childhood was difficult.' There was curiosity and sympathy in Tori's look, but instead of pressing for details she went on. 'But I don't see how that applies to Oliver.'

Ashraf shook his head. 'I want Oliver to have the best in every way. I can declare him legitimate, and that will give him legal status, but I want him to be part of a *real* family. To give meaning to the bare legality and make it something more.' He paused and turned to look at the innocent child who, he knew, would suffer if Ashraf wasn't careful.

Suddenly his lungs ached, pain searing deep.

'I want him protected from scorn and prejudice.' He took another slow breath that still didn't fill his chest. 'Above all I don't want him to believe, for a moment, that I'm not committed to him or don't want him here. I won't have him growing up in the shadows, unsure where he fits.'

Tori's arguments stilled on her tongue as she read the lines of tension wrapping around Ashraf's mouth and pleating his forehead. An icy wave washed over her, despite the balmy evening.

Here was something she didn't understand. Something important. Ashraf wasn't posturing. Whatever the problem was, it was deep-seated. She felt the ache of it just watching his still frame as he stared at Oliver.

'What do you mean, growing up in the shadows?'

Ashraf turned and for the first time she could recall, his dark eyes looked utterly bleak. But only for a moment. Just as she was registering what looked like anguish, his expression became unreadable.

He lifted wide shoulders and spread his hands. 'I wasn't meant to be Sheikh, you know.'

Slowly Tori nodded. 'You said your older brother was supposed to inherit. Is this something to do with him?

'*No.*' The word was emphatic. 'Karim's reasons for rejecting the throne are his own and private.' He paused as if to make sure she got the 'no trespassing' message.

Tori got it, all right, but that didn't stifle her curiosity. She watched as Ashraf swung his legs off the lounger to sit facing her, elbows on his thighs. The stance emphasised the power in his athletic frame and awareness fluttered through her, making her hurry into speech.

'So you weren't first in line to the throne... What's that saying? Having an heir and a spare lined up?'

Ashraf's huff of laughter was humourless. 'Good in theory, but I was never the spare—not as far as my father was concerned. He hated me because I wasn't his.'

'Not his?' Astonishment gripped her.

'My mother left him for another man when I was tiny. The official story in Za'daq is that she died. My father couldn't bear the thought of the public knowing the truth. In those days the press was carefully controlled. Nothing went public that would offend the Sheikh.'

Tori shook her head, still grappling with the first part of what he'd said. 'She left to be with another man? The man who'd fathered you? Yet she didn't take you?'

She couldn't imagine leaving her baby behind.

'She knew the Sheikh wouldn't denounce me as illegitimate because his pride wouldn't permit a public scandal. She was right. Publicly, he didn't.'

Ashraf's expression, as hard as cast bronze, confirmed that in private things had been different.

'Surely she could have taken you?'

'You didn't know his pride.' Ashraf shook his head.

'Once he'd acknowledged me as his son he'd never release me. Anyway, she probably thought I'd be better off here. Her lover wasn't wealthy.'

Tori stared, her mind racing. 'You never *asked* her why she left you behind?'

His mouth tightened. 'I didn't get a chance. She died of complications from influenza when I was a child. I only discovered that later—when I set out to locate her.'

Tori sank back, stunned. Ashraf an unloved child… abandoned by his mother and left to the mercy of a proud, arrogant man for whom he was a reminder of his wife's desertion. Her skin crawled.

'I never had what you'd call a family life.'

Ashraf's voice was uninflected. He might have been talking about the weather.

'Except for my brother, Karim, no one cared about me.'

He drew a breath that made his chest rise, then turned to lock his gaze with hers.

'My father never told anyone about my parentage but he made his disapproval clear to me in every possible way. There was no warmth or encouragement. He constantly found fault and his attitude rubbed off. The courtiers, all the people who mattered in Za'daq, took their cue from him. Everyone viewed me as useless, shallow, lacking the virtues my brother possessed. Whispers and innuendo followed me no matter how hard I tried.'

'So you acted up?'

She thought of those press reports about the Playboy Prince, spending his time flitting between scandalous parties and shockingly dangerous sports. Because he'd had nothing better to do with his time? Or because he too had believed he had nothing better to offer?

Tori's hand went to her throat. It was hard to imagine Ashraf, of all people, so vulnerable.

His mouth twisted. 'As a kid I tried hard to please my father. But nothing was good enough. Later…' He shrugged.

'Later it seemed a fine revenge to make him squirm a little by living down to the reputation he'd built for me.'

She didn't know what to say. Finally she asked, 'Did you ever meet your real father?'

Ashraf's expression had been wry before, his features taut. Now, though, it was as if an iron shutter slammed down, blocking out even the cynical amusement that had gleamed in that half-smile a moment before.

'That's the ultimate irony. When the old Sheikh was taken ill he needed a bone marrow donor. Even though he was so sick he still couldn't bring himself to countermand the suggestion that I get tested for compatibility. That's when we discovered I *was* his son after all. He'd spent years despising me on the basis of unfounded suspicion. Just because he'd found an old letter that predated my birth, sent to my mother by the man she later ran off with. He assumed—wrongly—that she'd slept with him and conceived me as a result.'

'Oh, Ashraf.'

She sat up, instinctively covering his clasped hands with one of hers. It was like touching warm but unforgiving steel. All that hate. All that distance between father and son for nothing but pride.

One of those large hands moved and covered hers. Eyes dark as a stormy night captured hers.

'I want Oliver to have what I never did. A family. Parents together in one place, loving him, caring for him—'

He broke off and Tori wondered with a wobble of distress if Ashraf's throat had closed as convulsively as hers had. She swallowed, trying to dislodge the choking knot of emotion blocking her larynx as she imagined his childhood.

'I don't give a damn what people think of me. But I don't want him subjected to prejudice because he's not in my life full-time. Because he's not seen to belong.'

Her gaze slewed to their precious boy, who'd woken and

was now staring at them with lustrous eyes so like Ashraf's that her chest squeezed.

'He *does* belong. He's ours.'

But as she spoke Tori's heart sank. Ashraf was right. Oliver could be legitimised, but to some his birth out of wedlock would for ever leave a taint of scandal.

'Whether he's in Australia or Za'daq he'll attract public interest. It's inevitable. I want to do everything to protect him from the negatives of that. I want to support him. I want him to feel safe and secure, proud of who he is. Sure right from the start that we're united and on his side.'

Ashraf's voice rang with sincerity. Tori wanted that too. She could understand Ashraf's reasoning now, and her heart ached for the boy he'd been, a victim of circumstances beyond his control, abandoned by both parents.

Part of her wanted to nod and say of course she'd do anything for her son. Yet even as she opened her mouth her own survival instinct kicked in. Everything rebelled at the thought of marrying for appearances' sake.

Flashes of memory filled her brain. Of her parents' marriage where whatever tenderness there might once have been had died. All that had remained was a sham, a pretence of a happy family constructed to salvage pride and win votes.

Tori had vowed never to have a marriage like that. Since childhood she'd known she wanted more. She'd promised herself she'd never settle for anything less than love.

'I...' She met Ashraf's gaze and her throat dried. She was torn between determination to do what was best for Oliver and fear that she'd become like her mother, living an unhappy half-life. 'I need time.'

After what seemed like a full minute he nodded. 'Of course. I understand.'

But that wasn't what his eyes said, or the pressure of his hand on hers. He was a determined man. A king. How far would his patience stretch?

CHAPTER EIGHT

FOUR DAYS LATER Tori knew Ashraf's patience was far stronger than hers.

Heat climbed her cheeks as she realised she almost *wanted* him to break the impasse between them. She lived on tenterhooks, feeling the tension screwing tighter with each hour.

Despite her reservations about marriage, Tori couldn't switch off her intense response to Ashraf's magnetism. The yearning for his touch, his tenderness, his body, just wouldn't fade. She remembered being in his arms, lost in a sensual abandon so profound the world had fallen away. The memories were fresher than ever and more tempting.

Late each day he came to her rooms to share a meal and spend time with Oliver. From that they'd begun to develop a new type of intimacy which was simultaneously challenging and precious.

Despite the unanswered question hanging over them, those hours were relaxing and companionable. Ashraf never mentioned marriage. He was an easy, amusing companion, sharing anecdotes and asking about her day, fascinated by what she and Oliver had done.

Nor did he shy from answering her questions. His frankness intrigued her, especially when she discovered areas of common ground or subjects in which their differing views led to stimulating debate.

Debate, not argument.

Unlike her father, Ashraf never tried to browbeat her into accepting his views.

It was her favourite time of the day. A time she recalled

late at night, long after Ashraf had left and she'd retired to her lonely bed.

Tori shivered and stared absently at the tiny shop's display of bright fabrics. She lifted the filigreed glass of tea to her lips. The scalding liquid warmed her and might even explain the flush she felt in her cheeks.

What she recalled most often, and in excruciating detail, was how Ashraf, after kissing Oliver on the brow, always took her hand and pressed a lingering kiss there as he said goodnight. His eyes shone like polished onyx and he held her hand so long she was sure he must feel the throb of her pulse racing out of control.

Every night she wondered if *this* would be the moment he'd break his self-imposed distance and pull her close, giving in to the ever-present spark of desire between them.

And every night, just as she decided she couldn't stand the suspense or the longing any more, he'd say goodnight and leave her alone in her sumptuous apartment.

'I won't be much longer, Tori. I promise.'

Azia's voice interrupted her thoughts. Tori looked towards the crimson curtain that hid the small shop's changing room and smiled.

'Take your time. I'm enjoying all these fabulous silks. It's like being in Aladdin's cave.' She nodded to the shop owner, who beamed and pulled down a bolt of sea-green silk threaded with silver before taking it to Azia.

It was a treat to be on a girls' shopping expedition with Bram's wife, while a nanny looked after Azia's little daughter and Oliver. Two days ago, when Bram had introduced her to his wife, Tori had been reluctant to accept Azia's invitation to coffee in the city. She knew all about duty visits, having done her share while supporting her father.

But Azia's smile had been warm and Tori had longed to get away from the palace's gilded luxury. She loved her apartment, with its pretty courtyard and pool, but she didn't know her way around the massive building and didn't feel comfortable wandering through it.

To her surprise, their coffee date had been fun and Tori had laughed more than she had in ages. Azia had an irreverent sense of humour and a kind heart. The next day they went to lunch and visited an exhibition of exquisite beadwork by an upcoming designer.

Today they were at the silk shops in the bazaar, where Azia was determined to find fabric for a special outfit.

'How about this?' The curtains swished back to reveal Tori's new friend draped in green and silver.

Tori tilted her head. 'It's very beautiful...'

'But...? Come on, tell me.'

'Personally, I loved that bright lime-green. This one is pretty, but that bright pop of colour really complemented your colouring.'

Azia laughed, but her expression was uncertain. 'I liked that one too but it might be a bit too bright.'

'Too bright?' Tori frowned. 'Why shouldn't you wear bright colours? You look fantastic in them.'

Her friend shrugged. 'It's for a royal event and...' She glanced at the shop owner, who took the hint and moved towards the front of the shop, giving them some privacy.

Azia shrugged. 'I don't really fit in there. I'm not high-born and nor is Bram. Last time I went to a reception I overheard comments—' She shook her head. 'It doesn't matter. I just want to fit in.'

Her words echoed Ashraf's, jolting Tori's composure. Who *were* these people who busied themselves making others feel out of place? What gave them the right to judge? Because they were rich or born into powerful families?

Tori knew about the flaws hidden in many powerful and 'perfect' families.

'Which colour makes you happy?'

'The lime,' Azia answered instantly.

'Then buy the lime. You look beautiful in it.'

Azia wavered, then nodded. 'You're right. I will. Thank you.'

With a rattle of curtain rings she stepped back into the changing cubicle, leaving Tori alone with her thoughts. Inevitably they returned to Ashraf. He'd spoken of not being accepted. How had that moulded him into the man he was? He wasn't uncertain or insecure. In fact he was one of the most determined people she knew.

But what if Oliver wasn't strong enough to endure the censure of others so easily? Her spirits plunged. Was she selfish, refusing to marry Ashraf and give Oliver a conventional family? Not all conventional families were like hers, where only one parent had loved and supported her.

Her father had been too wrapped up in his career to care for anyone but himself. He'd married Tori's mother because she came from a family with money and political influence. Tori had always thought if she married it would be to someone who wanted *her*, not what she represented.

She sighed and put down her tea. At least she and her mother had been close. How Tori wished she were here now, to talk over this enormous decision.

For the first time she understood why her mother had stayed with her father. For the security he offered while she raised Tori. A woman would put up with a lot for her child.

Not that Ashraf would be a hands-off father, like her dad. On the contrary, he'd be very hands-on—

'You look flushed.' Azia emerged with a bolt of bright silk under her arm. 'I'm sorry, I shouldn't have taken so long.' She paused. 'Do you already have something for the reception or should we look now?'

'I'm not going.' Tori got up from the visitor's chair.

'You're not? But...' Azia looked confused. 'It's a very special event, hosted by the Sheikh himself. You'd enjoy it. There's music and traditional dancing as well as a spectacular feast.'

Tori shrugged, suppressing a pang of regret. It did sound interesting. 'I don't have an invitation.'

Azia's brow knotted. 'That's impossible. Bram wouldn't forget your invitation. He *never* forgets—' She broke off as the shop owner bustled forward to complete the sale.

Hours later, as the sun paused above the horizon, making the sky ribbons of scarlet and tangerine, Tori entered her private courtyard. It was beautiful, with its delicate marble arches and fragrant garden.

Her gaze strayed to the long green-tiled pool. Ashraf had been delayed. She had time to swim before he arrived. She liked swimming, but hadn't done much since Oliver's birth—partly from lack of time and partly because of babysitting costs. This was a wonderful luxury.

Tori was grateful to Ashraf. If nothing else, she welcomed this break from solo parenting. She felt better for more sleep and proper exercise. Nor did she miss the early starts, getting herself and Oliver ready each day, or dealing with Steve Bates and office politics. Her job was good, but not the workplace.

She reached the end of the pool and turned, the rhythmic strokes inviting her mind to drift to the upcoming royal reception.

It was curious that Ashraf hadn't mentioned it. According to Azia, there'd be hundreds of guests. But not Tori. Silly to feel left out. She didn't *want* to attend stuffy official events. She'd done enough of that for her father.

Except this didn't sound stuffy. Invitees would enjoy displays by acrobats, swordsmen, riders and archers, including a feat where galloping horsemen shot flaming arrows into impossibly tiny targets.

Strange… Wouldn't Ashraf see this as a chance to showcase his culture? To introduce her to his friends? Instead he kept her secluded like a woman in an old-fashioned harem.

Or an embarrassment he didn't want anyone to discover.

The thought slammed into her and she swallowed water. An embarrassment? Was that how he saw her and Oliver?

Tori flicked her hair from her eyes and gasped in a lungful of air. No, Ashraf wasn't like that.

Except the day they'd arrived he'd spoken to her like a casual acquaintance, not a lover. Anyone watching wouldn't guess they'd been intimate. At the time she'd been grateful to him for helping her to save face before strangers. But what if he had another reason?

He'd sent her off immediately, not even introducing her to the man who'd met them. Plus he hadn't accompanied her to the palace as she'd expected.

Despite refusing him, you still want his attention, don't you? You want to be with him. Want him to want you.

The truth taunted her and she shied away from it.

Ashraf—hiding her?

She recalled that first day. The limo avoiding the palace's main entrance to use the back gate. Bram hurrying her inside—to avoid curious eyes? Bram telling her that this apartment was at the rear of the palace and quiet. She'd thought that considerate, but maybe it was because she and Oliver were an embarrassment.

It fitted with what Ashraf had said about prejudice. And with what Azia had hinted.

Bile was sour on Tori's tongue as she swam to the poolside and levered herself out. She shivered and turned to grab her towel—only to see it being held out for her.

'Ashraf!'

Tori's voice was harsh, as if he was the last person she'd expected. No, it was more than that. She didn't sound surprised as much as put out. As if she didn't *wish* to see him.

Impatience stirred. And a trickle of annoyance. He'd looked forward to the end of an interminable yet necessary meeting so he could enjoy a few hours with her. Didn't he deserve a warmer welcome?

Tori should be used to his presence. Yet the pool's underwater lights and the antique lanterns around the colonnaded courtyard revealed a face set in severe lines. And a body as arousing as ever.

Usually she smiled when he appeared, though it took her a while to relax fully. Ashraf had told himself that she needed time to adjust. But part of him—the part that had always taken for granted his ability to attract any woman he wanted—felt it like an insult.

He'd been patient. Beyond patient. He'd ignored his own needs to put hers and Oliver's first.

Since his accession he'd put the needs of his people and his country before his own and he didn't regret a second of it. But with Tori his altruism faltered when he looked into her wide blue eyes and felt the tug of desire in his loins. And when she stood before him in a skimpy scarlet bikini he had to pretend not to notice her sumptuous sexiness.

'Sorry I'm late.' The day had been difficult and he'd looked forward to her company. Clearly she didn't feel the same. 'I've already checked on Oliver. He's fast asleep.'

Tori took the towel and hurriedly wound it round her body. Annoyance jagged him again. Didn't she trust him? He had treated her as his honoured guest. He'd put no pressure on her for intimacy. He'd been scrupulous about giving her time and space to consider the arguments in favour of marriage.

For a man used to quick decisions and immediate follow-through his restraint had been remarkable. Yet did she appreciate it?

His mouth tightened. 'Is something wrong?'

She tucked in the end of the towel firmly, as if daring it to slip.

Ashraf forced down his irritation. It would achieve nothing. 'You're frowning.'

'Am I? No, nothing's wrong.'

One stubborn woman resisted him. One woman whose

fears he understood, which was why he'd held back rather than forcing the issue between them.

'Shall we go in? Supper has been laid out inside.' Hunger for food was one appetite he *could* satisfy.

'Not yet.'

Tori's tone was over-loud, her words quick. Her jaw had firmed, the way it did when she argued and when she'd masked her fear during their abduction.

Ashraf's frustration dissipated. How could he blame her for being cautious? She was facing such major changes.

'I have a question,' she said.

Maybe it was about what her life would be like in Za'daq. Pleased, Ashraf nodded. 'Go on.'

Tori crossed her arms over her chest and fire kindled in her eyes. 'Are you *ashamed* of me and Oliver?'

'Ashamed?' The idea was outrageous.

'Or just a little embarrassed?'

Tori's expression morphed into a searing disapproval that would have done his father proud. Even with her moonlight-pale hair dripping rivulets down her shoulders and chest she looked strong, compelling. And angry.

She wasn't the only one. 'Where did you get such an idea?'

'You're not answering the question.'

Her hands went to her hips, pulling the towel down to reveal more of her breasts. Ashraf dragged his attention back to her face and her perplexing words.

'That's ridiculous. Who suggested that?' If one of his political enemies had been bothering Tori he'd—

'No one. I'm able to think for myself.'

Ashraf frowned. 'But you *can't* think that.'

Surely his actions showed that he respected her? He'd gone out of his way to ease her into this new world. It was true he'd rushed her back to Za'daq because he couldn't afford more time out of the country right now, and because instinct had demanded he keep her and his son close. But otherwise he'd been the acme of consideration.

'You haven't answered me.'

That rounded chin tilted and Ashraf felt an urge to angle it even higher, so he could slam his mouth down on hers. He'd stop her insults and take out his frustrations as he ravished her mouth, then moved on to ravishing her body.

'I'm neither ashamed nor embarrassed about you and Oliver.' He held her haughty stare with one of his own and watched her eyebrows twitch in confusion. 'What gave you such an idea?'

Tori held herself stiffly. She clearly didn't believe him.

The realisation ground through him like glass grating beneath his heel. Except he felt it inside—as if his windpipe and belly were lined with shards. No one, not even those vultures waiting for him to fail as Sheikh, had ever accused him of untruth. Ashraf's hackles rose.

'It's the way we live here in the palace…alone, not mixing with other people.'

'I understood that you and Azia had been out together for the last three days?'

The fire in Tori's eyes flickered. She hadn't expected him to know about that. He breathed deep, biting back the impulse to tell her it had been *his* suggestion that Bram's wife visit her.

'Yes, we have. But if it weren't for her Oliver and I would be isolated here. Except for your visits late in the day.'

Ashraf stared. In other words, his presence counted for nothing. The hours he carved out of his packed schedule weren't appreciated. *He* wasn't appreciated.

Fleetingly Ashraf felt something dark and hurtful—a whispered memory of all those times when he'd tried to please his father and failed. But that boy was long gone. Ashraf had moulded himself into a man who would *never* be needy.

'Is that all?'

She must have heard a trace of suppressed anger in his tone for her hands slipped from her waist and she wrapped her arms around herself. Yet still she held his gaze.

'No. There are other things. The way we were hurried off from the airport without being introduced to anyone except Bram. Even when we got here Bram hurried us inside so fast that I wonder if he was worried we'd be seen. We always use the back entrance, and this apartment is at the rear of the palace. Is it because you don't want anyone knowing about us?'

Ashraf opened his mouth to respond but she hurried on.

'You spoke about marrying because of people's prejudice when your father believed you were illegitimate. You're worried about what other people think. And...' she sucked in a quick breath '... I'm obviously not good enough to attend your big celebration next week.'

He stared down into her flushed face, torn between fury at the insult and regret that Tori should believe that for a second. His hands clenched so tight the blood was restricted and his fingers tingled. He flexed them and shoved them in his pockets.

'First, Bram probably hurried you inside because he was worried about you coping with the heat—especially when you were tired from a long journey. Second, I didn't introduce you to the man who met our plane because his sole purpose in being there was to find out about you so he could make trouble. He's the Minister for the Interior, one of my father's oldest cronies, and he's devoted to the idea of unseating me from the throne. Call me prejudiced, but I didn't want him to be the first Za'daqi you met.'

Ashraf rocked back on his feet, forcing further explanations through clenched teeth.

'As for you being at the rear of the palace—that *was* intentional. Because I believed you needed rest. And I thought you'd appreciate some peace while you acclimatised and thought through your options for the future.'

So much for her appreciating his efforts on her behalf!

'You haven't been isolated. I moved out of the royal suite to be near you and Oliver.' He nodded to the windows on the side of the courtyard adjoining her rooms. 'I've spent every night since you arrived right next door. If you care to check, there's a concealed door between the suites. The staff have instructions to wake me if you call for assistance in the night.'

'I… I had no idea!' Tori's eyes rounded. 'Why didn't you say?'

'Foolishly, I thought you might feel pressured. As if I were encroaching by wanting to help out if Oliver had teething pains.'

Strange how he missed those night-time sessions, pacing the floor with a fractious baby. But holding his son in his arms, knowing he was building a bond that would last a lifetime, had stirred new and incredibly strong emotions.

Those hours in Tori's home, watching her feed Oliver, doing what he could to ease the burden, had held an intimacy and significance against which everything else paled. Even his royal responsibilities couldn't eclipse that.

Tori unwrapped her arms and the towel slid off, revealing her bikini-clad body, but she didn't notice. She stared as if she'd never seen him before.

'And I haven't introduced you to people at court yet because I respect your wish for privacy. You insisted this was a private visit, to test the waters. You *know*—' his voice ground low '—that I want to introduce you as my future bride.'

Ashraf's lungs tightened again at all her unjust accusations.

'I am not and never will be ashamed of either you or our son.' He paused, giving her time to absorb that. 'Yes, I've faced prejudice because of my father's attitude. No, I don't want Oliver to suffer anything like that. But I'm not *afraid* of public opinion.' He barely restrained his bitter laughter.

'I've lived with scandal so long I'm used to it. Most of the time it's in the minds of others rather than based on something I've actually done.'

Deliberately he moved into her personal space, leaning so close that her evocative scent blurred his senses.

'I want to marry you to give Oliver the best start in life. Not because I'm scared of tittle-tattle.'

'Ashraf, I—'

'And you haven't received a written invitation to the reception because I wanted to invite you myself. It's a perfect chance for you to see something of my culture, meet people and enjoy yourself. I wanted to give you time to rest and acclimatise before mentioning it.'

He'd been sure his painfully patient approach would bear fruit. That Tori would see the wisdom of his proposal and accept. It appeared patience wasn't working.

Tori blinked up at him. Finally she cleared her throat, moistening her lips in an unconsciously provocative movement that, to Ashraf's annoyance, shot a bolt of lust through him.

Even angry, he wanted this woman. Even after she'd questioned his honour and tested his patience to the limit.

Eyes the colour of a soft spring sky met his. 'I'm sorry, Ashraf. I got it completely wrong.'

'You did.'

Indignation still ran like a living current under his skin, heating his blood. This woman drove him crazy. She fought him over things that were, in his opinion, patently obvious, yet at other times was so reasonable it surprised him. Like accepting his need to see Oliver immediately and to be involved in his life.

And it wasn't just her contrary reasoning that exasperated him. Her ability to ignore the rampant attraction between them was unprecedented and provoking. While *he*, damn it, was distracted by the sight of those lush breasts rising and falling beneath the skimpy triangles of fabric. And the gleaming abundance of slick, pale skin.

'I should be thanking you, not accusing you.'

She lifted her hand to his sleeve. Ashraf stilled. Her touch was light, barely there, yet he felt it acutely.

'It's no excuse but, nice as it is to relax, I feel dislocated, cut off from work and home. I've overreacted. Can you forgive me?'

A huff of laughter escaped Ashraf. 'I don't suppose you feel chastened enough to marry me?'

Her eyes widened, as if he'd suggested something shockingly debauched instead of honouring her with a proposal that would make her a queen and the envy of half the women in Za'daq.

The anger that her apology had quenched spiked anew. Impatience surged.

'Is that a no?'

He turned his hand, capturing hers. His fingers encircled her wrist and he detected the wild pulse hammering there. Was she really so timid? Or was that arousal?

Ashraf was tired of tiptoeing around Tori's doubts. Tired of waiting. Tired of holding back.

'In that case, this will have to do.'

He tugged her close and she fell flush against him, her breasts to his torso, her other palm on his chest. To steady herself or to push him away?

Ashraf didn't wait to find out. In the same instant he roped his other arm around her slick body, lowered his head and kissed her full on the lips.

CHAPTER NINE

TORI SAW THOSE mesmerising eyes glitter and knew a moment of sharp, shocking anticipation.

Not dismay. Not even a second of doubt. Just anticipation.

It thrilled through her like an electric current, making all the fine hairs on her body lift and her breath seize. Then Ashraf's mouth was on hers, hard and demanding rather than coaxing.

She didn't need coaxing. Tori was primed and ready for his kiss. Had been from the moment he'd walked back into her life and some primitive part of her had hummed with excitement and want.

She wanted him so badly.

Relief was profound as she finally gave in to what she'd secretly craved. In this moment she didn't need to reason, or argue, or try to unknot the tangle of her mixed emotions. All she needed to do was feel.

She loved the taste of him, the heat and extraordinary *maleness* of him, hard and unrelenting. From that first instant there'd been no coercion. Just a demand that she was eager to meet. It had always been like this with him.

Her lips softened beneath his, inviting him in, all but begging him for more. He took up her offer and a shudder racked her as his tongue plunged deep, swirling against hers, exploring with a thoroughness that mixed determination and expertise. It was like tumbling through bright starlight, ceding control to this man whom she knew would never let her fall.

Ashraf scooped her closer, his hard frame solid muscle against her wet body. Tori clung tight, one hand clutching his robe, the other slipping from his grasp to slide up the back of his neck.

She heard a muffled grunt of approval as her fingers channelled through thick hair to splay possessively over the back of his head.

Her tongue danced with his, hunger cresting as she went up on her toes, trying to meld herself to him. His taste, his scent, his mouth were achingly familiar, as if it was just a few days since they'd made love.

Had they kissed like this in the desert? Surely not. Then they'd been strangers. Ashraf didn't feel like a stranger now. Remarkable to think they'd been together such a short time, for it seemed they knew each other at some deep level beyond words. He was the man who filled her thoughts and dreams. Who had done so since that night together. He was the one man who'd woken her dormant libido after the rigours and exhaustion of pregnancy and motherhood.

The one man she needed as she'd never before needed anyone.

The realisation made her freeze in his embrace.

Instantly he lifted his head, eyes glinting like black gems as they searched her face.

Tori heard the stertorous rasp of heavy breathing, felt her lungs heave and the push of his chest against her breasts as he too hauled in oxygen. Reaction juddered down her backbone and quivered across her skin. Being so close to him, touching him, undid her carefully cultivated caution. It allowed something wild inside her to take hold.

The air was smoky with desire, thick and scented with arousal. Yet the unspoken question was clear in Ashraf's expression. Did she want to stop?

She was bent back over his arm, plastered to him, so she felt the uneven catch of his breathing and his waiting stillness. They were on the brink of far more than a kiss. It was there in the taut awareness singing between them. But even now Ashraf would release her if she wanted.

Emotion swelled. As strong as the desire emblazoned in

her bones. Tenderness for this man who put her needs before his own. It struck her how remarkable that was, given that Ashraf literally had all the power in this kingdom of his.

Now her earlier doubts about him seemed absurd. She'd never met anyone with such innate integrity.

Tori shivered at the enormity of her feelings. Yet still she shied away from investigating them too closely.

Ashraf straightened and pulled away. He'd misread her.

'No!' She fastened both hands on his shoulders, fingers digging into fine cotton, pads of muscle and beneath that implacable bone. 'Don't.'

'Don't kiss you or—?'

'Don't stop.'

Yet instead of closing the gap Ashraf surveyed her as if he felt none of her urgency. Only the flare of his nostrils betrayed that he'd been affected too.

'So there's at least one thing about me you approve of.'

He wanted to *talk*? Frustration surged—and suspicion. 'Are you fishing for compliments?'

She spied a flicker of movement at the corner of his mouth and a tingle of delight teased her.

'No. But I'll take any you want to throw my way.' His lips firmed. 'You're not a woman easily swept off her feet, Victoria Miranda Nilsson.'

Tori shook her head, a snort of bitter laughter escaping. 'Really? Don't forget I'm the woman who had sex with a stranger in a prison cell after just a couple of hours' acquaintance.'

She shivered, remembering her father's disgust even at the airbrushed version she'd recounted to him.

In the desert what she and Ashraf had done had felt utterly right—a blessing rather than anything else. But after her father's talk of hushing up a dirty secret and Ashraf's talk of illegitimacy—

'And I'm the man who found solace and hope in sharing my body with a stranger in that same prison cell.' Firm fingers cupped her chin, easing it up. 'You're not ashamed of us, are you?' He didn't wait for her answer. 'I'm not. You gave me a precious gift that night. Not just your body but your kindness, your passion and strength. Believe me...' his mouth rucked up in a wry smile '...to a man on Death Row they were a gift from Heaven.'

His words sank deep, warming her. Despite her determination not to relive the past, sometimes she couldn't quite believe she'd had sex with a man she didn't know. A wounded stranger she should have been nursing instead of seducing.

Yet memories of that night held magic as well as trauma.

Tori surveyed him intently. 'You're not on Death Row now.'

Every sense told her he shared the passion she felt. But could she trust her instincts? Was it possible that Ashraf's kiss had been motivated by pique at her questions and her refusal to accept marriage?

Her uncertainty surprised her. Surely the attraction between them was self-evident? Yet adrift from the world she knew, plonked into a fairy-tale palace with a handsome, powerful prince and experiencing an ardour she'd only known once before, it was easy to feel this wasn't real.

Maybe it was wishful thinking.

Her experience of sex was pretty limited. She might work in an industry dominated by men, but that just meant she'd got into the habit of shutting down attempts to engage her interest. Having a relationship with a co-worker was a complication she didn't need.

At her lower back one large hand splayed wide then pulled her close. Closer. Till she felt his arousal. A hot shiver raced through her and internal muscles warmed and softened.

'No.' His voice was rich and low, eddying deep within her. 'And you're not in prison here. You understand that, don't you? You're free to make your own choices.'

Ashraf regarded her steadily. She nodded. The claustrophobia she'd felt in this beautiful building was of her own making. Everyone here had been friendly and helpful. *She'd* been the one imagining she was confined to this part of the citadel. She'd found it easier to stay cloistered in this gorgeous apartment than to learn more about Ashraf's home.

Was she intimidated by his royal status, or by the fact she was being forced to share Oliver?

If Bram hadn't introduced her to Azia she'd probably never even have left this courtyard apartment. She'd have blamed it on tiredness. Or the need to protect her son from possible prejudice. When had she become so timid?

'And so...?'

His hands went to her hips. Tori loved his touch. Pleasure shimmered through her.

She tilted her head. 'And so...?' She refused to admit she'd lost the thread of the conversation.

The gleam in Ashraf's eyes told her he'd guessed, but for once she didn't mind that he found her easy to read.

'And so what would you like now? You're my honoured guest. It's my responsibility to see that your wishes are met.'

'My wish is your command?' Tori couldn't prevent the laugh bursting from her lips. It sounded like an *Arabian Nights* fantasy. Yet Ashraf's hard hands on her bare flesh turned her thoughts away from storybooks into an earthier direction.

'Something like that,' he murmured.

This time there was gravel mixed with the thick treacle of his voice. Tori shivered as it scraped her nerve-endings, drawing shuddery awareness in its wake. This, she realised, was the mesmerising voice of a man with the sexual experience of a playboy and the single-minded determination of the warrior Prince she'd come to know.

Was it any wonder her defences lay in splinters?

What was she defending herself against?

Ash… Ashraf…sought only what she longed to give.

Tori slipped her hands down over his cream robe. Her palms lingered on the swell of defined pectoral muscles and her belly clenched. Ever since that night she'd found him half-naked, cradling Oliver in those strong arms…

'There must be something you want.' His grip on her hips firmed and his warm breath trailed across her brow.

She nodded and licked dry lips. Then sucked in a fortifying breath as she saw the flare in his eyes. That look sent need quaking through her. She'd spent ages grieving this man's death and now he was here, so very alive. Contrary to what she'd told herself, absence hadn't exaggerated her reaction to him.

'I want you, Ash.'

It really was that simple.

Just as well that he held her, for his sudden smile undid her at the knees. She swayed and clutched his shoulders, her pulse sprinting at the sheer glory that was Ashraf's smile.

He leaned so close that Tori thought he was going to kiss her, but he stopped a tantalising breath away.

'Your wish…' his words caressed her face '…is my command.'

Then he swept her up in his arms as easily as if she weighed no more than Oliver. He made her feel small, something she'd never experienced before, being on the tall side of average. And he made her feel treasured which, she realised in a flash of revelation, no man except Ash, her desert lover, had made her feel.

Tori wrapped her hands around his neck and smiled. 'You do that very well. I think you've had practice.'

It was a sign of her infatuation that she didn't care. He might have been a love-them-and-leave-them playboy once. But for this moment he was all hers. She'd given up fighting the inevitable.

* * *

Ashraf stared down into eyes the colour of heaven and thanked all his lucky stars that he hadn't died that day fifteen months ago. One brief taste of this amazing woman was far too little.

Did she realise she'd called him Ash? As if time had peeled away and they'd just met?

In what he thought of as his exile years, deliberately courting scandal, he'd answered to Ash just to fit in more easily with the westerners with whom he partied. He'd automatically used the short form of his name when he met Tori.

But the way she said it, her voice soft with longing, was unique.

No other woman had made his name sound like that.

No other woman had made him feel this way.

He hauled Tori closer, losing himself in her bright smile and inviting eyes. In her scent, alluring and fresh as spring itself. In the sense of utter freedom, of triumph, that was his body's response to her invitation.

His clothes clung to her wet body, but the dampness couldn't douse the heat burning inside. He felt as if he'd waited for this moment half a lifetime.

Dragging his gaze away, he strode into the sitting room. Pillar candles had been lit in ornate lanterns and more candles were clustered on the table, where a feast was spread. The room looked romantic. Had Bram noticed Ashraf's frustration and decided to play Cupid?

Ashraf gave the room one brief, curious glance but kept going. In the bedroom, he was about to kick the door shut when he remembered Oliver. They needed to be able to hear if he cried out.

At the bed he slowly put her down, gratified when her hands stayed locked around his neck. She swayed, and satisfaction stirred at her neediness. It matched his.

Lamps cast the room in a golden glow, yet Tori outshone it. She looked vibrant, delectable.

Ashraf's hands slid up from rounded hips, past the inward sweep of her waist and around to her back. One tug and the back of the bikini top loosened. Her breath hissed but she didn't move, just stood, her fingers clasped at his neck. Her expression notched his ardour even higher.

It was a moment's work to undo the bikini top and drag it away. Now Tori's hands at his neck shook and her breasts wobbled. He felt unsteady himself, his lungs cramping at the sight of the bounty of her pearly flesh. Some small part of him was surprised that he, once reviled by his father as a voluptuary, was undone by the sight of a woman's breasts.

Reverently, greedily, he cupped them, their plump softness perfect in his hands. The rose-pink nipples were hard and trembling under the swipe of his thumbs. Tori bit her lip and he was torn between the need to capture her mouth again, to plunder her breasts or strip off the rest of her bikini and thrust himself deep inside her.

Ashraf bent to skim kisses around one breast. Tori's weight on his shoulders grew as she sagged closer. With one arm he caught her around the waist, pulling her to him. Her breathing roughened, hoarse and aroused, as he closed his lips around her nipple and sucked.

'Ash!'

It was a protest and a plea, possibly even a prayer. And it shot all the blood in his body to his groin. He was buried in her scent, her flesh, her yearning. Needy fingers clamped his skull, pressing him closer as if she feared he might stop.

He did stop, but only to lavish attention on her other breast, drawing a groan from her that tightened his belly. Ashraf's need grew urgent, especially when Tori spread her legs around his and pressed close.

It was an invitation he couldn't resist.

Ashraf pulled back, ignoring her protest, and dropped to his knees. He smelled damp flesh, sweet woman and the musky, smoky scent of arousal.

His gaze fastened on her belly, which had once cradled

his son. Pride, wonder and possessiveness gave added depth to carnal arousal. He stroked the tiny striations running across her skin.

'Stretch marks…' Her voice was breathless.

Wondering, he shook his head. 'You're amazing.'

Tori's laugh was uneven, as if she didn't believe him, but he was lost in wonder at the miracle her body had made and in sheer, blistering lust. He was afraid that if he wasn't careful he'd push her onto the floor and take her with the finesse of a rutting stallion.

Ashraf forced himself to slow, watching the contrast of his dark olive-skinned hand on her pale, satiny skin. But despite his best intentions his patience was negligible. Seconds later his fingers had insinuated beneath the narrow sides of her bikini bottom, sliding it down.

She was blonde there too, the damp V between her legs pale gold.

'I've found treasure,' he murmured, running his hands down her thighs and then back up and around to anchor in her buttocks. Her muscles squeezed beneath his touch.

Tori's hands were in his hair. He grabbed one, nipped the fleshy part of her palm with his teeth, then kissed the spot, feeling a voluptuous shiver race through her. She was deliciously responsive. So responsive that he couldn't resist leaning in and nuzzling the pale golden hair that pointed the way to Paradise.

'Ash!' Her voice was reedy and weak, but her grip spoke of robust feminine need as she tilted her pelvis forward.

Ashraf explored with his tongue in thorough strokes that turned her shivers to deep shudders. Her gasps were the most satisfying music and the perfume of her arousal was heady, beckoning him to delight.

He'd intended to take his time, to seduce her so thoroughly that he'd overcome her scruples about marriage. But now he discovered a flaw in his plans. He wanted her too much to wait. This time, at least. He had never felt so strung out. It shouldn't be possible, but he felt as if he'd spill himself here and now, bringing her to climax.

After a lingering kiss he pulled back and rose to his feet. Unfocussed eyes met his and satisfaction warmed him. He liked her dazed with need for him.

'Undress me, Victoria,' he ordered, enjoying the sound of her full name, an intimacy they alone shared.

His satisfaction cracked as she reached for his long robe and pulled it up his legs with clumsy hands. He liked her touch, but even the brush of her fingers tested his control, teasing him when he was already stretched to breaking point.

He'd left his shoes at the door, so when she lifted his robe off he was bare but for silk boxers. This time Ashraf was the one to shudder as her gaze raked him. He felt it as if she'd stroked her slim fingers across his skin. He stood proud, lifting towards her, hardening still further.

'Your scar healed well,' she said finally.

Her touch slid along his ribs, tracing the knife mark. Where she touched he burned, as if she trailed ice over searing flesh.

'You haven't finished,' he gritted out, capturing her fingers and securing them in the waistband of his boxers.

Amusement flickered in her eyes. 'How remiss of me.'

But instead of pulling the offending garment away she sank to her heels before him. Ashraf's lungs atrophied at the sight of her there, naked and alluring, a carnal fantasy made flesh. His brain and lungs stopped when she tugged his underwear down and leaned in, taking him in her mouth.

Ten thousand volts jolted through him. He felt soft lips, moist heat, the tease of silken hair and then incredible, sweet delight as she drew hard on his flesh.

For a moment that lasted half a lifetime he gave himself up to carnal gratification. The feel of what she did to him, the sight of her there on her knees…it was too much.

Ashraf grabbed her shoulders and gently pushed her away, almost relenting when he saw her heavy-lidded eyes and moist lips.

'Later...' His voice cracked right down the middle.

'You didn't like—?'

'Of course I liked.' He sounded angry—probably from the effort it took not to pull her back. 'But I want to be inside you. *Now.*'

A flush crested her cheekbones. Amazing, given what she'd just been doing. And charming. Utterly charming.

'Come.' Ashraf drew her to her feet.

They stood so close she swayed and he pulled her in against him, revelling in the slide of her body against his. Every part of his flesh was an erogenous zone. One more touch, one more look from this woman, might send him over the edge.

How exactly they got onto the bed he wasn't sure. And that was remarkable to a man used to taking the lead in sexual encounters.

Their legs entwined as they lay facing each other. The way she looked at him made his chest swell. But there was no time to ponder unaccustomed feelings. His need was too strong. Especially with delicate feminine fingers urging him nearer.

It was the work of a moment to roll her onto her back and settle between her splayed thighs. Ashraf's mouth curved in a tense smile. He appreciated her complete lack of coyness now she'd decided to stop fighting.

The only fight now was his own as he battled sensory overload—her silky skin, the beckoning heat teasing his groin, her piquant feminine perfume and the sight of her achingly beautiful breasts jiggling with each breath.

Tori stroked his shoulders restlessly, her eyes brilliant as gems. Ashraf knew he should take his time, savour every second, but he also knew his limits.

'Next time, *habibti*,' he murmured as he captured one of her hands.

'Next time what?'

'Next time we'll take it slow.'

He caught her other wrist and lifted both hands above her head, holding them with firm fingers. He watched her eyebrows lift, but though she could have broken his grasp she didn't try.

'I don't want slow.'

Her words ignited the blaze he'd tried to bank down. She'd barely stopped speaking when he pushed her thighs wider, grinding himself against her core. His gaze fixed on her face and the arrested expression there. Her look, the feel of their bodies together, were delight and torture together. More than flesh and blood could withstand.

'Nor do I.'

He slid his free hand between them, feeling her lush wetness, the hungry pulse of her body as he probed, hearing her swift intake of breath. A second later his hand was beneath her bottom, tilting her towards him as he bore down in one long, steady push that left him centred within her.

Sweat broke out at his nape and his brow. Muscles seized as the full reality of their joining penetrated his brain.

He had waited so long for her. Since that night in the desert he'd taken no lover, telling himself he was too busy. Now he understood with a flash of terrible insight that he hadn't wanted any woman but this one.

The realisation took a millisecond—less time than it took to draw breath. Yet it rocketed through him like the rush of a desert sandstorm, blanketing all thought.

Then primitive instinct took over.

Ashraf's mouth went to her breast, drawing hard, making her cry out and wrap her legs around his waist, rising against him in hungry desperation. A desperation that matched his own.

He erupted in a storm of movement. He withdrew and

thrust harder, deeper than before, setting up a rhythm that matched the hammer beat of blood in his ears and the rough syncopation of their breathing.

It seemed only seconds before he felt the first fluttery tremors deep in her body. Setting his jaw and stiffening his arms, he tried to withstand the drag of delicious sensation as her climax shuddered through her. But the expression in those eyes locked on his, the sound of her desperate gasps, even the way she clutched him, as if he were the only solid point in a swirling universe, amplified the ecstasy he felt as she convulsed into orgasm.

'Ash! Ash, please!'

It was too late. Her pleasure became his. The clench of her muscles blasted him off the edge and into an oblivion so deep he knew nothing but the pleasure-pain of rapture.

When his senses returned he was trembling all over like a newborn foal. His pounding heart filled his ears and his strength was gone, leaving him plastered across her pliant body.

'Victoria…' It was a silent gasp against the fragrant skin of her throat. There was nothing else except this woman and the aftershocks of explosive passion racking a body he was sure would never move again.

She filled his every sense. He nuzzled her throat, needing even now to be connected to her. And then the hands grabbing his shoulders slid down his back. Her arms wrapped tight around his middle as if she, too, needed to be as near as possible.

She planted a kiss on his shoulder and he felt her lips curve. 'Thank you, Ash.'

With a superhuman effort he lifted his head. Forget-me-not eyes met his. They were heavy-lidded and she wore a dreamy smile. This was how he wanted her—sexy, warm and biddable. And the way she used the shortened form of his name pointed to another barrier smashing down between them.

Ashraf's mouth tilted up in an answering smile. 'Thank *you, habibti.*'

They might be together because of the child she'd borne, but he knew in the very marrow of his bones that this was the right thing.

His hold on her tightened.

His woman. Soon to be his wife.

CHAPTER TEN

TORI SIGHED AS pleasure trickled through her. The bed was soft, she'd had the best sleep she could remember and, half-awake, she sensed all was well with the world.

It took her a few moments to realise that the delightful sensation that had roused her was a trailing caress. The brush of fingers across naked skin.

Naked skin.

For a moment her dulled brain couldn't compute that till, in a flurry of excitement, memories swamped her.

Ashraf, even more potent and magnificent in the flesh than in her dreams, powering into her with a single-minded focus that had been almost as arousing as the feel of his hard body.

He'd been strong yet tender, urgent yet considerate. She trembled, recalling how his body had made hers sing. How his touch had reduced her defences to rubble. How the pleasure had gone on and on and—

'Ash!'

Her eyes popped open as that wandering hand strayed across her breast, pausing to circle in ever-diminishing rings towards her eager nipple.

Dark eyes held hers—eyes that danced with devilry and hunger. By the pearly light filling the room she knew it was very early morning and she felt a fillip of delight that Oliver had slept through, leaving her and Ashraf uninterrupted. Soon, she guessed, he'd wake...

Then Ashraf pinched her nipple and her thoughts shattered. Tori all but rose off the bed as arousal shot through her. His leg across hers held her down and even that, she discovered, excited her.

Mouth dry, she licked her lips. His eyes followed the movement. At his throat a tiny pulse flickered hard and the tendons at the base of his neck pulled taut.

Tori breathed in sharply, excited by his arousal. It was a heady thing, discovering she had power over this man she found impossible to resist.

'Good morning, Victoria.'

Even the way he said her name—her full name, that no one but her father used—tugged at unseen cords in her belly. She used the name Tori partly because its less feminine sound fitted her work environment, but mainly because she hated how her father expressed his disapproval by drawing out the syllables.

Now, on Ashraf's tongue, her name sounded sensual and inviting.

'Good morning, Ashraf.'

His hand slid down to circle her navel and feather her belly, drawing a shiver from her and an eager softening of muscles. Her legs quivered.

'Last night it was Ash.'

'Was it?' She remembered, but pretended not to. Because last night he'd flattened every barrier between them.

When they made love it was as if time ripped away and she was with Ash again, the vital, viscerally exciting man she'd known in the desert. The man who tried to protect her, who'd given her the gift of his support when she'd been terrified. Rather than Ashraf, the man whose intentions worried her, despite his attempts to allay her concerns. For nothing could take away the fact that he was supreme ruler in this foreign land and that he wanted her to relinquish her freedom and everything she knew.

If he knew the full extent of his power over her...

She shivered.

His hand paused just inches away from the apex of her thighs and, despite her worrying thoughts, Tori felt the sharp bite of frustration. No matter her concerns for the future, she needed more.

Tori pressed her palm down on the back of his hand, holding it against trembling skin.

Their eyes clashed.

'Why did you stop? You want me to call you Ash?'

Broad shoulders shrugged above her. 'Call me whatever you like.'

Yet he made no move to complete what he had been doing just moments before.

An ache set up inside her, deep in that hollow place he'd filled last night. And in her chest, as if her heart or lungs were bruised.

Tori shook her head, bemused by her imaginings. Yet she wasn't imagining the bone-deep yearning for completion. Or her lover's waiting stillness as he looked down at her.

Her lover. The words washed through her, and with them a kind of relief. Whether she thought of him as Ash the honourable stranger or Ashraf the determined King, she wanted him.

What more did he want from *her*?

She'd already proved she was no match for the desire he ignited in her. It was a mere week since he'd come back into her life and she was amazed she'd withstood his allure so long.

Desire made her limbs tremble as she looked up into eyes that beckoned and challenged at the same time.

Tori's mouth firmed. If he was waiting for her to say she'd changed her mind about marriage he'd have a long wait. Or was it something else he wanted?

She lifted her hand from his and cupped his shoulder, pushing him back. Her pulse accelerated with excitement as he let her, falling back onto the bed.

He lay there, big and bold and utterly still, like a bronzed cat lazily sunning itself in the pale light spilling across the rumpled bed. Yet there was nothing lazy in the eyes that meshed with hers. A frisson ran through her at the invitation she read there.

Shedding any hesitation, Tori rose to straddle powerful thighs. Ashraf was all heavy muscle and heat—incredible heat. His mouth tugged wide in a satisfied smile but otherwise he didn't move. Until Tori leaned forward to lick to one dark nipple and a tremor ran through his supine body. Hard hands grasped her hips. She licked again, then nipped with her teeth, hearing his breath catch as he lifted beneath her.

This time she took the lead. She brushed kisses across his torso, with its scattering of dark hair, then drew on his other nipple and heard what sounded like a low growl. His fingers tightened on her. Lifting her gaze, she found his eyes locked on her and a thrill of empowerment zigzagged through her.

Levering herself higher, Tori stretched up his body, letting her breasts skim his chest. It felt so good she had to stop and stiffen her wobbly arms.

There was no laziness in Ashraf's face now. Watching the convulsive movement of his throat as he swallowed, feeling the swell of his arousal beneath her, Tori knew for the first time that he was at her mercy. It was delightful—if short-lived. For then Ashraf lifted his hips, letting her feel the full force of his appetite for her. Tori's pulse hammered in her throat, her lips firming over a moan of need.

'Ride me, *habibti*.'

So much for being the one setting the pace. But how could she object as he urged her up onto her knees? Besides, his voice was more gravel than velvet, and his hands on her hips betrayed his desperation.

Tori knelt above him, dragging out the moment of anticipation, one hand on that broad chest the colour of old gold. Beneath her palm his heart raced. That was what undid her—feeling Ashraf equally at the mercy of their mutual desire.

Closing her other hand around him, watching his hooded eyes, she lowered herself so slowly that the sensation of him rising to complete her seemed to take for ever.

When, finally, she rested fully against him, Tori experienced again that sense of quiet magic. As if time stood still in the presence of something extraordinary.

But it couldn't last. Already the need to move was unstoppable. Tori rose high, then slid down with an exquisite friction that made everything inside her quiver.

Ashraf's body was fiery hot, his eyes glittering fiercely as she moved again and again, arching in an instinctive dance against him. She set the pace and every movement took her closer to bliss.

The threads inside her body tightened, pulling into a coiling knot where every feeling converged. Then, without warning, a searing white light engulfed her. Tori heard a threadbare voice in the distance calling for Ash. Felt the sudden, cataclysmic wave of ecstasy and could do nothing but ride it out, her eyes locked on his.

She watched as the wave took him too. And the sight swept her from rapture to oblivion.

All Tori knew was the fire-burst of bliss and Ash—everywhere Ash, within her, around her, below her, his hands anchoring her, his body worshipping her, his rough voice praising her.

She didn't even remember falling. Just knew, as Ash's arms roped her to him and she inhaled the familiar cinnamon and spice scent of his skin beneath her cheek, that she never wanted to be anywhere else.

Ash emerged from the shower in Tori's suite wearing a mile-wide smile.

Life was good. The afterglow of spectacular sex filled him, but it was more than that. Everything was falling into place. He'd announce their impending marriage at the upcoming royal reception.

Now he'd cleared up Tori's fears that he'd hidden her and Oliver out of shame all would be well. He'd reassured her that she was free to make her choices and she'd chosen *him*, coming to him utterly of her own volition.

It was good that they'd had that confrontation. It had clarified things, allayed her doubts. And it had showed him another facet of his future wife. She was a woman who would stand for no insults against her son, a woman who'd defy anyone, even Ashraf, to protect Oliver. The way she'd argued her points, standing toe to toe with him, had aroused his admiration.

And his libido.

He grabbed a towel and rubbed his hair, remembering the spark in his belly as she'd faced him. Even his annoyance at her misconceived doubts hadn't quenched that.

Nor, he realised as he towelled his body, had a cold shower. Despite his heavy schedule he'd happily have spent another hour in bed with Tori. Only the sound of little Oliver, awake and hungry, had stopped him.

And even that interruption had its positives. Going to Oliver's room to find his son looking up at him curiously, Ashraf hadn't felt impatience but a surge of tenderness. Getting to know his child, having a real role in his life, meant everything to him.

Ashraf flung the towel away and dressed, his thoughts returning to Tori.

She was a strong mother. She'd make a superb queen, given time. And they had plenty of that—a lifetime.

Satisfaction warmed him—and the familiar pulse of desire. It was still early. There might be time before his first meeting...

No. He had other priorities. Namely, hearing Tori say she'd changed her mind about their future together.

Quickly combing his hair, he strode back to the bedroom—only to pause in the doorway.

Tori sat in bed while Oliver sucked at her alabaster breast.

Lust pierced Ashraf. He recalled the taste of that breast, and the way his mouth on Tori's sensitive skin had catapulted her from languorous acquiescence to raw desperation. He breathed slowly, savouring the memory, and the peaceful picture of his woman and child.

Early sunlight turned her hair into a gilded angel's crown. Against the sumptuous coloured silks and satins her pale beauty shimmered like rare, fragile treasure. But her smile as she met his eyes sent a kick to his belly and told him that Tori was a robust, flesh-and-blood woman.

'I like watching the pair of you.'

The admission surprised him. He hadn't intended to say it aloud. At the sound of his voice Oliver half turned, then resumed feeding. A curious feeling filled Ashraf. Satisfaction? Excitement? And something bittersweet.

It seemed his son responded to him. That he recognised his father's voice.

Whose voice had Ashraf known as a child? Only his mother's, and then only for a short time. Oh, there'd been servants, even some kindly ones, but no adults to whom he was the wellspring of the world.

The only love he'd really known was his brother's. But Karim had been kept busy by their father, learning all that a future sheikh had to know. He'd had little time to spend with his kid brother, especially since he'd had to sneak time with Ashraf behind their disapproving father's back.

Ashraf would like Oliver to have a sibling. Several, if Tori agreed. He wanted Oliver to have the things he'd never enjoyed and would never take for granted.

'How do you feel about large families?'

Tori's brow furrowed, her smile fading. 'Why do you ask?'

Ashraf shrugged and walked to the side of the bed. 'We didn't used protection last night.'

At the time he'd been too busy exulting in how freely Tori gave herself to him. He hadn't paused for contraception. After all, they were to marry and he had no objection to more children.

'We didn't?' Her voice struck a discordant note and she suddenly sat straighter, making Oliver grumble. Her brow crinkled. 'No, we didn't, did we?'

Ashraf read her concern and understood. For Tori's sake a longer gap between children would be better. He'd seen her weariness and understood how pregnancy and single motherhood had taken a toll. There was no rush for more children. They had plenty of time.

'But they say the chances of getting pregnant are less while you're breastfeeding.' It sounded as if she was trying to reassure herself.

Ashraf reached down and touched her leg, stroking satiny skin. 'You're probably right.' Though he knew nothing of such things. 'And even if there is another baby sooner than we expected we'll manage together.'

'Sorry...?' Her eyes shone large and lustrous. But her expression wasn't what he expected.

'Next time you're pregnant...' He paused. 'Whenever that is, you won't have to manage alone. I'll be here to support you.'

Ashraf smiled and was surprised when she didn't reciprocate. Instead her features froze. Abruptly she closed her robe around her and put Oliver against her shoulder. Then she shuffled higher up the bed, sliding her leg away from his hand.

'There won't be a next time.'

'Sorry?'

'There won't be another pregnancy.' Tori paused, her breasts rising on a sharp breath. 'At least...' She shook her head. 'If it ever happens it will be far in the future. If I marry.'

'*If* you marry?' Ashraf saw her tilt her chin high and realised he was on his feet, looking down at her.

She shrugged, but there was nothing easy about the movement. She looked as rigid as he felt.

'Who knows what the future holds? If, later on, I fall in love, I might consider having another child.' She paused and glanced down at Oliver, nestled quietly at her shoulder. 'A brother or sister for Oliver *would* be nice one day...' she mused, as if the idea had just struck her.

Ashraf stared, outraged that she was still apparently rejecting him, even after tacitly accepting him last night. Forget tacitly. She'd been *blatant* in accepting him. Choosing him. Could she have been any more forthright? And that sultry smile she'd given him this morning as she straddled him...

His hands fisted as all his fighting instincts roused.

The idea of Tori, *his woman*, in love with some other man, *giving* herself to that unworthy stranger, filled him with a taste for blood he hadn't felt since he'd been a teenager, facing his father's sneering contempt.

'You gave yourself to me.'

His voice sounded strange, as if it came from a distance. Ashraf felt a constriction in his throat that matched the sudden cramp in his gut.

Her gaze turned to him and he watched understanding dawn.

'That was sex.'

She had the gall to make it sound like nothing.

'You wanted me. You accepted me.'

'Yes, I *wanted* you.' She said it slowly, enunciating each syllable. 'And you wanted me.' That was pure challenge— as was the flash of defiance in her fine eyes. 'But it was sex. It had nothing to do with...' Tori waved her hand, as if struggling to find the words.

Ashraf found them easily enough. 'My marriage proposal?'

Tori shook her head, her pale hair slipping around the deep rose-coloured robe that reflected the colour cresting her cheekbones. She wriggled to the side of the bed, holding Oliver close.

Ashraf caught tantalising glimpses of her slender thighs, then she stood, clutching her robe closed with one hand, the other cuddling Oliver.

'You never *proposed* marriage. You put it forward as a solution to a problem. Oliver isn't a problem.' Her voice rose to a wobbly high note.

Ashraf felt his forehead knot. What had happened to last night's passionate, accommodating woman? The woman who, he was sure, had finally agreed to be his?

Impossible as it seemed, his intended bride was rejecting him. *Again.* He clenched his teeth so hard that pain radiated from his jaw.

Never had a woman rejected him. Yet this woman made a habit of it.

'Is that what you want? Me on bended knee? Or would you prefer a candlelit meal with violins playing and a shower of rose petals? Would that satisfy you?'

Anger tightened every muscle. Disappointment, sharp as acid, blistered and scorched its way through his body.

And there was more.

Hurt.

Ashraf told himself it could only be hurt pride. He'd never considered offering any other woman what he offered Tori. His name, his honour, his loyalty.

'There's no need for sarcasm, Ashraf. I thought men were supposed to be good at separating sex and love or marriage.'

Despite the jibe, and the arrogant angle of her jaw, Tori's voice was brittle, her mouth a crumpled line. And abruptly, despite his roiling emotions, Ashraf realised something his anger had blinded him to.

Tori was scared. He read it in the obstinate thrust of her jaw and those over-wide eyes. In the protective way she held their son and the tremor she couldn't hide.

Scared of committing herself?

Or scared that he'd take Oliver?

That, as absolute ruler, he'd force her into a life that terrified her?

Drawing in air through his nostrils, Ashraf reminded himself that Tori barely knew his homeland except as a place of peril. He hadn't really helped her acclimatise. He'd deliberately left her alone during the day, believing she needed rest. And their evenings together had tested his determination not to seduce her.

How right he'd been. Sex had resolved nothing.

Tori hadn't tried to tease him or mislead him, giving him a night of unfettered passion and then withdrawing. She'd simply surrendered to a force too strong to withstand.

'Say something.' Her voice sounded stretched as if from tight vocal cords. 'What are you going to do?'

That was easy. He'd do whatever was necessary to secure Oliver and Tori.

Marshalling control, he smiled and watched her gaze drift to his mouth. 'I'm going to spend the day with you.'

And the next and the next. However many it took to convince Tori that life in Za'daq, with him, was the right choice. He'd court her till she stopped putting up barriers and surrendered.

CHAPTER ELEVEN

Tori looked at the vast landscape spread below the chopper and felt a mix of awe, curiosity and unease. The desert plain seemed to wash up to the edge of ragged mountains that fringed the border.

She gulped, tasting remembered fear. It was somewhere there that she and Ashraf had been abducted.

A warm hand closed around hers, making her turn to the man beside her.

'Okay?' The expression in those ebony eyes told her he understood the fear closing her throat.

Tori nodded, refusing to succumb to panic.

'I enjoy travelling by helicopter,' Ashraf added, as if suspecting she needed distraction, 'but I know some find it challenging.'

'I like it,' she finally admitted. She'd often flown to remote locations for work.

Why they were venturing so far from the city, she didn't know. Yet the opportunity to spend time with Ashraf, seeing him in his own environment, had been too precious to pass up. Tori had important decisions to make about Oliver's future. Getting to know Ashraf and his country was part of that.

Even if, after last night, part of her wanted simply to succumb to his demand for marriage.

If she'd known how profoundly making love to him would affect her she'd never have gone to bed with him.

Who did she think she was kidding? It would have taken a far stronger woman than she to say no. From the start he'd been irresistible.

She shivered and Ashraf stroked his thumb across her

hand. Darts of arousal pierced low in her body. It worried her, how easily and how deeply she responded to him.

'Here we are.' He leaned across and pointed to a valley between two trailing spurs, where she saw traces of green and the sinuous curve of a river. 'That's our destination.'

'It's a long way to travel for a picnic.' When he'd suggested leaving Oliver behind for a couple of hours, she'd imagined they'd go to a beauty spot near the city.

His hand squeezed hers. 'I wanted you to see something of Za'daq apart from the capital.'

She turned to meet his eyes, trying to decipher that intent stare. 'And you wanted to show me how safe this part of the country is now?'

It was a guess, but the curling groove at one side of his mouth gave Tori her answer. He *had* chosen this location deliberately. Did he know she was still anxious about returning to the desert? Did he read her so easily?

'I don't want you afraid of shadows, Tori.' His eyes held hers. 'Plus, I want you to meet my people. For a long time this region hasn't had the benefits found in the rest of my country.'

The helicopter descended and he gestured towards what looked like irrigation channels following the contours of the land, and a surprising amount of green vegetation.

'They are proud and hard-working. And things are changing here now Qadri has gone.'

Tori took a slow breath and nodded. She hated the anxiety niggling at her insides. Surely facing her fear would help her overcome that? It would be good to replace those terrifying memories with something else.

'I'll be interested to see them.'

Ashraf's smile as he threaded his fingers through hers made something hard inside her shift. Logic told her to keep some distance between them. He'd so readily assumed she'd changed her mind about marriage because she'd gone to bed with him. But she didn't have the energy to hold herself aloof. Basking in the warmth of his smile, in his company, was too tempting.

It was impossible to switch off the current of connection between them. Just this morning she'd gloried in his body and he in hers. She'd found heady delight and a sense of personal power in their lovemaking. How long since she'd felt powerful, much less mistress of her own destiny?

Since the kidnap she'd felt as if she was at the mercy of forces beyond her control. First her abductors, and then as her body altered to accommodate a new life, and later as she changed her life to put Oliver's needs first. She'd taken her current job so she could work child-friendly hours, not because she especially wanted to work there.

'Tori? Are you all right?'

Ashraf squeezed her hand. She looked around to discover they'd landed.

He leaned close, looking concerned. 'If you'd really rather go back...?'

But a crowd had gathered. A cluster of serious-faced older men in traditional robes, and behind them people of all ages.

'No. They're expecting you.'

From what she could see of the village, with its tumble of mud brick houses, Tori guessed a visit from their Sheikh would be a special event. She couldn't make him leave and disappoint them.

'How will you introduce me? Won't people wonder who I am?'

Ashraf grinned. 'Don't worry about that. Just come and meet them. Be yourself.'

Undoing his seatbelt and headset, he alighted from the chopper.

Tori hesitated, a hand going to her hair when she noticed most of the women wore headscarves.

'I'm not really dressed for this.' She'd worn a bright red

top which usually made her feel good, but now it made her
wonder if she should have dressed in a more conservative
colour.

'You're perfect.'

His gaze lingered for a second, as if he could see through
her loose-fitting top and summer-weight trousers. Instantly
Tori's self-consciousness was swamped by awareness. Wind
rushed in her ears and her breath snagged at the look in
those gleaming eyes.

'Come.'

He reached out, took her hand and helped her down. The
dying rotation of the helicopter's blades made her hair whirl
around her face, but Ashraf didn't seem concerned that she
looked slightly dishevelled. Presumably it didn't matter.

Then Tori had no time for self-consciousness as she was
introduced not only to the village elders but it seemed to
every adult in the place. Children stared up at her with wide
eyes, but she was used to that. When she'd worked across
the border in Assara, people had been fascinated by her
pale colouring.

While Ashraf was deep in discussion with the elders one
little girl, held in her mother's arms, swayed towards Tori,
reaching out to her. Rather than pulling back, she let the
child tentatively touch her hair.

The mother looked horrified, trying to draw away, apol-
ogising. But Tori shrugged and smiled. 'She's just curious.
That's a good thing.'

The local schoolteacher, acting as interpreter, translated,
and suddenly, instead of hanging back, more women approached. There was no more touching, but there were
smiles and shy questions which gradually became a steady
flow. Not, Tori was relieved to hear, about her relationship
with the Sheikh, but about her homeland, so far away, and
what she thought of Za'daq.

'If you'd care to take a seat, my lady?'

The teacher gestured as the small crowd parted and Tori

saw, in the scanty shade of what appeared to be the village's only tree, a striped awning. Spread in the shade beneath it were richly coloured rugs and exquisitely embroidered cushions.

When they were seated a woman arrived with a bowl and a small towel. Another carried a jug of water, offering it to the guests to wash their hands. Then platters of food arrived—dried fruit and nuts, and pastries dripping with syrup. Coffee was prepared with great ceremony and offered in tiny cups.

'Thank you,' Tori said in their language. 'It's delicious.' She stumbled a little over the pronunciation but knew by the smiles around her that she was understood.

Ashraf turned and his expression warmed her even more than the pungent coffee.

'After this I'll inspect the irrigation scheme behind the village but I won't be too long. I promise to get you back to the city in good time.'

Because Oliver would be ready for a feed. It seemed incredible that a king would so readily fit his arrangements around that. As incredible as him changing his schedule at short notice to take her out.

'Would you like to come with me? Or you could stay here and chat? Or maybe see the school?' Tori saw him glance towards the teacher.

'I'll stay.' She turned to the teacher. 'Perhaps you could show me around?'

Her choice was a popular one. While most of the men went with Ashraf, the women and children accompanied her. The children pointed out places of interest like the well, now with a pump powered by a solar generator. And then there was the tower on the hill, which had brought modern communication to the valley for the first time. They also stopped to look inside one of the houses, where a loom was set up for silk weaving, and Tori admired the fine fabric.

The school was a one-roomed stone building. But to Tori's surprise it wasn't the bare little space she'd expected. It was well-stocked with books, colourful posters and a couple of computers.

Seeing her surprise, the teacher explained. 'The government is keen to ensure all Za'daqis have a good education. In remote areas where children can't travel to bigger schools we now have smaller schools, each supporting a village or two. In the old days children here didn't get any formal education.'

'It seems to be working well,' Tori said, watching the children talk to their mothers about the art on one wall. 'They seem very engaged.'

'They are. The difference here in just a couple of years is amazing.'

'Only a couple of years?'

'The school is very new.' He paused, as if choosing his words. 'Until Sheikh Ashraf there was no funding for local schools here. Now even the children in small settlements have access to education. It will give them a brighter future.'

Tori felt pride stir at his words, as if she had a vested interest in Ashraf's achievements. Perhaps she did. She was well past the stage of pretending indifference.

'Sheikh Ashraf tells me there have been a number of changes in the region?'

'There have, indeed.' The teacher said something to the women surrounding them and received nods and eager comments in response. 'Life is better here now, with plenty of food and even visiting doctors. It's peaceful too.' He shot her a sideways look. 'In the past there was a problem with evil men...lawless men who did bad things.'

Despite the warmth of the day ice slid down Tori's spine. 'Yes. I've heard about that.'

The man nodded. 'But now they are gone and we have the Sheikh's law. Things are much better. The people are safe.'

His words stayed with Tori through the rest of their visit, as she watched the boisterous children and the women's smiles. *Safe.* Ashraf made her feel safe too. Except for her doubts about accepting a convenient marriage and living in a country where his word was law.

When she was with him she felt different. Better. *Happier.*

Were those feelings enough to compensate for accepting a loveless marriage? She was surprised even to be considering it.

'Is everything okay?' Ashraf asked as the helicopter took off and they left the waving villagers behind. 'You're very quiet.'

It was because she was distracted by conflicting feelings. The more she learned of Ashraf, the more she understood his idea of marriage was rooted in good intentions. He didn't plan to take advantage of her.

Yet good intentions weren't always enough.

Tori looked down at the silk scarf on her lap, a kaleidoscope of sumptuous colour.

'This present is so beautiful but I didn't have anything to give in return.' It had been pressed into her hands by the woman whose house she'd visited—the silk weaver. 'Weaving is her livelihood and I'm not sure she can afford to give it away.'

Ashraf shook his head. 'Your interest in her life is enough. That is something these people haven't had much of in the past. Besides, they're proud. They brought out their very finest for our visit, but they didn't expect an exchange of gifts. You did the right thing, accepting this.' He paused. 'Don't worry. No one will be worse off because of our visit.'

Tori knew without asking more that he'd be as good as his word. She leaned back in her seat and turned to watch the foothills slide into the distance. This time she felt no nervous tingle of apprehension at the sight.

'It sounds like they're already better off because of you.'

In her peripheral vision she caught his shrug. 'We've had some useful initiatives. They're beginning to bear fruit.'

'Like medical services, education, electricity and reliable clean water.' She ticked them off on her hand. Most men she knew would crow about their personal role in such successes. Her father especially.

Ashraf wasn't like the men she knew.

He caught her gaze and a surge of emotion enveloped her. Tenderness, yearning and something more. All sorts of feelings that she knew made her weak but which she couldn't suppress.

Ashraf captured her hand, setting off whorls of eager sensation just under her skin.

'What are you thinking, *habibti*?'

His voice had dropped to an impossibly deep note on the endearment.

Tori opened her mouth, about to give voice to the tremulous emotions that filled her. But at the last moment caution surfaced. She forced a casual smile. 'Just wondering how Oliver is doing with the nanny.'

Was that disappointment in his eyes?

The impression was gone in an instant, yet Tori couldn't banish the feeling that she'd been cowardly and less than generous with Ashraf.

That suspicion grew as her first week in Za'daq became a second. Instead of seeing Ashraf only in the evening she began to be taken out daily, introduced to his country and his people.

Despite her reservations, Tori looked forward to their outings and his company. She told herself she was relieved that he no longer pressed her to marry. Yet, to her chagrin, nor did he come to her bed.

Torn between pride and fear at how easily he dismantled her defences, she didn't dare initiate sex, not trusting herself. And that left her frustrated with herself and him. If it hadn't been for the smoking hot looks Ashraf sent her when he thought she wasn't watching, and his palpable tension when she stood close, Tori might have imagined him indifferent.

Was he trying to prove they could build a relationship based on more than sex?

She could only admire Ashraf's self-control. Hers frayed dangerously. Each day she fell further under the spell of this place and this man. And while Oliver settled into life in the palace she discovered so much in Za'daq to like.

Ashraf took her to the old parts of the city, with quaint buildings, narrow streets and hidden courtyards. They went to a vast covered market that sold everything from carpets and brassware to jewellery, perfumes and spices in all the colours of a desert sunset. Then to a dazzling art gallery, and a technology park where they visited fascinating new enterprises, and public gardens filled with families enjoying the green space. They drove out to a spectacular gorge where a rare breed of eagles nested and the scenery stole her breath as they watched the sun sink.

Tori met nomads in a desert encampment, traders, teachers and so many others who made her feel welcome. Wherever they went people were respectful but friendly, and gradually her nervousness about being in Ashraf's country eased.

He took her to a horse-trading bazaar on the edge of the city. Breeders had come from throughout the country and beyond, and the event had a holiday atmosphere. There was a great open-air feast and dashing displays of horsemanship. Tori watched in surprise when Ashraf agreed to take part, unable to take her eyes off him. He had the grace of a natural athlete, and when he rode it was like watching a centaur, man and horse moving as one.

It was late as they returned to the palace. The limousine's privacy screen was up, separating them from the driver, and Tori wished Ashraf would reach for her. She missed his touch. Missed the intimacy they'd shared. Her resolve to keep her distance was bleeding away like water in the desert sands and a new sort of tension filled her.

She turned to him, sucking in a sustaining breath as her pulse quickened. 'It was kind of you to give me such a lovely present but I really can't accept—'

'Of course you can. I watched your reaction when you saw that mare. It was love at first sight.'

Tori wrinkled her brow. If she didn't know better she'd say that Ashraf sounded *envious*. It was a bizarre thought that she hurriedly put aside.

'She's beautiful.'

It was true that Tori had fallen for an Arab mare being sold at the bazaar, but if she'd thought for a moment Ashraf would buy it for her she'd never have let her gaze linger on the gorgeous animal. She loved riding, but hadn't had a chance to indulge her passion for years, and it just wasn't practical now.

'But she needs someone who'll care for her full-time. I may not be here—'

Ashraf raised his hand and Tori was struck by the sudden austerity of his features. He looked handsome yet remote. More distant even than a week ago, when they'd argued after that glorious night together. When he'd believed she'd marry him because she'd gone to bed with him.

'She's yours, Tori. No strings attached. If you accept my offer and live here she'll be stabled at the palace. If you return to Australia she'll be shipped to you and I'll arrange stabling.'

It was the first time Ashraf had spoken of her possibly remaining in Australia. Instead of welcoming it as a sign that he'd finally seen reason Tori felt her stomach drop like a weight through a trapdoor.

She swallowed hard, trying to understand her reaction. Surely that wasn't disappointment she felt?

Increasingly she felt she clung to her determination not

to marry out of obstinacy rather than anything else. But to marry without love—

The sound of her phone interrupted her agitated thoughts. Frowning, she fished it from her bag. She'd kept in contact with her friends via social media while in Za'daq. She wasn't expecting any calls.

'Victoria? Are you there?'

The familiar voice cut through her thoughts like shrapnel through flesh. He hadn't even waited for her to speak and that tone, the way he said her name, told her he wasn't happy.

Her lips flattened as she sat straighter. 'Hello, Dad. I'm afraid I can't talk. I'm—'

But it took more than that to stop Jack Nilsson. 'What are you playing at? Why did I find out from a bunch of diplomats that you're living with the King of Za'daq? I had to read it in the diplomatic post reports. The press there are already speculating about you and it won't be long before the media here gets hold of the story. *Then* what am I supposed to say?'

His voice grew more strident with every word and Tori shut her eyes, cringing at his tone despite the years she'd spent telling herself she wasn't responsible for his bad temper. She leaned back into the corner of the wide seat. She knew how her father's voice carried, especially when he was annoyed.

She shot a sideways glance to Ashraf and found him regarding her steadily. No polite fiction that he couldn't hear her every word. For a second she thought of simply hanging up—but her father would ring back, more incensed than ever.

'I told you Oliver and I were coming here.'

'But not to the bloody *palace*! You didn't even mention you knew the King, or that you were in a relationship. Are you *trying* to make me look like a laughing-stock?'

'Hardly.' The word was snapped out and actually succeeded in stopping the acid flow. 'I wasn't thinking about you when I agreed to come here.' She had been thinking of Oliver.

'You should have thought of me! You know there's an election looming. If I'd known you had such *personal* connections there, we could have pressed for exclusive rights in that Za'daqi mining exploration project...'

The rest of his words faded into a blur as nausea rose. Her father had discovered she was the guest of a stranger on the far side of the world and his first thought was what he'd say to the press. His second was whether he could trade on her intimate relationship for commercial and thereby political gain.

Tori swallowed convulsively, fighting back bile. She should be used to her father's ways but sometimes he outdid himself in callous self-interest. There'd been not a word about how she was, or Oliver. How did he still have the power to hurt her even now?

'Dad, I can't talk privately.'

'Why? Aren't you alone? Is *he* there?'

Tori opened her mouth to say goodbye when a hand reached for the phone.

'If I may...?' Ashraf couched it as a question but there was no mistaking it for anything other than a command.

For a second she hovered on the brink of cutting the connection. Then she shrugged. Fine. The two alpha males could battle it out between them.

But as she listened to Ashraf's smooth voice she realised her father had met his match. Ashraf was gracious but firm, making it clear that their relationship was private, assuring her father that she and Oliver were safe and with every amenity at their disposal.

Her father's tone changed from blustering to friendly, almost eager. Tori rolled her eyes. He thought to use this situation for personal advantage. The idea made her queasy.

* * *

Ashraf ended the call and handed her the phone. 'He's concerned about you.'

'*Concerned* about me?' She shook her head, her expression disbelieving. 'He's never been concerned about me—except to make sure I don't embarrass him publicly.'

Ashraf inclined his head. Tori's words confirmed his impression of the man.

'You don't like him?'

Nor did Ashraf. Her blustering father had turned slyly obsequious, talking about building stronger links between their countries. His concern for Tori and Oliver had been surface-deep.

'He's hard to like.'

'Go on.' He'd been curious about her relationship with her father, but hadn't pressed for details since he and Tori had other priorities. Maybe knowing more about it might help him understand her better.

'I'd rather not.'

Ashraf considered her steadily. 'I prefer to be prepared. He mentioned negotiating a marriage settlement.'

She goggled at him. 'He *didn't*? That's outrageous! I never mentioned marriage to him and nor did you.'

Ashraf shrugged. 'Nevertheless… I have a feeling he'll be calling my office again soon.' Not that he anticipated any difficulty in dealing with one whose motives were so transparent.

Tori sank back, rubbing her forehead, the picture of distress. 'I'm sorry.' She shook her head. 'I never—'

He reached out, capturing her hand, relishing its fit against his as he closed his fingers round hers. 'You've nothing to be sorry about, Tori.'

She met his eyes and sighed. She looked so upset Ashraf almost told her it didn't matter, that they didn't need to discuss this, but instinct told him it was important.

He waited patiently as the car drove towards the palace.

'He's completely self-focused,' she said at last. 'He married my mother for money and her family's political leverage. He wasn't interested in us, except to trot us out as the perfect family when it was time to impress the voters or the VIPs.'

Ashraf heard the hurt she tried to hide and vowed that Jack Nilsson would learn to respect his daughter.

'Fortunately my mother was lovely. We were close.'

Presumably it was from her mother that Tori got her sweet, honest character.

'Your father…he hurt you?'

'Not physically.' She paused. 'Really, I was lucky. He wasn't around much. He was away when parliament sat and the rest of the time he had other priorities.'

As if his family wasn't a priority. Ashraf's teeth clenched. He hated the idea of Tori with an uncaring parent. Yet surely that should make her more willing to create a real family for Oliver?

'Everything I did was judged on how it would look. I wanted to play soccer but he thought it more ladylike if I learned piano.' She shook her head. 'As a kid I couldn't get dirty or be seen in public with a hair out of place. It was extreme and unnecessary. I knew other politicians' kids who didn't live like that, but he saw me as an extension of himself. Everything was about appearance, not about being a real family. Our only value was as props to make him look good.'

Tori grimaced.

'I think eventually it destroyed my mother. She stayed with him because of me. She thought any family was better than none. But I *know* we'd have been better just the two of us, without him.'

Now Ashraf began to understand. Did Tori see parallels between his proposal that they marry to create a family for Oliver and her mother sticking at a bad marriage for her child's sake? Worse, did she compare his motivations with her father's?

The idea revolted him.

'And even now he tries to manage your life?'

Tori laughed, the sound sharp. 'Hardly! I rebelled when my mother died and I went to university. He wanted me to study law and follow in his footsteps.'

'But you chose geology.' He smiled. 'An act of rebellion *and* a chance to get your clothes dirty?'

Her chuckle warmed him, expelling the chill he'd felt since they'd begun this conversation.

'You could be right. It also gave me a career that would take me far away from him.'

'When you found yourself pregnant you didn't seek his assistance?'

He found it perplexing that she'd moved to the opposite side of Australia from her father. Without family support things must have been tough.

Her hand twitched in his, as if she'd withdraw it. Ashraf placed his other hand on hers, holding it steady. 'What is it?'

Her gaze met his then slid away. 'I told him what had happened and he told me to abort the baby. He said there was nothing to be gained from having it and that it would make it hard for me to secure the right sort of husband.'

Ashraf's hands tightened around hers. His throat choked closed on a curse. He drew a slow breath, searching for calm. 'Maybe he thought a permanent reminder of what you'd been through—'

'Don't try to excuse him!' Tori's voice rose to a keening note. 'He wasn't interested in me or how I was doing. He didn't even want me to see a counsellor in case my story leaked to the press.' She shook her head. 'He said my behaviour was *sordid*. He washed his hands of me and he has no interest in Oliver.'

Indignation exploded through Ashraf. Tori had been kidnapped and traumatised and the best her father had been able to do was tell her to abort the baby. He knew by her expression that her father had said far more too. Had he blamed Tori for what happened?

For her sake Ashraf had to stifle his incandescent fury. With difficulty he sat, outwardly calm. Yet he imagined getting his hands on the man who'd dared talk of marriage settlements and closer relations when he hadn't the common decency to care for his own flesh and blood.

'In that case you're better off without him. While you're in Za'daq I can make sure you never have to deal with him again.' It was little enough, but he'd take pleasure in doing it for her.

She nodded. 'Thank you.'

It was a good thing for Jack Nilsson that he was on the other side of the globe. Ashraf wasn't a violent man but he'd enjoy making an exception in this case.

No wonder Tori was wary of a pragmatic marriage. He'd mentioned the importance of public perception in Za'daq and maybe she assumed his motives were like her father's. The idea sickened him.

He stroked his fingers down her hot cheek, then lifted her chin so she had no choice but to meet his eyes.

'I give you my word, Tori. I'm not like your father.'

'I know that.'

But her smile was crooked. It cracked his heart to see her look that way. He was used to her being defiant, strong and independent. He hated it that perhaps some of the pain he read on her face was because of *him*.

'I make you a promise, Tori.' He placed one hand over his heart, his expression grave. 'If we marry I will be devoted to you and our children. Always. To be Sheikh is a privilege and an honour, but I know, I *understand* that family is more important than power and prestige.'

How could he not know? He'd grown up unloved and unregarded except by his brother. Ashraf would have given anything to have had an atom of love or even liking from his father. Or a genuine memory of a mother's tenderness.

'My family will be the centre of my life. You have my word on it.'

CHAPTER TWELVE

FOUR DAYS LATER Ashraf's words still echoed in Tori's ears. She recalled each nuance, the deep cadence of his voice, the searing look in those impossibly dark eyes, the feel of his hands, hard and warm but so gentle, clasping hers.

He'd made her feel cared for.

Special.

Tori bit her lip. She'd never been special to anyone except her mother. It was a strange feeling, both wonderful and nerve-racking.

If she believed him.

That wasn't fair. She *did* believe Ashraf. He meant every word. Tori had no doubt his intentions were good. But would good intentions be enough when his heart wasn't engaged? For, despite the shivery excitement his words, his look, his intensity had conjured in her, it was impossible to believe that after spending just a few short weeks together the King of Za'daq had fallen in love with her.

And without love how could she commit to marriage? She knew what a lack of love did to a family.

Yet Ashraf wasn't her father. He'd told her that but she'd known it from the first. Ashraf was—

'What's taking you so long, Tori? Do you need help with the zip?'

Azia's voice came from the bedroom, jerking Tori into the present. She blinked and took in the unfamiliar image in the mirror. It had been so long since she'd dressed up she barely recognised herself. And she'd never looked as she did in this dress.

'Just coming,' she called, smoothing her palms down the

black velvet. It was reassuringly soft…like Ashraf's voice when they made love.

The thought sent another flurry of nerves jittering through her. Instead of making life easier, abstinence from sex had left her a wreck. The wanting hadn't stopped. It grew stronger daily. Especially since she knew Ashraf slept in the room neighbouring her own bedroom, connected to hers by a single closed door.

She caught her wide eyes in the mirror and dragged in air. This wouldn't do. She couldn't think about that if she was going to get through tonight's reception.

Smartly she stepped across the tiled floor and opened the door to the bedroom, sweeping in, her long skirts flaring. Azia waited, looking fabulous in the shimmery lime-green that complemented her sable hair and dark eyes.

'Ah…' Azia drew the syllable out, gesturing for Tori to turn. Obediently she did. When she faced her friend again, Azia nodded. 'Perfect. You'll stun them all.'

'That's what I'm afraid of.' Tori grimaced. 'You're sure it's not too much?'

'Too much?' Azia laughed. 'You're the guest of one of the richest men on the planet. How much is too much?'

'Well, the glitter, for a start. Though I love the silver embroidery. It's exquisite.'

Azia nodded. 'It's some of the best work I've seen, especially given how little time they had to make it.'

The dress had been made by a friend of Azia's, a designer just starting her own business with a couple of seamstresses.

'I wouldn't change a thing.'

'It's not too revealing?'

Tori had wondered about that, but left the detail to the designer, who'd been so excited and grateful to make a gown for a formal court event. Tori had told herself a local designer would know what was appropriate in Za'daq. But the narrow silver straps over her shoulders left a lot of bare flesh.

'Does it *feel* revealing?'

Tori shook her head. It felt wonderful. If she weren't so nervous she'd feel like Cinderella heading for the ball. She'd never possessed a dress so glamorous, or one that made her feel beautiful.

'Of course it doesn't.' Azia's tone was firm. 'The neckline's not too low and though the dress is contoured to your body it's not tight. You look sophisticated and elegant. I can't wait to see the look on Ashraf's face.'

The thought of him washed heat across Tori's cheeks but Azia, bless her, pretended not to notice.

'I'm glad you chose black instead of the deep red. It's perfect with your colouring. Besides,' she added with a twinkle, 'you can wear red for the next one. Or maybe that gorgeous kingfisher-blue we saw.'

Tori smiled automatically but her heart wasn't in it. Would there *be* a next time? She remembered Ashraf talking about having her horse shipped to Australia. And he hadn't pressed her again to accept marriage.

Maybe his offer for her to stay in Za'daq was no longer on the table, with or without marriage. She couldn't expect it to be open-ended. There must be limits to Ashraf's patience.

Yet returning to Australia didn't appeal. Was she getting used to a life of royal luxury? Of ease and comfort?

More likely she was growing used to basking in Ashraf's attention. The more time they spent together, the harder it was to imagine leaving. Even if it was for her own good. Ashraf was more, so much more even than she'd imagined.

A knock sounded on the door and before she could answer Azia was there, curtseying low.

'Your Majesty.'

Ashraf stood framed in the door, looking debonair and so handsome that Tori felt her insides roll over. She'd expected him to wear traditional robes tonight but instead he wore a dinner jacket, superbly cut to his rangy, powerful frame. The crisp white shirt accentuated the rich bronze of his throat and his hair shone black as jet.

'Majesty? Why so formal in private, Azia?' He took the other woman's hand and pulled her upright.

Azia dimpled up at him but her eyes were serious. 'Just practising my curtsey for tonight. I'm told I still haven't got it right.'

Ashraf frowned and kept hold of her hand. 'I can imagine who told you that. Just ignore them. I'd rather have your genuine smile than perfect court etiquette.' He paused. 'Just as I'd rather have your herbed lamb with lemons and pilaf than any ten-course royal feast.'

Azia blushed. 'Then you must come to dinner again soon. I'll talk to Bram about setting a date.' She darted a look at Tori. 'I'd better go. He'll wonder where I am. See you there, Tori.'

Then she was gone, surprising Tori, who'd expected to accompany her to the reception.

The door closed and Ashraf faced her. There it was again. The throb of sensation as if all the oxygen had rushed out of the room while heat pooled low in her body. She should be used to it. Instead of familiarity lessening the impact of Ashraf's presence, it only heightened her response.

'Victoria.'

His voice was a rough purr, drawing out the syllables of her name into something exotically beautiful.

'You look magnificent.'

She felt her shoulders push back, her lips curve at the extravagant compliment. 'Thank you. So do you. Though I expected to see you in traditional robes.'

He paced towards her. It felt as if the room shrank till there was nothing beyond Ashraf.

'It's good to mix things up. A change from tradition and court formality can be useful occasionally.'

Tori read the lines still bracketing his mouth. 'Is this something to do with Azia? With the people who don't think she and Bram are good enough to be here?' She'd finally prised that out of her friend and still reeled from what she'd learned.

'Some of the older courtiers look askance at anyone different, or any change. But they'll learn.'

The determined set to Ashraf's jaw told its own story. Tori knew Ashraf would make that change happen. Azia had explained how Ashraf and Bram had become friends—one a prince, the other literally a pauper.

Bram's mother had been a servant and his father a foreigner who'd left her pregnant, unmarried and struggling to feed herself, much less a baby. She'd been shunned and Bram's blue eyes had been a constant reminder of her shame. Doing his military service with Bram, Ashraf had saved him from a vicious whipping by some men who had objected to serving with a clever upstart from the gutter. Bram still bore scars from the attack, but he and Ashraf had been stalwart friends since.

The tale had left Tori seething with outrage. And warmed by Ashraf's actions and the men's friendship.

She blinked now as Ashraf moved into her personal space, pulling something from his pocket. A small leather box.

Tori's heart leapt. Surely he wasn't—?

'For you to wear tonight.'

Once more that low voice curled through her, like smoke caressing her senses. She breathed deep, registering Ashraf's warm cinnamon scent, and knew that soon she'd be begging for more from him. Days of companionship and those searing, unsettling looks had done nothing to satisfy her craving.

Slowly she opened the box and found a pair of stunning earrings. 'Are they…?' She peered more closely.

'Diamonds and obsidian.'

The diamonds were large and exquisitely cut, and beneath them the long teardrops of pure black obsidian were flawless.

'I've never seen anything like them.' She might be a geologist, but she usually saw stones in their raw state. She estimated that these were unique and incredibly expensive. Yet it wasn't their monetary value that mattered. It was Ashraf's expression as he offered them.

Her heart stilled. Could it be...?

'You like them?'

Ashraf cringed inwardly at the neediness of that question. Like a kid seeking validation from an adult, or a lovesick youngster mooning over a girl he could never have.

Yet he knew Tori would eventually come to him. He'd seen hints that she'd begun to see the sense of his arguments. Plus there were clear signs of her sexual frustration. Her hungry stare as he entered the room had been like an incendiary flare. He still felt the sparks in his blood.

'They're stunning. But I can't—'

'Of course you can. And it would please me if you wore them.' He paused, watching her waver. 'Azia will be disappointed if you don't. She made a point of telling Bram what colour you were wearing, knowing he'd tell me.'

Tori's mouth rucked up ruefully. She liked Azia, which pleased him. Azia and Bram had kept him sane these last couple of years since he'd taken the throne. True friendship was in scarce supply in the royal court.

'In that case, thank you.'

Colour streaked her cheekbones. Ashraf knew she wasn't used to accepting gifts. He liked that. Liked knowing she'd never been beholden to other men. She'd been shocked when he had procured that horse for her, protesting at length though it had been clear she adored the mare. His Tori was very independent but he enjoyed giving her presents.

He watched her replace her plain silver studs with the new earrings. As she turned the light caught the gems, drawing attention to the pale pearl lustre of her skin and her slender throat.

Ashraf's pulse quickened.

His. His magnificent Victoria.

She *would* be his—and soon.

Not just because she was the mother of his son. But because he wanted her. He'd never want any other woman but her.

It should have been a shocking revelation. Instead the knowledge was like the final piece of a puzzle slotting into place. Ashraf felt a buzz of excitement and at the same time the peace of acceptance.

His gaze fell past pale skin down to a dress that glittered like the fathomless night sky in the desert, awash with stars. Traceries of delicate silver thread gave way to pure black where the dress skimmed her gorgeous body.

Ashraf swallowed hard. His baser instincts urged him to forget the people already gathered in the royal audience chamber. He'd rather spend the evening here with Tori.

He read her eyes, which had turned misty with awareness. It would take little to persuade her into bed...

But he had a duty to his people. A duty to Tori. To show her what her world would be like in Za'daq. That included events like tonight—not as much fun as visiting a souk or a village. She had to know the worst as well as the best. He just hoped, with a nervousness he hadn't felt in years, that the reality of court life didn't terrify her.

As expected his arrival, with Tori on his arm, caused a ripple. Cronies of his father raised eyebrows and matrons who'd shoved their unmarried daughters in his direction since he'd ascended to the throne barely hid their chagrin.

Ashraf surveyed them undaunted from his superior height. Tori was his personal guest. When she married him people would have to accept his choice.

None of them were courageous enough to say what was

on their minds. That the woman at his side wasn't a Za'daqi aristocrat. That he'd actually *touched* her in public—even if it was just a guiding hand on her elbow. That he'd broken custom by wearing western clothes.

They'd put up with his changes to government policy because even the most hidebound had begun to see the benefits. But alterations to court tradition, and by extension to their own sense of superiority, would be harshly judged by some. There had already been dismay because he'd been seen holding Tori's hand on a rural visit.

However, he sensed change wouldn't be as difficult as it had been when he'd inherited the throne. His nation was altering. Ashraf had enjoyed the evening more than usual. There was a wider mix of social groups and foreigners attending. Plus the atmosphere became more relaxed after the crowd had gone outside to watch feats of horsemanship, archery and acrobatics. He'd seen Tori's delight and viewed it all through new eyes, enjoying her enthusiasm.

Now, late in the reception, he was enjoying a joke with an army officer who'd been a friend in the old days. When he'd believed he'd found his future in the military. Before his father had cut short his career, outraged at the thought of the despised cuckoo in the nest excelling at something.

Ashraf saw Tori, stunning in silver and black, eyes bright as she laughed with Azia, another woman and a man he recognised as a foreign diplomat. Tori was gesturing towards Ashraf, as if pointing him out.

At that moment an older couple broke in on the group. The irascible Minister for the Interior and his haughty wife. They spoke and Azia flushed furiously. Tori's chin lifted. The two foreigners with them looked startled.

Ashraf started forward but a voice in his ear said, 'No. Wait.'

It was Bram.

'Is there a problem?' his army friend asked, craning to look past the crowd.

'Only a little one,' said Bram. 'Not worth worrying about. Besides, I think… Yes, it's taken care of now.'

He was right. Whatever poison the older couple had tried to spread clearly hadn't worked. Tori was speaking now and his nemesis looked discomfited, his wife embarrassed. Then Tori and the foreign woman began chatting again. Colour flushed Tori's cheeks but otherwise she looked serene.

'Nevertheless, I'll make sure,' Ashraf murmured. 'If you'll excuse me?'

He reached the group and all eyes turned to him. The Minister opened his mouth to speak but Tori was faster.

'Your Majesty.'

Tori said it as easily as if she called him by his title daily. Her eyes glittered bright as diamond chips, and the slight flare of her nostrils hinted at displeasure, but otherwise her expression was calm, her smile welcoming.

'I don't believe you've met Ms Alison Drake, the new American ambassador.' She turned to the slim brunette, 'Alison, I'm pleased to introduce you to His Majesty Sheikh Ashraf ibn Kahul al Rashid of Za'daq.'

Not by a flicker did Ashraf betray surprise at her remembering his full name, or at her deft handling of the introduction. Hadn't she spent her youth at her father's side, mingling at official functions?

'Ms Drake, it's a delight to meet you.' He shook her hand, preventing her from curtseying. 'I understood your flight had been delayed? I expected you tomorrow.'

'The pleasure is mine, Your Majesty. Apologies for my very late arrival. I managed to get an alternative flight and was advised…' she glanced at her companion from the embassy '…that it would be okay to attend—though I haven't yet formally presented my credentials.'

The Minister for the Interior cleared his throat but Ashraf silenced him with a look. He had no role in diplomatic matters and he'd tried to stir up trouble for Tori and Azia. Ashraf wouldn't tolerate that.

'Of course. It's a pleasure to welcome you. We'll leave the formalities till tomorrow. In the meantime, I hope you're enjoying yourself?'

'Oh, yes. I've had such a wonderfully warm welcome to your country.'

He didn't miss the way her eyes flickered towards the older man. Or how Azia bit her lip and focused on adjusting her shawl. His curiosity deepened.

'Excellent. Let me introduce you to some more people.' He looked across the crowd to Bram, who was already ushering forward a number of dignitaries to meet the ambassador.

Ashraf turned to the couple standing stiffly to one side. 'Minister, your wife looks very tired.' He offered her a charming smile and watched her swallow nervously. 'You have my permission to leave. We'll talk tomorrow.'

It was hours before Ashraf could be alone with Tori.

The guests had been encouraged to leave and the staff had shut the doors, leaving them the sole possessors of the audience chamber. They stood before the large arched windows looking over a city washed in the national colours of crimson and gold from a final flourish of fireworks.

But Ashraf's eyes were on Tori, not the view. She'd never looked more beautiful. Nor had the connection between them, invisible as spun glass but strong as the desert sun, been more palpable. She'd spent the last part of the evening at his side and it had felt right.

It was where she belonged.

Tonight, for the first time in a week, he dared to hope she felt the same. The way she smiled at him, the sense of understanding, the fizz in his blood when their eyes met, had to mean something.

Any fear he'd felt that she might be scared off by the

pomp of a royal event had been short-lived. She'd shone. She was charming and interested in people. Those qualities had endeared her to his people on their excursions. Plus those years of supporting her father had stood her in good stead.

'You were magnificent tonight.'

He caught and held her hands. Their eyes met and he felt the impact square in the centre of his chest.

She shook her head, her mouth curving up. 'That was you, Your Majesty. Magnificent.'

He tugged her closer, almost close enough to kiss. But there was one matter to clear up first.

'What was that scene with the Minister for the Interior?'

Tori's eyebrows pinched. 'You saw that? I didn't think anyone had noticed.'

'That he'd been insulting?' Again, Ashraf felt fury burn. 'I don't think anyone else did—only me and Bram.'

Both had been watching their womenfolk. Yet only Bram had been sure that the women could handle the problem. Ashraf had underestimated Tori.

'You handled him well. Now, tell me.'

She sighed. 'He had no idea who Alison was. He saw us laughing and assumed she was simply a friend of mine or Azia's and therefore unimportant.'

Ashraf had learned tonight that the ambassador had once been posted to Australia. She was an old friend of Tori's mother.

Tori lifted her shoulders. 'He made disparaging remarks about court standards slipping since shopkeepers and…and others had been invited to such events. He suggested we leave as we must feel out of place.'

Ashraf understood the reference to shopkeepers. Azia's parents ran a shop in the main souk. But 'others'…

'Others?' He was sure the colour washing Tori's face had nothing to do with the fireworks. His jaw clenched. 'Tell me.'

'I've forgotten his exact words.'

Tori wasn't a good liar, but before he could call her on it she continued.

'He lost his air of superiority when I stared him down, mentioning how kind and welcoming most Za'daqis were to guests.'

Ashraf didn't miss the emphasis on *most*.

'I introduced him to the new ambassador and Alison mentioned that her parents had run a grocery store back in the States.'

Despite his anger, Ashraf laughed. Hospitality was something Za'daqis prided themselves on. The Minister would have hated being called out on his rudeness. 'I like your friend Alison more and more. Nevertheless, I want to know—'

Tori put her finger to his mouth, stopping his words. Touching him felt so good. How had she kept her distance this last week?

'I'd rather forget him. He's rude and self-opinionated— but you know that.' She felt Ashraf's surprisingly soft lips against her flesh and longing shivered through her. And something more profound. 'Don't let him spoil what's been a wonderful night.'

'Wonderful?'

Eyes gleaming, Ashraf captured her wrist and kissed her palm, turning that shiver into a pounding torrent of awareness.

Tori gulped, her throat closing as she looked into that strong, dear face.

She prided herself on her honesty and her willingness to face facts, no matter how unpalatable. But tonight she realised she'd hidden from the truth.

Far-fetched as it seemed, if she counted on the calendar the time they'd actually spent together, Tori was in love with Ashraf al Rashid.

In love. Not just in lust. Not just admiring of his determination to do right by Oliver and his people or grateful
for his understanding of her doubts.

In love.

Totally.

When he'd given her these fabulous earrings and she'd
caught his tender look the truth had struck. She'd wondered
if his feelings were more deeply engaged than she'd suspected. Had she resisted his proposal so adamantly because
she cared too much for him? Because she didn't want to
commit herself till she knew he felt the same way?

The thought of loving Ashraf but never having his love
terrified her. It was a roiling wave in her belly whenever
she dwelled too long on doubt. But tonight, as she watched
him with his people and basked in his attention, she couldn't
hide from her feelings any longer.

If her abduction in the desert had taught her one thing
it was to live for the moment. You never knew what was
around the corner. Whether you'd have another chance to
do what really mattered.

What really mattered was Oliver and Ashraf.

'Victoria? You're miles away.'

Ashraf curled an arm around her waist, securing her
against him, and everything inside her rejoiced. *This* was
where she wanted to be.

She licked her bottom lip and saw his eyes zero in on
the movement. Heat drenched her. But as well as physical
need she recognised now the deeper sense of contentment
that swelled her heart.

Life in Za'daq would have challenges. Life with Ashraf
would be a learning experience. But love couldn't be denied. She'd made up her mind.

'I've come to a decision.'

Ashraf's grip tightened, his brows furrowing. 'Don't let
one bigoted man—'

'Shh...' She reached up on tiptoe and silenced him, this time with her lips. How she'd longed for his kiss!

He gathered her in with both arms and would have deepened the kiss but Tori leaned back just enough to speak. She felt secure in his embrace—not because she needed protection or looking after but because Ashraf made her feel as no other man had. Because she loved him.

'If the offer is still open, I'll marry you.'

For a moment she thought he hadn't heard. Or that she hadn't said it aloud, just thought the words. He looked down at her, his expression unreadable.

Then, to her amazement, he dropped to his knee. Her hands were in his and he kissed first one and then the other. Not in passion but with a deliberate reverence and a formal courtesy that belonged in a world of warrior knights and beautiful maidens.

'You have my word, Victoria, that you won't regret this.' His voice made it a solemn vow. 'I will do all in my power to make you happy. To support you, honour you and care for you. And our family.'

His words sent a flurry of emotion through her.

Care. That was good. More than good when combined with the rest of his promise.

Tori shut down the querulous inner voice that said care wasn't love. That the chances of Ashraf ever loving her were slim, given how he'd grown up unloved. The fact that he loved Oliver was enough for now. It had to be. And maybe, just maybe, over time—

Her thoughts stopped as Ashraf surged to his feet. That sombre expression had vanished, replaced by a smile so brilliant it undid something inside her.

'Thank you, Tori.'

Then, before she realised what he was about, Ashraf swooped low, scooping her up in his arms, swirling her around and striding across the room.

She laughed. 'Where are we going?'

As if she didn't have a fair idea.

'To bed. To show you how good our marriage will be.'

Because he was afraid she'd change her mind? No. She'd decided. She wouldn't expect the impossible. Tori would accept what was offered and make the most of it.

She didn't believe in fairy tales.

CHAPTER THIRTEEN

ASHRAF SEETHED AS he marched into his office. There'd been satisfaction in sacking the Minister for the Interior, but not enough.

'Meeting didn't go well?' Bram looked up from his desk.

'It went as expected. We now have an opening in the Ministry.' And an offended ex-minister, shocked that his King had actually dismissed him. The old goat had thought himself untouchable.

'Good. The Council will run better without him.'

Ashraf shoved his hands in his pockets. 'I expected you to counsel patience.' That had run out last night.

Bram shrugged. 'You gave him chance after chance, compromising to bring the old guard along with you and allow him some pride. But he's dead wood, holding the government back.'

Ashraf lifted his eyebrows. Bram really was speaking his mind today. 'What's happened?' He knew his friend. Something had prompted his militant attitude.

Bram nodded to his computer. 'The press reports are worse than we first thought. Somehow they've got a photo of Tori and Oliver, taken in Australia. Speculation is rife that he's your son.'

Ashraf ploughed his fingers through his hair. It had been a gamble, waiting to legitimise Oliver. Ashraf had wanted to announce a wedding simultaneously, but he'd respected Tori's need for time.

'The cat's out of the bag, then.' He took a deep breath. 'Arrange a press release. I'll—'

'That's not all.' Bram looked grim. 'I've received a petition from a small group of Council members. They've heard about Oliver and know that you've moved out of your apartments to be with him and Tori. They insist you give them up or abdicate.'

Ashraf snorted. 'As if they have the power to *insist*! Let me guess.' He named three cronies of the sacked Minister and Bram nodded. 'They seem to forget it's only by *my* pleasure that they have a role in government.'

'They threatened to approach Karim and ask him to assume the throne.'

Ashraf gritted his teeth. The last thing Karim wanted or needed was a delegation of old fogeys bothering him. 'Karim rejected the throne. He can't simply change his mind. Even if it were possible, he'd never agree.'

Bram lifted one eyebrow but Ashraf said no more. Only he and his brother knew the reason for his action. A medical test had revealed that Karim, not Ashraf, was the cuckoo in the nest, the son of another man.

Privately Ashraf thought that had precipitated his ailing father's death. The revelation that the son he'd groomed as heir wasn't his while the despised younger child was his true son.

Karim had stayed after the funeral only long enough to see Ashraf crowned and then left Za'daq. He had no plans to return.

'Is that all?'

'One of the latest press reports has a particularly nasty edge. It makes a great deal of Tori's work in isolated areas, often as the only female on a team. It draws conclusions about her morals and insinuates…'

Bile rose in Ashraf's throat. 'I can imagine. Where, precisely, was this from?'

Bram mentioned a media outlet owned by a friend of the sacked Minister. Ashraf nodded. 'Show me, and call the legal office. They can check the libel laws.'

He'd end this *now*, before it came to Tori's ears.

But as the afternoon wore on Ashraf's fiery indignation was overtaken by something far harder to bear. Especially when the lawyers dithered over whether the law had actually been broken. Ironically, if Tori were Za'daqi, or if she'd already married him, the reports could have been taken down and the outlet closed. As a foreigner, her situation was less clear.

Ashraf had grown up being vilified by his father. He was used to people assuming the worst about him. But to see Tori belittled and be unable to stop it tore at something vital within him.

He stalked the offices, trying to find a solution but finding none. He either abided by the laws he'd introduced, allowing more freedom for the press, or he gave up all pretension of being anything other than an autocratic ruler, thus destroying the hard work he'd put into turning Za'daq into a more democratic country.

He was caught by his own insistence on reform, and his inability to sweep the ugly innuendos away and protect his woman ate at him. He'd expected scandal. But seeing the negative focus shift to Tori, with such snide inferences, sickened him.

His wonderful woman had been through so much. Now, generously, she'd finally agreed to marry him for their son's sake. She'd signed on for a marriage without love, though it wasn't what she wanted. She'd agreed to learn a new way of life—not only in a country foreign to her, but as a royal, under constant scrutiny. He'd promised she wouldn't regret her decision.

And now… How could he ask this of her?

The answer was simple and terrible.

He couldn't.

Tori was on the floor with Oliver, watching his eyes grow round with excitement as, wobbling, he managed to stay sitting up before losing his balance and falling onto the cushion she'd put behind him.

Smiling at his achievement, and his delight, she was taken by surprise when Ashraf appeared.

'You're early.'

Pleasure filled her. All day she'd wondered if she'd done the sensible thing, agreeing to marry Ashraf. In the end she'd given up wondering if it was sensible, contenting herself with the fact that it was her only option if she wanted to be with the man she loved.

The glow inside her as she looked up at him told her she'd done right. Better to love than to turn her back on the chance of happiness.

'Gah-gah-gah.' Oliver, on his back, waved his arms and legs as he saw his father.

'Hello, little beetle.' Ashraf bent and scooped him up, lifting him high till Oliver crowed with excitement.

As ever, the sight of them together tugged at the sentimental cord that ran through her middle. It was stronger today, after she'd spent all night making glorious love to Ashraf.

Tori told herself that was why she felt emotional. Lack of sleep. *And finally admitting you're wildly in love with this man.*

'We need to talk.'

Ashraf looked down at her and that warm, squishy feeling solidified into a cold lump of concern. Something was wrong. She read it in the lines bracketing his mouth.

'Of course. I'll ring for the nanny.' Tori scrambled to her feet.

'No need. I've called her. Ah...' He turned at a knock on the door. 'Here she is.'

He took time to buss Oliver's cheek and let his son grab his fingers, all the while murmuring to him in his own language, before handing him to the nanny.

Finally they were alone. But Ashraf didn't pull Tori close. He didn't even take her hand, though when she'd last seen him he'd been reluctant to leave her bed. He'd lingered, stroking her hair, kissing her and murmuring endearments in a voice of rough suede that had made her feel maybe she was wrong. Maybe he might learn to love her one day.

Now, Ashraf didn't even look at her. He seemed fixated on the view from the window. His brow was pleated and his mouth was set so grimly that the back of her neck prickled in anticipation of bad news. Her stomach churned.

'What's wrong?' She came up beside him, put her hand on his arm then dropped it as he instantly stiffened. 'Ashraf?'

Tori had a really bad feeling now. During everything they'd been through never once had Ashraf shied away from her touch. Shock slammed her. It did no good telling herself that it wasn't revulsion she read in his grimace, even if the idea seemed crazy.

He turned but didn't reach for her. Instead he shoved his hands deep in his pockets, broad shoulders hunching. Tori felt his rejection like a punch to the solar plexus that sucked out her breath. What had happened to the tactile man who couldn't get enough of her?

'I'm sorry, Tori. I was distracted. Let's sit, shall we?'

She shook her head and planted her soles more firmly on the silk carpet. 'I'm fine here.' If it was bad news she'd rather have it standing up. 'Is it my father?'

'No, no. Nothing like that. There's no news from Australia.'

Tori's swift breath of relief surprised her. She didn't *like* her father but it seemed she did care for him at some level.

'So it's news from Za'daq?'

She looked into fathomless eyes and wished she knew what Ashraf was thinking.

Just when she thought he wasn't going to speak he took her hand, enfolding it in long fingers. Warmth trickled from his touch but dissipated with his words.

'I'll always treasure your generosity in agreeing to marry me, Victoria.'

For the first time the sound of Ashraf saying her full name sent a cold shiver through her—nothing like the shimmer of lush warmth it usually generated.

'But I'm freeing you from your promise.'

Tori felt his encircling hand tighten as she stumbled back, away from him, till finally she broke his hold.

'You don't want to marry me?'

In another time, another place, she'd have winced at the sound of her ragged voice. But it matched the way she felt. Off balance, as if someone had ripped that beautiful handwoven rug from beneath her feet.

But the only ripping here was her heart. Her sad, foolish heart, which had opened itself up to Ashraf's kindness, strength and caring.

'I'm sorry.' He held her gaze, his own unwavering. 'It's for the best. I was selfish to ask you to give up your life and home and live in Za'daq. I see that now.'

Tori wanted to protest that living with him in Za'daq was what she craved, but he continued.

'As you wisely pointed out, Oliver will still have a family even if we live apart.'

Live apart.

Tori pressed her hand to the place below her ribs that felt hollow, as if an unseen hand had scraped out her insides. He didn't even want her in his country!

Out of the miasma of shock and hurt, indignation rose. 'That's not good enough.'

'Sorry?'

He'd obviously expected her simply to accept his decree. He wasn't the enlightened man she'd thought. All those generations of absolute rulers had left their mark. She read surprise in the lift of his eyebrows and determination in those haughty features.

'If you're going to jilt a woman you need to do better.'

For a second—a millisecond—she saw something pass across that set face. Then it was gone. If anything he stood straighter, imposing and rigid, like the soldier she'd discovered he'd once been. Or an autocrat looking down on a lesser being.

Yet even in her distress Tori couldn't believe that of Ashraf.

'Of course. I apologise. Again.'

He paused, and if she hadn't known better Tori would have said he was the one struggling for breath, not her.

'I should have started by saying I'm sorry for changing my mind.'

Changing his mind? Tori stared, incredulous. He wanted her to believe he'd simply *changed his mind*?

She shook her head, wrapping her arms around her middle to contain the empty feeling which threatened to spread and engulf her whole.

'Still not good enough, Ashraf. I need to know why.' A thought pierced her whirling brain. 'Is it someone else? Have you found a better bride?'

Someone local who understood Za'daqi ways. Some glamorous princess.

'Of course not!' He actually looked insulted.

'There's no "of course" about it.' Tori's voice grew in strength as anger masked pain. 'This morning, *in my bed*, you were happy with the arrangement. What changed?'

He winced and half turned away. Tori began to wonder if the caring, wonderful man she'd fallen in love with had been an illusion.

'You're right. You deserve to know.' He paused, breathing deep. 'The press, stirred by my opponents, have learned about Oliver. About us. The stories they're printing…' He spread his hands and grimaced. 'They're not to be borne. The filth they're spouting will only continue and I can't allow that. I have to stop it.'

'I see.'

It was clear from Ashraf's expression how important this was to him. Tori recalled his talk of past scandals, how he hadn't been accepted by the political elite, how he'd had to strive to win support for his schemes.

Was his situation so precarious? It seemed so. And so was the crown he wanted to pass to Oliver. Tori wanted to tell him that it didn't matter. That Oliver could make his way in the world without a royal title. But it did matter. This was Ashraf's birthright. He'd worked all his life to prove himself. Since becoming Sheikh he'd worked longer and harder than his predecessors to improve the nation. Tori had had that from Azia, who was forever singing Ashraf's praises.

This was his destiny. His purpose in life.

But that didn't stop her searing anguish as she faced facts. The man she loved was rejecting her because when it came to the crunch he, and his people, believed she wasn't good enough to stand at his side.

CHAPTER FOURTEEN

TORI TURNED AND marched away from the window into the shadows.

Ashraf wanted to follow and haul her close.

He didn't do it. If he touched her his good intentions would collapse and he wouldn't release her.

He swallowed and it felt as if he'd swallowed a desert of sand, his mouth so dry the action tore his throat to shreds.

This was the cost of releasing the one woman he'd ever cared for. *The one woman he could ever love.*

That, above all, gave him the strength to weld his feet to the floor.

He loved Tori. Loved her with such devotion that watching her struggle with his decision felt like the most difficult thing he'd ever done. Harder than facing the threat of death at Qadri's hands.

What would it be like, living the rest of his life without her?

The laceration in his throat became a raw ache that descended to his chest, intensifying to a sharper pain with each breath.

But he had to protect her. In his arrogance he'd assumed they'd face the scandal together. That it would be directed at *him*, with his notorious past, and that Tori would be seen as a victim of his licentious ways. He hadn't bargained on her being represented as some…

He frowned. Was that a sob?

Tori stood with her back to him, facing the courtyard. Her shoulders were straight but her head was bent. As he watched another quiver passed through her.

Seconds later he was behind her, hands lifted but not touching those slim shoulders. 'Tori, are you all right?'

Stupid question. Of course she wasn't. But how could he comfort her?

'Does it matter?'

Her steady voice made him feel, if possible, worse. 'It's my fault. I shouldn't have let this happen.'

'Which? Suggesting marriage or fathering Oliver?' She snorted. 'Don't answer that. Clearly you regret both.'

'No!' His fingers closed on her shoulders and he gritted his teeth, fighting the need to spin her round and into his arms. To hold her properly one last time. 'You can't think that.'

'There are a lot of things you control, Ashraf, but what I think isn't one of them.'

'Parting is for the best.' How he wished there were another way.

'Whose best? Yours? Not Oliver's or mine.' She shrugged from his hold and swung to face him.

Ashraf stared into eyes that glittered with tears she refused to let fall. For the first time he felt himself to be the failure his father had accused him of being.

The one woman in the world he wanted to protect from harm and he'd brought her infamy and scandal. The sight of her, brim-full with pain, knotted his conscience and stole his resolution.

'Don't lie, Ashraf. Just say it. It's too risky for your crown to take on a woman with a bastard son, even if you're his father.'

His breath hissed at the words and her eyes narrowed.

'That's it, isn't it?'

For a second she stood stock-still, eyes wide. He'd seen the victim of an accidental gunshot look exactly the same— that moment of disbelief before he crumpled to the ground. But Tori didn't crumple. She turned and stalked to the bedroom.

'It won't take me long to pack. We'll leave today.'

It was what he wanted. What was best for Tori. Yet Ashraf couldn't let her do it. He was too selfish.

'Wait!'

She kept walking, head up, shoulders back, but she stumbled as if she wasn't watching her step.

His heart twisted. 'Tori.'

'There's nothing to say.'

But there was. So much he barely knew where to start. He inserted himself between her and the bedroom door, frustrating her attempt to shove him aside.

'This isn't about me protecting my position—it's about protecting *you*.'

'You're not protecting me. You're banishing me.'

His heart, the organ he'd so long thought dormant, beat harder at the torment in her voice.

'If you're not here they'll focus on me, like they always have. You won't be a target.'

Silence. Silence that lasted so long he wondered if she were trying to freeze him out. Finally she blinked, like a sleepwalker rousing.

'The stories aren't about you?'

'Partly. But…'

But the most negative ones made it sound as if he'd fallen prey to some avaricious *femme fatale* who went through men like a fish through water.

'They focus on me, then,' she murmured. 'That makes sense. It makes you look bad and you can't afford that.'

Unable to stop himself, Ashraf grabbed her upper arms and pulled her close. 'How many times do I have to say it? I'm used to bad press. It's *you* I want to protect. You shouldn't have to put up with this.'

Her eyes rounded and she stopped trying to pull free. 'Are you serious?'

'Yes, I'm serious!'

He saw her blink and realised he'd raised his voice. It

was something he never did. His father had shouted all the time when he was riled—at him, at servants, at inanimate objects.

Ashraf shuddered. Another sign he was losing control.

'Tell me what they're saying,' she said.

At first he refused, but Tori wore him down. When he'd finished she shook her head sadly and Ashraf knew he was right to send her away. If only he had the courage to do it.

'You'd really banish me so the press won't hound me?'

His chest rose high on a deep breath. 'It's not banishment. It's—'

'Sending me away from the man I love is banishment.' Her soft voice cut across his.

Everything inside Ashraf stilled. Even his pulse slowed, before speeding up to a gallop. He swallowed. This time the sand in his throat had been replaced with a choking knot of tangling emotion.

'You don't love me.'

It was impossible. Even his mother hadn't loved him, choosing instead to run off with her paramour and leave Ashraf to her husband's mercy.

'Why don't I?'

Tori's smile trembled and his heart with it. He shook his head, unwilling to say the words. It was too big a risk. Yet perhaps for the first time in his life he needed to open himself up, though it made him even more vulnerable.

'Because I've never craved anything so much. And life's taught me never to expect such a blessing.'

'You poor, deluded man.'

Her palm covered his cheek and his eyelids drooped as the pent-up tension was expelled from his lungs. One touch, just one, did that.

'I've been in love with you more or less since we met.'

'That's crazy. You didn't know me.'

Yet he greedily hoarded each precious word. His hands firmed around her waist, pulling her closer.

'It was instinctive, and everything I believed about you has turned out to be right.' She frowned. 'Even down to your managing ways. Do you *really* think I'll curl up and die because the gutter press prints lies about me?'

'You shouldn't have to face that.'

Her chin lifted. 'You're right. I shouldn't. And I'm sure you and your lawyers will help me make them stop. But if you think I'm going to be scared away by gossip, think again.' Her mouth tilted at one corner. 'I work in a male-dominated industry. I've faced prejudice and sexual innuendo all my working life. Most of my peers are great, but there are always some who can't cope. I won't put up with it and I certainly won't let it destroy my happiness. Besides, I've learned a thing or two from my father about dealing with the press.'

Ashraf stared, stunned by the pragmatic courage of his beloved. He'd known she was special, yet still she surprised him.

'Ash?'

Her use of the old nickname was even more intimate than the feel of her hand on his flesh.

'You do want me?'

'Of course I do. I never want to let you go.'

He wrapped her tight in his arms. Not kissing her but simply embracing her. Feeling her heart beat against him, her breath a warm caress against his collarbone, her body a perfect fit to his.

Tori's uncertainty made heat prickle at the back of his eyes. His breath shuddered. He had a moment's recollection of feeling this close to tears only once before. He'd been about four and he'd often gone to play in the courtyard that had been his mother's. The garden's fragrance had reminded him of a long-ago comforting presence that he guessed must have been hers. But someone had told his father of his secret visits and he'd arrived to find all the scented roses pulled out. The place was a barren waste.

But Ashraf's palace wasn't barren. He had Tori—his woman, his lover, soon to be his wife. A heroine strong enough to stand beside him through whatever life held. And there was Oliver too.

'You do know,' he murmured, tilting her chin so he could look into her glorious eyes, 'there's no turning back now.' His chest swelled with feelings he'd suppressed too long. 'I love you too much ever to let you go. If you get cold feet before the wedding I'll have the border closed and—'

'What? You'll kidnap me and ride off with me to your secret desert encampment? I like the sound of that.'

Her smile was wide and unshadowed. It seemed his Tori really had moved on from the trauma of their abduction.

Ashraf lowered his head so his mouth hovered above hers. 'I'd planned to honeymoon on my private island off the coast, but if you prefer the desert...'

'I prefer you kiss me and tell me again that you love me.'

He looked down, reading marvellous things in her gentle smile.

This. This was what he craved.

'Your wish,' he said against her lips, 'is my command.'

EPILOGUE

It was a long wedding. Days long. Filled with good wishes, lavish entertainment, music, feasting and enough pomp to convince Tori that she really had married a king.

She returned to the audience chamber after freshening up to find Karim waiting for her, a query in his moss-green eyes. Beyond him the room was filled with guests in their finery, the air buzzing with animated conversation.

Funny to think she'd been wary about meeting Ashraf's brother. Everyone spoke of him in glowing terms and she'd wondered if it was true that he really didn't want Ashraf's crown. Till the brothers had told her their story and Karim had welcomed her into the family with genuine warmth.

His smile had been almost wistful as he'd admitted he'd never seen Ashraf so happy. That neither brother had expected to find true love. Tori's heart had squeezed at his words and she'd hugged him hard, eliciting mock protests from Ashraf and a quaintly clumsy hug from Karim. Clumsy, she suspected, because like Ashraf he wasn't used to emotional displays. It certainly couldn't be from lack of female companionship, for despite Karim being only his half-brother he shared Ashraf's chiselled good-looks and potent appeal.

'How are you holding up?' he asked.

Tori beamed at him. 'I'm doing well. Especially since everyone is so happy for us.'

Contrary to expectations, the ghastly rumours had ceased almost straight away when it turned out that the die-hards who disapproved of Ashraf were completely outnumbered by those who thought him an excellent Sheikh.

As for Oliver being born outside marriage—that didn't seem to be a problem now Ashraf had legitimised him. If anything, many Za'daqis viewed it as proof of their King's masculine potency and thought it natural that Tori had been swept off her feet. She'd discovered a strong romantic streak in his people.

'Ashraf sent me to find you.' Karim offered her his arm and when she curled her hand around it he bent to murmur in her ear. 'Unless you'd rather skip this bit and rest?'

She should be tired but Tori had never felt so energised. 'I wouldn't miss it for anything.'

'You don't even know what it is!'

Karim laughed as he steered her through the throng, his deep chuckle reminding her of Ashraf's. Even after a few days she knew that Karim, like her husband, rarely laughed aloud. Both were so serious, though Ashraf was learning to relax more.

'So tell me.'

They were outside now, on the terrace, looking down at the wide space where she'd previously watched horsemen and archers perform stunning feats of skill and bravery. Now the space was filled with people. More than filled. They spilled down the slope beyond into the public gardens and streets as far as the eye could see.

Tori stumbled to a halt. 'Where have they come from?'

A deep, familiar voice reached her.

'From everywhere—all across the country.'

It was Ashraf, his eyes shining. He looked magnificent in white robes trimmed with gold as he strode up and took her hands.

Tori's insides melted. Her Ashraf. Her husband.

Beside them Karim spoke. 'They're not VIPs, just ordinary people who've made their way here to wish you both well.' He clamped his hand on Ashraf's shoulder, leaning close and lowering his voice. 'You've done well, little brother. They love you.'

Ashraf shrugged, making little of the praise, though Tori saw that it moved him.

He turned to her. 'There's even a delegation from that first village I took you to in the foothills. Where you got that scarf.'

Tori looked down at the deep jewel colours of the scarf she'd teamed with a dress of vibrant teal, embroidered at the hem with silver. Over the last three days it seemed she'd worn every colour of the rainbow, and each time her pleasure in the magnificent wedding clothes was outshone by the appreciation in Ashraf's eyes.

'What are we waiting for? There are a lot of people to greet.'

Ashraf's slow smile made her heart drum faster.

'Thank you, *habibti*. It will mean a lot to them.' He looked at Karim. 'You'll come too, brother?'

Karim shook his head. 'This is your day—yours and Tori's. I'll go and deal with the VIPs.' He turned towards the palace, leaving Ashraf and Tori alone.

As Ashraf led her towards the expectant throng he tucked her close against him. 'I'm afraid this will add extra hours to the wedding celebrations. You'll need to rest when this is over.'

'It's not rest I need. I have other priorities.'

Ashraf stopped and turned to face her. 'Have I told you how very much I love you?'

His deep voice resonated and a ripple ran through the watching crowd.

'Yes.' She knew there were stars in her eyes as she looked up at him. 'But I never tire of hearing it.'

'And you love me.' His declaration was loud and proud. 'I do.'

The crowd cheered, and Ashraf grinned, and Tori knew she'd just embarked on the most remarkable, wonderful adventure of her life.

* * * * *

THE PRINCE'S
PREGNANT MISTRESS

MAISEY YATES

This book is dedicated to the librarians. I spent countless hours at libraries, reading countless books. Thank you for giving the joy of reading to everyone.

CHAPTER ONE

IT HAD BEEN a perfect night. So beautiful, the white Christmas lights strung across the facades of the buildings in Vail glittering on the snow all around them. Like the stars had dropped down from the sky to light their way.

Yes, the night had been perfect and Raphael even more so. But then, he always was.

Bailey couldn't quite believe it was real. Even after eight months with him, she couldn't believe it. He was like something out of a fairy tale, and she was a girl who never thought she'd have a happy ending.

But then she'd met him.

Of course, she only saw him every few months, when he flew into Colorado on business, and never for long enough.

She'd been guarded all of her adult life. So cautious when it came to men and dating. But with Raphael...that caution had never been there. She'd just given herself to him with no thought of self-protection, no thought of anything but how much she wanted him.

She was like a different woman with him. A woman in love.

It was always so frantic when he was there. Tonight

was no exception. They'd finished dinner, a walk through the town, then back to the hotel, where he'd consumed her.

There had been an edge to him tonight, an intensity. Not that she was complaining.

She stretched out on the sheets, curling her toes. She was still recovering. She giggled and rolled onto her side, looking toward the bathroom.

The door was closed, a sliver of light visible beneath it. She sighed heavily, waiting for him to come back to bed.

Waiting *impatiently*.

Tonight felt different. Significant and special.

She loved him so much. She ached with it. She'd never thought she could feel this way about someone. Never thought someone could feel this way about her.

She was ready for more. She was ready for everything.

The bathroom door opened, and her heart skipped a little. That made her smile. It was ridiculous how giddy she was over him. But then, she'd never let a man close enough to her to have this kind of intimacy.

In her waitressing job she got hit on by men all the time. She just wasn't…swayed by it. At all. She had been thoroughly disenchanted with men by the time she'd moved out of her mother's home at sixteen. She'd seen too much. Too much heartbreak. Too much screaming.

Bailey had decided to make her own life, her own future. She'd made it to twenty-one a virgin because she'd been so determined to wait until it was right, until she was ready.

And then she'd met Raphael. Her friends barely believed he existed. She'd stopped talking much about him when all she'd gotten were skeptical eye rolls and *Raphael? Bailey, are you dating a Ninja Turtle?*

He'd never met them because he was so busy whenever he flew in. And then she wanted him all to herself. So yeah, she was giddy. She had a feeling she always would be.

"Bailey, shouldn't you be getting dressed?"

She frowned. She hadn't expected him to say that. She spent the night with him all the time when he came through town. "I thought…well." She swept a hand over her bare curves. "I'm ready for more if you are."

"I have an early flight out—I thought I told you."

He looked grim suddenly. She hated that grimness. It grabbed her by the throat and held her tight, filled her lungs with dread, and she couldn't quite pinpoint why. "No. You didn't." She forced a smile because there was no point fighting with him if these were their last few minutes together before he had to leave again. "You have to go back to Italy?"

"Yes," he said, reaching for his pants and tugging them on, covering up his gorgeous body.

She watched him dress the rest of the way, the reverse strip show still arousing even if it had a more depressing ending than the alternative.

His muscles rippled with each movement, his fingers blunt and efficient as he buttoned his shirt. Reminding her of just how *efficient* they were with her.

"Bailey," he said again, his tone vaguely…irritated. She couldn't recall Raphael ever being irritated with her before.

"I'm comfortable," she said, sighing heavily and rolling out of bed. "There. Now I'm not. I hope you're happy." She purposefully wiggled her hips a little bit as she made her way to where he'd torn her dress off earlier. "I hope this survived," she said, picking it up gingerly.

"I'll replace it if it didn't."

"I'm more worried about what I'll wear home." Another sigh escaped her lips. "When are you coming back?"

"I'm not."

She felt like all the air had been pulled from her body. She just stood there, blinking in the dim light, totally frozen while her fingers went numb and her insides went cold. "What do you mean, you aren't coming back?"

"I don't have any more work here in Vail. We're finished up with our meetings."

"Right. So. But… I'm here."

He laughed, a hard, low sound that wasn't like Raphael at all. "Sorry, *cara*, that is not enticement enough."

She was dumbstruck. Completely. And she hated herself for it. "I don't understand. We just had the nicest date and the best… I don't… I don't understand."

"It was goodbye. You have been an especially lovely diversion, but that's all it could ever be. I have a life back in Italy, and it's time I got back to it in earnest."

Dumbstruck turned into sucker punched. "A life? Are you… Raphael, are you married?"

"About to be," he said, his tone hard. "I can't afford distractions any longer."

"You're engaged. Of course you are," she said, words tumbling out of her mouth without her permission. "I bet you…live with her. Of course you only come and visit me every couple of months. I'm such an idiot."

She covered her mouth and stifled a scream. She was too angry to be humiliated. Too wounded to care if she bled all over him. "I was… I was a virgin, and you knew that," she threw at him. "I told you it was a big step for me!" Angry tears welled in her eyes, rolling down her cheeks.

"And I appreciated the gift, *tesorina*," he said, his tone now like iron. "We were together for eight months. It was hardly a fling."

"It's a fling if one of you isn't taking it seriously at all!" A sob rose in her throat, shaking her whole body. "If one of you knew it would end and was sleeping with someone else." She bent down then, picked up her shoe and threw it at his head.

He dodged it neatly, an Italian swear word on his lips.

She bent again, picking up her other shoe and flinging that at him too. This one hit him square in the chest. He closed the distance between them, grabbing hold of her wrist. "Enough." He released her as quickly as he'd taken hold of her. "Don't embarrass yourself, Bailey. Not more than you already have."

"You should be embarrassed," she said, her voice shaking. She pulled the dress on, then moved to pick her shoes up. She hadn't put her nylons back on, but who had the time for that ridiculousness when your heart had just been ripped out through your chest? "You are the one who *lied* to me." She sniffed much louder than she meant to, pulling her coat on over the dress, trying to ignore the fact that she was shaking so hard now her teeth were chattering.

"I never lied to you," he said, his dark eyes burning. "You created the story you wanted to believe."

She let out a feral growl and rushed past him, heading out the door as quickly as she could, feeling like a disgraced hooker walking out of his hotel room in the middle of the night, wearing high heels and a beautiful dress that she was going to have to burn now.

It wasn't until she was outside, until the cold wrapped itself around her, overtaking her, that she fell apart. Completely, utterly. She sank to her knees in the snow, sobbing until her throat hurt.

It felt like her life was over. And right now, she did not have it in her to put herself back together.

Three months later

I'm sorry, Bailey. But I can't have a waitress falling asleep in the kitchen in the middle of her shift. Especially not a fat waitress.

Her boss's voice played over and over in her head as she trudged back to her apartment. She had been right, that night three months ago when Raphael had broken things off with her. Her life pretty much felt like it was over.

She was so far behind in her classes it didn't look like she had the credits she needed to graduate, she didn't have a job anymore and she was so sick and tired she barely cared about either.

Now she was going to have to tell Samantha that she couldn't make rent. Well, this was the crowning achievement on the past months' humiliations, really. She had become everything she had felt so far above for most of her life.

When she had left home, left town, she had blistered her mother's ears with her rant about how she was off to make a better life for herself. One that wouldn't be all about men and an intense dedication to being a victim.

She'd gotten the hell out of metaphorical Dodge. Leaving behind that life of destitution. Where she'd been nothing but unwanted. Nothing but resented, and she'd vowed to do better.

She'd been wise to men, and what they might say to get into your pants, from the time she was way too young to know any such thing. Because she'd heard her mother rant at length on the subject after whatever boyfriend had broken up with her. As a result she had imagined herself as inoculated against such things. Had imagined that she was immune to that kind of behavior.

The truth of it was, she simply hadn't met a man who made her crazy enough. Then she met Raphael. And now, here she was, single, out of a job and pregnant. And all at the age of twenty-two.

She was the cycle. The cycle that she had so proudly and grandly told herself she wouldn't perpetuate. Now here she was. Perpetuating. She was a statistic. A sad statistic wandering around in the chilly, early spring air with nowhere in particular to go.

She stopped, turning to face the small general store across the street. Candy. She needed candy. Since she couldn't have wine. *Damn pregnancy.*

She ducked into the store and made her way to the nearest candy aisle, stopping abruptly when her eye caught the tabloid just above the chocolate bar her hand hovered over.

The man on the cover looked…far too familiar.

Prince Raphael DeSantis jilted by Italian heiress Allegra Valenti just weeks before royal wedding!

"What the actual *hell*?" The shoppers around her

startled when she all but shouted the words, but she didn't care. She reached out and grabbed the magazine, flipping through it with shaking fingers.

Raphael. *Prince* Raphael.

She flipped the pages until she saw it. The article about the scandal that was apparently rocking the principality of Santa Firenze, a tiny dot on the map of Europe. One she'd never even heard of.

It was him. There was no mistaking it. With his arresting good looks, more like a god than a man, and his incredible body...a body they had on show in the article, thanks to a few creeper beach pics. Those broad shoulders, washboard abs and lean hips...

She knew that body better than she knew her own.

"Oh, my..." She reached into her purse and pulled out a stack of tip money, throwing a ten down onto the counter. "Keep the change." She ran out with the candy bar and the magazine, her entire body starting to shake.

What *Twilight Zone* episode had she stumbled into? What kind of a joke was this?

By the time she got back to her apartment she felt like she was going to be sick all over the floor. And, given the theme of the last couple of months, she wouldn't be surprised if she did. Attempting to keep food down was sometimes a superhuman feat. Not that you could tell by her expanding waistline. Which her ex-boss had made clear to point out along with the firing.

She was tragic. So tragic that all she wanted to do was throw herself down on the bed and sleep for the rest of the day.

She made her way into the living room, where Samantha was sitting, looking wide-eyed.

"Are you okay?" Bailey asked, mostly to stave off the question of whether or not she was.

"You have a visitor," her roommate responded.

"Who?" she asked, feeling like the only possible option was that it was someone from the IRS telling her she owed back taxes, or maybe a police officer letting her know she had a warrant for a parking ticket she didn't know she had...something awful. Because that was the theme of the day. The theme of the past few months, really.

"*He's* here," Samantha said, sounding dazed.

There could only be one he. There was only one *he* that would make a woman's voice sound like that. Only one man Bailey had ever met who could render a woman completely stunned by his very presence.

And, as Bailey was processing that bit of information, she heard shoes on the hardwood floor and looked up, up into the dark eyes of Prince Raphael DeSantis just as he exited her bedroom.

He was here. In her crappy little apartment. Looking as out of place as a lion among house cats.

She wrapped her coat more tightly around herself, doing her best to conceal her figure. To hide the bump that she knew was pretty plainly visible without her woolen shield.

"What are you doing here?" she asked. She realized she was also still holding the tabloid with his face on it. She looked down at the magazine. Then back up at him. "What are you doing here?" she repeated.

"I came to tell you that I wanted to start seeing you again," he said.

"Oh, *please*." This exclamation came from her roommate, who had watched Bailey weep into her pillow for weeks now.

"What she said," Bailey affirmed, crossing her arms even more tightly beneath her chest.

"Could we have a moment?" He directed the question at Samantha, then, without waiting for a response, grabbed hold of Bailey's arm and guided her back into her bedroom. He closed the door, enclosing them both in the space.

And for a moment, she was completely lost in him. In his strength, in his very presence, which reached to every corner of the room, and around her. She wanted to lean into him. To rest her head against the solid wall of his chest and release hold of all of the heartbreak, fear and stress she had been enduring for the past few months.

She just wanted to fall into his arms and lose it all. Lose herself.

But that was impossible. He was…he was a liar. On so many more levels than she had realized.

"My engagement is off," he said, as though she were not holding a magazine in her hand proclaiming exactly that. "And, given that, I see no reason why the two of us can't resume our liaison."

"Our…*liaison*. The one where you come and visit me every couple of months for sex?"

"Bailey," he said, his tone exceedingly hard done by. It made her want to punch him. "I have a certain life, certain expectations, and…"

"These expectations?" She turned the tabloid around, thrusting it toward him. "You're a prince? What strange fairy tale did I fall into, Raphael? You said you were a pharmaceutical rep."

"You said I was a pharmaceutical rep, Bailey," he said. "Don't you remember?"

"I…" She remembered everything about the night she met him. The way that her world had stopped completely when their eyes had met. How out of place he looked in the sleazy diner that she worked at, Sweater Bunnies, where the waitresses all wore sweaters with plunging necklines and short shorts, with glittering tights and high heels.

His plane was delayed because of the weather. He had come into town on business. They had ended up talking. And then she had done something she had never done before in her life. She went home with him.

They didn't have sex. Not that first night. But he had kissed her, and she had…well, she'd learned an entirely new definition for the word *want*. Her entire body had caught fire with the touch of his lips, the touch of his hands. They had been talking one moment, and then the next, he had her down on the bed.

"I'm a virgin," she said.

"I don't need you to be," he responded, his voice rough, his hands tangled in her hair. "We don't have to play that game. Unless you want to."

"No," she said, "I really am. Like, a really, real virgin. Who has never done anything like this before, ever."

He sat up. "Never?"

"Never. But, I like you. And…maybe if the weather is bad tomorrow…"

"You want to wait, but you might be ready tomorrow?"

"I don't know."

"We'll wait," he said, kissing her cheek.

And he hadn't thrown her out. Instead, he had poured her a glass of soda and then continued to talk to her.

She hadn't made him wait long after that. The next night she'd made him her first, and she'd already been spinning fantasies about him being the only.

Then...well, then he'd turned out to be a frog. Except he was actually a prince. Which was just insane.

"Of course I remember," she snapped.

"Then you remember that you were the one who laughed at me, and said, 'You aren't a pharmaceutical rep or something, are you?' And I did not correct you. In fact, you will find, Bailey, that a great many of the things you think about me you created."

"So now you're gaslighting me? You're making this whole thing about what I chose to believe? And somehow, you think that will make me want you back. Not as a girlfriend, or anything like that, just as your little Colorado-based... Tell me, Raphael, where do your other women live?"

"I never thought of you that way," he said, his tone fierce. "Never."

"Actions speak louder than words and all of that. You treated me like one. You're still treating me like one. Get out of my apartment, Your Majesty," she spat.

"I am not in the habit of taking orders, you will find. I was all right playing your game before, but now you know. I am a prince, *cara mia*. And what I want, I have."

"Well," she said, flinging her arms out wide, "you don't get this."

He reached out, cupping the back of her head and drawing her forward. "You don't mean that."

"Oh, but I do." She pressed her hands flat against his chest—the better to shove him backward—only then he felt…so much like home. Like everything brilliant and perfect that she'd been missing while her life had been upended.

It was easy to forget he was the one who'd upended it.

He curved one arm around her waist, drawing her body flush against his. And then he frowned.

And she came back to reality, hard.

"Don't touch me," she hissed, pulling away and straightening her coat a little bit frantically.

She didn't want him to see that she was pregnant because…

Because she didn't know why. She'd resigned herself to her fate as a single mother because he was supposed to be married to someone else. Because the text she'd sent out to him after the fact saying she needed to talk to him had gone unreturned.

But he was here now. And he was a prince, damn it all.

Her own father had never been around, and she and her mother had suffered financially for it. Raphael could support their child. Could make sure they didn't struggle.

She flicked the top button of her coat open, her heart pounding. "I'm not going to be your lover, Raphael," she said, her voice trembling as she continued undoing buttons. She let her coat fall free and revealed the bump that was only just now visible beneath her tight-fitting sweater. "But whether you want to be or not, you are the father of my baby."

CHAPTER TWO

IT WAS RARE that Prince Raphael DeSantis was rendered speechless. But then, it was rare for him to be rejected.

And that had happened twice in the past week.

Were he a man with any insecurity, he might be wounded. However, he was the Crown Prince of Santa Firenze, a man who had been born with the world in hand and every advantage available to him. A man who—upon his birth—had been worshipped by the palace's many servants, simply because he existed. Reverence was a gift bestowed upon him from his first breath. And he had spent his life ensuring that he maintained the admiration of his people.

And this little waitress had refused him. Then gone on to reveal a surprise he certainly hadn't seen coming.

"You are certain it's mine?" He knew the question would earn him more of Bailey's ire, but he suddenly felt as though everything was hanging in the balance. This woman, who looked at him as though she wanted to do him bodily harm, was carrying the heir to the throne of his country.

She recoiled from him. "How dare you ask me that?"

"I would be remiss if I did not."

He tried to ignore the hurt in her blue eyes. This

changed things. It changed everything. Bailey had been a diversion he wasn't looking for. And he had allowed himself to get caught up in it. To enjoy the fiction that she had built up around them. That he was a business-man, coming to Vail once every couple of months for meetings and to spend time with her.

Somehow she hadn't seemed to know who he was. But then, part of maintaining the admiration of his peo-ple had been keeping himself out of baser things like tabloid news. Which he had clearly failed at recently. He attributed that to his former fiancée, Allegra.

But it had all come to an end three months ago. He had known that he couldn't continue his assignation with Bailey right up until his marriage. He had never touched Allegra, and he didn't love her, but he had in-tended to be a good husband to her. A faithful hus-band. Or at least—depending on the agreement they ultimately reached—a discreet one.

When the engagement had ended, however, he had immediately thought to come back to his mistress.

The world was crumbling as he knew it—a slight exaggeration perhaps, but the cancellation of a royal wedding could hardly be deemed insignificant. It had made him tabloid fodder.

His father, the late ruler of Santa Firenze, had de-spised all forms of media and had felt it wholly beneath a leader to become a headline when he should be aim-ing to be part of history.

He had instilled this in Raphael, along with strength and steel. There had been no softness allowed in his childhood, and Raphael could see it for the benefit it was now that he was a man, both of his parents long dead and an entire nation left to him to oversee.

In fact, his marriage to Allegra was a testament to that strength. That he had been more than willing to set aside the desires of his flesh for the betterment of his kingdom.

Bailey, no matter that he desired her, could offer no political advantage to his country. Allegra, on the other hand, would bring an alliance with one of Italy's oldest families and a great deal of influence within the business community thanks to both her father and brother.

Bailey heated his blood. But his time with her was outside the norm…something separate from Santa Firenze. Something he could not afford to bring back there, he had known with certainty. Not only was she beneath him in status, she was a distraction. The sort his father had always warned against.

The only thing Bailey had…was his heir. And that was something that could not be ignored.

He had not foreseen this complication.

"Yes, Your Royal Jackass, it's your baby. Since you were the one to take my virginity, I would think you would know that."

"Nearly a year ago, Bailey. Many things could have happened since that first time we were together. I was not always here. And it has been three months since I left you. For all I know, in your grief, you sought solace with another man."

"Yeah, it's been a nonstop orgy since you dumped me. I figured, why not just go for it? After all, your royal scepter paved the way. Might as well allow the common folk a chance."

"Enough. You are being crude, and it doesn't suit you."

"Yes it does. It suits me perfectly. As you well know.

I am not the kind of woman that you could ever take back to your country, so you *must* think that. I'm a waitress. A lowly server that you met in a sleazy restaurant better known for the waitresses breasts than the chicken breasts. I would say this behavior suits me perfectly."

She was vibrating with rage, angry like she'd been the night he had ended things with her. When she had screamed at him, thrown a shoe at him. *Hit* him with a shoe. It had been the exact response he'd been looking for. He could not have her coming after him. Could not have her being tempted in any regard to find him, not when he was ready to get married and begin producing children. He had made their separation as devastating as possible so she would not seek him out.

Better to spoil her memory of him than leave her longing. Of course, he had changed his mind about that. Which he reserved his right to do. He was a prince, after all.

"You are carrying my child," he said, looking down at her stomach. She wasn't showing dramatically, just a vague bump beneath her sweater. Her curves looked a bit more abundant. He considered himself an expert on Bailey's curves, so he was certain his assessment was correct. "How far along are you?"

"Close to four months," she said. "It happened before we broke up. But I didn't know until after."

"Did you try and get in touch with me?"

That question seemed to make her angry, too. "Yes. I did. Though, since I didn't know your actual identity, it was a little bit tricky. I texted you."

The only number that Bailey had was to the phone that only she used. He had been careful to keep everything with her separate. Particularly when he had discovered that she truly didn't know who he was. There had been something so enticing about it. The chance to come here and be with a woman who had no expectations. To be more himself than any other venue allowed.

And when he had ended things with her, he had gotten rid of the phone. Cutting off his temptation. He didn't need to save messages from her. Or the occasionally suggestive photographs that she had provided.

"I no longer have that phone," he said.

"Wow. When you break up with a girl, you really go hard-core."

He frowned. "You keep using that word, Bailey. As though you were my girlfriend. From my point of view, we never had that kind of relationship." He realized, even as he spoke the words, that he was being extraordinarily unfair to her.

With most women, he laid out the ground rules from moment one. He had not been seeking Bailey out. Not at all. He had come to Vail to visit a friend's resort and see about investing in the property and its expansion. And then a blizzard had waylaid his travel.

Not even a man such as himself could control a storm.

He had wandered into a restaurant not far from his hotel, and had nearly walked right back out when he'd seen what sort of establishment it was. But then he had seen her. Somehow, in spite of the tacky surroundings, the horrendous uniform and the dim lighting, she had shone.

He had been able to think of only one thing. One word. *Mine.*

And there had never been a single thing in his life

that he had wanted and had not gotten. He had purposed in that moment that the waitress would be one of them.

When she had made assumptions about who he was, he had allowed her to do so. He had encouraged it. And he had not done as impeccable a job as he usually did of ensuring that the relationship stayed in the bedroom. But he had reasoned that he only ever saw her for a long weekend every couple of months. And it would be wrong to keep her in a hotel room the entire time.

So he had taken her out. He had no connections to Vail other than that one visit to see about investing. The press never had any reason to take an interest in him being there. Or even think that he would be there.

There were a great many advantages to having a relatively low profile.

"What I mean," he said, attempting to soften his tone, "is that I have lovers, not girlfriends. Women that I carry out affairs with. I don't date. That's the issue with being a prince. You cannot simply go public with women, not without expectation being attached. However, I was hardly going to live my life celibate."

"You had a fiancée." The words were low, carrying with them an edge of violence.

"Allegra was nothing more than a convenience. She is from one of Italy's most revered families. She was a reasonable choice for a man in my position. She was not my lover."

"Well, I guess that's something," she said. "So. I figure we need to come to some kind of child support arrangement? I'm having your baby. If you need me to get a paternity test, fine, whatever. I'll hate you, but I already do. Whatever you need. A cheek swab, my blood. Though I'd prefer not to give blood. I've already bled for you. I'm not doing it again."

"What are you talking about? A child support?"

"Presumably you have a castle. I would like to not live in a heap."

"And so you want money?"

He found her fascinating. This woman who had not known who he was. This woman who was standing there with a tabloid featuring him at her feet, who had been a virgin when he'd first taken her. Who was asking for child support, and not threatening to go to the press. Not demanding a pied-à-terre in various cities or pieces of the crown jewels.

Clearly, she had no understanding of the situation she found herself in, in spite of what she thought.

"I don't think it's unreasonable," she said. "My own mother was single. And my father didn't give us anything. I'm not going to consign my son or daughter to that life if I can make it better. I have a responsibility. And so do you."

"Undeniably I have a responsibility to this child, but I do not think you understand exactly what you're dealing with here," he said, staring at her, mystified.

"I'm dealing with an unexpected pregnancy and the best way that I can think to handle it. I want to make sure that you are not living in the lap of luxury while your son or daughter has nothing."

"Oh, I have no intention of my son or daughter lacking for anything. But if you think that I'm leaving them here in Colorado to be raised alone by you, you have failed to understand the man that you are involved with."

Her entire face turned pink, her rage seemingly

silent for the first time since he had aroused it three months ago.

"I am not sending child support checks, *cara*. There will be no more discussion of it."

"What do you mean you aren't allowing me to raise my child in Colorado? Under what authority? This is America! And last I checked, you probably aren't a citizen."

"Diplomatic immunity," he said, waving his hand, "and a desire to preserve relations with my country, will no doubt see any kind of court battle you should wish to wage fall in my favor. Who would give custody to a waitress from Sweater Bunnies when a prince is on hand to raise the child to rule?"

"You're going to take my baby from me?" Her voice had turned shrill, and he could see that she was looking around the room, her eyes darting back and forth. Probably looking for a weapon.

"It should not come to that."

"Start speaking slowly, and spelling out what exactly you're implying. Obviously I'm not picking up on it."

"Of course," he said, "there will be no discussion of my sending you child support checks, and no discussion of the child being raised here, because you will both be in Santa Firenze."

"I thought I wasn't fit to be brought back to your country."

She wasn't. Even now, looking at her, that intense possessiveness had him in a stranglehold. Taking her, claiming her seemed to be the most obvious choice.

Which was what gave him pause. A ruler was meant to be cool. A ruler was meant to direct his actions with his mind, his sense of honor, not with anything half as fickle as desire or heat.

He wondered what his father might have done in this instance. And then had to concede that his father would never have been so foolish as to get himself in this situation.

He was forced then to weigh his options. To bring back a woman such as this, one he had already decided was unsuitable for his kingdom…it was unfathomable.

But honor. Honor and duty were at the center of all of it, regardless of what she made him feel. His duty was to his child.

"That was before I knew you were carrying my heir." He took a step toward her, the word *mine* pounding itself through his head in time with the thundering of his heart. "Of course you are coming back to my country with me now. But not as my mistress. Bailey Harper, you are going to be my wife."

CHAPTER THREE

"You have a private jet."

"Of course I do," Raphael said, brushing past her and walking up the stairs into the sleek-looking aircraft.

"Were you in your private jet the night that we met?"

He treated her to a withering look. "I wasn't flying economy."

"I just…" She let the words trail off. There wasn't much to say. Not really. He was not the man she had thought he was. That had become apparent when he'd broken her heart the way that he had, when it had been revealed that there was another woman in his life. This was just another layer to it. She supposed that some people would view this as good luck. The fact that the man who had gotten her pregnant was wealthy, titled and powerful should be some kind of boon.

She looked up at the plane. She didn't really feel like it was a good thing. Not now.

She just felt small. Small and so desperately out of her depth.

She had argued with him about the marriage thing, and she intended to argue with him even more. But… what could be done? He presented a pretty ironclad case when it came to how he would go about getting custody. And she didn't want to lose her baby.

Are you sure part of you just doesn't want to go off with him because it sounds easy?

She banished that traitorous voice, began to walk up the steps and into the jet. And that feeling of being tiny only increased. She was nothing. No one. Just a girl from Nebraska who had gone to Colorado seeking mountains and a fresh start. A girl raised by a single mother in a drafty house built in the 1920s with a sagging foundation and a crack in the ceiling.

She looked around the cabin, her jaw a little bit slack. It was…she had never seen anything like this on the internet. She had idly scrolled through the odd slideshow on various lifestyle websites showing the ridiculously luxurious way that the rich and famous traveled, but she had never imagined she would be standing in the middle of it. Much less ready to fly on board.

"There are bedrooms back that way," he said, gesturing past the plush living area and bar to the back of the plane. "There is also a bathroom and a shower."

"There's a shower?"

"Of course there is." And that was it. No further explanation. As if it really were the most typical thing on the planet for a man to have a shower on his plane, and she was the absurd one for thinking otherwise.

"Okay then. I will keep that in mind in case I feel a little bit travel stale."

Her heart began to hammer loudly, her hands shaking as the door to the plane closed.

"You know," she said, "we don't have to go now. I have… I have school to finish."

"You mentioned. In your rant as you packed your things."

She was failing right now, but still. "Well, it was a valid rant. I worked hard to pay my way this far through school, and if I don't finish this term, I'll be out the money for the classes."

He sat down on one of the tan leather couches, spreading his arms wide over the back, his posture laconic. She had to wonder how on earth she hadn't realized he was royalty. Sure, she had never been in the presence of anyone who could be considered royal, but he exuded it. How had she ever thought he was a normal man?

You never did. You saw him and the world stopped.

"Come now," he said, "*cara mia*, the cost of your college tuition will be the least of your concerns. I can arrange to have you complete your courses remotely. Or you may transfer to one of the universities in Santa Firenze. Of course, you will have to take classes at the palace and not on campus should you choose to do that."

"Why can't I go to the campus?"

"You would create a circus." He tapped the back of the couch with his fingertips. "I am not a man accustomed to getting tabloid attention. My family name has always been upheld, whispered reverently, spoken of with great respect. We are not part of the nouveau riche royal set who takes great pride in posting our social engagements on various online accounts. We take pride in the title. My father did before me, and I do it now. That headline you saw today was an aberration. There is a reason that you were not aware of my identity. I simply don't court publicity. That is the vocation of celebrity, and I am not a celebrity. I am the ruler of my country." He sighed heavily. "I dislike the position I find myself in. Because you…you will be a problem."

"Oh, will I? Excellent. One hopes that I will be too much of a problem for you to want to take on."

He waved a hand. "Not at all. You see, *cara*, you are carrying my baby. The most important thing on this earth is the birthright of that child. You must be married to me in order to secure that birthright."

She blinked. "Is this the Middle Ages?"

"No, this is Santa Firenze. And this is the cost of being royal."

"Good thing you're rich. It seems damned expensive."

"You have no idea. But, suffice it to say, your tuition is not my concern. In fact, it isn't your concern, either. You have no more financial concerns."

His words were strange. Made her ears feel fuzzy. She could hardly comprehend them. All she had worried about—from the time she had known what it was like to be hungry, from the moment she had experienced her first night in winter with the heat off because the electricity had been interrupted by the power company—was money. To have this man look at her, snap his fingers and say it was no longer a concern was…it was beyond surreal.

"I don't… I don't understand…any of this."

"It is simple," he said as the engines to the plane fired up and the aircraft began to glide down the runway. "I am a prince, I cannot have a bastard. I would have preferred a more suitable wife, a wife with a title or a pedigree of some kind. However, you are the one carrying my baby. That means I will have to make do with what I have."

"More flattering words have never been spoken, I'm sure."

"This is not about flattery. This is about reality."

The aircraft lifted off, and as it rose higher, Bailey's stomach sank into her feet. The longest plane ride she had ever been on was the short trip between Nebraska and Colorado. And nothing more. Which brought to mind other concerns. "Wait," she said, her heart kicking desperately against her chest, thinking that perhaps she had found a reprieve. "I don't have a passport."

He laughed. "That is of no concern to me. I can arrange to have one secured for you."

"Not by the time we reach your country."

"That is the thing. It is *my* country. No one is going to deny you admittance if I say you may have it. And as for coming back to the States, you certainly will eventually. So, we will secure you documentation for that eventuality. However, either way you'll be fine. You will be traveling with me."

He was maddening. Nothing fazed him. Nothing even made him pause. He was going about this with all the ruthless efficiency of a commander going into battle. And each and every protest issued from her lips, he struck down like an enemy of war.

"Does none of this bother you?" she asked. "I mean, you say you don't like being in the tabloids, but you say it with all the fire and passion of an iceberg. Meanwhile, I feel like my life is falling apart. I feel like I've been dropped into some third-rate reality show."

"That's insulting. This is first-class," he said, his tone dry, "all the way."

"Is this a joke to you? Your life has been easy, I get that. It radiates off you in waves. Your privilege. Your wealth. Everything I've had I've worked for. Every day of my life has been infused with some kind of struggle. Every single thing I own was purchased at great cost. You spend more on bottled water in a week than I spend on groceries in a month."

"That is probably true. But now this is your life. Do not worry about your roommate, by the way. I made sure to give her several months of rent so that she would not feel your absence too keenly."

"Nice of you to consider her feelings," she said, though she was grateful that Samantha wouldn't be left high and dry. Suddenly a wave washed over her, leaving her feeling adrift. Weightless. "I think I'm in shock," she said, sinking further back into the chair across from him, her limbs suddenly feeling very shaky.

"Bailey," he said, his expression concerned. "Are you able to breathe?"

She laid her head back, feeling dizzy.

"No," she said.

Suddenly he was next to her, his large hands cupping her face. He was warm, and he was so very Raphael. "Bailey," he said, his tone stern. "Keep breathing."

Her vision went fuzzy around the edges for a second, then dark…

It came back, with too much clarity, too much brightness. She felt sick to her stomach, a cold sweat on her forehead, her fingers icy. "What happened?" she asked.

"You passed out," he responded. He looked…he looked genuinely concerned. Though she wondered if it was for her or for the baby.

"Don't touch me," she said, pulling away from him. He complied, removing his hands from her face. She hated it. Hated that when he touched her she still felt something. Hated that he wasn't touching her anymore. Hated herself for caring.

"Have you been passing out regularly?"

"No," she said, trying not to watch him as he stood up and crossed to the bar. Trying very, very hard not to pay total and complete attention to his every movement. "I've had a little bit of a shocking day. I walked into a grocery store and saw that my ex-lover was a prince. Seeing as I knew I was having his baby, it suddenly occurred to me that I was having a prince's baby. Then I went home, and said prince was in my bedroom. Then he dragged me onto a private plane, all the while demanding that I marry him or he'll take my baby away. I think I'm just suffering the aftereffects."

He opened up a bottle of sparkling water and poured it into a glass, his movements deft and swift. Then he crossed the space to her, handing her the drink. "I found out I was going to be a father today, and I seem to be handling it well."

"Because you're a robot," she replied, taking a sip of the bland, fizzy liquid.

"I think that you can attest to the fact that I'm all man, Bailey. Not a robot."

"Not all. Parts of you," she said. "You seem to have Tin Man syndrome. No heart."

"I love my country," he responded, his tone cool. "I am eternally loyal to it. And I will do whatever is necessary to preserve the legacy. There is no reason for me to panic about the situation we find ourselves in. There is no question that I must marry the mother of my child. And while who you are will require a little bit of damage control, I was already set to be married in the next month. And, presumably, sometime after my wife would have given birth to a child. That has always been the course plotted out before me. All in all, only the bride has changed."

"So...women and the children they bear are interchangeable to you?" she asked.

"A wife and child are necessary components to my life," he said, his tone hard. "Essential to the continued health of the kingdom and bloodline. The importance cannot be overstated."

"But who the woman..."

"Matters in terms of bloodline, political affiliation and the ability to have children. You have one out of three—I think you're smart enough to guess which."

He said it with such calm. As though the bride were the most incidental part of the marriage. As though he didn't care at all whether he was married to her or to the shiny brunette she'd seen in the tabloids. "You're horrible. Just horrible. How did I manage to convince myself for eight months that you were Prince Charming? No reference to your *actual* royalty intended."

"We see what we want to see, Bailey. You wanted to see me as something that I wasn't. It was convenient for you at the time. I was an easy lover for you to have. Don't pretend that it didn't suit you on some level to be with a man who was only around part of the time."

"Or I was an idiot virgin who had finally found a man that she wanted to sleep with, and had her judgment completely clouded by her orgasms."

Her words hung between them, tense and heavy. She despised herself for bringing that up. For bringing up the pleasure they had found together. She would rather forget it. It kept her up at night. All day, she would drag herself around, feeling exhausted and heartbroken. But night was worse. Because then she would dream. And when she dreamed, it was that Raphael was in bed with her. Touching her, kissing her. And when she woke up, she was alone. Hideously, depressingly alone, and she ached. For a touch she would never have again.

"I am sorry you were hurt," he said, his tone clipped. "That was never my intention. But I have known who I was to be, what sort of woman I was to marry, from the time I was a boy."

"And that woman isn't me."

"No." He pushed his hand through his dark hair. "It is important to make the best choices I can for my country. And someday my child will do the same. It is what was instilled in me from the beginning. My mother reinforced my father. She had been raised to be the wife of a prince, and she knew her place. That is what it takes to raise the heir to a throne, Bailey. You must understand it is not snobbery on my part—at least not entirely—when I say you are not suited."

"I…" She swayed slightly in her seat. "I really don't even know how to have this conversation."

"You should get some rest," he said, stunning her with that declaration. "When we land we will be very close to the palace, and you can get settled in. In the meantime, I am afraid that you are overtaxed."

"I don't feel like you've earned the right to comment on my level of taxation."

"As ruling government of an entire nation, taxation falls under my purview."

"Oh, well, that's fabulous. I guess we know which things are certain. Death, taxes and Raphael."

"I'm hardly going to kill you, *cara*. I'm going to make you a princess."

Suddenly, she felt so tired she could barely hold her head up. She could not be a princess. She was a waitress. And waitresses didn't become princesses. "I'm going to have that nap now."

Bailey wandered to the back of the plane, opening the door to the bedroom, then closing it tightly behind her. It was bigger than her bedroom in her apartment. With a large, ornate bed that looked like it was designed for much more than sleeping. It was ridiculous. *He* was ridiculous. This whole thing was ridiculous.

She kicked her shoes off, crossing to the bed before throwing herself down on her face like some tragic cartoon princess. She shut her eyes tight, trying not to give in to the tears that were building behind them.

This had to be a dream. All of it. When she woke up in the morning, her head would be clearer. She would be single, alone and pregnant. Her ex-boyfriend would be nothing more than that jerk pharmaceutical rep from Italy who had left her in the lurch. He would absolutely not be the prince of some obscure country, and she would not be a future princess.

The alternative was unthinkable.

When they disembarked in Santa Firenze, Raphael had them pull the car right up to the plane. He was feeling more than slightly concerned for Bailey's health. Or, at the very least, the health of their unborn baby.

She had been especially pale ever since he had first seen her in her apartment, and she had gotten only more waxen as the trip had worn on. Though he had only seen her once after she had gone to the bedroom to sleep, and that was only to use the restroom about a half hour before they landed.

He was confused by her. By their every interaction. She was not grateful for the offer of marriage. Not especially pleased that he was giving her the chance to be a princess. His wife. A position of great honor. One that most women would fight over.

And yet the two who'd had it offered to them both seemed to have rejected it.

Allegra was a separate issue.

"The car is waiting," he said through the closed bathroom door.

Bailey emerged a moment later, wet-haired, gritty-eyed and cranky, wearing a university sweatshirt and a pair of stretch pants.

"I see you availed yourself of the shower," he said.

"How often do you get a shower at thirty thousand feet? I thought that if I didn't at least give it a try, I would be seriously failing in the luxury stakes."

"Well, you will have ample opportunity to use the facilities again. Even if I upgrade jets, it will still have a shower."

"You're assuming that I will be making use of your jet in the future."

"Of course, you're marrying me. Pretending otherwise is ridiculous." He grabbed hold of her elbow, leading her from the plane, carefully helping her down the steps. "Now, come get in the car."

She sputtered, "Just because you say nothing else makes sense does not mean that nothing else makes sense."

He opened the door to the car, gesturing for her to get in. She shot him a deadly glare, then complied. He got in beside her, slamming the door shut. "You seem to be misunderstanding," he said, feeling very much like he was speaking a different language. Because Bailey seemed to persist in misunderstanding him. "I am the ruler of Santa Firenze. No one in my family has produced an illegitimate child. Not one. No one in my family has ever been divorced. We are a hallowed and storied lineage. I am offering you a chance to become part of it. The fact that you have rejected me is outrageous on so many levels I cannot even begin to list them all."

"By all means," she said, leaning back in her seat. "List them. If you have time."

"It isn't that long of a drive to the castle."

She blinked. "Castle?"

"What part of *prince* are you having trouble comprehending? I speak very good English, though Italian is my first language. You, however, are making me question my linguistic skills."

"I would hate to be the cause of you questioning your linguistics. I'm sure that they're fantastic."

"They can't be overly fantastic, because you do not seem to understand anything of what I am telling you." There was no point arguing.

She would understand the moment his family home came into view. It was the jewel of Santa Firenze. Settled in the middle of the Alps, overlooking one of the deepest and bluest lakes in Europe, craggy peaks rising up around it. She would understand then. What he was offering. Understand what a gift he was presenting her with.

As the car made its way down the narrow, winding two-lane road, Bailey insisted on shifting constantly in her seat and letting out long, huffy sighs.

"Your distress is noted," he said.

"Not overly. You keep accusing me of not understanding, and yet I think you're the one who has not fully taken on board that I am not happy about this."

"I am offering you marriage. Legitimacy for your child, an end to your financial concerns."

"About that," she snapped. "Where was your offer to end my financial concerns when I was working double shifts at that horrible restaurant? As I was killing myself to get through college, and you were presenting yourself as a businessman there on your company's dime?"

"Would you have accepted my offer of financial assistance?"

Her face went blank then, her mouth settling into a stubborn line. "Yes," she said.

"You're a terrible liar. You would not have accepted. Not from Raphael the businessman. And you seem to like Raphael the prince a lot less."

"That's because the first time I met Raphael the prince was when he was breaking up with me at midnight after what I had thought was a very romantic date. Only then you threw me out into the snow."

"I wanted a clean break. I felt it was better for both of us."

"Don't try to convince me that you lost any sleep over any of that."

He *had*. She had no idea. He had lost countless hours of sleep, lying there hard and aching, wanting something that only she could give to him. She had cast a spell over him from the moment he had first seen her, and he had never been able to explain it. He only knew that she affected him in a way no other woman ever had. And it had nothing to do with skill.

He could remember the first time she had knelt

down before him and taken him into her mouth. The way that she had tasted him, with shy, timid strokes of her tongue, how she had taken him in as deep as she could, her every movement uncertain. It was not her skill that enticed, but her sincerity. Her intense dedication to him. He was a man who had always felt a certain level of worship was his due, but it meant so much more coming from such a willing supplicant, rather than a trained one.

So yes, he had lost sleep. He'd had no desire to touch another woman, and, in fact, that had worked to his advantage, since he had purposed that he would not until his wedding night with Allegra. In that time he had attempted to drum up some kind of enthusiasm for the woman he was engaged to. But he had found none. Allegra was beautiful, with golden skin and dark, shimmering curls.

But he had craved the pale, flaxen-haired beauty of Bailey.

It was all vaguely ridiculous. He was fantasizing about a university student named *Bailey*. Princess Bailey.

But that was the thing with honor. It was supposed to matter even if it was hard. A truly strong oak didn't bend in the wind, and neither could the ruler of Santa Firenze.

As a boy, when he'd hurt himself, his father had not allowed his mother or the servants to comfort him. It had been up to him to breathe through the pain and carry on. That, his father had told him once, was how a man learned to soldier on in all things. If you could do it with a cut, you would do it with an emotional wound, too.

When he was older, his father had told him it applied to other physical aches, as well. A man might want a certain woman, might burn for her, but if there was potential a dalliance would harm the country, that craving—like all other harmful desires—had to be cast aside.

The prince of Santa Firenze could have whatever his heart desired. And that was why his heart, soul and sense of honor had to be made strong.

Raphael knew that he was strong. Had been, utterly and completely all his life.

Until her.

It was *truly* ridiculous. But here they were. And she, somehow, felt like she was in a position to play hardball.

The limo wound itself around the last curve, and, finally, the stately palace gates came into view. Wrought iron and scrolling, the family crest emblazoned upon them. They parted for the car as if by magic, and the limo rolled through a lane lined with hedges until they reached the magnificent courtyard in front of the palace.

The ground was overlaid with brick. A giant fountain dominated the center. At its top was a golden statue and there were many others fashioned from marble all around, representing the great leaders of his country. His very bloodline carved into stone in front of this hallowed castle that had housed generations.

He looked over at her and was satisfied to see that, finally, she had the decency to look impressed. She was staring up at the castle, at its turrets, with ivy climbing up the side and the blue-and-white flags of his country waving in the breeze from the very top of the shining palace.

"This is my home," he said, stating the obvious for

dramatic effect. "And when you are my wife, it will be your home. When our child is born, it will be his home. Do you still think you should raise him in an apartment in Colorado with your roommate?"

"I… I had no idea."

"It is not my fault you don't pay attention to current affairs. Or perhaps it is my fault, for keeping my country financially sound and free of most of the conflicts that happen in the world. We have very few reasons to be in the news because the citizens are happy, the coffers are full and we have no national security crises or natural disasters to speak of."

"Is this Narnia?"

"If it were, then a breath would turn all of the statues back to flesh. However, it is the real world. And they are only stone."

"That's a shame," she said. "Then all I would have to do is walk back to the wardrobe and I could be free of you."

She was mutinous. And he had never dealt with mutiny before. Like his father before him, he'd made Santa Firenze his life. Nothing had ever come before it. And as such, no one in his country had ever had cause for complaint.

"You don't actually want to be free of me," he said. How could she? "You're putting up a fight because you have an idea of what your life should be. I would argue that you are putting up a fight additionally because you have an idea of what consequences you should suffer for your sins."

"My sins?" she asked.

"Yes," he said, "your sins. You think you should be punished for this. Because you allowed yourself to get pregnant. And now you must pay penance. The sad, single mother, waiting tables, having been abandoned by her lover. It's a very nice narrative, but it is not a situation you find yourself in. You have a man willing to step up and take responsibility. More than a man, you have a prince. Saying anything but an emphatic yes is a waste of your resources."

She looked up at the palace, her eyes wide, her lips parted slightly. He was struck in that moment by the fullness of her beauty. Just as he had been the first time he'd seen her. And now she was carrying his child. She would be his wife.

Mine.

He pushed that word to the back of his mind. This wasn't about that. It was a necessity. What he must do. It had nothing to do with want. With that thing Bailey made him feel that was so perilously close to weakness.

"Come," he said, opening the door and extending his hand to her. "We must get you to your room."

CHAPTER FOUR

BAILEY TRIED NOT to stare too gauchely as she entered the palace, her heart thundering loudly. Loudly enough that she was pretty sure it was echoing off the marble walls of the massive antechamber they were standing in now. She had never seen anything like this in her life. It was like something out of a movie, except in a movie she had a feeling she would be heading toward some sort of fun montage where she would try on lots of dresses and upbeat pop music would play in the background while a sassy stylist told her how amazing she looked.

Instead, she was standing there wearing nothing more than a sweatshirt and pants that had seen better days, feeling like something a very large, overly self-satisfied cat had dragged in.

There were servants wandering around the palace, not making eye contact with Raphael, as though any unsolicited contact would be far too presumptuous on their part.

They did not look at her, either. Not with any kind of curiosity. In fact, she seemed beneath their notice. As though she were merely a package he had brought in after a day of shopping.

"It's so quiet in here," she said, her voice reverberating around them even though she was speaking softly.

"There are so many people in the palace at all times, it would be difficult to think if everyone were carrying on a conversation, don't you agree?"

"So you have a…silence policy?"

"There is no policy. But my father was one to train the servants to ensure they were rarely seen and rarely heard. I have done nothing to revise that code of conduct, as it suits me." He, on the other hand, didn't seem to feel like he was speaking too loudly. His voice echoed across the room, and he was not bothered by it in the least.

"You are definitely an *elevated* personage," she said, following him just slightly behind. "Aren't you?"

"This is my palace," he said, making a broad, sweeping gesture. "Of course I am elevated."

"It's just… I had the feeling royalty was a bit more modern nowadays. Prince Harry is out greeting soldiers and things."

"And getting caught with his trousers down at hotels in Las Vegas."

"We both know your trousers have been down, Raphael—it's just that nobody was there to take pictures. Actually, I could have taken pictures. I should have. I sent you some scandalous shots and sadly, never got a nude pic from you. Think of the leverage that would provide me."

His eyes sharpened. "I see you're finally considering the angle of using the press against me."

"I don't want to. Not particularly. To what end? So that we're both embarrassed? So that our child can look at the headlines in the future and see all the ugly things we said about each other? That isn't what I want. We both know that even if I were able to disgrace you by giving sordid details of your secret affair with a waitress, I would be the one who was called a whore."

"You speak the truth," he said, resting his hand on the solid marble banister, one foot on the first stair. "That is how it has always been."

"Yes, indeed," she snapped.

He arched a dark brow. "Don't look so angry with me," he said. "I don't rule over the whole world."

She sniffed. "You act like it." He continued up the stairs. She followed. "What about my things?"

"They are being handled. Though I sincerely doubt that any of your things will be deemed suitable for your new position."

She thought of her collection of clothing, all relatively dear to her, since she was a pretty intense bargain shopper who saw the experience as something of a covert ops situation. "I like my clothes."

"You will have new clothes. Better clothes. More than you could possibly wear."

"I don't understand the point of all of this."

"The point is that you are to be my queen. And you will look like my queen. When we break the news of our impending marriage, it will be with the view of presenting you in the best way possible. It does not benefit me to embarrass you, either."

"Well, at least there's that." Her stomach sank, tightening a little bit. "I don't…what is all of this going to entail?"

"You have seen movies where the people stand out on the balcony and wave at their subjects below?"

"Of course. It's a cliché."

He didn't miss a beat. "Prepare to become a cliché."

She took the steps quickly, trying to keep up with him. "You can't be serious. We're not really going to… that isn't…you don't expect to present me to the entire nation."

"Don't be silly," he said, and she felt herself start to breathe again. "I will be presenting you to the entire *world*."

Her heart slammed against her sternum. "The *entire world*? The entire world isn't going to care about me. I'm just… Bailey Harper from Nebraska. And two days ago I was a waitress."

"That is exactly why the world will be interested in you," he said, his tone fierce. "They will hold you beneath greater scrutiny than they ever would have held Allegra. They will turn over your every potential scandal. They will bring up the fact that you were waiting tables in a restaurant designed to flaunt the female figure. They will bring up the fact that you were pregnant prior to our marriage. The fact that I very likely had to marry you. They will find out the details of your childhood, of your parentage, and they will use it against you. Because that is what the media does."

"You make it all sound so exciting," she said, deadpan, trying to keep the abject horror out of her voice.

"It is simply the truth," he said. "It is why I have done my very best to stay on the right side of things. But I cannot do anything about the fact that this is going to create a scandal."

"What if I just went back to Colorado? What if we just…forget this happened."

He stopped again, turning to look at her, his eyes

fierce. "I cannot forget this happened," he growled. *"Ever."*

"But you could marry a more suitable woman. And you could kind of do it like they did back in the days of yore. You know, pay off your mistress, pretend that your bastard doesn't exist. That's kind of the way they did it, right?"

"It is not the way *I* do it. I am a man who is more than able to own his mistakes."

"Oh," she said, "excellent. I get to be something you own. A mistake you own, even. I'm the luckiest girl in the world."

"Whether or not you realize that, you are," he returned. "You are to be my princess—is there something degrading about that in your eyes?"

"No, there is something degrading about being seen as so far beneath someone that they lie to you about who they are, keep you as their dirty little secret, then abandon you so that they can marry someone who's more suitable, only bringing you back to their country when they realize that you are pregnant with their baby. None of this has anything to do with me. So why would you expect me to be flattered?" The words came hard, fast.

She didn't even know why she was so angry, because she shouldn't care. She should be happy, come to think of it. She should be happy that she didn't have to worry about the future of her child. That she wouldn't be destitute, waiting tables for the rest of her life. That she could give her baby something more than the kind of unstable situation she'd had growing up.

Except she didn't feel triumphant. Because at the end of the day, she hadn't really broken the cycle. She had still fallen into it. It was just that she had gotten pregnant with Raphael's baby, and not some random auto mechanic she'd met while passing through a dusty town in the Midwest, as her mother had done.

Bailey had just been more fortunate in her mistake, that was all. She couldn't feel triumphant about it. She couldn't feel anything but stupid.

"We will argue no more," he said, his voice hard. Then he turned and continued on up the stairs.

She let out a hard breath and followed after him. "Does the staircase ever end?" she asked.

He said nothing. Rather he let the answer become self-evident when they reached the top and a grand corridor opened up in front of them. Art that looked to be painted by the masters hung on the walls, various suits of armor positioned between each grand painting. The place was a museum, from the intricate scrollwork carved into the stone to every painting, every artifact displayed throughout.

"Your room is just here," he said, opening up a set of broad blue double doors that revealed a lavish sitting area that graduated up to a bedroom set. The bed itself had a velvet canopy that hung down and enough pillows stacked on top of the plush bedspread that it looked like it was prepared to accommodate an entire harem.

"Just how many people are supposed to sleep in that bed?"

He said nothing. Instead, he simply looked at her. And it burned all the way down to her toes.

"I didn't—"

"You have your own bathroom, shower and bath, as well," he said, cutting her off. "And this door here connects to my room, which shall make things convenient for us."

Her heart stopped cold. "How will it be more *convenient* for us, Raphael?"

"We are to be man and wife, *cara*. There are certain expectations that go along with that."

She seriously thought her head might explode. His outright arrogance knew no bounds. She was astounded. *Enraged.*

"You honestly think I'm going to sleep with you?"

"You have done so before," he said, gesturing toward her midsection.

"Yes," she said, "I did. When I thought you were a normal man. A man with a heart. A man that I might have a future with."

"Clearly you have a future with me. We are to be married."

"We are to be married only because your fiancée dumped you at the last minute." She took a step toward him, seething. "Only because I'm carrying your child. And had your fiancée not broken things off, you wouldn't even know that I was having a baby, because you never bothered to respond to my text."

"As I told you before, I had gotten rid of the phone you used to contact me."

She blinked. "And a prince wasn't concerned about missing calls or texts going to an old number?"

"It was a phone that was only for you," he responded.

"A burner phone." She shrieked the words. "You had a burner phone for me. I really was your filthy secret, wasn't I? What would have happened if people had discovered your assignation with me? How *humiliated* you would have been." She laughed, and once she started she had a hard time stopping. It wasn't funny. It cut her down deep. But it was either laugh or curl into a ball and weep. "Well, now the entire world is going to know. Funny how things work out, isn't it?"

"I am going to do my best to make it as painless for both of us as possible."

"You're a saint, Raphael," she spat. "You really are. But if you think you're a saint that's getting anywhere near my body again, you are fooling yourself."

"I don't understand what the issue is. We share a mutual attraction…"

"I trusted you," she said, her voice low, vibrating. "I trusted you with my body, and you knew that cost me. I didn't even know who my father was," she said, "and I was determined that I would never be like my mother. That I would make better decisions. Instead, I met you. And you set out to make sure that I became exactly like her. I don't trust you anymore." Her voice was trembling now. "I don't think I will ever trust you again. I will marry you, Raphael. I will marry you because it is truly the best thing for our child. I will marry you because I don't know what else to do. Because I want this baby, because I want to not be a waitress forever. Because I don't want my child to go to bed hungry, to go to bed cold. For those reasons, I will marry you. But I will not be your wife. Not really."

His face hardened, his eyes growing cold. "Do you expect me to be celibate for the rest of my life?"

"I don't care what you do. As long as you don't come anywhere near me."

"We shall see," he said, his tone made of pure ice now.

"There is nothing to see," she said. "My decision is made. And unless your particular brand of bastardry extends to forcing women into bed with you, I can safely say that you will not be having me in yours ever again."

"I have never had to force a woman into my bed," he gritted out, "you least of all. The reason I said *we shall see* is that I hold out very little hope for your self-control, *cara*. I believe that I can have you begging for me with the proper flick of my wrist between those pretty thighs."

She ignored the desperate well of longing that opened up inside her, making her conscious of how empty she was, of how lonely. Of just how much she desired him. "Never," she said, tilting her chin up.

He said nothing. Instead, dark eyes burning into hers, he closed the space between them, wrapping his arm around her waist, his grip like an iron bar. He looked… she could see almost nothing of the man she had known in Vail. This was the prince. Commanding, ruthless and so beautiful she could scarcely breathe for it.

Perhaps this was more evidence of just how weak she was. Or perhaps it was simply a testament to Raphael. Either way, she found herself looking back at those black, fathomless eyes, desire yawning through her, stretching all the way down to her toes, hitting everyplace in between.

It didn't matter that only a few hours ago she felt like she was near death. It didn't matter that she was wearing nothing but stretch pants and a ratty sweatshirt. It didn't matter that her hair was unkempt, unstyled, and that any makeup left behind was a mere ghost of what had been applied the night before. Nothing mattered but this. But him holding her, and her wanting him.

Before she had a chance to protest, before she had a

chance to even consider if she might want to, his lips crashed down on hers.

It was as fast as it was ruthless, a claiming of her mouth that mirrored the way he had stormed back into her life today. Taking ownership, making her his.

She left her arms at her sides at first, and then she could no longer resist. She clung to him, curling her fingers around the soft fabric of his shirt, holding tightly to him, because if she didn't, she would fall to the ground.

Three months.

Three months she had been without this. Without him. It was so much better than she remembered. So much more.

And then he released her, his top lip curling. "As I said. We shall see."

Then he turned and walked out of the room, leaving her there with her shame and with a burning desire that refused to be quenched no matter how much her brain and her heart tried to put it out.

CHAPTER FIVE

THE NEXT MORNING when Bailey did not appear for breakfast, Raphael went in search of her. She was not in her bedroom. Which was a surprise. He had expected to find her there, sleeping late, as Bailey had often done when she had spent nights in the hotel with him. But she was nowhere to be found. He wandered the halls, wondering if there was any way she had possibly made an escape. And to what end. She must know that he would find her. There was nowhere on earth she could go to hide from him. As evidenced by this morning's headline, the paparazzi had already identified her as his potential lover. And were speculating about whether or not she figured into his breakup with Allegra. She was not anonymous. Already she was conspicuous.

And he had almost infinite resources. There was no way she could avoid him for too long.

He remembered then that she had no passport. And his lips curved into a smile. She could go no farther than the borders of his country. And that meant he wouldn't have to cast a very wide net at all to find her.

One of his servants rushed by, her eyes downcast.

"Where is Bailey?" he asked.

The woman stopped and looked up, her expression

serene. "Ms. Harper is taking her breakfast in the library."

Well, he had to give her full marks for knowing exactly who he was talking about and where she was.

"Thank you," he returned. He made his way down the corridor, flinging the doors wide when he reached the library. Bailey, who was settled into an armchair with a book in her hand, startled.

"How did you know I was here?"

"I have staff."

"Yes, I am aware of that. They're the ones who brought me breakfast," she said, lifting up a cup. "And tea. They're all very nice. Maybe you should talk to them instead of ignoring their very existence unless you have a pronouncement."

"I do not ignore them. They maintain distance out of respect. If I were to stop and speak to each and every one of them, no one would get any work done, myself included. I am a fair ruler and a very good employer. They do not need me to co-opt their time in order for them to feel that. Just as I do not need fawning to know that they revere me."

"Wow," she said. "You're…a whole thing."

"So very nice of them to aid you in hiding away in my home," he continued as though she hadn't spoken.

"I'm not hiding. It's just that this place is the size of a small city. I practically need a cab to get across it."

"Dramatic as ever. I have taken the liberty of procuring you a new wardrobe."

She set her teacup down. "Like…you personally?"

"Don't be ridiculous."

"Right. Well, you procuring me a wardrobe is somehow not ridiculous?"

"There is nothing ridiculous about me."

She laughed. "Are you kidding me?" Bailey stood, stretching, the soft fabric of her T-shirt conforming to her breasts and to the soft swell of her stomach as she did. "You, who were carrying on a secret affair with a university student in Colorado but is secretly a prince with a castle and a superiority complex that would suggest you have little going on in your…trouser region."

"Well, we both know that isn't true."

She waved a hand. "I have nothing to compare it to."

"Regardless, you know every inch of me. And know I am not ridiculous." Her cheeks turned a deep shade of pink, and he felt an answering fire in his gut.

"That's one man's opinion," she said, her tone arch.

"The only opinion that matters in this country."

"Ridiculous," she muttered.

"The press conference will be today."

"What?" she asked. "I'm…jet-lagged still."

"It cannot be helped. The wedding must take place as quickly as possible. I'm sure you understand that."

"But weddings take time to plan?" It was phrased as a question, her voice slightly tremulous.

"Not when you have infinite wealth and power."

"Well, I really wouldn't know anything about that."

He frowned. "No. Nor will you. But we should discuss your monthly stipend. It will be quite generous, of course."

"I…" She blinked. "I don't know what to say to that."

"You'll need your own card, naturally. You will want to shop. Dine out with friends."

"Are you offering me an allowance like a child?"

"No," he said. "I am offering some independence."

"To spend your money. At least, an amount you determine is acceptable."

"I can give you a credit card without a limit, conversely. I'm not worried about your spending habits. You're a *terrible* gold digger, Bailey. You failed to recognize you had hooked yourself a prince. Then you didn't go to the tabloids, and when I mentioned you were getting a new wardrobe your eyes did not glitter with anything like triumph. In fact, you look slightly like you want to kill me."

She pursed her lips in thought. "*Kill* is a strong word. I don't want to kill you. *Maim*, possibly."

"Well, that is reassuring. I would try to keep jokes about harming my royal personage at a minimum around my Secret Service. They take a dim view on that."

She cocked her head to the side. "Where were they when you were with me?"

"As I told you already, I have a fairly low profile. If I don't want to be recognized, casual dress and a pair of sunglasses generally does it."

"The Clark Kent of royalty."

He frowned. "Excuse me?"

"Because nobody recognizes that you're Superman when you have your glasses on."

He found himself laughing, which caught him by surprise. That was more like the relationship he'd had with her before. She always had a way of amusing him, often when he least expected it. They should have nothing to talk about. He had often thought that when the two of them had been together. And it wasn't because he wanted to get to know her that he had initially pursued that connection with her.

Attraction. That was what had hit him upon first seeing her. Need. Want.

He had expected to sleep with her. What he hadn't expected was to spend hours talking to her. And enjoying those conversations.

A man in his thirties, raised to be royalty of a small country in Europe, should have little in common with a university student in her twenties from the United States. And perhaps they didn't have much in common. But she intrigued him. She surprised him. And he found he quite enjoyed it.

Surely, since she was going to be his wife, that was okay.

"I suppose that's true," he said. "I didn't make any announcements about coming into the States. I was there to visit a ski resort owned by a friend. And see about investing. That night, as you know, there was a blizzard, and I was unable to fly out."

"Then, to paraphrase, of all the diners by the airport, why did you walk into mine?"

"I nearly walked back out. I didn't realize what sort of establishment it was. And while I was reasonably confident no one from the press was nearby, I cannot take the chance that I might be seen somewhere of that nature. But then I saw you."

Color rose in her cheeks. "I made you stay?"

"I wanted you," he said, his voice rough. "From the moment I saw you."

He didn't know what he had expected. Really, he needed to stop expecting anything when it came to Bailey. She did not behave in any way that made logical sense to him. But he did not expect for her to frown.

"You make it sound like I was a watch."

"You're going to have to clarify," he said, his tone dry.

"Like, you saw me, and you wanted to buy me. Like I was something you might see in a store."

She wasn't wrong. It was the exact same thing to him. He wanted something, he got it. Women were no exception. Much like watches or cars. All of them were expensive, and often a lot of trouble. And yet he went to great lengths to acquire them. He didn't see how that was offensive.

"People are not things," she said, her tone hard, her expression matching it. As though she had been able to read his thoughts.

"Perhaps not. But things have value. It is not the insult you make it sound like."

"You're not supporting your case."

"I do know that people are not things," he said. Still, the acquisition of things, favors or the affections of women all often went much the same for him. What he saw, he soon had.

"I'm skeptical."

"You are welcome to remain skeptical. However, we must get you ready for today's conference. We have three hours. I have someone coming in to do your hair and your makeup. Then your dress will have to be fitted quickly. I imagine it will be close enough. Still, your figure has changed a bit since the last time I saw it completely uncovered. I did my best to guess."

"I...that all sounds a little excessive."

"Not at all. Your face is going to be on magazines around the world. On the front page of newspapers everywhere."

Her lips twitched. "Okay. I suppose I can submit to having a little bit of assistance."

"What's that?" he asked in mock surprise. "Is Bailey Harper actually submitting?"

"To my vanity. Not to you. Don't get used to it."

"I will see you in two hours. And I expect for you to look like a princess."

Bailey had spent the past few hours being waxed, styled, plucked and polished until she glowed. And when she looked in the mirror, she couldn't help but marvel at the incredible work a professional could do.

She had only ever had her makeup done for her once. And that was when she was in high school, and she'd decided to check out one of those makeup counters in a department store. She had come out of that experience looking like a 1980s reject, with far too much blue eye shadow and a generous helping of glitter.

This was an entirely different experience. She could hardly recognize the woman staring back at her. Her eyes were large, smoky, the charcoal gray of the shadow emphasizing her blue eyes. Her lips were painted a lovely pink color, dark and matte, very subtle.

Somehow, they had managed to style her hair into a smooth, sleek bun, the likes of which she never would have been able to manage on her own.

And the gown…it was beyond anything she had ever imagined wearing. A light shade of pink entirely covered with some sort of netting. And sewn into it were thousands of little glass beads, concentrated around the middle and dispersing over the bodice and the skirt.

With her every movement, she sparkled.

Even she could almost believe this. Even she could almost believe that she was a princess.

The dream, the fantasy hovered at the edges of her consciousness, made her soul feel like it might grow wings and fly. Or might be crushed once and for all if it went wrong.

You're nothing but a weight. You've held me down for sixteen years, Bailey. Don't think I'll spend one day missing you.

Her mother's words rang in her ears, quick to dull some of the brightness of the moment.

Whatever. She was a princess. How much of a weight could she be?

"Look at me now," she said.

She wasn't sure what she thought about all of it, not in the grand scheme of things, but in this moment, she felt pretty good.

There was a heavy knock on her bedroom door, and she assumed it was another servant, come to add another layer of makeup or perhaps to take her to meet Raphael.

"Come in," she said, not looking away from her reflection in the mirror.

The door opened, and she looked up, meeting Raphael's dark gaze as he entered the room. Her heart was thrown forward, slamming hard into the front of her chest.

"You are ready," he said.

She kept her eyes on his in the mirror, the fact it was a reflection acting as a slight buffer. "Yes. Your team of experts is in fact quite expert."

She saw a lick of fire in his eyes. "They are indeed."

"I thought we were going to meet somewhere."

"We are. Here."

She didn't want him in here. She didn't want him

looking at her like that, not with the bed so close by. She didn't want to acknowledge her own weakness.

"Well, here we are," she said, looking everywhere but at him.

"You're missing the most important part of what you'll need today," he said, stepping toward her.

She whirled around, gripping the edge of the vanity. "What's that?" she asked. "Your royal visage?"

"Not quite." He reached into the interior pocket of his jacket and pulled out a little black box.

She was pretty sure her heart stopped completely. "What are you doing?"

He opened the box, revealing a square-cut diamond on a thin band that was also encrusted with stones. Beneath it was another band, glittering yet brighter. She didn't think she had ever seen something so valuable this close. All she could think of was how much money it represented. How many months of rent it could've paid. How many months of groceries and electricity it could have provided.

It was impossible to think differently. When she had gone through life as she had.

"These are for you. Of course, just the engagement ring for now." He took hold of it, grasping it between his thumb and forefinger and holding it out to her.

And suddenly, it wasn't the value that concerned her. Her heart felt like it was shriveling, like everything was being squeezed from it. She had imagined this. Raphael proposing. Before she knew.

The ring she'd pictured had been nothing like this, and the setting had been something entirely different. She had thought he might do it that night in Vail. Out on the snowy streets, or even in his hotel room. When they were both still naked, flushed with passion.

She had fantasized about him getting down on one knee. Looking up at her, telling her she was beautiful. That he loved her. That he couldn't live without her.

Here she was, in a castle, wearing the most beautiful dress imaginable, being offered the most incredible ring. And it paled in comparison to that small, dark fantasy she'd had of him kneeling before her wearing nothing but the naked longing he felt for her on his face.

He was a different man here. There was nothing human or vulnerable about him. Nothing real. His face was stone. As though he were already preparing to become a statue on the grounds.

He wasn't asking. And she was in no position to do anything beyond taking the ring and putting it on her finger. So that was what she did. As she slipped it onto her finger, it killed her by inches.

She looked down, not quite able to believe that she was looking at her own hand. That she was wearing something quite so ostentatious.

"You do not seem pleased, Bailey. Is the ring not large enough for your taste?"

She tried to formulate a response, but the words stuck in her throat. How did she tell him that she had never imagined getting engaged, until she had met him? And then she had imagined it endlessly. And that this, though it was so much more spectacular than that initial fantasy, was nothing more than a pale imitation?

She hadn't imagined the ring.

She had imagined how full her chest would feel. How happy she would be to move forward in her life with someone by her side. To have the kind of relationship she had never dreamed she would.

Well, this was something she hadn't imagined, but she didn't feel full. She felt drained. Missing someone who had never really existed. Suddenly, she resented the man in front of her. It was easy to think he had stolen her lover from her. That they were two different people.

"You think the size of the ring is the problem?" she finally asked.

"You look upset."

"Because. Because this should have been the most romantic moment of my life. But this is all for show. There's no romance in it. There's no feeling. Just a diamond."

"A diamond would be enough for most women. And if it were not, the title of princess would supplement."

"I never dreamed of any of these things." She had never dreamed of love, either. Not before him. Dreaming was dangerous. Devastating in ways she hadn't fully realized until she'd seen those same dreams ground into ash.

"Does not every woman dream she perhaps might be a secret princess?"

"No. Sometimes a woman just dreams that she will be able to escape instability. Get an education, work for a better life. I was never afraid of that. But I was afraid of destroying my hard work. I was afraid of losing my head with a man and ending up in the exact same position as my mother. And so I did." Her voice broke on that last word, and she despised herself. For being so vulnerable with him. For giving him any more information about herself. She had been in a whole relationship all by herself back in Vail. She could see that now.

She had told him so much about who she was, what she wanted. And he had given her nothing in return. He was so skilled at keeping things focused on her, of making small talk that filled the hours but never became personal.

In combination with the physical intimacy, it had been so easy to believe that they were close. But she had never known him. And he had never intended to allow her to.

"You keep saying that. You keep comparing yourself to her. But you are here." He swept his hand across his body, indicating the space they were standing in. "As am I. I fail to see how your situation equates with hers."

"Because," she said, feeling like she was on the verge of screaming herself raw. "If you weren't a prince, if your fiancée hadn't broken up with you, I would be her. It's only your obligation and your money that separates us."

"But you have it. And you have me."

"As though that solves all of my problems without creating more."

"Yes. Terrible problems. Such as which car will you take out shopping today, which of the many forks on the table will you use to eat the delicacy laid out before you, and how on earth will you become accustomed to referring to yourself as princess?"

"Those are things," she said. "That's all."

"It is everything. As you said, you dreamed of a better life. This is a better life."

"I would have been happy with a house in the suburbs and a husband who wasn't too arrogant to function."

"I function just fine, Bailey. As you know. Though perhaps I need to refresh your memory?"

She pressed herself flat against the vanity, trying to put some distance between them while he advanced on her. Her heart was hammering a steady rhythm, so loud she was sure he could hear it. She didn't know what she wanted.

She hated that most of all.

The certainty that she shouldn't. The certainty she wished she could. Jumbling together to create a complex tangle of need inside her.

She needed him to touch her.

She needed him to stay away.

He moved to her, extending his hand and tracing her features with the tips of his fingers. She couldn't breathe. She couldn't think.

She just wanted.

"Regrettably," he said, dropping his hand back to his side, "I will have to remind you later. It is time to introduce my people to their new princess."

CHAPTER SIX

BAILEY FOUND HERSELF being ushered down a corridor of the palace at high speed. Raphael was holding tightly on to her arm as they made their way to what she presumed was the clichéd balcony they had discussed earlier.

Heels clicking loudly on the marble, an aide of some kind ran up to Raphael, her cheeks flushed, her expression tense. She handed him a piece of paper, offering no explanation. Raphael didn't pause, instead, he looked at the scrap, frowning deeply. Then he shoved the paper into his pocket, speaking past her in Italian.

He didn't bother to try to clarify what had just happened. And the only words she knew in Italian were dirty, because he'd taught them to her in bed.

She did her best to keep those thoughts at bay as they kept on rushing. Then they stopped suddenly, in front of double doors with heavy brocade curtains over them.

"You will not have to speak," he whispered into her ear, his breath hot, fanning over her neck. "Just stand next to me. Smile and wave when I do. And for God's sake, Bailey, try and look poised."

And then the doors parted. She found herself being whisked out into the fresh air as quickly as she had been dragged down the corridor. The sun was stunningly bright, washing over the mountain view. It was a shocking blue, with sharp peaks and slashes of bright white snow, fading down to the crystalline lake below. It was so intense, so beautiful that it seemed more like a painting than real life.

More surreal still was the immense crowd of people who had gathered below in the courtyard. They were hushed, standing there, still, waiting to hear from their monarch. She had never seen anything like it. And she had certainly never been in front of this many people. It was like some bad dream from junior high. Except she wasn't naked. She was wearing a designer gown.

"I am aware," Raphael said, speaking in front of a microphone that amplified his deep, rich voice, "that there has been some confusion regarding my future, and the future of this country as a result. Regrettably, my engagement to Allegra Valenti came to a rather abrupt end. And, as you have already seen in a great many of the tabloids, there has been speculation on the reasons for such a thing. I cannot deny that there is some truth to those rumors."

She had no idea what rumors he was talking about. The only headline she had seen was about the dissolution of his engagement, nothing more. She thought back to the scrap of paper he'd been passed in the hall. Had he been given all of this information only a few minutes ago? She knew Raphael was smooth. But that was impressive, even for him.

"Allegra and I wanted to do the right thing, both for my country and for her future," he continued. "But it has become abundantly clear that we were wrong in our methods. Otherwise, we would not have found ourselves in the situation. It is true—Allegra is now with someone else. And I will not deny that I am, as well. It took Allegra's courage for me to see the light, but now that I have, I hope that you will trust what I am giving to you now." His voice was solemn, sincere, and Bailey found herself being drawn in. Hanging on his every word, wondering what he might say next.

"What I am sharing with you now," he continued, "is my heart. I had thought there was perhaps no place for such a thing in politics. But I have faith in my people. Bailey Harper is the choice my heart has made. She is not from a wealthy family. Not from a blue-blooded lineage. But she is going to be my princess, and I believe in time you will all grow to love her as I do."

Bailey was sure that she was dreaming. Any minute now, she was going to wake up in her bedroom back at her apartment in Colorado. Any minute.

Rather than gaining any lucidity, things only got stranger. The crowd erupted below in a roar. Cheering. Cheering him and her and…well, both of them.

She'd never had so much positive affirmation in her life.

And then Raphael wrapped his arm around her waist, drawing her close.

He gripped her chin with his thumb and forefinger, pressing his nose against hers, his dark eyes blazing a trail of heat all the way down to her core.

She couldn't pull away. Not now. Not when they were putting on a show for the country. So, she simply had to stand there, held captive as the crowd was below. Knowing with every fiber of her being that all of the things he just said—all those words that had been so carefully crafted to sound sincere—were exactly that. A meticulously woven fiction designed to spin a tale that would sit well with a nation. Designed to create an impenetrable argument.

Anyone who rejected her now would seem spiteful. Shallow and petty. He had acknowledged that she was beneath him, and even though the words had been beautifully chosen, that was the thrust of all his argument.

Yes, she was lowborn. Yes, she was beneath him. Yes, he had tried to want someone more suitable.

But he had also lied. He had said she was the choice of his heart, when in reality, he had only chosen her because she carried his child in her womb.

She wasn't the choice of his heart. She had been the temporary choice of his libido, and that was not at all the same thing.

But he was looking down at her with such ferocity, such possessiveness, that it was difficult to reason all of that out. And anyway, there was nothing she could do now. She couldn't protest. Not even for an infinitesimal moment, because there were cameras everywhere, the entire world poised at the ready to find fault with her. And so she simply let her eyes flutter closed. Allowed him to lean in and press the softest of kisses to her lips. Almost like a brush of a feather.

Except there was such weight in it. Enough that she thought it might destroy her. That it might crack her irreparably. Reduce her to nothing where she stood.

They parted quickly, and then he raised his hand in a stiff, formal-looking wave. And she knew this was the part where she was supposed to imitate. So she did, feeling like she was playing a part in the theater. Trying to imitate her best approximation of the royal wave as she knew it from movies and parades.

Then, just as quickly as they had appeared, she was being whisked back behind the doors, carried away.

"That was it?" she asked.

"I don't answer questions. I give speeches. I do not give explanations for my decisions. What I decree is law."

"Wow. You really should see someone about that ego."

"It is not an affliction for me."

"It is for those around you," she countered.

"My ego prevents me from feeling overly concerned about that. As I am quite comfortable."

He was so handsome. Even when he was being ridiculous, so arrogant it was amazing she hadn't hauled off and slapped him. He was utter perfection. Those dark eyes and blade-straight nose. The sharp jaw. And his lips...the only soft thing about him where everything else was unyielding as granite.

"What was on that paper they gave you?" She asked the question mostly because she needed something to distract her from how very *Raphael* he was.

"Headlines are already set tomorrow to announce the engagement of Allegra Valenti to Cristian Acosta."

"Your ex is marrying someone else?"

"More importantly, she's pregnant with his baby. Which will also appear in tomorrow's headline. We will be lucky if your pregnancy doesn't appear either. Rumors are apparently already circulating. I didn't want to bring it into today's announcement, as I didn't want to undermine my points. But I saw no reason to sidestep the issue of Allegra being engaged."

"Oh. Well, that was quite the good off-the-cuff speech then."

"I have my moments. I know what my people want to hear."

"Well, that's…romantic."

"As you well know," he said, reaching up and loosening the knot on his tie. Her fingers itched to wrench it free completely. As she'd done so many times before. "There is little that is romantic about this. It isn't about romance. It's about doing what's right."

And just like that, desire turned to anger. "Oh, I do hope we can have that engraved on my wedding band."

"We *could*."

Such a strange, arrogant creature he was in his natural habitat. He could scarcely recognize her sarcasm. "No, thank you," she said, speaking slowly. "I have no desire to have that inscribed on my wedding band. I was messing with you."

"Messing with me?"

"Yes. Which I did often when we were together in Vail. It just seems sometimes like you don't remember."

"I think maybe I wasn't listening to you very closely back in Vail," he said. "Typically, I was blinded by the desire to have you."

Those words were like a clean, vicious stab through her chest. "I see. So the contents of my bra were a lot more interesting than the contents of my brain?"

"Talking to you never served a purpose," he responded, neatly sidestepping the question. "I always knew that our association would be temporary."

"But sex somehow made sense?"

"Most people assume that a sexual liaison will be temporary in some way. Unless you're looking at marriage, and often those end, too."

It was so simply put. So pragmatic. And really, not

wrong. It enraged her. Because she wanted to feel mortally wounded. Wanted to feel justified. Wanted how blindsided she had been to be about him, and not about her.

She sniffed. "Well, you lied to me."

"By omission."

Anger burned through the last shred of her pride. "You're so full of crap." She stamped, her gorgeous dress swirling around her legs. "You *absolutely* let me believe, and build off those assumptions I made early on. You did it so easily. Effortlessly. And I saw that reflected in the way that you made the announcement today. You're very good at saying what people need to hear."

"I would say that's a good quality in a leader."

"It matters much less than *doing* something. Than being sincere. What does it matter if your words make somebody feel warm all over when they listen to you talk, and then your actions leave them cold? In my case, *literally* out in the snow."

"Any dramatic tossing into the cold was your own doing. I didn't chuck you into a snowbank."

"Well, I collapsed in the snow." She watched his expression, neutral and shuttered. Maddeningly still. "In *distress*," she added. "I hope you're happy."

"It does not make me happy to have hurt you. But I fail to see how your unrealistic expectations were my fault."

"I think you fail to see how anything could be your fault ever," she spat.

"I am held to a different standard. As a result, I live my life by a different set of rules. Again, that is hardly my fault. I am under greater scrutiny. I carry heavier weight—there must be some perk to that."

"What perk? The feeling that the entire world is a trinket box you can reach into and rummage around, pulling out whatever you want and then casting it aside when you're finished? The idea that people are as disposable as *things*? That everything is here for you to use to your satisfaction? I think that goes a little bit beyond the benefits you could expect for being royalty."

"I see. And what benefits do *you* suppose I deserve? For bearing the weight of an entire nation and all of the people in it?"

"Dental? I don't know. But definitely not the right to lie about your identity."

"I wanted you," he said, grabbing hold of her arms and pressing her back against the wall, his movements sudden, swift, shocking.

He held her tight, his voice suddenly low, rough. Gone was the prince. Somehow she had managed, with a few words, to strip him back down to the man.

"I thought of nothing else but having you," he continued. "I was engaged to someone else. I knew that there was no future, and I took you anyway, because I could not imagine living in a world where I had seen you, and desired you, but not satisfied that desire. I am not a man who understands failure. I'm not a man who understands *no*."

"So you approached me as a child throwing a tantrum over a toy might?"

He growled, rolling his hips forward, the evidence of his arousal plainly felt, even through the layers of her gown. "I am not a child. And what I had was nothing like a tantrum."

He leaned closer to her, and she nearly melted. His smell, his touch, his heat…it was all too much. Too good. "Have you ever felt like your blood was on fire?" he rasped. "Have you ever felt like you would die if you didn't have something? When I saw you, that's what it was. Nothing but fire and need. I cannot explain it. Perhaps I acted uncivilized. Perhaps I played the role of villain in this. But I would do it again."

"Even knowing it ends here?"

He looked stricken by that. His dark eyes haunted. "I… I can still see no other option. Because the alternative is walking through life ablaze, and never having a chance to try and put it out."

He didn't know what was happening to him. He was… shaking.

And he knew with certainty it had nothing to do with facing a crowd of thousands, nothing to do with the eyes of the world being trained on him. Not in the least. That attention, that deference, was his birthright and he wore it with the ease he wore his own skin.

Only one thing had ever made him do this. Tremble like a child.

Bailey.

Always Bailey.

From the first.

It enraged and invigorated him in equal measure.

Because she was out of his reach. She had been. Always. He had carved out a moment of time when he could have her, just a moment. Swaths of time removed from Santa Firenze, spent in a town in the States, mostly in a hotel room with a woman he'd known he could only possess for a short while. And then a change in the tide had brought him back to her. Only now she had made it clear she wouldn't touch him. That he could never have her again, and had happily given rights to his body to other women. But there were no other women.

There hadn't been. Not from the moment he'd first met her.

Never in all his life had Prince Raphael DeSantis wanted anything that compromised the future of Santa Firenze. Never had he taken such an inconvenient mistress. Never before had he chosen a woman on the other side of the globe. A woman he could see for only snatches of time. Going more than a month without sex, often, because he couldn't slip away to Colorado. And because he could find no excitement in himself for anyone else.

The entire point of a mistress was to bring pleasure. It was the meaning of their existence.

He had certainly found pleasure in Bailey's arms, but there had been a cost. She didn't conform to his schedule, his map or his station in life. He'd had to bend to accommodate her.

He'd had her...countless times over days that were easily counted. And still, she made him shake.

Still, she treated him as if she was above this. As if she could turn away from their attraction so easily while he could not.

"I am on fire," he said, the words strong, hard. "And there you stand like ice."

"You doused the fire, Raphael. It's a bit late to regret it."

"More insipid jokes about me throwing you into the snow?"

"That's not a joke," she said. "A part of me *died* that

night. A part of me that believed in something other than my own grit for the first time in…ever. I believed in you. I believed in us. And you took it from me. You're a liar. You're a liar who would have abandoned me to raise a baby alone if not for a twist of fate."

"We met by a twist of fate," he said, releasing his hold on her arms and pressing his palms against the wall, trapping her between them. "How could our reunion have ever been anything else?"

"It could have been anything. You're a man who acts like he controls the entire world, but you're going to pretend you couldn't control what happened between us?"

"If I could have controlled what happened between us, I never would have touched you."

"Rail at fate, Raphael. Not at me. Or maybe for once rail at yourself."

She moved, as though she were going to try to dodge his hold, and he pressed himself closer. Her blue eyes glittered, anger visible there. She was ready to lash out at him if he did something she didn't want. But that was fine. He was more than ready to lash out in his own way.

Quickly, he removed one hand from the wall, sliding it around to cup the back of her head. Then he pulled her forward, claiming her mouth with all the arrogance he possessed that she claimed to be so disdainful of. She was not disdainful of it. She was weak for it. Needy. And he knew it. No matter what she said. No matter how she pretended she didn't want him anymore.

She could play it like she was disgusted with him. With all of his perceived flaws, which she was more than willing to list at the drop of a hat. And yet, without them, she would not go up in flame like this.

She pressed her hands against his chest, attempting

to push him back. But he would not be moved. Instead, he closed the distance between them, pressing her head up against the wall. His hand was trapped between her head and the hard surface, crushing his bones. But he didn't care.

She wiggled, as though she were attempting to get away. Then he angled his head, sliding his tongue across hers, the movement slow, sensual. And he felt the exact moment she went limp. The exact moment she gave in to this thing that raged between them like a starving beast.

He heard footsteps behind them, sensed that household staff members were wandering this very corridor looking the other way. He didn't care. They could stare all they wanted. She was his. She was his princess. She would be his wife. She carried his child in her womb.

Mine.

That was the word. The one that he had been a slave to, driven by, that first night he'd seen her. And he saw it now for what it was. A prophecy. He possessed her now, in every way that mattered.

And this moment, this capitulation, made it clear that he would possess her body again. She would not resist. Could not. Because regardless of how she tried to act, she was as helpless as he was. She was. He was not the only one who shook.

This little creature who seemed to imagine that she was too good for this, too good for him, was shivering in his arms like a leaf in the breeze. He was not beneath her. But, soon enough, she would be beneath him.

He rocked his hips forward, pressing his hardness into her softness, glorying in the soft gasp that he sipped from her lips.

He abandoned her mouth for a moment, kissing her

neck, down to her collarbone. He could bare her breasts here in the hall. Suck her glorious pink nipples into his mouth, so sweet, like candy. He could lift her skirts, free himself from his pants and thrust himself deep inside her.

Not a single servant in his employ would report what they had seen. They were all far too discreet, and far too well taken care of to take a chance at compromising their position in the palace.

And he did not care for his own modesty. This was his palace, after all. If he wanted to have a woman against the wall, that was his prerogative. Of course, he never had. But Bailey...he needed her. He needed her like water. Like air.

And he could feel the deprivation keenly, just as he could those other things.

He raised his hand, curling his fingers around the top of her gown, tugging the bodice down, exposing one rosy peak.

She gasped, wiggling away from him. And he was so shocked that he didn't stop her. He had lost himself. Had lost his sense of time and place.

"What are you doing?" she hissed, pulling her dress back in place. "There are...people." As if to underscore her point, a staff member, dressed all in black, rushed by quickly, her head down.

"All that you see here is mine. Mine to do with as I will. The people that work here have no other purpose but to see that my will is done. If my will is to have you out in the open, I will hardly curb my behavior for the sensibilities of those who live to serve me."

"You arrogant son of a—if you aren't concerned for your servants, if you aren't concerned for your own modesty, what about mine? And even more than that, what about the fact that I said you were not to touch me?"

"You are welcome to make edicts, Bailey. That does not mean I will comply with them. I am a law unto myself. What I want, I will have."

"So you have said. But, Raphael, do you have me?" She tilted her chin up, arching one pale brow, her expression defiant. He had never had anyone look at him like that before. As though he were something beneath contempt. "No." She supplied the answer herself. "You don't."

And then she turned on her heel and stormed down the hall, leaving him standing there, aching, desperate and in a position he did not understand.

He had shown her power. He had presented her to his people. He was giving her a title. Had installed the ungrateful creature in his palace. He had aroused her body, had proven that the fire between them was not gone.

Still, she had turned him down. Still, he had failed at an objective.

He had offered her everything in his possession, and it had not brought her to heel.

Bailey Harper was an enigma. Raphael deeply disliked enigmas.

But he would have to put the mystery of Bailey on hold. A royal wedding had been planned to take place in a few weeks' time. And by God, it would.

If not by God, then by his own hand. That, at least, would not fail.

CHAPTER SEVEN

IT WAS SURPRISINGLY simple to be the bride in a royal wedding. Given that such a thing was a worldwide spectacle, Bailey supposed it would be a great deal of work. It appeared it was not a great deal of work for the stars of the show.

It was probably helpful that most of the details had been in place already. Invitations already sent out. When she had found out that an amendment had been sent, letting people know that the name of the bride had in fact changed, she had wanted to melt into the floor and die a thousand deaths, and any number of other overdramatic and fatal things.

Focusing on her humiliation at being Raphael's pregnant replacement bride was a lot easier to handle than thinking about her disgrace in the hallway a couple of weeks back.

He had…well, he had been perilously close to having her in a public space. Had been perilously close to breaking her resolve absolutely and completely.

But then, after her foot-stomping tantrum, he'd been distant. Nothing if not circumspect. Which was just weird. Because Raphael was never circumspect. He had all the subtlety of a wrecking ball.

She startled as Raphael entered the dining room, his manner purposeful, his gaze direct. "Good evening, Bailey."

"What are you doing here?"

"Is that the customary greeting we give each other nowadays? Manners really are a dying art form."

"I haven't seen you at dinner for two weeks. And here you are. To what to do I owe the pleasure?"

"We have a menu to plan."

"Isn't the menu already planned?"

"Yes. But to Allegra's specifications. She had chosen the design for the cake and the flavors. In addition to the meal that will be served to the guests. I thought you might want your own preferences considered."

"I...well..." She didn't actually. She sort of wished that none of it was up to her. That none of it had anything to do with her. She wished that he could feel impersonal. That she could feel a victim, like she was being dragged along on this crazy, luxurious journey against her will. But when he did things like this, like acting as though there would be consideration for her as a person, and not just a trinket...

Not just another weight.

It tugged at tender, recently wounded spaces inside her. Made her hope where she desperately needed hope to be dead.

"It's cake, Bailey. Do you want to help choose it, or not?"

"Sure," she said, crossing her arms and sitting back in her chair. He had a way of taking all of his nice gestures and twisting them. Making them feel like a grievance.

"Come in," he commanded.

Bailey was confused for a moment until two members of staff came in pushing two different carts carrying covered platters. It was all set in front of her and the lids were removed quickly, revealing an array of entrées, and behind them, plates filled with miniature cakes.

"I…" She could feel her eyes go wide, could feel her entire face lighting up. She couldn't disguise it. Couldn't disguise that she thought this was pretty cool.

"A tasting menu. For your enjoyment."

"And for you?"

In answer, a new staff member came in, carrying a single platter.

"Steak for me," he said.

Then, as quickly as they had come in, the staff melted back out, leaving her alone with Raphael and several beautifully colored cakes.

Honestly, she preferred the company of the cakes.

She looked at the entrées, unsure of where to begin. There was salmon, steak, chicken and some kind of vegetable mixture.

"Vegetarian option," she said, lifting her fork and poking at the eggplant. "How very inclusive of you."

"I am nothing if not generous and exceedingly modern."

She snorted. "If you say so."

"I have to. No one else will."

"That does not surprise me." She took a bite of the vegetables, shocked when rich, buttery flavor exploded over her tongue. "Okay, that's better than I thought it would be."

"I have one of the most accomplished chefs in the world at my disposal."

"Honestly, food has been slightly difficult for me. Just hasn't tasted right for the last few weeks. I'm surprised that I'm enjoying anything." She took a bite of the chicken this time, then went down the line sampling. "I don't know how I'm supposed to choose!"

"You could choose everything."

She laughed. Because it was absurd. "Okay," she said, "I choose everything."

"Done." A member of the waitstaff came back, this time with a carafe and two cups. "Decaf for you," Raphael said, pouring a mug of coffee and passing it across the table to her.

The cakes, she saw, had little labels. Lemon chiffon with raspberry filling. Chocolate with a ganache icing. Hazelnut with mascarpone.

"I can guarantee you I'm going to need to be rolled out of here when I'm finished," she said, picking up a fork and holding it poised, unsure of which delicacy to take a bite of first.

"Go ahead," he said.

She bit her lip, trying to decide where to start. Then Raphael stood, rounding the long table and striding purposefully down the other side toward her. She stopped, watching his movements. He shoved the chair out of the way, sitting on the edge of the high-gloss surface. She blinked, a wave of shock and heat coursing through her. It had been…well, it had been two weeks since she'd been this close to him.

She had begun measuring her days in terms of how long it had been since she and Raphael had first started their relationship. She always knew exactly how long it had been.

Two weeks since they had kissed. Since he had touched her.

Three and a half months since she had said good-bye to him at the hotel. Since he had been inside her.

Suddenly all of that time felt weighted. Like it was pressing down on her, making it difficult for her to breathe. She looked up, her eyes clashing with his. His lips curved upward into a slow-burn smile that scorched her through and through.

"You like chocolate," he said, sliding his fork down through the rich, dense cake. Then he held it out to her, poised in front of her lips. "You should try that first."

Her heart was pounding, the blood rushing through her veins, hot and fast. "Haven't you ever heard of saving the best for last?"

"I believe in having the best all the time." He leaned in, the intensity in his gaze touching her deeply. "Open for me."

Those words sent an echo of sensual memory through her. Of times he had spoken those words when she was down on her knees in front of him. His voice rough, demanding. When she had wanted nothing more than to please him. And to please herself.

And, just as she had then, she parted her lips eagerly for him.

Sweet flavor burst on her tongue, dark, bitter notes following. It was like a metaphor for their entire relationship. Decadent. Intense. And something she couldn't resist, even if she should. Something she knew she shouldn't have too much of, but that she craved. All of it. Every bite.

He set the fork down, lifting up her coffee cup and handing it to her. "To cleanse your palate."

"I'm not sure coffee is a palate cleanser," she said, taking a sip anyway, her fingers brushing against his as she took the cup.

Lightning streaked through her. Would she ever be able to touch him and feel nothing? Would his skin ever just be skin? Or would it always be gasoline against her lit match?

He slid the fork through the lemon and raspberry. "Now, I think this is good, too. And it reminds me of you."

"Why is that?"

"Because," he said, bringing the fork to her mouth again. "It's tart."

He slipped the cake between her lips. "Did you just call me a tart?" she asked after she'd swallowed the bite.

"No. You aren't a tart. You are *tart*. You don't let me get away with anything. There is nothing I have done that you won't force me to answer for, is there?"

"Do you think you should be allowed to get away with not answering for your actions?"

"Yes, damn it," he said, humor playing with the edges of his mouth. "No one has ever expected me to be responsible for my actions."

"What kind of childhood must you have had?"

"One filled with everything I could have ever wanted. My needs were anticipated before even I knew them. I had a dedicated staff all to myself from the moment I came home from the hospital. Actually, I had a dedicated staff at the hospital. To hear tell of it, the entire floor was reserved for my mother when she gave birth."

"That's an extravagant beginning."

"I have never been anything but extravagant from the moment I came into this world."

"Did your dad hold you out over the balcony like *The Lion King*? Or maybe like Michael Jackson."

"I was presented to the nation when I was three days old."

"And you were adored by all," she said.

"Of course." His grin took on a decidedly arrogant tilt. "Though it was not all parties and presentations. I had to learn to be strong. For the kingdom. I could not be indulged. However, we are both indulging now. Try the next one." This time, he cut a slice off the cake, then picked it up between his thumb and forefinger. His fingertips brushed her lips. "Open for me," he said, his voice getting deeper, huskier.

She did, and he slipped his fingers and the cake into her mouth, retreating slowly, the salty flavor of his skin lingering. Arousal shot through her, need. Memory.

She couldn't really concentrate on the cake. Everything in her had zeroed in on him. On her desire for him. On this moment they were in. This little bit of connection that made her feel like maybe she did know him. Or, at least, that maybe she could. It was difficult to remember why she was so angry with him. Here, in the silence of the dining room, with the night sky beyond the window clear and bright with stars.

The two of them at this massive banquet table, with a private feast. It felt much more like fantasy than reality. These past weeks had, but this was something more. Something different. Not like some overblown princess fantasy, but something intimate. Something real.

It made her feel like she was cracking apart inside. On the verge of giving in to something she had sworn she wouldn't. But he was right there, and so warm and so very much what she really wanted.

And he was trying to make this work for her. Having her taste the food, having her sample cake. Trying to make this a little bit about her, instead of just an amendment to the wedding invitations. Almost as if he understood how she felt. As if he cared.

"There," he said, his eyes molten. He lifted his hand, dragging his thumb slowly across her cheek. "I think I have proven that I am not the selfish beast you think I am."

Something about those words sliced through the haze she was lost in. "You knew that this would…make you look like you cared."

"Of course."

"This is part of your plan. It's a thing you're doing to try and make me like you. Try and make me think you care."

"I thought of it. I thought you might care what kind of food and cake you had at the wedding."

"That's not the same as caring about me having something that I wanted."

"Yes, it is."

"No, it isn't," she insisted.

"Perhaps we are experiencing something of a language barrier. I knew you would care—therefore, I set out to do this for you. I fail to see how that proves my overwhelming selfishness."

"Did you do it because it would mean something to me, and that mattered to you? Or did you do it because you knew it would manipulate me?"

"If the result is the same, does it matter?"

"Of course it matters!" She pushed down on the table, launching herself into a standing position. "It isn't enough for you to simply know how to pull my strings. In fact, it's abhorrent."

He laughed, a hard, mocking sound. "Yes, how dare I? What a monster I am. I have brought you into my home, given you an entirely new wardrobe and presented you with a feast of cake. Truly, the abuses you suffer are beyond what anyone should be expected to endure."

"I can't be a game to you for the rest of my life. Some little puzzle that you're trying to work out constantly, and if you can make all the pieces fit, maybe you'll get me back in your bed."

He frowned. "I don't understand you," he said, frustration wearing through his aristocratic tone.

"You don't care. That's the problem. You're playing with me as if I'm a toy, and it is completely different than giving something to me because it came from a desire to please me. You only cared about what it would make me do, not what it would make me feel."

"That isn't true," he said. "I cared about what it would make you feel."

"Because if I felt good, you thought it might make me fall in line." He said nothing, his square jaw set as though it were stone. "That's what I thought."

"Why do you insist on being impossible?"

"I don't know. Why do you insist on being a liar? Why do you insist on being a prince? Why do you insist on being nothing like you were supposed to be?" She turned away from him, beginning to storm out of the room. He grabbed hold of her arm and pulled her back.

"I'm sorry there are no snowbanks outside. Nothing to fling yourself into dramatically. Perhaps you could stay here and talk to me like an adult instead of storming off like a little girl."

"I'm not a little girl," she said, consciously echoing words he had spoken to her, "as you well know."

"You do throw a very convincing tantrum."

"It's the only control I have," she launched back.

"You have me parading around the palace, putting together tasting menus and miniature cakes. Is that not control, Bailey? You have me jumping through hoops to try and gain something other than a sour expression from you. And you claim you have no control?"

"What does it cost you?"

He said nothing to that, his dark eyes inscrutable.

"Exactly," she said, turning away again.

"I don't understand the point you're trying to make," he said finally, when she was halfway between him and the door.

She turned. "You act like you're so aggrieved because you had to do something considerate for me. Something that was going to benefit you anyway. But your kitchen staff prepared the food—all you had to do was ask. You didn't give me anything at cost to yourself. It was all in service of yourself."

"If all that will ever matter to you is my reasoning behind my actions, and not my actions themselves, then we will never reach any kind of accord. I don't see what my motives matter."

"My mother kept me alive, but she let me know every day what a hardship it was. Do you think that didn't matter?"

"Of course it did," he said, his tone clipped. "But I have a responsibility. I am who I am."

"A stone?"

"Maybe so," he said, his voice hard. "But that is what withstands. It is what a nation needs. It is what our child needs. If you're going to flail around dictated by your emotions, one of us has to be firm. I am built to withstand storms, anything that might befall my country. I have to be willing to do my duty at all costs. I must be willing to sacrifice. If I am hard, it is only because it is an essential quality in a leader. I am everything I am supposed to be. I will not apologize to you."

"Good. I wouldn't want it anyway. Because you wouldn't mean it." She turned and stalked out of the room, rage making her limbs feel weak.

Dimly, she thought she might be overreacting. But she didn't really care. She had been manipulated by him from moment one. From the first moment they had seen each other. Everything he had done was suspect now. All of the things he had said since she'd come back to the palace were building on top of one another, a boulder that lodged in her chest, blocked her throat and made it impossible to breathe.

She was unsuitable. Beneath him.

You make him feel like he's on fire.

That traitorous thought glowed in her chest like an ember. Refusing to be doused. It would have to be. It just had to be. She had to get some control where he was concerned, so she wasn't continually taken in by his machinations.

She had two weeks. And then she would be his wife. It all felt so permanent. So final. Yes, there was always divorce, but she doubted it would be easy in her current position.

She was already bound to him. He wasn't just going to let her escape. She wandered over to the end of the corridor, looking out the window, over the view below. The scenery here was so beautiful, crisp and vast. It gave her the sense that she might be able to melt into it. But she couldn't. He had an army, and she had nothing. She didn't even have a passport. They wouldn't let her back into her own country.

Her throat closed tight, a sudden feeling of helplessness overwhelming her. She was marching toward this wedding day, whether she wanted to or not.

She was already in shackles. It was just that once this was over, she would be a princess in chains, rather than a commoner.

She supposed that was as good as it was going to get.

CHAPTER EIGHT

THE DAY OF the wedding dawned bright and clear, and Bailey felt it made something of a mockery out of just how stressful all of it was.

Of how much she wanted to escape into the mountains, regardless of the fact that she was pregnant, and starting to show in a completely undeniable way, in spite of the fact that there was no escape from the long arm of Raphael. Logistics were beginning to matter less and less. There was only a sense of gnawing desperation.

The only thing she could really do was try to keep her head together. Try to remember exactly what this was. It was an agreement the two of them were entering into. She would have to find a place, of course. She wasn't going to be his wife, not really. She was determined on that score. She had pride. And she had a heart to protect.

But she also wouldn't be able to sit around being idle. Motherhood would certainly take up a good portion of her time. But she wondered if there were any other things she could busy herself with.

She was in the process of getting a business degree, because she had thought it was a nice all-encompassing goal. That way, she would have the opportunity to work in a lot of different environments, and ideally start a company of her own. She had no idea what a princess might do with a business degree. Sort of moot, since at the moment, she couldn't see herself finishing it.

She had been consumed since the moment she had gotten to the palace, and studying had been low on her list of priorities. As had figuring out how to make up classes. She was in survival mode. Midterms had no place in that.

Someday, maybe. But not now. As much attention as had been paid to her appearance the day she was presented to the country, the preparation for the wedding was even more intense. She had been given some sort of scrub that was supposed to make her glow, and indeed it did.

Then she'd been made up, her hair expertly arranged, a work of architectural brilliance, and her wedding gown given a final fitting, to ensure that it flowed over her stomach so as not to draw too much attention to her expanding figure.

The announcement about the baby would wait until after the wedding, and she definitely understood why. There would be no hiding the fact that she had been pregnant prior to their marriage, but she had a feeling that once everything was settled, it would all be accepted with a bit more equanimity.

The fait accompli was definitely one of Raphael's preferred methods of operation.

In fact, it was his exclusive method of operation. If he had ever given her a choice in anything, she couldn't remember.

Liar.

She thought back to that first night. That night they

had met and he had kissed her. When passion had nearly carried her away and into his bed only a couple of hours after their first meeting. And she had told him the truth. That she was nothing more than a nervous virgin.

He had given her a choice then. He hadn't pressured her at all.

But he had seemed so different then. Yes, he had still had notes of the same arrogance she saw now. And, yes, he had definitely still liked getting his way. But it hadn't been quite so hard, or so heavy-handed.

She looked around her bedroom while the women who had been hired to prepare her for the big day continued to fuss with her hair, adding little bits of flowers to her curls and adding to the bouquet she held in her hands at the same time.

But of course, in Colorado, he hadn't been the prince of anything. Well, of course he had been, but it had been different. All of this was under his domain, which he was always the first person to remind her of. It was only just now that she realized the enormity of that.

It was about more than just a palace. It was about all the generations that had lived in it. His entire line that had ruled this country for…she didn't know for certain how many years, but she was certain that he did. Was sure that it was written on his heart. Because for all that he was insufferable, and in general kind of a beast, she had no doubt that he would bleed for his country.

As one of the women assisting her settled a necklace over her collarbone, clasping it, the weight suddenly felt excruciating. So heavy on her chest it was almost like it was suffocating her.

Bailey Harper, originally of Nebraska, was stepping into this legacy that wasn't meant for someone like her.

And he was well aware of that. He was carrying extra weight because of it.

His family tree went back hundreds of years. Hers stopped at a garage somewhere in the middle of nowhere where her mother had hooked up with a random guy.

It made her feel small. Rootless. Adrift.

Suddenly, she felt completely unequal to the task. And it had nothing to do with being his wife, or sharing his bed, which she was still determined not to do. But everything to do with the fact that she was being set up as a symbol for this country. This country that she didn't even know anything about. She hadn't even known it existed until last month.

She could see why he had chosen someone else. Why he had attempted to leave their relationship back in Colorado, where at least it made some sense.

She took a deep breath, trying to steady herself. And then the door to the bedroom opened.

"Are you ready, Princess?" It was one of Raphael's closest aides. And it was the first time he had called her princess.

She wasn't ready. She didn't think she ever would be. But it was happening all the same.

"Yes." She swallowed hard. "Yes, I'm ready."

The crowd overflowed the massive old church, just as expected. Thousands of people were in attendance, ready to see the Crown Prince of Santa Firenze finally claim his princess.

Raphael stood at the head of the altar, surveying the traditional surroundings. In this church, generations of his family had married. Generations of political alliances had been struck. That was what his marriage to Allegra was supposed to be. A marriage for his political gain. To gain the ally status of one of Italy's oldest families. It was always best to be on friendly terms with a close neighbor, and he had intended to make inroads via his wife.

Now here he stood, poised to become the first person in his family to marry for a reason other than politics. Perhaps Bailey was right. Perhaps there had been other illegitimate children, swept under the rug and cast aside. But every single marriage in the history books of the DeSantis family had been one of political importance.

Except for this. Except for him.

Raphael wondered what his father would say about such a thing if he were still alive. Would he be disappointed?

He shoved that thought off to the side. His father would have understood that this was the most expedient thing to do. This was an age of transparent media, and bastards were not so easily hidden. Not when every person on earth had a platform thanks to the internet. It would have been easy for Bailey to broadcast the fact that she was pregnant with the DeSantis heir. Easy for her to make a spectacle of his family name and his country.

His father would understand this marriage. It was not a decision driven by emotion. But a decision driven by necessity. He had weighed the cost, and he had acted.

Anyway, even without Bailey his marriage to Allegra would not have gone forward.

Yes, this was purely logical.

As the back doors to the church opened, and the music changed, his heartbeat changed, as well.

She was like an angel. An angel with a mouth that was made for sin.

She took her first step into the sanctuary, and everything in him seized tight. Her dress flowed over her curves, but it was plainly obvious to him that she was pregnant. The soft chiffon gown conformed to that small bump, and her breasts were much fuller than they had been only a few months ago. But perhaps not everyone was so in tune with changes in Bailey's figure. Likely, no one else was.

But she was his. So of course he noticed. He noticed everything about her.

He had done his very best over the last couple of weeks not to notice her at all.

They had barely spoken. Had barely made eye contact when passing each other in the hall. She had seemed happy to keep it that way, and he would not be the one to break the silence. He had refused. His pride refused. He would not bend, not for this woman.

A *nation* bowed before him. He would be damned if he bowed before one petite blonde.

And yet, as she continued down the aisle toward him, there was only that one word. That one word that he always heard echoing in his mind when he looked at her.

Mine.

And after today, she truly would be his. She would be bound to him, legally, yes, but also with vows that were as old, if not older, than the church they were standing in. She would make promises to him here, in this place where every royal baby in his family had been christened, where every royal couple had been consecrated.

He was a man of practicality. He did not believe in

mysticism. However, he felt that making vows here had to carry more weight. That there was something truly binding in the stone walls that had witnessed so many other reverent and sovereign occasions.

All of these thoughts tripped around his mind, but none of them were as loud as the word.

Mine.

She held her head high, tilting her chin up, and he could see that her eyes were glittering. That she was fighting back tears. Bailey, his Bailey, had every emotion so close to the surface. She was hotheaded. Temperamental. And so completely genuine it was difficult to feel any annoyance about it.

She had more conviction in her every word than he had in all of his body.

But his country didn't require conviction. It required a cool head and clear leadership. That was all that had ever been required of him. He fulfilled that position without equal. Still, she seemed to find fault. She always could, his Bailey. No one else ever seemed to say anything negative at all.

Everyone else worshipped him.

Her blue eyes locked with his, and he saw no worship, no deference at all. He saw a challenge. He saw a will of iron, anger that refused to be extinguished and desire that still burned bright.

He saw a woman who was most certainly an asset to his country. Strong enough to be his princess. Strong enough to rule. How had he ever thought she was not royalty? She was. Down to her core. A woman of immovable conviction. Of deep feeling and moral standing.

She would care for his country as he did. He knew

that she would. He knew beyond anything that she would give to Santa Firenze all that he did and more. If for no other reason than to try to show him up.

Such was her stubbornness.

In that moment, he treasured it. Valued it. Because he could see that it was her strength.

She had told him about the way she had worked herself through school, how she had scraped, saved and struggled for everything she had ever had.

How had he ever seen that as anything less than equal to his own standing?

When she reached him, he took her hand in his, drawing her close. And as the priest intoned the words of the service, he let it all wash over him like a wave, absorbing it all rather than hanging on every word.

When it came time for the vows, he spoke without hesitation. He was not a soft man, not a man geared toward romance. But he was a man who knew commitment. A man who kept his word. He did not give it easily, and he had not given it to her at all prior to bringing her here, but he was giving it now. And that meant it was cast in stone.

"Upon my life," he said, his every word ringing out true and clear through the sanctuary, "I will bind myself to you. Keep myself only for you. Pledge myself to you. Body and soul. Until death separates us."

Color washed over her face as he said the words, and they resonated deep inside of him, ringing with a truth he could not deny. There was no question then of whether or not she would be his wife in body, in soul. He had spoken the words, and so they were.

For his part, he could never touch another woman, ever again. It had been so from the moment he had seen her. As deeply imprinted in his soul as that sure and knowing possessiveness that had gripped him from the first moment he'd laid eyes on her.

Mine.

And he was hers, and no one else's.

She repeated his same words back to him, her voice muted, her eyes downcast. And he could see that that same certainty that he felt, down to his very soul, was not shared by her.

It could not be so. She was *his*. His and no one else's. He had bound himself to her. And he had meant his every vow. He would keep it. He would keep every one.

And then it was announced that he could kiss his bride.

He wrapped his arm around her waist, pulling her close, gripping her chin as he brought his face down to hers, and kissed her like it was a brand. As though he were trying to burn that same mark onto her soul that he bore on his.

When they parted, her eyes were bright, her breathing swift, rapid.

He looked at her, everything in him on high alert, determined.

Then, as the crowd cheered for them, for their marriage, he leaned over, his lips brushing against her ear. "You are mine," he whispered. "And I have decided that I will have my wedding night."

It was absolutely impossible to concentrate on the wedding feast, on the chocolate cake that she had chosen and the delicious steak that she had been served earlier. Difficult to do anything but smile brutally as well-wishers filtered through, telling them how pleased they were to have her as princess.

Every voice was a dull, murky mumble. Every taste bland. Because all she could think of was that husky whispered promise he had made up at the altar. Not his public proclamation, but that carnal vow made only for her ears.

That he would have his wedding night.

She had been determined that he wouldn't. And she had been certain he had understood. After all, they had barely spoken at all for the last couple of weeks. Why would he think anything had changed?

She was…she didn't know how she felt. She didn't know what to think. Except she wished that this interminable reception would continue to be interminable. Wished that it would go on so that she didn't have to face being alone with her new husband.

Her *husband.*

She had just stood in front of a nation, in front of the world really, and made promises to this man that she would never be able to break.

She was his captive. She could see clearly enough that she had been from the moment she had first stepped onto his private plane. Perhaps from the moment she had taken his hand outside the diner and said she would, in fact, go home with him on that first night they'd met.

The marriage was just a formality.

She had fooled herself into believing that she had some kind of bargaining power. That he had seen her side of things. That perhaps he understood that things would be better if they didn't have an intimate relationship. Clearly, it had all been a ruse. Something to lull her into a false sense of security.

Or maybe to keep her from screaming at him every day for the last two weeks.

She looked over at him, her eyes catching hold of his. Her heart felt like a bird fluttering in a cage, desperate to get out. At least if her heart escaped, it might be able to fly away from this place. Away from this man who had the potential to be so devastating. If she could only keep her heart safe, then maybe the rest would be okay. She enjoyed having sex with Raphael.

She pressed her mouth into a thin line. That was such an insipid description of what being with him was. It was never about the physical. It never had been. Yes, it felt amazing. Yes, he gave her pleasure unlike anything she'd ever known. But it had never ended there. Not for her.

She had felt connected to him from the moment she'd met him. And when his body had joined with hers, she had felt like everything made sense. Like he had uncovered hidden pieces of her that made so many other things fall into place.

She could not separate that from emotion. Couldn't excise it from what she felt for him.

Whether it was anger or love, there was always something. Always something bigger than she was.

She had loved him back then. Truly. Desperately. Had been ready to spend the rest of her life with him. But then she had to face the fact that she didn't know him. Then he had broken her heart. Then he had swept her off to a castle and shown her demonstrations of power the likes of which she had never seen before.

She had loved the man he was. She didn't know how she felt about this man. This man she had just married. This man who was, sadly, the reality of her fantasy lover, who she'd had over long weekends every couple of months.

She felt silly just then. That she had managed to create such intense feelings for someone that she really hadn't spent all that much time with. That she had allowed herself to fall in love with a man who was so clearly a work of fiction. And that she was now bound to his true self, someone who would never love her. Someone who would only take.

They continued to make their way through the reception, managing to speak to just about everyone but each other.

And then came the time for their grand exit. It was very traditional, with rice thrown as they walked out of the elegant reception hall. She tried to smile. Tried to look like a new bride should. But she found she could not. It was far too difficult. Not when she felt like she was made of lead.

They made their way outside. It was cold and crisp, the night air like a baptism, washing away the events of the day.

But only for a moment.

He led her to the palace, up the steps and in through the massive doors.

They stopped in the entryway, and he regarded her closely. "This is your home now," he said. "Truly. It is a part of you."

She looked around, her pulse throbbing a steady rhythm at the base of her throat. "And to think, my biggest aspiration was perhaps to one day own a house in a nice neighborhood."

"Well, look at it this way. You won't have to deal with a homeowner's association here."

"Just legions of staff and a husband who thinks he rules the world."

"Only a country," he responded. The heat in his dark eyes grew more intense, and he lowered his head, his face a breath away from hers. "Let's go to bed."

"I told you. I told you that I was not…that we were not…"

Something changed in his expression then. He was still perfectly pressed. Still dressed in that meticulously tailored tuxedo he had worn to the wedding. His hair was perfectly styled, not a bit of it out of place.

But it was like a switch had been thrown, and every last vestige of civility was gone from his face.

He was wild just then. Feral.

A predator who had most definitely set his sights on her.

"I know what you said," he responded. "But I made vows to you before my country. Before my ancestors. And I, for my part, intend to keep them. You may not wish to have me as your husband, but I am going to make you my wife."

And then he swept her up into his arms, holding her against his hard chest. She was too shocked to protest. He propelled them both toward the stairs, toward his room.

She knew then that the decision had been made. That, as with all things, once Raphael had set his mind to something, he would not be deterred.

She held on to him, because, after all, she didn't want him to drop her. Held on to him until he brought them both to his chamber, a set of rooms that she had not been in before. He carried her over the threshold, as though he were any groom on his wedding night.

He turned and shut the doors, the sound one of absolute finality.

Then he faced her, his expression all lean hunger.

"And now, my wife," he said, taking a step toward her, "you will be mine."

CHAPTER NINE

BAILEY SEARCHED HIS face, looking for a hint of calculation. Searching for an indication that this was part
of his plan.

But there was nothing. That cool sophistication was
gone. Burned away. He wasn't the man she'd met in
the diner back in the States, and he wasn't the prince.

He was something else entirely. Something foreign
and familiar all at once.

He advanced on her, his eyes a broad spectrum of
flame, burning with every dark emotion. Rage. Need.
Fear.

Of himself or her she didn't know.

It didn't really matter, either, because an answer to
that wouldn't change his course. Wouldn't change what
was about to happen here. She backed against the wall,
letting him advance on her.

He reached out, grabbing hold of the delicate neckline of her wedding gown and tugging hard. The whis-
per-thin layers of fabric tore, the bodice separating at
the seams, exposing the strapless, lacy bra she wore
underneath.

She gasped, pressing herself more firmly against
the wall.

"Is that how you look at me now?" he asked. "As though I am your enemy?" He cupped her cheek, sliding his thumb across her delicate skin. "As though you don't know me? As though I have not known your body in nearly every way possible?"

"That was different," she said, her tone stiff. "It is different. I don't know you. Not anymore. I never did. The man that I met, the man that I thought you were, doesn't exist. And I'm not going to have sex with a stranger."

"A stranger?" He chuckled, a humorless sound. Then he leaned in, pressing a kiss to her neck, his lips hot and enticing against her skin. "Would a stranger know that if he were to touch you here," he said, sliding his hand down to cup her breast, his thumb resting beneath the lower curve, "that you will start trembling?"

Her traitorous body did exactly that. Shaking beneath his touch, a quivering, needy thing. She was every inch his creature, and he knew it. The bastard knew it.

"Would a stranger know," he said, "that if he were to taste you like this—" he slid his tongue down the side of her neck "—that you will go up in flames?"

She did. Just like that, she did.

"Trust isn't the same thing," she said, panting. She was ashamed that she was so transparent, but she didn't know if there was anything for it.

"I don't care about your trust, *amore mia*. I care about this." He kissed the edge of her mouth, and a lightning bolt shot through her.

She turned her head to the side, closing her eyes tight. "No," she said.

He growled, gripping her arms and looking into her eyes. "What will it take? What do I have to do? I have already lowered myself to admit to you that you make me burn. That I have not been the same since the moment that I saw you in that diner. I have confessed these things to you, and it is not enough. What will it take?" he ground out.

"N-nothing," she said, the lie tasting bitter on her lips. "There's nothing you can do."

"Do you want me to beg?" he asked, the words hard, full of disdain. "Is that what you want? My waitress wife, do you suppose that you are worthy of me lowering myself for you?"

"I suppose that I deserve nothing less than absolute contrition from the man who abandoned me when I was pregnant with his child. The man who would never know that he was having a baby were it not for a freak change of circumstances." And that was not a lie.

"Contrition doesn't come for free." His black eyes glittered like obsidian. Hard. Sharp. "Perhaps you should remind me of what I enjoyed about you in the first place. Because at the moment, I am having a difficult time remembering."

"Or, perhaps," she said, "you can go to your room and find comfort with your right hand. I am not a thing that you can use. I am a woman. You cannot treat me like something you can simply retrieve at will, then toss back when you're finished."

He dropped to his knees in front of her, curling his fingers around the material of the gown as he went, dragging it down into a pool of ruined material on the floor. "Begging is what you require then?"

Her breath hitched. "I didn't say that."

"You would have me beg to be with my own wife. Then so be it." He looked up at her, his expression hard, and then he grabbed hold of the waistband of her white lace panties, tugging them to her knees. "Consider this my supplication."

"Raphael—"

Whatever she had been about to say was lost as his strong, firm hands grabbed hold of her hips, steadying her. Then, he leaned in, inhaling deeply, pressing his face against the tender skin of her inner thigh. "I have dreamed of this," he rasped. "I have dreamed of you."

He moved to her center, sliding his tongue over wet, needy flesh, tasting her deeply. She shivered, pleasure cutting into her like a knife. She reached out, grabbing hold of his shoulder, curling her fingers around his jacket, clinging to him.

Was she so weak?

As he moved even more deeply, his tongue created a wicked kind of magic that moved through her body like a dark enchantment.

She wanted to cry. Because of how good it felt. Because of how weak she felt. Because she was failing herself. But she realized she wanted to have him force this seduction on her. She wanted to submit to it. To tell herself that she was unwilling. That all the power was with him, so that she could absolve herself of any sin. Of any guilt.

You want it. You want him.

She squeezed her eyes shut, letting go of him. But she didn't move away from him. She raised her arms up over her head, pressing her knuckles firmly into the wall, as though she were releasing her culpability in this.

Her heart beat a steady rhythm, each and every pulse calling her a liar. As Raphael continued to push her higher, further, faster. He was ruthless in his exploration of her, his tongue and fingers seeking out each delightful point of pleasure.

He dragged his fingers through her slick folds, pressed a finger deep inside her as he continued the wicked assault with his tongue.

She hadn't allowed herself pleasure since he had left her. It had been punishment for her stupidity, and then, when she had come here to the palace, something she refused to allow herself because she would only be imagining Raphael.

She was strung so tight she was certain that it would take very little to snap her in two.

He knew it, too. He could feel how wet she was for him, how needy. She knew that he could feel her now, her internal muscles tightening around him as he continued to pleasure her. He knew how close she was to the edge.

That bit of humiliation should have pulled her back. Instead, it spurred her on. Brought her arousal up to impossible heights.

"Raphael," she gasped. "Raphael... I can't."

"You can," he said, his breath hot on the source of her pleasure. "And you will. Come for me, Bailey."

The command was as arrogant as any he'd ever issued. As though he, and he alone, had dominion over her body. As though she were powerless to resist any command he might issue, even one such as this.

He was right.

The words pushed her over the edge, sending her hurtling down toward the very bottom of an abyss. And when she hit, she shattered. She became a thousand sparkling pieces, shimmering with pleasure, with the glorious release that made her feel weightless, free. For the first time since her life had been broken apart and glued back together, badly, she felt free.

She felt like herself.

As though he had not just given her a physical release but had released a part of her she had ruthlessly squashed, shamed, left for dead.

She inhaled sharply, and then, suddenly, he was in front of her again, claiming her mouth with his, the taste of her desire on his lips. Carnal. Wild.

He swept her back into his arms, carrying her across the room and depositing her on the bed. Her heart tripped over itself as she watched those deft, blunt fingers working the buttons on his shirt, wrenching his tie free, casting the last vestiges of civility down to the floor.

She drank in the sight of him, hunger roaring through her, as though she had not just found release.

The dim light cast his muscles into sharp relief, the dips and hollows of his abs exaggerated in the glow cast over him by the one lamp that was lit. She was breathless. Caught up in her desire. Just as she had been from the beginning.

There was no thought of consequences. No deference paid to self-preservation. What was the point? She might live a life preserved, but she wouldn't be herself. She would be squished and hidden. Safe but unused. Like a book that had never been read.

She watched, transfixed, as he worked his belt through the buckle, slid it slowly through the loops on his pants. She looked up, looked into his eyes. They burned her, straight down to her center, down to her soul. It wasn't enough that he had complete and total reign over her body, he seemed to demand it in every other capacity, as well.

Nothing more could be expected of Raphael, not really.

His arrogance knew no boundaries—why should it find any here?

She let her eyes drop again, and this time she was held transfixed by the outline of his erection, the absolute evidence of his desire for her. That he was just as weak, just as mortal as she was right now.

It had been so easy to remember the control this yawning, needy thing had exerted over her that she had forgotten about the power she held over him. How had that happened? Hadn't he demonstrated it when he'd fallen to his knees in front of her?

He had shown her, at every turn, that she held sway over him, and yet she had focused on the needy sense of powerlessness inside herself.

Something inside her turned, like a key in a lock, and she felt as though she was seeing all of this differently now. As though a revelation had tumbled down upon her, and she couldn't go back to viewing it quite as she had before.

She rose up onto her knees, reaching behind her and undoing the four little hooks that held her bra in place. She threw the insubstantial confection down to the floor, kneeling there before him, completely naked now. She refused to hide, refused to cower.

Refused to feel ashamed.

That had nothing to do with Raphael, or anything he had ever made her feel. But with herself. She had been bound up in this idea of failure. That desiring Raphael, that desiring anyone, had led her to her doom. That it made her lesser.

But all of that was her baggage. Bound up in cracked pride, because she had always been just a little bit disdainful of her mother and her actions. But it was only pride. Pride that kept her bound and lonely, that would never keep her warm at night, that would never bring her any sense of fulfillment. And maybe Raphael wouldn't either. Maybe this was simply the road to fresh heartbreak.

But she wanted him. And he wanted her back.

It was enough for now. For this moment.

"You made me wait too long," he said, his voice rough.

He shoved his pants down his lean hips, uncovering his body. Her breath rushed from her lungs. It had been way too long since she had seen him naked. Of course, images of him were burned into her brain, fantasies that wouldn't leave her alone even when she desperately needed them to.

But it wasn't the same. Wasn't the same as being so close to him she could touch him. Could taste him.

She moved to the edge of the bed, reaching out slowly, curling her fingers around his shoulder. Then she bent down, kissing his chest lightly. His muscle jumped beneath her lips, his entire body jerking backward, as though he had been burned.

Oh, yes, she had power here.

She nibbled her way up to his jaw, traced that square angle down to his chin with the tip of her tongue, then worked her way up to his lips, sliding her tongue between them, tasting him in a way that mimicked what he had done between her thighs only a few moments ago.

He wrapped his arm around her waist, growling, pushing her down onto the bed, onto her back. He kissed her deeply, taking absolutely no quarter, employing no gentleness at all. But that was fine. That wasn't what she needed. She needed him out of control, as he had been from the moment they had first come into this bedroom. That realization made something bloom, hot and hopeful, in her chest.

This wasn't calculated. This was nothing like their cake tasting two weeks ago. He wasn't doing this to manipulate. He was doing it because he had no other choice. Because he was at the end of his control.

Satisfaction pooled hot and low in her stomach, arousal wrenching itself tighter inside her. His hardness was settled between her legs, sliding against where she was already beginning to feel needy for him again. But an orgasm alone wouldn't be enough this time. She needed to be filled by him. Needed him inside her.

The words hovered on the edge of her lips, but she felt like they might cost her something much dearer than she was willing to pay. There wasn't room for that.

"I want you," she said. "I want you inside of me."

He groaned, the sound a prayer and a curse all at once. Then the blunt head of his arousal pressed up against the entrance to her body, and he tested her, slowly, taking all the care he had taken with her the first time.

Tears stung her eyes. She didn't want tenderness. She wanted fierce, hot and fast. She wanted to satisfy this growling beast inside her.

She braced her hands on his back, then slid them down to his rear, grabbing hold of him tightly and urging him deep inside her. She gasped as he filled her, wholly and completely, nearly to the point of pain.

She relished it. All of it.

She looked up at him, at the tension in his face, the cords of his neck standing out, evidence of the intense amount of power it was taking for him to control himself. She loved that. Seeing how profoundly she affected him. Truly realizing that she wasn't alone in this insanity.

He had lied to her. He had broken her trust.

But this was true. It was real, and it was honest. It was everything. She wasn't entirely sure she knew everything of who he was. Wasn't sure where the truth of the man she had first met ended and the reality of this prince who she'd married began.

She didn't know. She wasn't sure she ever would. But this, this meeting of their bodies, this intense, deep connection that occurred when the two of them were together, was honest. It was the same now as it had been then. He didn't feel like a stranger.

She knew him in her soul.

She knew him in this honesty. In his every touch and his every thrust as he began to move inside her. This was real. Pure and true, and the fact that she had ever felt ashamed seemed wrong now.

She exulted in it. In him. In the rightness of it. Nothing had felt right for so many months now, but this did.

She was caught up in it, in him, swept away on a tide of pleasure as release washed through her again and again. And when he shattered, when he found his own, she gloried in that, too. In his big body shuddering as he spent himself deep inside her.

When it was over, there was no sound but their fractured breathing echoing off the walls, nothing but a profound feeling of finality. It was no longer a question, whether they would end up here. Because they had. No longer a question of whether he would continue to pursue, and she would continue to resist. It was done. And now that it was, she knew there would be no going back.

And now she wondered why she had wanted to in the first place. Raphael was the only man she had ever wanted. It didn't matter whether she thought he was a businessman or knew that he was a prince. It didn't matter if it was back in the United States or if it was here.

He was the thing her heart desired, more than anything. And she was justly entitled to her anger and her heartbreak over how he had treated her. But they had this chance. This chance to be married. To be together. And she had been choosing to cling to anger.

Anger was a hot, destructive shield to use. And she was beginning to realize there was a great cost to protection anyway. For the sake of pride, for the fear of being hurt, she had been intent on keeping something she wanted from herself.

All of it tangled up in that self-flagellation she'd been lost in for so many months.

If she was going to live with him, raise a child with him, be his wife, there was going to be a certain amount of letting go involved. Of deciding to put the past behind them. Of making where they ended up more important than where they had begun.

She breathed in his scent, wrapped her arms around his neck, held him close. And she let all the rest go.

CHAPTER TEN

WHEN RAPHAEL WOKE up in the morning there was a woman wrapped around him. It was notable, because it had been so long since that had happened. He opened his eyes, looking out across the broad expanse of his chamber. And he saw a wedding dress, torn into two pieces and left on the floor like a moth that had been stripped of its wings.

He remembered then. Backing Bailey against the wall. Tearing the top of her gown. Holding her tightly against his mouth while he had unleashed all the pent-up anger and need that roared through him like an untamed animal.

Yes, suddenly he remembered all of that.

He sat up, and the swift motion disturbed Bailey, who had been wound up in him in such a way it was impossible for him to take a breath without affecting her.

She opened her eyes, the foggy, sleepy blue sending a wave of longing through him that made his teeth ache. He had no idea what that meant. No idea why. She was here, and she was naked, which meant there was absolutely nothing for him to long for. He had everything.

This woman, who was now his wife, this palace and

his kingdom. There was nothing else. No reason for the hollow, bone-chilling ache that pervaded him now.

And yet it persisted.

"Good morning," she mumbled.

"Is it?" he asked, clipped.

He found himself extricating himself from her hold and getting out of bed, walking across the room, kneeling down to examine the damage he had done to the dress.

"It's a little bit late for regret," she said, sitting up, holding the sheet up over her breasts. Her cheeks were extra pink this morning, her mouth a bit swollen. He could not remember how many times he had reached for her last night, desperate to sate the desire for her that had built itself inside him to a fever pitch.

She bore the marks of that. Of his passion. Of his selfish desperation. As did the dress.

"I should have thought it was never too late for regret. In fact, you have been demonstrating that to me over the course of the past month. Just how very much you regret me. I'm beginning to think that perhaps you're not entirely crazy to feel that way."

She frowned. "Yes, well, nice to know you won't become completely crazy, now that you've married me."

"I wasn't myself last night."

"Yes, you were. You were completely yourself. You felt you were entitled to something that you weren't being given and reacted as you do."

"You said you wanted me," he said. He was thinking of that moment when she had told him, with that desperate, needy sigh on her lips, that she wanted him inside her. She had said that. She had wanted it.

"Yes, I did. I have. From the moment you came back to me, I've wanted you. That isn't the issue."

"What is?" He stood, holding the remaining pieces of the dress in his hands. "Because, for someone who claims to want me, you did an admirable job of resisting me at every turn."

"I don't want to be a salve for your wounded ego. And I don't want to be a challenge to your masculine pride. That's what I was saying. You're a man who is accustomed to having everything he wants. I don't want to be just another one of those things. I want to mean something more than that to you."

"You want to cost me something," he said, understanding filling him slowly. "That is what you said the other day. That my gesture with the cake was empty because there was no cost to me."

"You've cost me an awful lot, Raphael. I don't suppose it's extremely selfish to wish that I cost you a little something, too."

"You think you have not? I have vowed never to touch another woman."

"The bare minimum requirement for marriage, I should think."

"I am the first person in my family to marry for a reason other than political gain." Finally, finally that elicited some reaction from her. Finally that caused a change in her expression. "I broke centuries of tradition to marry you. You have no connection that could possibly benefit Santa Firenze. What I did, I did for our baby. Yes, I could have hidden you away. I could have paid you off, given you some exorbitant sum of money, but that isn't what I wanted. I wanted my child here. With me."

"And me?" she asked, her voice small.

He let the dress fall to the floor, and he crossed the space between them. He looked at her, and she turned her gaze away. He reached out, taking hold of her chin, directing her eyes back to his. "I have not been with another woman since the day I met you. When I broke things off with you, I did my very best to try and turn my focus to Allegra. She and I never had much of a connection. We hardly had anything to do with each other. She and her entire family would accompany me on various holidays, but she and I were never tempted to spend time alone. She was ideal, in other words."

"How is it ideal to not want your wife?"

"It is ideal to not find your wife a…a distraction. I hoped… I sincerely hoped that when I ended things with you I would be able to find some sort of desire in myself for her. She was going to be my wife, after all, and a life wanting someone else was unthinkable."

"And how did that go for you?" she asked, looking comically hopeful.

"The next time I saw her after you and I broke up, I purposed that I would kiss her." He cleared his throat. "A real kiss. Not just a kiss on her head. But then I saw her and… I could not. I kept seeing you. Every time I saw a woman with blond hair, I would hope that she would turn around and it would be you. I want you to distraction, Bailey. It is wholly inconvenient."

"So, I'm not a completely negligible part of this package?"

"I suppose I wasn't being entirely truthful when I said that I didn't marry for any kind of gain. When I saw you walking down the aisle toward me yesterday, I realized that your strength is only going to be an asset to me, and to this country. You may not have political connections, but I admire you. You worked very hard to get where you are in life, and I don't know very many people who can say the same."

"You work hard, Raphael."

"Undoubtedly," he responded. "But I was given all of this. That's different."

As soon as the words left his mouth, he realized how true it was. How his confidence, his power, was built on something handed down. And in order for it to be handed down effectively, his father had handed his arrogance and certainty down, as well.

He had molded him perfectly. Taught him with so many gestures that there was nothing he could not have while demonstrating at the same time there was nothing more important than the country.

"That's more impressive in some regards," Bailey said. "Seeing as when you haven't earned something often it means less. And it would be easy for you to feel less of an obligation to your country because you didn't achieve your position through hard work. So, I can easily make an argument to support the fact that you're actually pretty amazing."

"Suddenly you have kind words for me, Bailey? Please tell me you did not sustain a head injury last night."

She smiled, a rather impish expression that tugged something deep inside him. It was strange, and not entirely unpleasant, to have a moment where she wasn't at odds with him. He had told himself that it didn't matter, that the only thing that was really bothering him was the prolonged celibacy.

He had told himself that he didn't miss her companionship, just her body. That the entire relationship they'd had back in Colorado was something of a farce. A strange experiment on his end. Being with a woman who had no idea who he was, interacting with her as a typical man would.

But her smile sent such a ferocious flood of warmth through his body that it was difficult to believe that now.

He wanted to do something for her. But he couldn't think what. He had married her, after all. Made her a princess. He wasn't exactly sure what you did to top that gesture. Though, perhaps, a honeymoon.

"Have you ever been to Paris?" he asked.

"No," she said. "But I still don't have a passport."

"You are the princess of Santa Firenze. Your travel documents will be sorted by the palace." He watched her cheeks turn pink, her pleasure obvious. "You are excited about the idea of going to Paris?"

"Of course I am. Who wouldn't be? I've dreamed about seeing it, but I never thought I would. My fantasies ran toward cutting myself above the poverty line. Getting a good job. World travel never really featured."

"Well, world travel is essentially in your job description now."

"Lucky me," she said. "And I mean that. That was not sarcasm."

"No sarcasm?" he asked, with mock shock coloring his tone. "It's amazing you didn't injure yourself."

"You're giving me Paris. I felt, at the least, I owed you a little sincerity."

His chest tightened. He wasn't sure why, but he had the strange feeling of impending doom, rolling over his shoulders like a dark, heavy cloak. "I wouldn't give me too much. But I shall alert the staff of our plans, and they will pack your things."

"We're going now?"

"Paris has waited for you long enough."

CHAPTER ELEVEN

THE FIRST SIGHT of the city took Bailey's breath away. Everything was so old. She had noticed the same thing in Santa Firenze. Maybe that was a strange observation, but everything in the United States was relatively new, particularly things in the West. They didn't have this sort of history, embedded into every brick, into each and every fine scroll carved into the stonework.

The art, the history, was like a living thing, making the architecture, the very air around them, seem like so much more.

They drove along a road that bordered the Seine, the gray water reflecting the clouds above, the row of buildings, old churches and museums on the other side of them like an impenetrable sentry wall.

The penthouse that Raphael had secured for them was rich in details, from the crown molding down to the gold fixtures in the kitchen and bathroom. There was a spread of cheese and bread waiting for them upon arrival, along with a bottle of champagne that Bailey would not be availing herself of.

The master suite was brilliantly appointed, and the closet was already full. Full of beautiful garments that,

Raphael informed her, a personal shopper had chosen specifically for Bailey.

Among them was a rich, green gown made of flowing silk. Silk that would undoubtedly show her growing pregnancy.

"When am I supposed to wear this?" she asked, brushing her fingertips down the fine fabric.

"Tonight," he said, his tone nonchalant.

"I didn't know we had plans."

"There is a private dinner and art exhibition at the Musée d'Orsay tonight. I thought it was something you would probably enjoy, and I thought that the man in charge of the event would likely enjoy the attendance of royalty, even if it were last minute. I was correct. At least on that score. I hope I was correct about you, too."

His expression was so sincere, his tone hopeful. It was…it was so unusual to see Raphael looking something less than certain. But he did. Just as he had done this morning after their wedding night. He had been concerned that he had crossed a line. The fact that he was capable of such concern was encouraging.

He wasn't pulling that veil of arrogance back into place at every opportunity. At least, not today.

"Of course I want to go. A beautiful dress, wonderful food, famous art. What's not to like?"

His smile was slow, and he nodded. "Yes. You are correct."

"You were afraid that I wouldn't like a beautiful dress and a private evening at a museum?"

"I am eternally at a loss with you," he said, his frustration clear. "I had imagined that you would fall to your knees in gratitude the moment I told you I would marry you. That you would see what an honor I was bestowing upon you when you caught sight of my palace. So far, you have been distinctly unimpressed with me."

"It's not you I'm unimpressed with," she responded. "Just the things."

"I am the things," he said.

She frowned, taking a step toward him, reaching up, pressing her palm to his cheek. "How can that be? Didn't I meet you before I knew you had any of that?"

"That was different."

Her heart sank a little bit. "Yes," she said, "it was different."

It was different because it had been completely genuine on her part and a ruse on his. Different because she had imagined they would have a future, while he knew for a fact they wouldn't.

"We will leave in a couple of hours for the party."

"I might want to… I mean, I might take a walk. Just for an hour or so."

He frowned. "You can't do that."

"I'm in Paris. I would like to have a look around." And she needed just a little bit of distance to catch her breath. It was difficult to be under the influence of Raphael. He was so very much. She was trying to find that line between protecting herself and sacrificing herself.

She didn't want to wall him off, not completely, but she needed to have some defenses in place, surely.

"You are royalty. You cannot simply walk around the streets by yourself."

"You really think anyone will recognize me?"

"You are the favored headline at the moment, *cara*. I think you would be recognized within seconds."

"Then I guess I'll get ready," she said, monotone.

"What else could I possibly want to do in Paris but apply makeup?"

"How quickly the tide turns." His expression was grim. "I'm not trying to ruin your life. I'm just being realistic."

She frowned. "Okay." She let out a long, slow breath. "I'm sorry. I'm actually being a little unreasonable. I'll just get ready."

By the time she got herself beautified, it was time to go. She looked at herself in the vanity mirror, frowning. Yes, it was very apparent that she was pregnant.

"I hope you're prepared for the fact that we are essentially making an announcement tonight," she said, walking out into the main living area of the penthouse.

Raphael looked up from his newspaper, his jaw going slack. "Oh," was all he said. More of a noise than an actual response.

"What does that mean?"

He stood, closing the distance between them. He stopped just short of her, not touching her at all.

"Come on, Raphael—you have to say something, or I'm going to go back into the bedroom and change into my sweats."

"No, you will not," he said, his expression fierce. "You are perfect. A jewel come to life."

"I didn't even have a professional makeup artist tonight," she said, pressing for yet more compliments, because this one made her feel warm all over. "And," she added, reaching up to play with a strand of loose hair, "I did my hair, too."

"It suits you. Possibly because it is you. Utterly and completely."

He leaned in, kissing her forehead. It was a strange,

affectionate gesture, void of the usual carnal sexuality that was typically laced through their other kisses.

Then he angled his head and kissed her lips. This one had all the usual carnal sexuality and then some.

"We have to go," he said. "Or I will have you out of that dress, and we will never make it to the museum."

"People are going to know I'm pregnant," she prodded. "You didn't say anything about that."

"I'm proud of your pregnancy. Of the fact you are my wife, that you are carrying my child. I'm pleased to show the world."

"That was the right thing to say," she said, stretching up on her toes and kissing him.

"There's a first time for everything," he said, amusement in his voice.

Somehow they managed to make it to the museum with all of Bailey's makeup intact, which was a miracle, seeing as Raphael had done his very best to kiss most of it off in the car. The museum was beautiful, set for a dinner in one room with ornate table settings and large bouquets of lushly colored flowers.

Men in black suits and women in gowns that ran the spectrum of the rainbow milled about the room making conversation, moving through the large building, looking at the various exhibits that were open to the guests.

The hors d'oeuvres that were being served looked lovely, but Bailey found she was more interested in examining the art.

She managed to tear herself away from one of the overly enthusiastic women who had grabbed her upon entry, excited to meet a princess. And had been obviously angling to get Bailey to comment on her condition. Bailey found it all extremely strange. Being the center of any kind of attention.

Only a few short weeks ago, she'd been the wait-staff. Now she was a princess. A guest of honor. It was enough to make her head spin. And definitely enough to make her seek out a quiet moment.

She made her way to the wing of the museum that housed the sculptures. Bailey wandered through the exquisite marble figures, marveling at the expressiveness of the features. They weren't cold, in spite of the smooth, white stone that was used to fashion them. In fact, she could almost believe that any moment they might come to life.

She paused in front of the statue of a kneeling woman, one of the rare female figures that was fully clothed.

"Here you are."

She turned to see Raphael coming toward her. Her heart clenched tight. And so did other things. Really, he looked amazing in a tux. He shouldn't wear anything else. Unless he was naked. He could be naked.

"Over relating to the plight of Joan of Arc?"

She looked down at the statue's small plaque. "I guess I was."

"Great is your martyrdom."

"Sometimes it feels like it is."

"A very brave creature you are, Bailey Harper."

"That's Princess Bailey DeSantis to you," she said, keeping her tone arch.

"My apologies for the grave error." He moved closer to her. "You're enjoying the art?"

"Yes. I've never seen anything like it. I mean, I've been to museums before, but nothing with works like this. This is…it's exquisite."

"You know, only this floor is open to guests tonight."

"I know."

"I made arrangements to get us up to one of the top floors. I thought you might like to see Manet."

She looked over at him, her heart pounding heavily. "I would… I would love that. But it isn't supposed to be open."

"I am Prince Raphael DeSantis," he said. "The rules of mere mortal men do not apply to me. Nor should they."

She laughed. She couldn't help herself. "I'm sorry—sometimes I forget I'm married to a demigod."

"You wound me so. Only a demigod?"

"I'm sorry. Jove reincarnated?"

"Much better." He extended his arm. "Shall we?"

They took an elevator until it was required they take the stairs, then made their way to a silent floor, high above the activity that was happening below. The settings were sparse, nothing but blocks of black walls dividing a large space. But that was because the show belonged to the artwork that was hanging there.

Raphael stayed silent while they wandered through the displays, while she paused at the paintings. Strangely, while standing in front of one that featured a woman at a picnic—the men were dressed, and she was naked—Bailey could suddenly relate to that woman. Uncovered like that for all to see while her companions were covered still. Out of place, where they blended.

Bailey's eyes filled with tears.

One tear tracked down her cheek, and she tried to wipe it away before Raphael saw.

"What's wrong?" he asked.

"Nothing is wrong," she said, her throat tight. "Except…this is beautiful. And it's so much more than I ever thought I would have. It just feels wonderful right now, and I can't believe that something won't go horribly wrong."

It all rolled over her like a thunderstorm, lightning and rain lashing at her soul. She was in this beautiful place, this place that had only ever been a dream to her, a place she had imagined would always only be a dream, with a man who transcended fantasy. A man she hadn't known she was waiting for, a man she had never imagined she could possibly have.

She was…she was a princess. She was going to be a mother.

She was suddenly standing in a life she had never expected, one she could still barely believe she was living.

"What if I wake up and it's all just a dream?" she whispered.

He put his warm hands on her shoulders, sliding them down her bare arms, holding her tight. Then he leaned in from his position behind her, his breath hot against her neck. "Does this feel like a dream?"

"No," she said, her voice trembling now.

"Why would you think this was a dream?"

"Because. I used to have such vivid dreams when I was a child. I would go to bed hungry, and then spend all night dreaming that I was somewhere warm. About to have dinner. And then I would wake up just as hungry as I'd been when I'd gone to sleep and I would cry. Because it wasn't real. And that was when I realized it wasn't enough to dream. Because dreams aren't real, Raphael. They aren't." She swallowed hard. "When I met you…that was the first time I'd dreamed since I was a child. Only then I woke up. And you weren't any more real than all those other dreams. I was still hungry." She forced a smile. "And now I'm here, but it's just so difficult to believe that I won't wake up again and find it all gone."

He wrapped his arm around her waist, his large hand flat on her round stomach. "I am here," he said, his voice fierce. "I am your husband. I made vows to you, and I will keep them."

She nodded, unable to speak around the lump in her throat.

"This is beautiful," she said finally, dashing away another tear. "So beautiful it made me cry. So perfect... I can barely believe it." She turned to face him, his face another piece of art in a room filled with masterpieces. And she realized then that she was all his. Always and forever. That there was no self-protection to be found, and there never had been.

She loved him. With everything she was and everything she would be.

"Are you ready to go back down for dinner?"

"Yes," she said.

They began to walk back toward the stairs, and then she stopped in front of a massive clock built into a window, overlooking the city below.

The buildings were lit, casting a golden glow onto the river. She stepped up, moving nearer to it, leaning against the railing that was designed to keep people a safe distance from the glass, and gazing at the scene.

"Do you still feel like you're dreaming?" he asked, moving closer to her.

"No matter where you come from, I'm not sure this can feel real."

"A private art showing? One of the most beautiful

views in the world? That feels all too real to me. But you...you might very well be a dream."

She turned to face him, her heart thundering fast and hard. "Me? I thought it was a lot closer to a nightmare."

"Bailey," he said, and not for the first time she was struck by the absurdity of her extremely American name spoken in his cultured accent.

But he made it sound sexy. And no one else had ever managed to do that.

He pressed his hand between her shoulder blades, drawing his fingertips down the line of her spine until his hand reached the rounded curve of her butt.

Her breath hitched as his touch became more and more intimate, something about the effect of his hand over the silk making her feel extra sensitive.

He leaned in close, pressing a kiss to her neck. "I promise you—this is very real."

She closed her eyes, then forced them back open. Forced herself to keep her eyes on the incredible view below as he began to gather the fabric of her skirt into his hand. Began to draw it up her legs.

She gasped as the cool air hit her skin, and he moved his palm over the bare curve of her bottom.

Then he moved his hand, dipping it between her legs, his fingers delving beneath the edge of her panties.

"Raphael," she said, her voice a fierce whisper. "Someone might come up."

"No one is allowed to come up here." He shifted his movements, pushing his fingertips forward, grazing that sensitized bundle of nerves at the apex of her thighs. "And even if they did, I would simply order them to turn back around."

"But they'll see."

"Then let them," he said, his voice firm, authoritative. "You are my woman." There was something about that proclamation that affected her on a visceral level. He had called her his wife, he had called himself her husband. But there was something different about this. Something that laid elemental ownership that went beyond legal paperwork.

She let out a slow, shuddering breath as he continued to stroke her. "Do you...do you mean that?"

He wrapped his arm around her, grabbing hold of her chin, his forearm braced against her chest as he held her against him. "My word is law," he growled, rocking his hips forward, his hardness brushing against her.

"Of course it is. But...but I need to know."

"What do you need to know, *cara*?"

"Am I your woman? Or am I a burden? A duty?"

He hesitated for only a moment. "Everything I have was presented to me. That is my duty. What was passed to me. What I inherited. But you... I chose you."

Relief washed through her, tears prickling her eyes. She just couldn't face being a millstone around his neck. Not after her mother.

He *chose* her.

Raphael held her tight for a moment, stroking her until she was gasping for breath. Until she could hardly see straight, the city lights blurring in front of her, turning into a glittering, impressionistic work of art right before her eyes.

She clung to the railing. It was the only thing keeping her upright.

Then his fingers were replaced by his arousal, as he flexed his hips forward, pushing his erection through her slick folds.

"Bend forward," he commanded, pressing his hand against her stomach and drawing the lower half of her body back slightly as she complied with his order. He slipped his hand to her hip, holding her tight as he tested her entrance with the blunt head of him.

"We can't do this here," she said, her whisper swallowed up by the expansive room.

"Do you want to?" he asked, pressing in another inch.

She lowered her head, pleasure chasing need down her spine. "Yes." She shuddered.

"Then we can."

He pushed home then, a harsh groan on his lips as he seated himself fully inside her. He turned her face, kissing her as he established a maddeningly slow rhythm that was designed to torment her—it must have been. He kept her poised, on the brink, sending little ripples of pleasure that promised to become waves but never did, as he kept himself in firm control.

She began to rock back against him, meeting him thrust for thrust, trying to increase the pressure, to entice him to go harder, deeper, faster. And when those subtle enticements failed to fracture his command, she said the words. Over and over again, until she felt him splinter, until he began to break apart, piece by royal piece.

His hold became punishing, his blunt fingertips digging into her flesh as he pounded himself into her, over and over again. He was saying things, harsh, broken things, in a language she didn't know, his breath hot on her neck as he whispered promises her body understood even if her brain did not.

His arm was an iron bar across her chest, his grip tight at the base of her throat, while he slipped his other hand between her thighs, working wicked magic at the center of her pleasure.

"Please," he said, his voice as fractured as the rest of him. "Please. I can't hold on much longer."

His desperation, his plea, was the thing that turned the key, unleashed the flood of pleasure inside her. She came hard, a hoarse cry on her lips as her internal muscles clenched tightly around him.

He held her up as he thrust into her two more times, shaking as he cried out his own pleasure, the sound echoing off the walls around them, a new addition to the gallery that already contained so much beauty. Now it held this. Them.

Surrounded by so much history, it made everything feel more weighty. Made this feel more real. Made it feel like perhaps it wasn't just a dream.

As he held her tight, clung to her while they waited for the aftershocks to stop, she realized there was no way on earth this could be a dream. She never could have spun this out of thin air. She didn't possess the raw material to do it. Her life, that life of hunger and vague neglect, hadn't allowed her to dream of anything half so big.

And it had nothing so much to do with Paris, or the beautiful gown she was wearing, or the fact that Raphael was the most incredibly handsome man she'd ever seen. It was just him. The warm press of his chest against her back, that tight grip he kept on her. Making her so very aware of his strength, and yet so very safe at the same time.

"Would you still like to go down to dinner?" he asked, moving away from her, smoothing her dress back down and turning her to face him. He began to tuck her hair back into place, smoothing her, wiping away a smear of lipstick from below her lip.

"Is there another option?" she asked, sounding as shaky as she felt.

"Perhaps we could take that walk around the city?"

He whisked her quickly back through the museum, with such an air of command about him that no one dared to try to stop them. His hold on her was so possessive, so protective, and she gloried in it. In belonging to him. In feeling like she mattered.

"Are you going to call your driver?"

"No," he said, "we should walk."

He released his hold on her, shifting so that he could clasp her hand, just as he had done that last night in Vail, just before he had broken her heart. That simple, sweet gesture that had meant so much to her then and felt amplified now.

He led her down the sidewalk, the streets still alive even at this late hour. She had a feeling they looked out of place, she in her long black coat, her green dress shimmering around her feet, and Raphael in his tuxedo strolling along the river.

She looked up, her breath catching as she saw the Eiffel Tower in the distance, lit up for the evening.

"I never thought I would see that in person," she said.

"The Eiffel Tower?"

"It's surreal. I've seen it in so many movies…and there it is. Right in front of me."

"Then I think you will enjoy what I have in mind next."

She did. A small café just across the street from the tower. The base was visible from the little alcove they were seated in. They had coffee and simple sandwiches with bread, cheese and ham that tasted anything but simple. It wasn't the lavish, elegant dinner that they would have had if they'd stayed at the museum, but it meant more to her. It meant everything.

Hours passed that felt like minutes, and it was time to start walking back. It was late now, and her feet hurt, but she didn't want to get a car. She wanted to keep walking. She wanted to extend this night, forever. To keep existing in this moment, with the man as he was now. His guard had dropped somewhere along the way, and she wanted to keep him here.

Far too soon, they were back at the penthouse, but it was quickly clear to her that the night wasn't over. He took nearly as long getting her undressed as she had taken to get dressed before they went out.

When he pressed her into the soft mattress, he spent time thoroughly tasting each and every inch of her. Then he went over all those tender places with his hands, taking her to the brink over and over again.

When they both went over, it was together, and with all the pleasure pounding through her, images from earlier in the evening, from their time together in Colorado, mixing together inside her, painting a picture of a reality more beautiful than dreams, there was only one thing she could think to say.

"I love you."

Much later, when Bailey was asleep, Raphael stood on the balcony of the penthouse, gazing out at the city lighting up the night sky below. He wrapped his fingers tightly around the balustrade, Bailey's admission ringing inside him.

He had said nothing in return. And she had fallen asleep soon enough. But a response would be needed. Still, he could not give her the response she wanted.

If he had learned one thing about ruling from his parents, it was that there could be no greater attachment in the entire world than the attachment to the country. To the cause.

Certainly, a man could care for and treat his wife and children well, but love was an entirely separate issue. Love was something reserved for citizens, for the land and old stone buildings, the family history. Love was something much more like patriotism than what Bailey was talking about. At least, in his world.

Love kept its distance. It served others, not always those closest. His father had always made that so very clear. In the rules he established, the limited time he allowed his mother to spend with him.

When you were royalty, love wasn't personal. It was broad, spread out over everything that fell beneath your rule.

It could be expressed least of all beneath your own roof. Not in the ways that were shown on movies and in TV shows. A ruler cared for his subjects by seeing to their needs, and his father had always done much the same with Raphael and his mother.

The things he presented them with were there in his stead.

But still, he would have to say something to her.

He could say the words. They would cost him nothing.

His chest seized up tight at the thought. He had never told a single person that he loved him or her, ever. He didn't like the idea of starting now, particularly not when it was simply to soothe her feelings.

No, there had to be something else.

He took his phone out of his pocket, tapping the screen as he continued to formulate a plan in his mind. Then he dialed the palace in Santa Firenze.

"I'm going to need gifts sent up to the penthouse in Paris by tomorrow morning. A diamond necklace, flowers—enough to fill every surface in the place—and a lavish spread for breakfast. The best croissants you can find, meat, cheese. Something for the princess to drink that doesn't contain alcohol."

He cut the call off, turning and facing the doors to the penthouse. This would suffice. He would make her happy. He knew that he could. He was a man with near limitless power and deep pockets. Whatever she desired, he would give her.

He thought of her face tonight as she had looked at the art, of the way she had begun to weep with happiness. Yes, he could continue to give her things like this. Continue to make her happy. Keep her in this dream she was afraid of losing. She never had to lose it. He would make sure she didn't.

She would not be hungry with him. She would never be cold. She would never want for a damn thing.

As long as she didn't continue to ask for his love.

CHAPTER TWELVE

WHEN BAILEY WOKE up the next morning, Raphael wasn't in bed. There was something niggling at the back of her mind, but she couldn't quite think of what it was. She got up, putting on one of the silk nightgowns that were hanging in the closet. She had slept naked. Honestly, there was no point wearing clothes when Raphael was around.

Still, she was not going to walk into the living room naked.

She stopped the minute she walked out of the bedroom, shocked. There were red roses everywhere. Like grand-gesture-at-the-end-of-a-romantic-comedy level of everywhere.

She walked farther out into the room, noticing a tray set on the coffee table in front of the couch. There was a French press with coffee and a tray laden with pastries. Her stomach growled, a welcome sound after waking up too many mornings feeling vaguely nauseous.

And still, something continued to bother her.

But she figured she would work that out over some *pain au chocolat*.

"You're awake," Raphael said, striding into the room, a wide, flat velvet box clutched in his hand.

"Yes. I am. What's going on? Unless a morning order of flowers and pastries is business as usual for you. Which I kind of think might be a great tradition."

"All for you, *cara*." He moved nearer to her, holding the box up. "As is this."

Inside the box was the most incredible piece of jewelry she had ever seen. An ornate, glittering necklace composed of delicate strands of white gold braided together with gems sprinkled over it like dewdrops. And then, at the center, one large teardrop-shaped diamond that looked like it belonged at the center of a jewel heist.

And then she remembered. Last night, she had told him that she loved him. He had said nothing.

She looked around the room. This was...this was his response.

"That's...it's a lot," she said.

"Not too much for you," he said, his tone sincere, as though he were issuing her the greatest of compliments.

"Thank you," she said, waiting for...she didn't know what she was waiting for. He wasn't going to make a grand pronouncement, not today. But then, maybe it wasn't reasonable to expect one. Maybe she just needed to be patient.

"You don't sound very pleased."

He moved toward her, extending the jewelry box out to her. "I am," she said, taking it from him. "Who wouldn't want diamonds and butter?"

"Would you like to put the necklace on now?"

"No, thank you. I'm still in my pajamas. That would be a little bit ostentatious, don't you think?"

"You're free to be as ostentatious as you like," he said.

"That is a dangerous bit of permission. You have no idea what I'm going to do with it."

"I'm intrigued. I hope to see great acts of ostentatiousness in the near future."

"I will do what I can to oblige you."

"We are a headline this morning," he said casually. "As you suggested we might be."

"Oh," she replied, wincing a little bit. "How unflattering is it?"

"A couple of publications dared to be snide about how I was clearly forced to marry you. But others talked about how longingly you gazed at me during the party last night. And some of them even had photographs of us eating at the café, suggesting that the two of us clearly choose to spend time together in venues that are invisible because we enjoy each other's company, not just to court media attention."

That made her stomach sink. It made her wonder what his motivation had been for last night's impromptu walk through the city. She wondered if it had been a bit more calculated than it had appeared. She gritted her teeth, shutting that thought out. It didn't really matter. What had happened in the museum, in front of the clock, the entire city down below, that had been for the two of them.

So that had to count for something.

Sure, it meant that he wanted sex.

No, it was more than that. It was.

"I'm glad that we turned out a pretty good PR performance," she said, keeping her tone neutral. She was still deciding how she was going to handle all of this.

What it meant that she had told him she loved him and he had responded by buying her more things.

"If you have to be in the headlines, it is best if they're favorable."

"Oh, right. I forgot that all of this was a bit beneath you."

"It's a distraction," he said.

"From what?"

"From the actual job. There should not be so much glory in running a country. It should never be about you."

"Okay, that's interesting coming from the most arrogant man I have ever met."

He lifted a shoulder. "Perhaps you see me as arrogant. But from my point of view, it seems that it would do my country no good to see their ruler as a man who did not possess the utmost confidence in everything he did. Why should they trust me if I don't trust myself?"

"Well, sometimes there is strength in asking for help."

"No, that's a lie that helpless people tell themselves. People who don't want to feel weak, when they are in a desperate position. I don't blame them. If one finds themselves in a desperate position, one must handle it as they see fit. And I suppose there is strength within that. But I am not desperate. Not now, nor have I ever been. My father ruled in this fashion. And he created a nation that was strong, one that has weathered worldwide financial crises and war, without ever entering into either. Should I seek to change the way things are?"

"I suppose not," she said, taking those words and holding them close, turning them over. It was clear to her that he felt showing weakness of any kind was detrimental. Not just to himself but to an entire nation. It was difficult to argue with that. The most she'd ever been in charge of was a goldfish.

What did she know?

"The entire country trusts in me confidently." He lowered his voice then, looking at her, something in his dark eyes softening. "You can, too."

Those words warmed her, comforted her. After a morning of feeling off balance, they were exactly what she needed to hear. Well, if an *I love you* was unavailable, anyway.

"If you say so."

"I do. And my word is law."

"Oh, Raphael." She stood up, pressing her hand to his chest, emotion coursing through her. "I do love you."

She felt him stiffen beneath her touch. But she didn't really care. And suddenly, she was well aware of how she would proceed.

He might not love her yet. But he'd *chosen* her. He'd said. So she was just going to love him. There was no other alternative. Nothing more than keeping everything stuffed down inside, and she didn't want to do that. It would hurt her far more than honesty would.

"Do you have a list of things you wish to see today?" he asked.

Her heart twisted. But she kept her smile firmly in place. "Why don't you surprise me?"

He liked that. She could see it in the satisfied expression on his face. The gesture of trust, her simple admission that he could possibly do a good job with anticipating her needs.

"That," he said, "I can do."

The week in Paris went by too quickly, and when they returned to the palace, Raphael threw himself into dealing with affairs of state. Which, she supposed, was unavoidable seeing as he ran the entire country. He had left it in the capable hands of his staff for a while, but there were most certainly things that only the prince could see to.

She told herself she wasn't lonely. That she didn't miss having him around. That it was fine that she only saw him at night when he came to bed and took her with the kind of passion he withheld from her during the other hours of the day.

Most of all, she told herself that it was okay when he didn't say he loved her, too.

Oh, he had given her absolutely everything. More clothing than she could conceivably wear, especially considering it was maternity wear, and she would only need it for a few more months. Jewelry, books and then last week, an entire wing of the palace. All for her.

One day he had come in with a petite woman clutching a book at his side. "I know that back in Colorado we had discussed you finishing your degree," he said. "I have employed a teacher to assist you. She has compiled accredited curriculum and a university you can work with remotely. I want to make sure you have everything that you were promised and more."

The woman had smiled, looking down at Bailey's increasingly obvious bump. "Of course, we will work around your schedule," she said kindly. "I would not want you to feel overtaxed, Princess."

Nobody had ever cared if she was overtaxed when she was going to the University of Colorado. Nobody had cared that she was sick and tired of waiting tables when she had gotten pregnant before she had a title. Nobody at all.

It was strange to have people care so much about her condition.

And care they did. From the media to the staff at the palace, everyone was doting on her.

She had become a kind of icon for style when it came to pregnancy, but she really didn't feel like she could claim the glory for that. Raphael had appointed her a stylist who assisted her every time she went on an outing. If it were up to her, she would probably be in sweats. Though she had to concede that it wasn't really any more work to put on a dress and leggings.

She was very well taken care of. Possibly more than she had ever been in her entire life. But she still felt… empty. Because things weren't love. All of this wasn't love. It was deference, and it was…well, it was definitely care. But it wasn't what she felt for Raphael.

If there was no baby, she would have wanted him. If there was no title, and there was no expectation about marriage, she still would have wanted him. She had wanted him when she had thought he was just some kind of middle managing pharmaceutical rep.

But he hadn't wanted her. And even though he was doing a wonderful job of taking care of her now, even though he clearly still wanted her, she had doubts. And those doubts were insidious.

The doctor visit today had yielded results she knew would make him happy. The fact that she was having a boy. The kind of heir men like him were best off with. Or so she'd heard.

For some reason she was having a hard time finding the right moment to tell him.

"How are your studies going?" he asked, coming into the room that night.

"They're going very well. Professor Johnson has been extremely patient and helpful. I feel like I haven't even really fallen behind, because getting the one-on-one help has been so valuable."

"Perfect. What exactly are you going to do with a business degree?"

"Well, back when I was in Colorado I imagined that I might open my own business someday. And I thought it might just help me get more comfortable jobs until then. Maybe with slightly better pay."

"And now?"

"I feel like it's still valuable to understand the way things work. To understand a bit about the structure of these things, and where it all fits in with the economy. Surely there's value in that for a princess."

"If you find it valuable, then it is. And I'm sure that you can use it in any way you see fit. There are plenty of different charities you can get involved with. Organizations that would benefit from your insight, I'm sure. But I think a degree is one of the least things you have to offer something like that."

She sensed she was on the cusp of receiving a compliment, and so she pressed further. "Is that right?"

"You are fiercely determined. And a wonderful advocate. I can imagine you will get a great deal done. An iron will combined with the title is a wonderful thing."

"I'm glad you can appreciate my iron will."

"I appreciate it much more now that it isn't being turned on me with as much frequency."

She laughed. "Well, I make no guarantees."

Silence stretched between them, strange and slightly uncomfortable. She was so rarely uncomfortable with him anymore. She imagined it was because this silence was full of so many unsaid things. She wanted to tell him that she loved him again. Just to see what he would say. She told him every day. Had since that day in Paris. There had been no response. No response beyond giving her more and more.

"I have a very busy schedule tomorrow," he said, for no reason that she could discern.

"So, I won't see you?"

"Probably not."

"I haven't seen you enough lately," she said.

"I am very busy," he said, his tone getting hard. "It is something you will have to get accustomed to. I was around a little more than I would normally be when I first brought you back here out of courtesy to you. And because we were planning a wedding. And then, of course, we went to Paris, so we saw a great deal of each other. But it cannot continue. You will find a great many things to keep yourself busy."

"Is that why you're keeping me in school? Is that why you're talking to me about what I might do with my degree and all my spare time?"

"Yes, in part. You need to have something to keep you occupied. Something that will enable you to serve the country."

"I will also be parenting our child."

"Yes," he said, speaking slowly. "But mostly that responsibility will fall to nannies."

"No," she said, "it most certainly will not."

"You have a duty to the country, Bailey."

"I have a duty to our baby. Above and before anything else. I was ready to be a single mother, Raphael, because I had no idea if I would ever see you again. In my mind, I reshaped my entire life to accommodate this child. And while it seemed daunting, while I still don't know if I'm even half qualified to be a mother, I know that I want to devote my time to that."

"But it is not how it's done. Both because we will be busy ruling the nation, and because our child must be set on the right path from the first day, as I was."

"Being…bowed to by servants and held only by members of staff? Both worshipped and ignored all at the same time?"

"I was never ignored," he said, his tone hard. "I was essential. The heir to the throne. It will be the same for our child, and every portion of their childhood will be spent building to the moment they shall stand as I do, the prince or princess of Santa Firenze. It is how it has always been, and how it must continue to be."

"I don't care how it's been done for the past hundred years. I'm also the first nobody anyone in your storied royal lineage has married. Expect that I will do things differently. That I will have different expectations."

"So, your childhood was idyllic?"

"No," she said, "my childhood was awful. And you know that. My mother was eternally stressed and filled with resentment for me. She worked a job she hated and barely managed to keep us fed and clothed. We had no relationship. We have no relationship now. She resents me far too much for that. She made the decision to have me, and she regretted it ever since."

"So why," he said, his tone full of exasperation, "do you think the key to our child's happiness is you being around?"

"I don't think you understand. When I found out I was pregnant, I knew that I was in the exact same situation my mother was in. I knew that it would be so easy for me to spend my child's entire life resenting them. For interrupting my plans. For making things difficult. But they were my choices that led to that, Raphael, and I refused to punish my child for them. I thought long and hard about how I was going to avoid repeating the pattern that I had seen myself falling into. It was so important to me. But I realized, a few days after I found out I was pregnant, as I was lying in bed crying, ready to rend my garments in my distress, that it wouldn't be that way as long as I loved my child. As long as I loved my child more than I loved the dreams that I had built for myself. As long as I love my child more than my own comfort."

"Your child will be comfortable."

"But I want to be with them. I'm not going to fill up my days with busywork when I could be spending time with him or her. I like the idea of volunteering. I like the idea of having something of a vocation other than princess. But I'm not turning over the entire responsibility of my child to someone else."

"But it is how things are done." She could tell he was reaching the end of his temper. That he didn't understand—even after all this time with her—dealing with someone who wouldn't simply accept his word as law.

"Don't *you* want to spend time with our child?"

He waved a hand. "It has nothing to do with want, and everything to do with responsibility. It was thus for my parents, and it will be thus for me. You talk of love as if it is some kind of magic. As if it will move mountains, create time and keep a kingdom standing, but it is not. It is a potential distraction. Something that might prevent a ruler from acting in the best interest of his country. I cannot allow that. My father did not, and so I must not."

Her heart was pounding faster now, her stomach turning over. "You really think that love is the enemy?"

"I think it is an unnecessary distraction. I think a man in my position can afford to love nothing more than his country."

Those words hit hard, and she was reminded of that moment in the hotel room the night he'd first ended things with her. That grim finality. The evidence that he would not be moved. Not by tears or flying shoes.

"So, you'll never love me." It wasn't a question but a statement. Even as she spoke the words, they felt sharp in her throat, cutting into her, making it hard to breathe. "You're only ever going to love this country. You're not even going to love your own child?"

She had been willing to live in a situation where he didn't love her. Had been willing to try to figure that out. But the realization that he expected to have nothing to do with his own son or daughter was something she couldn't easily sweep under the rug.

"I told you this child mattered to me. There is a reason I had to marry you and not simply find someone else—"

"Will you love him?"

"I have never said those words to anyone," he said. "It has never been important to my existence."

"It is important now, Raphael. It's important to me."

"Have I not demonstrated how deeply I care for you?" he roared. "Have I not given everything to you that you could possibly want? And still, you behave as though it isn't enough."

"Raphael—"

"No. You are a waitress," he said, his tone harsh. "And I brought you here, to my palace, into my home, and I gave you all that it was in my possession to give. Still, you act as though somehow I am beneath you. You accuse me of being arrogant, and yet I think you best me on that score. Have I not given you an entire wing of this palace that has been in my family for generations? Did I not make you a DeSantis princess? You lived in a hovel, and I have elevated you in ways you never could have aspired to, and this is how you respond?"

"You're angry because I fail to be honored by the scraps that you've given me?" Rage was vibrating through her now, and she wasn't thinking entirely clearly. She didn't really care. She wanted to strike out at him. Wanted to hurt him the way that he had hurt her, all those countless times from that moment when he'd left her lying in the snow in Colorado. "That's what they are, and you have no idea. You think you can appease me with gold dust. Shiny things I never even wanted. That I should be grateful. But these are easy things, Raphael. So easy. For a man in your position, giving me a wing of your palace is nothing. You couldn't walk the length of it in an afternoon, so how will you ever miss a quadrant of rooms? You send me gifts, gifts that you have ensured I know are not extravagant enough to put a dent in your royal treasury. And you act as though you are somehow doing me a great favor. But how many necklaces can a woman wear? How many beautiful gowns?"

"That isn't the point," he said, sounding frustrated.

"Yes," she said, "it is the point. These things…they are easily replaceable. They are easily acquired for a man like you. But love? That is…it is so rare. And it is so beautiful. And so very, very costly. Don't you think that it has cost me every time I have told you that I love you and you've said nothing in return? That is a gift beyond price, and you don't even see it. You don't see everything that *I* have given to you. My body, my soul, my heart. I left my dreams, modest though they were, my dreams that you felt were somehow nothing, to come here and be with you."

Her angry words did nothing to cool his rage. "Look at all you have been given in return. Don't ask me to feel sorry for you. Don't pretend that you didn't love what we had in Paris. You didn't enjoy the extravagance."

"Of course I did. I'm only human. But all it will take is a financial crisis, a natural disaster, a war to wipe these things out. They are temporary. They are nothing. If the world catches fire, they'll burn away. And then what will be left? All that will be left standing is you and me, and without all of these shows of wealth and magnificence you don't know how to connect with me. You don't know who you are."

"But that will not happen," he said, his voice hard.

"Hopefully not. But you're still missing the point. These things are temporary. And they're not real. Not really. What I've given for you, that's real. What I feel for you? It *hurts*. It hurts whenever I breathe. It strips me of my pride by inches, day after day, every time I tell you I love you and you say nothing back. And what cost have I been to you? Truly."

"You are obsessed with that," he spat. "The cost. You wish to be an inconvenience? You wish to seem so high maintenance?"

"No. I wish to know that I'm not the only one sacrificing to have this. I wish to be something more than one of your possessions that you take out and put away at your will. That is what I want."

He exploded then. "You wish for the impossible. You wish to control how I feel. You have decided that my actions are not good enough. What good would it be if I felt things, and yet did nothing for you? If I told you that I loved you, and yet left you in that heap of an apartment in Colorado. Then you would not find these gestures so empty. If there was a lack of them, I imagine you would be saying that I clearly didn't love you because of what I failed to do."

"It's true," she said, her voice small. "I feel like those things kind of have to come together for them to matter."

"Is this how you were as a child?" he asked, the question hitting her like a slap. "Never able to be pleased? If your mother took care of you, but failed to demonstrate to you that her love was real, did you resent her?" His words dug beneath her skin, hit at her insecurity. But that wasn't fair. She refused to feel guilty for wanting someone to love her.

"That was low," she said, her voice vibrating. "Even for you, that was so damn low."

"It isn't throwing a shoe, I grant. But it's something to consider." He turned, his broad back filling her vision as he began to walk away.

"You're leaving now?" she asked.

"I can't talk to you at the moment. And so I refuse to."

"And your word is law," she said.

He turned again. "Yes," he said. "Yes, it is. And you would do well to remember that."

"Or what? You'll send me back to where I came

from? What does it matter if we are still together if you aren't even going to have me raise our child? If I don't mean anything to you?"

"I want you with me," he said.

"But why? To hear you tell it, I am nothing more than a waitress, and I am beneath you. You don't love me, and you never will. You don't need me to be there for our child. You think everything I came from is insignificant, that everything I want is something that doesn't matter. Why do you want me with you?"

He crossed the space between them, his expression lean and feral. "Because I want *you*," he growled, wrapping his arm around her and pulling her up against his body. It was hard and hot, everything she loved about him. Everything that always saw her weakening in his presence. She had to resist him now. She had to.

"It isn't enough. It's just another thing that will burn away."

"Never," he said, pressing his lips to her neck.

"Yes," she said, "it will. My body will change after I have this baby, and the years will soften it even more. I won't look like I did when you met me, when you first decided you wanted me. I'll be like every other old, unneeded thing littering this palace. And I will not submit myself to that."

"Have I not told you that your strength is valuable to me?"

"You have. But it isn't enough."

"And nothing less than what you want is enough?" He released his hold on her, taking a step back.

"Exactly. I've given you all that I am. All that I ever will be. I have submitted my future to you. And in return I want to know you. I want to have you. Every part of you. I want your love, I want your anger, I want everything messy and imperfect inside of you. I don't just want this distant arrogance, this blind insistence that you are law and above everything. I don't want it. I want all of that broken down and destroyed."

"Then you will never have it," he said.

She moved to him then, gripping his face, closing the distance between them and kissing him with all the pent-up rage that was inside her. Every twisted, ugly thing. All her selfishness, all her need. Her insecurity and her fear. And always, even now, every last bit of her love.

"Don't hide from me," she said, her voice vibrating.

"There is nothing to hide," he responded, his dark eyes blank.

"Liar," she said, claiming his mouth again.

He had told her more than once that she made him burn. That she had control over him no one else ever had.

Well, if ever he needed to go up in flames, it was now. And she was going to make sure it happened.

CHAPTER THIRTEEN

RAPHAEL KNEW THAT he should push her away. That he could not allow her to try to gain control in this way. He was Prince Raphael DeSantis, and no woman could manipulate him.

Except he could not bring himself to pull her lush mouth away from his. Could not deny the fire that burned between them.

He was being ripped apart from the inside out, piece by piece, and still, he could not bring himself to push her away. Still, he could not deny the desire that burned between Bailey and himself.

He would show her. He would prove to her, with this, that the need between them was enough. That it transcended use, that it went somewhere beyond beauty. There had been many beautiful women in his life. He'd always had his pick.

When he'd seen her, something had streaked through him, white hot and clean. It had been different than anything else ever had been. More. Deeper. It had been real. Real in a way nothing else before it had ever been. He would make her see. He would make her understand.

Raphael grabbed hold of her hair, twisting his fingers through the silken strands, tugging hard as he continued to kiss her, deep and long. As he took her seduction and flipped it against her.

Love.

They didn't need love. He didn't need it. It didn't matter. It wasn't important. And for a man in his position, it wasn't even possible. He had never wanted for it. Never once. He had always been given everything he needed.

But never love. Therefore, he could only assume that love was not among the necessary. Not for a man like him. If it were, his parents would have given him that, but they hadn't. Instead, he had been given education. He had been given staff. He had been given a room filled with the kinds of toys that would ignite any child's delight.

As a teenager, he had been given new cars. Well-fitted suits and private tutors who instructed him on how to best conduct himself in all situations.

Unlike Bailey, he had never been cold. He had never gone without. He'd had everything, always.

How dare this little witch come in and tell him that he lacked? How dare she make it seem as though he lived with a deficit? How dare she reduce everything that had always mattered to him to insignificant rubble? How dare she brush aside his gestures so casually?

He would not allow it. Not again. Not ever again. His blood was liquid fire in his veins as he ran his hands over her curves, reveling in her softness, in her heat. In her obvious need for him.

Yes, that was what he needed. He needed to feel how much she wanted him. And he needed it now.

He pushed his hands up beneath her skirt, his fingertips sliding easily beneath the edge of her panties. He felt that she was wet for him. Even angry, she still wanted him.

"You want me ugly?" he asked, his voice rough. "You want me out of control?"

He would give her all that and more. Here. Now. With his body. He would make her pay for this. For making him feel like his insides were made entirely of broken glass. For taking his well-ordered life and turning it completely upside down. For taking his perfect existence and proving to him that it was something less.

Yes. He would make her pay for that.

He pushed a finger deep inside her, watched as her mouth fell open, her eyes glazing over with pleasure. Yes, he wanted her like this. Mindless for him as he was for her, every damn day. Every moment, every breath. He wanted her to feel this desperation. To feel like it was all slipping away and there was nothing she could do about it. To feel hungry, aching, empty. As though nothing could ever fill the void. That was his entire existence with her. He wanted her to know that. To understand.

He had never felt like this. Everything he'd wanted, he'd had. And she insisted on keeping herself just out of reach. On making his best efforts not good enough.

She was ruining them. She was ruining him.

He would return the favor.

"Is this what you want," he rasped, adding a second finger to the first, rubbing the sensitive bundle of nerves at the apex of her thighs with his thumb. "You want me out of control?"

"I've *had* you out of control," she said. "From the beginning. But you won't admit what that means."

"It's sex. That's what it means. That we have very, very good sex."

He withdrew his fingers from her, rubbing her hips, sliding his hands down her thighs and lifting her, wrapping her legs around his waist, carrying her to the bed. He kissed her then, deep and long, with every ounce of his passion, every bit of his rage.

"No," she said, and he paused in his movements. "No, it's not sex. You chose me. You chose me, and that matters."

He said nothing, ignoring the pain those words inflicted on his heart as he pushed her skirt up her hips, dragging her panties down. Then he freed himself from his slacks. He didn't bother with more foreplay. Didn't bother with gentility. Instead, he thrust deep inside her, both of them gasping as he went deep. She was so tight, so wet and so undeniably his.

She could love him all she wanted. She did love him. Why couldn't that be enough for her? He didn't understand.

Don't you?

The howling beast inside him supplied the question, and he rejected it. Rejected all thought in favor of feeling. The feeling of her, the heat of her body, tight around him, the feeling of her fingernails digging into his skin. The sound of her needy cries as he pushed them both harder, higher. The feel of her hot breath against his neck as she panted, signs that she was getting closer to her peak.

That was his truth. It was all he cared about. He would exist in it now. Live in this moment, for as long as he could. He wanted nothing else. Nothing else, ever.

She was wrong. Wrong about him. Because if everything else was stripped away. If he ended up a prince with no palace, no kingdom, they would still have this.

She will love you. She will pour everything out for you. And what will you give in return?

He gritted his teeth, thrusting harder, losing himself in the fractured rhythm that only the two of them could ever dance to. The flames rose higher inside him, and he didn't fight it. He let it consume him, his release a shock of thunder inside him, shaking him, rattling him to his core. And as he spilled himself inside her, she found her own bliss. Her internal muscles clenched tightly around him, wringing more pleasure out of him, prolonging his orgasm.

It was always so with her. All of these things that he had never thought possible. That he had never thought to want.

And the truth of it all hung somewhere between them, hovered over him like a cloud, and he was desperate to hide from it. To push it away. Because those three words were the undoing of his entire life. Those three words undermined everything he was, everything he believed. They would shatter him. Utterly, completely.

He could not allow it.

He pushed himself away from her, forking his fingers through his hair, pacing the length of the room.

"I love you," she said.

He turned, that thing inside him savaging him now, tearing him to shreds from the inside out. "No!" He roared the words at her, satisfied when her face contorted with fear. With anguish. Because he had to make her see. He had to make her see that this would not happen. That it could not.

"But I do." The simplicity of it…that was the worst

part. As though it simply had been and now always would be. As though he had no control at all.

"You shouldn't," he said. "No one ever has. Why should you? Why should you find it so easy to love me?"

"An entire nation loves you."

"Because of what I was born to be. Not because of who I am." Those words were far too heavy. They landed against the top of the well he kept covered. That bottomless, needy well that contained the dark truth about himself. About who he was and what that meant.

He never wanted it to open. He never wanted that truth to come out.

"I love you," she said again, defying his orders at every turn, as she always did.

Bailey, so strong and defiant, always. How had she become his? How had she decided that she loved him? How had she decided that she could love at all? With a life as bleak and difficult as hers sounded, how had she arrived at the conclusion that love meant anything?

He could ask her. But his mouth wouldn't form the words.

There was no point to them anyway. There was no point to any of this. It had all been a fiction from the very beginning. A dream.

Bailey talked a lot about dreams. About how she'd been afraid to have them. He had spent his life living an existence carefully constructed to appear like a dream, the kind of life that prevented him from having any aspiration that fell outside duty.

He had no idea what it was to dream. To want. To hope for anything that extended beyond what was expected. He had no idea at all.

She was his first dream. She had been from the moment he had walked into that diner. His first foray into something that went beyond necessity and into desire.

He closed that off, ruthlessly, with great finality. He could not allow himself to think such things. It was nonnegotiable.

She was exactly what his father had always told him something like this would be. A distraction. She was a fatal weakness, something that could get right under his skin, changing everything he was, everything he was supposed to believe in.

She would become larger than Santa Firenze in his heart, in his mind, and he could not allow it.

"I don't love you," he said, his voice rough. "I never will."

Then he turned and walked out of the room, leaving behind a piece of himself he had never known existed. Leaving behind the most essential, vital part of his heart. But it was for the best. It was all he could do.

The only other option would make his world fall apart. And he couldn't allow that. Not when so much depended on him standing firm.

He felt in that moment that if there were a snowbank for him to throw himself into, he would do it.

The door to Bailey's room opened behind him, and he turned. She was there, her blue eyes glittering.

"I don't know what you think my response will be," she said. "If I will accept it and tell you that's okay. If I will continue on in this farce of a relationship simply because you will it, and your word is law. But I don't care about your pride, Raphael. Your pride needs to burn. If it's the thing that separates us, then it is the thing that has to go. I'm not staying."

"You have to."

"I will call the American embassy and tell them you're holding me captive."

"After we appeared in Paris together? After our wedding? The entire world knows you're carrying my child, Bailey. Do you honestly think you can pull something like that off?"

"I will, because I have to. Because you have finally killed the hope that I've been holding on to for all of these months. You built my trust back up, and now you've destroyed it again. And I'm not going to give you another chance. If you want to be involved in our child's life, you can. But you're going to have to come and visit us in Colorado. Because that's where I live. That's my world. And even if you never understand why it matters to me, that's the life I built for myself. It is not small. And neither am I."

She sucked in a sharp breath before continuing. "I was never just a waitress. I was never just anything. I have always, always been Bailey Harper. And that has always mattered. I pulled myself up with all of my own strength, and I will be damned if you reduce all of that effort to nothing. It will be good enough for my child, because it is what I built. And there will be love in my house. If your duty, or whatever you feel, is compelling enough to bring you across the world to visit, then I'll be happy with that. But I sincerely doubt anything less than love would compel a person to make that kind of effort. So I'll expect that you simply won't be involved."

"You can't do that," he said. "My child is my heir. The heir to this throne. He must be raised here. He must know of his heritage."

"A heritage of ice. A heritage so cold it will destroy him as soon as he touches it? No. That isn't the life that

I want for our child. And someday I think you'll see that I'm right. When your son grows up to be a more compassionate, more loving, more caring ruler than you will ever be. When he becomes the husband that you have been afraid to be."

"My son?"

"Yes. I had a doctor appointment today. And I was going to tell you. But then we fought."

"You tell me that you're having my son and are going to take him away from me?"

"You're taking him away from yourself, Raphael. That's the truth of it. But you don't want him. Not really."

"I do." He did. With everything. He didn't understand what was happening to him. Why he felt so torn, so bloody. So close to being destroyed.

"You like the idea of a wife. You like the idea of a son that you can raise and mold in your image. But you will always keep us at a distance. And I won't let that happen. You can break down that wall inside of you, that thing that keeps you from lowering yourself to accept my love."

"It has nothing to do with lowering myself."

"Maybe not. But you still won't do it. You're too proud."

"What are your demands?"

"Ready a jet to fly me back home. Arrange for me to gain entry into the US, and I will not make a scandal out of this. But I swear to you, I will strike your pride in any way that I can if you don't comply. Because I know that's the only thing you truly value."

Raphael could only stand there, stunned, wounded. And then he knew there was only one answer he could give her. That there was only one right thing to do. And it had nothing to do with pride and everything to do with the fact that he finally saw what she had been telling him from the beginning. What he had done to her was an insult. He had taken her, manipulated her and had never bothered to look deeper into his actions because he knew that doing so would require him to face deep, uncomfortable truths about his life and about himself that he had never wanted to face.

And so he did the only thing he could do. The only thing he could do and still survive.

"I will ready the jet. Be ready to leave early tomorrow."

Then he turned and walked away. Because he would be damned if he watched her leave.

CHAPTER FOURTEEN

HE WONDERED HOW a palace with so many people in it could feel empty. But it did. With Bailey gone it was empty.

And so was he.

He wandered the halls of the place he'd been so absurdly proud to bring her to. As if she would see it and crumble in humility and gratefulness because it was a palace, and there was no way she could have ever aspired to such a thing on her own.

She had worked for her life. For her education. For that apartment he'd insulted. He'd worked for none of this and yet held it up as some form of achievement.

Dio.

He was every bit as arrogant and unrelenting as she'd accused him of being.

But it was the only thing he had. The only thing that stood between him and the yawning void he tried so desperately to keep covered up.

It had cracked open now, and he was so terribly conscious of just how vacant and empty his entire existence was.

It made him question what he'd been taught. For the first time, he questioned his father. He'd never wanted to.

He'd so desperately wanted to preserve that image. Of a man who ruled a country with unfailing strength, who was the leader that Raphael had always aspired to be.

But he had been a terrible father and an even worse husband.

Raphael gritted his teeth, lowering his head and bracing himself against the wall. His staff continued to walk by, not speaking, not pausing. Why should they? That was the environment he'd continued to foster.

No connections. Nothing to interrupt business as usual.

Deference as a replacement for connection.

Prizing efficiency in a grand spectrum of days that all blurred together, instead of lingering in human connection.

He was breaking apart inside, and there was no one here to talk to. No one who would ever pause to ask why.

Oh, his Secret Service would take a bullet for him. But they would never talk to him.

Because that was what his father had taught him. What had been ingrained in him from childhood. He had never questioned it.

Never questioned when his father had yelled at his mother late one night for skipping an event because Raphael had been sick.

He knew he hadn't meant for Raphael to hear the argument, but he had.

"I needed you there tonight, and you were not. It split my focus!"

"Your son was sick," she hissed. *"I needed to be with him."*

"We have staff for that. An excellent staff. The boy wants for nothing. I, however, looked weak in front of

the ambassadors. Everyone's wife was in attendance except for you. You knew what this marriage was to be. You are to support Santa Firenze first. Above all else. Anything else is a distraction."

The next day he'd had a new toy. A gift from his father. The only contact the older man made during his illness. And after that his mother had been even more distant than before. An edict given by his father, because his son and heir could not be made dependent.

He'd done his best not to be a distraction. There and then he'd purposed to be the sort of man his father was. He never wanted his mother to be on the receiving end of his father's wrath for something concerning him, either.

The fault was his. It couldn't possibly be the old prince's. Not when the man was such a brilliant leader, not when he had done so much for the country.

He was also forced to remember the day his mother died. When his father had stood, stoic beside the grave of his late wife, and Raphael, only fifteen, had kept his face as hard as the old man's.

"Grief is a distraction, Raphael," he said later. *"A weakness only other men can afford. You must never love anything more than you love your country."*

"You don't?" he asked.

"No. And a good thing, because the nation won't pause for the loss of your mother. And neither can I."

Neither can you.

That had been the unspoken subtext of the conversation. That loss could never touch men like them. Because living life dictated by emotions was to walk on unsteady ground. He'd understood it.

And yet now he felt that even if it made sense, even if his father was right in his way, he was also wrong.

This kind of cold emptiness would break a man in the end. At least, it would break him. He was broken now, that was certain. Without Bailey, who had been the world's biggest distraction from the first moment he'd met her. The first spark of the unexpected in a lifetime of grim certainty.

Duty without love was empty. Life without love was empty. He could see that clearly now.

There was no cost to it. Bailey was right. If it cost nothing, it meant nothing. If you hid behind walls of control, and kept your wife and children at a distance, appeasing them with gifts...there was no love at all.

It didn't protect your country. It only protected you.

Building a wall like that, keeping out the elements... it could protect. But a life without sunlight could only leave you cold.

He had allowed it to make him a statue long before he'd been memorialized in death.

His father hadn't loved the country most. He'd loved himself and his protection most, and he'd taught Raphael to do the same.

He thought back to his mother's funeral. How much he would have given to get a hug from his father then. But the old man couldn't bend that way. Not for Santa Firenze, for his pride.

It had seemed like strength to Raphael then. But he could see now that the greatest strength would have been in showing weakness. For a son grieving his mother. A nation mourning a princess.

Instead, Raphael had been given a new car the next day.

A single moment sharing their loss would have been

so much more costly to his father. So much more valuable to Raphael.

The gifts had always been empty, but Raphael had wanted them to matter. So he'd believed his father. Believed him so that he could pretend he'd been loved.

You have been loved. You've been loved from the start by Bailey Harper, and just like your father, you pushed it away.

He pressed his hand to his chest, trying to staunch the flow of pain bleeding endlessly from his heart.

He had pushed away the best gift he'd ever received, because the cost of it had been too great.

What good was endless wealth if he couldn't afford love?

That was the damned rub. He couldn't buy love. He had to pay for it with the same. With humility and sacrifice. With discomfort. With his very soul.

As he looked around the palace and saw nothing but empty vanity, he knew that he had no other choice.

Her dream was over.

That was her predominant thought as the plane touched down in Colorado. It was what played in her mind over and over again as the car that Raphael had organized for her picked her up from the airport and drove her to a neighborhood that was unfamiliar.

"This isn't my house," she said when the driver pulled her up to a place with a well-manicured lawn that she had never seen in her life.

"These are the keys," he said. "My instructions were to bring you here and to give you these. Raphael said there would be an explanation inside."

Heart hammering, she took the keys from the driver's

hand and made her way up the front walk. She put the key in the lock, and it turned. She took a deep breath before walking inside. And then she did. It was beautiful. Modest, and certainly not a palace. But exactly the kind of place she had dreamed she might find herself in one day.

There was an envelope on the counter with her name written on it. She opened it, pulling out a simple note that was inside.

I know that you won't want to take this from me. I know that it will offend your pride. However, please consider this part of my child support. I am a prince after all, so you know that I can well afford it. This is the dream that you spoke about more than once when we were together. A house in a nice neighborhood. I wanted to make sure that you had this. That our child had this.

It wasn't signed. It didn't need to be. It could only be from one person. He was arrogant even when giving houses as parting gifts.

Her heart crumpled, and she looked around the room, feeling so adrift. This had been her dream. This little house, this kind of security. But it didn't feel like enough now. And that had nothing to do with the fact that she had just spent the last month being a princess. The last month living in a palace. No, all the feelings of inadequacy had to do with the fact that she had spent the last month sharing a bed with Raphael. And there was no room for him in this little house. In this little life.

Not for the first time, she wondered if she simply should have accepted what he'd given. Wondered if it would have been enough. If she shouldn't have pressed for more.

She shook that thought off quickly.

There was nothing else she could do, not really. It had been the right thing. The right thing for herself, and for her baby.

Anyway, it was too late to question it now. But this gesture, this one last gesture, which wasn't a whole giant mansion or anything crazy like Raphael would normally do, was the first sign she'd really seen that he had actually listened to her at all. That he saw value in her dream. Beauty in it the same way that she had.

It was a little bit late now, but she would accept it. Maybe, just maybe, he was starting to understand a little bit. Maybe there was still hope.

Or that's just what you want to think because you spent the entire plane ride back here crying and feeling like you'd been stabbed through the heart.

Yes, there was that. That couldn't be ignored.

She did feel a little bit stabbed.

The days began to bleed together. She went to class and came back home. She wasn't working, because she was allowing Raphael to pay for a few things. Maybe that was wrong. But he was the father of her baby and currently still her husband. They weren't going to divorce officially until after the baby was born. All contact she'd had with him had been made through his aides. She saw no reason to go against him on that. Mostly, she just didn't have the energy. She was close to six months pregnant, undeniably so, and unable to muster up much energy to do anything. Though she had a feeling the heartbreak was to blame, more than the pregnancy.

She sighed heavily, throwing her purse down onto the couch, her body following quickly after. This place was starting to feel like home. Maybe that was a betrayal, seeing as it had come from Raphael. But it was one of the few bright spots in her life. This gift from him that was still extravagant by the standards of most people, but actually showed his willingness to listen.

She heard footsteps and sat up, her heart hammering hard. She was pretty sure she was hallucinating. Except then she looked toward her bedroom and saw a glorious figure standing there. He was wearing the same sort of well-cut suit that he always wore, his expression as lovely and arrogant as ever.

She felt like she was having déjà vu. Flashing back to the moment he had been in her apartment that first time he'd come to find her after their breakup. She felt like maybe she was dreaming, just as she had imagined she might be back then. She pinched herself.

"What are you doing?"

"Making sure that I'm not asleep."

"You are not," he said, taking a step toward her. It was then that she saw he did look different than he usually did. She noticed that he had dark circles under his eyes, and that the lines by his mouth were more pronounced than they usually were. It was then she noticed how exhausted he was. That his hair was disheveled as though he had been constantly running his fingers through it. It was then she realized just how affected he was by all of this. The same as she was.

"What are you doing here? I didn't realize that part of the deal with you buying me a house meant that you got to come and go in and out of it as you please."

"That was never my intent," he said, his voice rough.

"It was my intent to leave you alone. To honor what you said to me. It was my intent to let you go. But I have spent the past couple of weeks in agony, and I... I needed to see you."

"So we can have the same fight? So we can yell at each other some more? You can say more hurtful things, and I can counter with meaner things."

"No," he said, sounding ragged. "That isn't what I want. It's as far removed from what I want as anything ever could be."

"Why are you here?"

Suddenly, Raphael dropped down, landing on his knees, looking up at her with dark, tortured eyes. "I came to bow."

"You came to...what?" Her heart hammered wildly, her hands shaking. She couldn't reconcile what she was seeing in front of her. This proud, arrogant man, on his knees before her. As though he were the servant, and she were royalty.

"I was bowed to from birth," he said. "Not because anyone cared especially much, not because they were awed by their....deep emotion for me. But because of my blood. I was given everything from the moment I entered this world simply because I am a DeSantis. I have never, not once, debased myself for another human being. I will crawl across broken glass if it means having you, Bailey. I would spend the rest of my life on my knees before you if that was what it took."

She put her hands on her temples, hardly able to believe what was happening. "Raphael...you never had to do this. This was never what I wanted."

"But it is what must happen. I have been the most unbending, inflexible person, and I realize that. But I have been afraid that if I were to ever bend, I would break completely. And when you left, I did. I shattered. And I have spent the last two weeks trying to figure out what to do with the pieces of myself that you left behind. I have spent the last weeks trying to figure out what all of this means. Why your declarations of love offended me so much. Why I couldn't give them back. Why I had never...why I had never heard them before. Why I had never spoken them."

"Oh, Raphael." It hit her then, just then, that he had never felt chosen, either. That he had been born, and his fate had been set. But no one had ever chosen him.

She was from nothing and nowhere, and he was from a family as old as time, and they shared the same pain. Hers covered with pride and determination, his with arrogance and the insulation provided by his position.

But it was all pain.

"My father told me," he said, his voice breaking, "he told me that a ruler must never love anything more than he loved his country. Day after day he told me this. He told me this every time he had not a moment to spare to say a few words to me. He told me this every time he and my mother were traveling for my birthday. Every time I had dinner by myself. Except for the household staff. And in the place of my parents' presence would always be gifts. Everything a young boy could ever want."

"Gifts meant a lot to you," she said, her voice muted. Suddenly she felt...she felt foolish for not seeing that. For not realizing that for him those things had meant something. "Raphael, I am so sorry I didn't know."

"Of course not. But you see—they had to mean something to me. They were all I had. That and the... edict to always stand strong. My father told me that I couldn't allow love or grief to distract me. Even at my mother's funeral."

She put her hand over her mouth and shook her head. "No. I…how old were you?"

"Fifteen."

"He didn't comfort you or…or anything?"

"He bought me a car."

"To replace your mother?"

He shook his head slowly. "I think he bought me a car because it was…all he could really give. That was what I learned to place importance in. That and the title. The directive that was placed before me. And after he died… I told myself the only thing that mattered was ruling over my country in a way that would make my father proud. Making myself invulnerable so that I could be the best leader that I could be. To me, that's what it meant. And you have to understand that everything you said undermined that. If gifts are truly empty gestures, if things do not compensate for human connection, if arrogance and confidence are not the same as emotion, then I am a hollow, empty person with no connection at all. My father never said that he loved me. But I was able to take those things and create words from them. To fashion sentiments out of them that didn't exist. And you challenged that. From the moment that you first walked into my life."

She swallowed hard. "I'm sure that your father loved you." She wasn't sure. Because she wasn't sure her own mother had loved her. She could hardly speak for his father.

Raphael shook his head, pushing himself to his feet. "I don't think he did. But it doesn't matter to me, not now. That was part of my rock-bottom experience, you understand. I had to lay there on the floor for a while and fully come to terms with that. To accept what you had done to my worldview. To me. I got so angry at you because if what you said was true, then it meant my entire life was so much hollower than I had ever realized. If what you said was true, then I was never truly loved."

"You have an entire country of people who love you."

"Who revere me because of my bloodline. And maybe even love the idea of me. But no person who has ever known me has ever loved me. And, as I said, no one had ever spoken the words to me before you did. I wasn't conscious of the absence of them until you brought them into my life. I wasn't aware that I had never spoken them until you spoke them to me. And it was confronting. Because it demanded something of me that I didn't want to give."

"What's that?" she asked, her voice faint, splintered.

"Humility. To get on my knees and confess to you that I needed those words. That I had been missing them my entire life. Everything in me cried out for a kind of connection that I was always denied. That I needed love. That I needed someone to be close to me. That I was desperately aching for someone to get past all of that arrogance, to love me through it, to want me no matter what. Admitting that—"

"Raphael," she said, closing the space between them and wrapping her arms around him. "I love you. But more than that, I choose you."

His big body heaved, a broken sob escaping his lips. "I love you," he said, the words untested, unfamiliar and beautiful on his lips.

She clung to him. So tight she never wanted to let go. Not because she was afraid he'd disappear, but because they'd spent far too much time not holding each other at all. "I am so honored to be the first person to hear those words from you," she whispered.

"And you won't be the last. I will say them to our son. I will say them every day. I will withhold no good thing from my child. Not now that I've allowed myself to see what really matters. What really lasts. You're right. Everything I've ever put stock in my entire life has been vanity. So easily burned away by the things of the world. But this, this is real. It's deep. It's something that can never be taken away from me. Never be taken away from you. And I... I am so grateful. Because you have given me the one thing on earth that I could never buy. That I could never force someone to give to me simply because of my title. And I think that's why it terrified me so. I knew it was something I had no power within myself to acquire. I knew it was something you would have to choose to give me. Something I could never manipulate out of you. It's why I got so angry every time you asked for me to feel something authentic. To do something other than to simply wave my hand and commit an empty gesture. You asked for real things. For deep things. I knew that in order to achieve that, I would have to allow myself to feel something real."

"I know it hurts," she said, the words choked. "I know it does. I know what it's like to let your hopes shrink smaller and smaller, so that you aim for something you can manage at least, something that you might be able to have. Something that doesn't seem too spectacular."

"I never knew to dream," he said, his voice rough. "I was given all of this and told I had the world. How could I begin to disagree?"

Her chest tightened, and she looked up into his eyes. Haunted. Wounded. That arrogance was gone for now. She felt like she should look away so that she didn't... embarrass him. So that she didn't see him like this. So raw and exposed in a way he never had been before.

She saw it all for what it was now.

His protection. Not just from the world but from the truth that lurked inside him. The fear that he, of all people, may forever want something that he wouldn't be able to have. That his birthright didn't ensure for him.

"I thought..." he began. "I thought that I didn't know need. I thought that I had never needed anything in all my life. But it turns out I am a creature made entirely from need. Who has spent all of his life covering deficiency with a host of things. With possessions and powers, as I told myself that needing was the same as devotion. That deference and worship would somehow fill a hole in my heart." He brushed his thumb over her cheek. "I didn't need. And I didn't dream. Until I met you, Bailey."

He closed his eyes for a moment, and when he opened them again they were bright. "I was furious. Furious that you could show me something about myself I had never before seen."

"A lowly waitress," she said, her tone dry.

"Do not ever say that." He shook his head, his tone fierce. "You made a prince bow down to you—how could you ever be lowly?"

"I like that your standard of greatness relates back to you."

"Naturally."

She smiled then. "I'm pleased to see your arrogance hasn't been destroyed. Only reduced."

"I am still me."

"Yes," she said. "And a good thing, too, because you're the one that I love."

And then he did the impossible one more time and got to his knees in front of her. "I want you to be my wife," he said.

"I already am." Her throat was tight, emotion building in her chest until it was impossible to breathe.

"But this time I am not demanding. This time I'm asking. This time, it is with the understanding that I am not a great gift. Not with my title and my palace. You are the gift, Bailey. You. You have changed me, changed my world."

"After I broke it," she said, a little sob breaking the words.

"It was always going to break. You uncovered the void in me—you didn't create it. And you were the only one who could ever fill it. You're my only dream."

A tear slipped down Bailey's cheek, and she knelt down with Raphael, bringing herself to the ground with him. She bracketed his cheeks with her hands, her heart so full she thought it would burst.

"I never thought a girl like me would dream of a fairy tale. But here you are, my very own Prince Charming. And do you know what the very best thing is?"

"What?" he asked, his voice rough.

She pressed her lips to his as tears slipped down her cheeks. "We're going to live happily ever after."

EPILOGUE

SANTA FIRENZE REJOICED the day their prince and his princess gave birth to their first son. Raphael felt that he got much more credit for it than he deserved, and he was the first to tell everyone so.

If anyone was surprised by the prince's sudden show of humility, they didn't say. Especially as it ran only so deep.

He was still Prince Raphael DeSantis, after all.

When he and Bailey brought their son home, he didn't allow the residents of the palace to bow to him. Instead, they had a party in the newest DeSantis's honor. They had cake of every variety, cake that Bailey heartily approved of since, as she told him, she was completely secure in her husband's heart now.

There was laughter and music, happiness that was perhaps not fitting of a man who would one day join the statues out in the courtyard, but he didn't care. Love was more important than tradition.

The oldest members of staff held the little prince, kissed his forehead. Showed him affection in a way that Raphael had never been allowed to receive.

The sight made him feel like just maybe he would do

right for this child. That just maybe he would be able to care for him in the right ways.

Much later, when he was in the bedroom with Bailey, and she was holding their son close, feeding him at her breast, he was struck with a sudden swift surge of emotion so deep, so intense that he had to go down to the floor so he didn't fall forward.

And that was how the prince, who had been bowed down to from the moment of his birth, and all throughout his life, came to kneel before a waitress. Brought down to his knees by love.

* * * * *

MATCHED TO A PRINCE

KAT CANTRELL

To Cynthia, because this book was so hard to
write and you were there for me every step of the
way. And because TPFKAD had to be
in it somewhere.

One

When the sun hit the three-quarter mark in the western sky, Finn aimed the helicopter for shore. It was nearing the end of his shift and, as always, he couldn't resist dipping low enough to let the powerful downdraft ripple the Mediterranean's deep blue surface.

A heron swooped up and away from the turbulence as fast as its wings could carry it, gliding along the air currents with sheer poetic grace. Finn would never get tired of the view from his cockpit, never grow weary of protecting the shoreline of the small country he called home.

Once he'd touched down on the X marking the spot for his helicopter, Finn cut power to the rotor and vaulted from the cockpit before the Dauphin blades had come to a full stop. His father's solemn-faced driver stood on the tarmac a short distance away and Finn didn't need any further clues to recognize a royal summons.

"Come to critique my landing, James?" Finn asked with

a grin. Not likely. No one flew helicopters with more precision and grace than he did.

"Prince Alain." James inclined his head in deference, then delivered his message. "Your father wishes to speak with you. I'm to drive."

Checking his eye roll over James's insistence on formality, Finn nodded. "Do I have time to change?"

It wouldn't be the first time Finn had appeared before the king in his Delamer Coast Guard uniform, but he'd been in it for ten hours and the legs were still damp from a meet-up with the Mediterranean while rescuing a swimmer who'd misjudged the distance to shore.

Every day Finn protected his father's people while flying over a breathtaking panorama of sparkling sea, distant mountains and the rocky islands just offshore. He loved his job, and spending a few hours encased in wet cloth was a small price to pay.

But that didn't mean he wanted to pay that price while on the receiving end of a royal lecture.

James motioned to the car. "I think it would be best if you came immediately."

The summons wasn't unexpected. It was either about a certain photograph portraying Finn doing Jägermeister shots off a gorgeous blonde's bare stomach or about the corruption charges recently brought up against a couple of his running buddies.

A blogger had once joked that Finn's official title should be Prince Alain Phineas of Montagne, House of Scandal. It wasn't so funny to the king, who had tried to combat the negative press with a royal announcement proclaiming Finn's upcoming marriage. A desperate ploy to get his son to settle down.

Hadn't worked so far. Perhaps if his father could actually name a bride, the ploy might get some traction.

Finn paused. Maybe his father had picked someone.

He hoped not. The longer he could put off the inevitable, the better.

But his life was never his own and whatever his father wanted, Finn would deal with it, like always.

Only one way to find out if he'd be announcing the name of his bride soon.

Finn allowed James to show him into the backseat of the town car his father used to fetch people and tried to swallow his dread. The Delamer Coast Guard administrative building disappeared behind them and Finn's homeland unrolled through the windows.

Tourist season had officially started. Bright vendor booths lined the waterfront, selling everything from outrageously priced sunscreen to caricatures quickly drawn by sidewalk artists. Hand-holding couples wandered along the boardwalk and young mothers pushed strollers in the treed park across from the public beach.

There wasn't a more beautiful place on earth, and Finn thanked God every day for the privilege of not only living here but the opportunity to serve its people. It was his duty, and he did it gladly.

Too soon, the car drove through the majestic wrought iron gates of the palace where Finn had grown up, and then moved out of as soon as his mother would allow it. He'd realized early on he was just in the way. The palace was the home of the king and queen, and eventually would house the crown prince and princess, Alexander and his wife, Portia.

Finn was so far down the line of succession, he couldn't even see the head. It didn't bother him. Most days.

A slew of workers scurried about the hundred acres of property surrounding the stately drive. Each employee focused on maintaining the famous four-tiered landscaping that ringed the central fountain bearing a statue of King Etienne the First, who had led Delamer's secession from France two centuries ago.

Another solemn-faced servant led Finn to the office his father used for nonstate business. That was a relief. There'd be no formality then, and Finn could do without royal addresses and protocol any day.

When Finn entered, the king glanced up from paperwork strewn across his four-hundred-year-old desk, which had been a gift from a former president of the United States. Finn preferred gifts you could drink, especially if they came with a cork.

With a small smile, his father pushed his chair back and stood, gesturing to the brocade couch. "Thanks for coming, son. Apologies for the short notice."

"No problem. I didn't have any plans. What's up?"

Since he didn't mistake his father's gesture for a suggestion, Finn perched on the fancy couch at a right angle to the desk.

King Laurent crossed his arms and leaned on the edge of his desk, facing Finn. "We need to move forward with finding you a wife."

Called it in one.

Finn shifted against the stiff couch cushions, determined to find a comfortable spot. "I said I'd be happy with whomever you picked."

A lie. He'd tolerate whomever his father picked.

If Finn and his bride ended up friends as his parents had, great. But it was a lot to ask in an arranged marriage. It wasn't as though Finn could hold out for love, not when it hadn't worked out the one and only time he'd allowed himself to care about a woman.

Juliet's face, framed by her silky light brown hair, swam into his mind's eye and he swallowed. A hundred blondes with a hundred shot glasses couldn't erase the memory of the woman who'd betrayed him in the most public and humiliating way possible. He knew. He'd tried.

"Be that as it may," the king said, "an option I hadn't considered has come to my attention. A matchmaker."

"A what?"

"An American matchmaker contacted me through my secretary. She asked for a chance to earn our business by doing a trial match. If you don't like the results, she won't charge us."

Finn smelled something fishy, and if there was anything he knew after spending the majority of his day in or near the sea, it was fish. "I'm reasonably certain we can afford her fee regardless. Why would you consider this?"

Was this another ploy to get him under his father's thumb? Had the king paid this matchmaker to orchestrate a match with a woman loyal to the crown, who could be easily controlled?

"This matchmaker introduced Stafford Walker to his wife. I've done enough business with him to know his recommendation is solid. If the woman hadn't mentioned his name, I wouldn't have given her idea a moment's consideration." His father sighed and rubbed the spot between his eyes wearily. "Son, I want you to be happy. I liked what she had to say about her selection process. You need someone specific, who will negate all the bad press. She promises to match you with the perfect woman to become your princess. It seemed like a fair deal."

Guilt relaxed Finn's rigid shoulders. "I'm sorry. You've been more than patient with me. I wish…"

He'd been about to say he wished he knew why he courted so much trouble. But the reason wasn't a mystery. She had eyes the color of fresh grass, glowing skin and a stubborn streak wider than the palace gates.

Perhaps this matchmaker might find someone who could replace Juliet in his heart. It could happen.

"I've had this matchmaker, Elise Arundel, thoroughly checked out, but do your own research. If you don't like the idea, don't do it. But I've had little luck coming up with a potential bride on my own." The king smiled, looking like his usual cheerful self for the first time since Finn had entered the room. "There's no shortage of candidates. Just the lack of one who can handle you."

Finn grinned back. "At least we agree on that."

Because Finn took after his father. They both had big hearts and even bigger personalities. And the absolute sense of duty that came part and parcel with being royalty. They shared a love for Delamer and a love for the people they served.

His father managed to do it with grace and propriety. Finn, on the other hand, tended to whoop it up, and photographers loved to capture it. Of course, a photo could never depict the broken heart that drove him to search for a method, any method, to erase the pain.

He got all that and didn't mind the idea of getting married, especially to save himself from a downward media spiral. Finding a woman he could love at the same time was an attractive bonus. Settling down and having babies appealed to him if he could do it with someone who gave him what he desperately wanted—a sheltered place all his own where he could be a man and not a prince, if only for a few hours.

The odds of a matchmaker pulling a name out of thin air who could do that…well, he'd do better betting a thousand on red and letting it ride.

"I'll talk to Ms. Arundel." Finn owed it to his father to figure out a way to stop causing him grief, and he owed it to his country to portray the House of Couronne positively in the international press. If it meant marrying the matchmaker's choice and making the best of it, so be it.

Relief filled the king's eyes and a double dose of guilt swam through Finn's stomach. His father loved him and wanted the best for him. Why couldn't Finn do the right thing as his brother always did? Alexander would be king one day and constantly kept that forefront in his mind. His behavior was above reproach and *he* never caused their parents a moment's worry.

Finn, on the other hand, was the spare heir. Unnecessary. The Party Prince.

An advantageous marriage was a chance for Finn to do something right for once, something of value to the crown. He'd hoped to keep putting it off. But clearly his father was having none of that.

"She'd like you to fly to Dallas, Texas, to meet in person," the king said. "As soon as possible."

Dallas. He'd never been there. Maybe he could pick up an authentic cowboy hat if nothing else.

Mentally, Finn rearranged his calendar for the weekend. He'd committed to attending a couple of charity fund-raisers and had planned to hit a new club in Saint Tropez Saturday night. Looked as if he'd be skipping all of it.

"I've got a shift tomorrow, but I can go the day after."

His father put a gentle hand on Finn's shoulder. "I think it's a good choice."

Ducking his head, Finn shrugged. "We'll see. What's the worst that can happen?"

As soon as the words left his mouth, he regretted them. Scandal followed him like a mongrel dog he'd fed once and couldn't get rid of. Juliet's betrayal had been the first scandal but certainly not the last. It had just hurt the most.

And that was the kicker. She'd hurt him so badly because he'd loved her so much, only to find she didn't feel the same way. If she had loved him, she'd never have participated in a protest against everything he held dear—his father, the military, the very fabric of the governing structure that he'd sworn allegiance to.

The irony. Two things he'd loved about Juliet were her passion and commitment to her family. Without them, she'd be uninteresting and lackluster. Without them, the protest wouldn't have happened.

It didn't matter. She'd killed all his feelings for her. Except the anger. That, he still had plenty of.

Grimly, he bid his father goodbye and let James drive

him back to his Aventador still parked at the coast guard headquarters. His entire life could be summed up in one phrase—dual-edged sword. No matter which way it was wielded, he'd be cut. He would be a man and a prince until the day he died, and it seemed fated that he could never satisfy both sides simultaneously.

Yet he held on to a slim thread of hope this matchmaker might change things for him.

Juliet Villere did not understand the American fascination with small talk. It was boring.

The packed ballroom wasn't her preferred scene anyway, but coupled with a strong desire to avoid one more conversation about the ridiculous game confused Americans called football, the wall had become her friend. It warmed her bare back nicely and provided a great shield from the eyes she'd felt burning into her exposed flesh.

Why hadn't someone told her that a makeover didn't magically transform your insides? All the makeup and fancy clothes in the world couldn't convert Juliet into someone who liked lipstick. Or parties.

But she owed Elise Arundel and her matchmaking-slash-makeover services a huge debt for taking her in when she'd fled Delamer in search of some magic to heal the continual pain of Finn's betrayal. That was the only reason she'd agreed to attend this glittery event full of Elise's clients.

Maybe Elise wouldn't notice if Juliet ducked out the side entrance and walked back to the matchmaker's house in the Dallas district called Uptown, where Juliet was staying until Elise found her an American husband. It was only a couple of miles, and she'd practiced walking in these horribly uncomfortable heels enough times that her leg muscles were used to the strain.

Then she caught sight of Elise heading in Juliet's direction, a determined look on her mentor's face.

Too late.

"Having a good time?" Elise asked, her dark page boy swinging in time to the upbeat song floating above the crowd.

"Fantastic."

The sarcasm clearly wasn't lost on Elise, who smiled. "It's good for you to be in social settings, dressed to kill. I invited you to this mixer so you could practice mingling. Hugging the wall won't accomplish that."

The reminder tightened Juliet's stomach, and she resituated the waistline of the form-fitting green dress her new friend Dannie Reynolds had helped select.

"I have nothing good to say about football." One thing was clear—the American husband she'd asked Elise to match her with would watch it. Therefore, Juliet would likely become well versed in the fine art of faking interest. "So I'm acquainting myself with the benefits of solitude."

Elise laughed. "Dance with someone. Then you don't have to talk."

Juliet shook her head. She'd never danced with anyone other than Finn, and she didn't want to break that streak tonight.

Finn.

Pain, sharp and swift, cramped her stomach. Crossing the Atlantic hadn't dimmed his hold over her one bit.

He'd shredded her soul over a year ago. Shouldn't she be finished healing by now? She wanted desperately to get to that place where he was just some guy she used to date, one she recalled fondly yet distantly.

But the announcement of his upcoming engagement had cut deeply enough to drive her from Delamer all the way to Dallas, Texas. Thank God she'd stumbled over that EA International ad in the back of a fashion magazine she'd thumbed through at the dentist's office back home—it had given her a place to go.

"I don't see the point in dancing with one of these guys."

As she didn't see the point in having fake nails or painted

lips. But it wasn't her place to argue with the formula Elise used in her matchmaking service.

"None of them will be my match," she continued. "And besides, they've all got sports on the brain. Does scoring more points feed hungry children? Right any wrongs? No. It's stupid."

Juliet started to make a face and remembered she couldn't do that anymore. Actually, she wasn't supposed to be so outspoken either. Her American husband would want a refined wife with the ability to mingle with the upper crust. Not a woman who had little use for propriety and fluff. Or the Dallas Cowboys.

How in the world was she going to pretend *that* much for the rest of her life?

The same way she was going to pretend her heart hadn't broken when she'd lost the man she'd loved, her sweet little brother and her life in Delamer.

Anything was manageable if it matched her with a husband who could keep her in the States, and save her from having to watch Finn marry someone else.

With a laugh, Elise shook her head. "No, no. Don't hold back. Tell me how you really feel. How about if I save you from further suspense and tell you I have your match?"

Juliet's heart stuttered to a stop. This was it. The reason she'd come to America.

What would her future husband be like? Did he enjoy swimming and sailing and could she ask him to take her on trips to the beach? Would he be okay with her family coming to visit occasionally? Did he have a nice smile and laugh a lot?

Most important, would she be able to develop feelings for him that would fill the Finn-shaped hole inside?

Even though Elise guaranteed a love match, replacing Finn was probably too much to hope for.

Contentment would be enough. It had to be.

She swallowed the sudden burn in her throat. "That didn't take long. I only finished your questions yesterday."

Shrugging, Elise turned to face the ballroom, her shoulder bumping Juliet's companionably. "Sometimes when I load the profile, I don't get a match against someone already in the system and then we have to wait until new clients are entered. Yours came back immediately."

Juliet wanted to ask for the name. And at the same time, she wanted to dive under the buffet table.

What was she doing here? This man in Elise's system expected a certain kind of woman, one who could host his parties and mingle with his friends, smiling through boring stories of business mergers and tax breaks. And football. That was so not her.

She wanted to go home.

Then she thought about living in Delamer day in and day out and how often she saw Finn's helicopter beating through the broad blue sky. Or how she'd stumbled over another photograph of him cutting the ribbon at the new primary school—that picture would never die.

A little girl who would attend the school had sneaked up and wrapped her arms around his thigh just before he cut the ribbon. Finn leaned down to kiss her cheek and presto. Instant immortalization via the hundreds of camera phones and paparazzi lenses in the audience.

The pictorial reminder of the prince's sweet and charming nature stabbed her in the stomach every time. He was such a good guy, with a sense of honor she'd once loved—until realizing it was a front for his stubborn refusal to see how much he'd hurt her by taking his father's side. There was no reasoning with Finn, and that trumped all his good qualities.

In Delamer, there were constant reminders of the void her brother Bernard's death had created.

Any husband was better than that.

"What happens if I don't like the man your computer

picked?" Juliet asked, though surely Elise's system had captured her exact specifications.

"There are no absolutes. If you don't like him, we'll find someone else, though it might take a while. However…" Elise hesitated. "I'd like you to keep an open mind about the possibilities. This man is perfect for you. I've never seen two more compatible people. Not even Leo and Dannie were this closely aligned, and look how well that turned out."

Juliet nodded. Dannie and Leo Reynolds were definitely one of the most in-love couples in the history of time and had never even met each other before they signed on with EA International and got married. If Elise said this man was Juliet's perfect match, why doubt it?

"I had an ulterior motive for inviting you to the party tonight," Elise confessed. "Your match will be here too. Soon. I thought it would take some pressure off if you met socially."

Her match. Already.

Juliet had hoped for some time to learn more about him before being thrown at his feet. She touched her pinned-up hair. At least she'd meet her future husband while looking the absolute best she could, a small victory in her mind.

Deep breath. Bernard would want her to be happy, to move on. The memory of her brother's smile bolstered her.

A disturbance in the crowd caught Juliet's attention. People craned their necks to peer over each other, whispering and nodding toward the ballroom entrance.

"What's going on?" she asked.

Elise uttered a very unladylike word.

"I was hoping for a little more time to explain. It's your match." Elise cleared her throat. "He's early. I think that's a good quality in a man. I mean, along with all of his other ones. Don't you think so?"

Her future husband, assuming everything went according to plan, had just walked into the ballroom.

Juliet's pulse took off, throbbing below her ears. "Sure. But why does it sound like you're trying to talk me into it? Does he have two heads or something?"

"I did something a little unorthodox to find your match." Elise bit her lip and put her hand on Juliet's arm. "Something I hope you'll appreciate. It was a test. I figured if the computer didn't match you, I wouldn't say anything. I'd never tell you and I'd find someone else for you both."

"What are you talking about? What did you do?"

Elise smiled weakly as the crowd pressed closer to the entrance, blocking their view of whoever had drawn so much interest. "You talked so much about him. I heard what was still in your heart. I couldn't call myself a matchmaker if I didn't give you an opportunity to rediscover why you fell in love in the first place."

The first wave of unease rolled through Juliet's stomach. "Talked about whom?"

"Prince Alain. Finn." Elise nodded toward the crush surrounding the entrance. "He's your match."

"Oh, my God. Elise!" Juliet wrapped her arms around her waist but couldn't stop the flood inside of...everything. Hope. Disbelief. The unquenchable anger at his inability to side with her. "You contacted Finn? And didn't tell me? Oh, my God."

Finn was here. In the ballroom.

He was her match.

Not a quiet American businessman who watched football and would save her from the heartache Finn had caused.

"Open mind," Elise reminded her and grasped Juliet's hand to propel her forward, parting the crowd easily despite being half a head shorter than everyone else. "Come say hello. Give me ten minutes. Let me explain to you both what I did and then you can blast me for my tactics. Or spend a little while reacquainting yourselves. Maybe give it a chance. It's your choice."

Greedily, Juliet's gaze swept the crowd, searching for a

familiar face. And found a solid figure in black tie, flanked by a discreet security team, moving toward her.

Finn. Exactly as her heart remembered him.

Tall, gorgeous, self-assured. Every bit a man who could support the weight of a crown despite the probability that he never would. Hard, defined muscles lay under a tuxedo that did little to disguise the beauty of the man's body. His short, dark hair that had a tendency to curl when he let it grow was the same. As was the winsome smile.

Until he paused in front of Elise and caught sight of Juliet. The smile slipped a touch as his gaze cut between the two women. "Ms. Arundel. It's nice to see you again."

Finn extended his hand and took Elise's, drawing her forward to buss her cheek as if they were old friends. To Juliet, he simply said, "Ms. Villere. What a pleasant surprise. I wasn't aware you were on this side of the world."

In spite of the frost in his tone, his voice flipped her stomach, as it always had. More so because it had been so long since she'd heard someone speak with the cadence intrinsic to people from Delamer.

"The surprise is mutual," she assured him, shocked her throat hadn't gone the way of her lungs, which seemed to be broken. She couldn't breathe. The ballroom's walls contracted, stealing what air remained in the room. "Though I'm reserving judgment on whether it's pleasant."

Stupid mouth had gotten away from her again. The laser-sharp eyes of the crowd branded her back and she became aware of exactly how many people were witnessing this public meeting between Prince Alain and a woman they no doubt vaguely recognized. Wouldn't take long to do an internet search and find videos, pictures and news reports of the scandal. It had garnered a ton of press.

His expression darkened. "Be sure to inform me when you decide. If you'll excuse me, I have business with Ms. Arundel which is not of your concern."

Finn was in rare His-Royal-Highness mode. She hated it when he got that way.

"Actually," Elise corrected with a nervous laugh and held a palm out, "Juliet is your match."

Two

"What?" Finn zeroed in on Juliet, piercing her with steely blue eyes she remembered all too well. "Is this your idea of a joke? Did you beg Elise to contact me?"

Is *that* what he thought? Her brother was dead and afterward, Finn had abandoned her when she'd needed him most. Juliet would never forgive him. Why would she extend one small finger to see him again?

"I had nothing to do with this!" Hands on her hips, she waded straight into the rising tension, eyes and ears around them forgotten as the emotions Finn elicited zigzagged through her torso. "I thought you were getting married. What happened to your princess? What are you doing signing on with a matchmaker?"

A muscle ticked in Finn's forehead. "My father does want me to get married, as soon as I find a bride. That's what I'm doing here. I was promised the perfect match. Amusing how that worked out."

Finn wasn't engaged? There wasn't even a potential

princess on the horizon? She'd left Delamer based on something that *wasn't even true*.

"Yeah, hilarious. I was promised the same."

In tandem, they turned to Elise. She smiled and escorted them both to an unpopulated corner, likely so the coming bloodbath wouldn't spatter her guests. Finn's muscled companions followed and melted into the background.

"Do you remember the profile question about love?" Elise tucked her hair behind one ear with a let's-get-down-to-business swipe. "I asked you both what you'd be willing to give up in order to have it. Juliet, what did you say?"

Arms crossed, Juliet glared at Elise and repeated the answer. "You shouldn't have to give up anything for love. It should be effortless or else it's not real love."

No compromise. Why should she have to completely rearrange her entire belief system to appease one very stubborn man? The right man for her should recognize that she'd tried to upset the status quo only because she'd been forced to.

The right man for her would know he'd been everything to her.

"Finn?" Elise prompted and he sighed.

His gaze softened and he spoke directly to Juliet. "You shouldn't have to give up anything. Love should be easy and natural, like breathing. No one asks you to give up breathing so your heart can beat."

He had. He wanted her to forget Bernard had died serving the king's ego, wearing the same uniform Finn put on every day. She slammed her lids closed and shoved that thought away. It was too much.

"Right. Easy and natural. That part of us wasn't hard."

And with the words, the good and amazing and breath-stealing aspects of her relationship with Finn lit up the darkness inside her.

Everything had been effortless between them. If Bernard

hadn't had that accident, she and Finn would probably be married by now and living happily ever after.

"No. Not hard at all." Finn shook his head, his eyes still on her, searching for something that looked a lot like what she constantly wished for—a way to go back in time.

Which was impossible and the reason she'd fled to the States.

But she'd left Delamer because she thought Finn was marrying someone else. If that wasn't true, what else might she need to reexamine?

Elise put her hands out, placing them gently on their arms, connecting them. "Do you remember what you each said you were looking for in a relationship?"

"The calm in the storm," Juliet said, and her ire drained away to be replaced by the tiniest bit of hope.

"A place where I could just be, without all the other pressures of life," Finn said, his voice a little raspy. "That's how I answered the question."

He didn't move, but he felt closer. As if she could reach out and touch him, which she desperately wanted to do. Curled fingers dug into her thigh. Her heart tripped. This was not a good idea.

"So? We answered a couple of questions the same way. That's no surprise."

Finn agreed with a nod. "I would have been surprised if we didn't respond in a similar vein."

They'd always been of one mind, two hearts beating as one. When they sailed together, they never even had to talk, working in perfect tandem to reef the main or hull trim. They'd met while sailing with mutual friends, then fallen in love as the two of them skimmed the water again and again in Finn's boat.

"So," Elise said brightly, "maybe the better question is whether you can forget about the past and see how you both might have changed. You're in America. The divide you had in Delamer doesn't matter here. It's safe. Take some time on neutral ground to explore whether that effortless love still exists."

That was totally unnecessary. She'd never fallen out of love with Finn and being here in his presence after a long, cold year apart solidified the fact that she probably never would.

But that didn't mean they belonged together.

"Are you a relationship counselor or a matchmaker?" Juliet asked Elise without a trace of guile.

"Both. Whatever it takes to help people find happiness."

Happiness. That hadn't been on her list when she came to Elise, broken and desperate for a solution to end her pain. But instead of an American husband, she'd been handed an opportunity for a second chance with Finn.

He was the only man on earth who could rightly be called her match. The only man she'd ever wanted to let into her heart. That had always been true and Elise had somehow figured that out.

That was some computer program Elise used. Juliet had hoped for a bit of magic. Perhaps she'd gotten her wish.

"Elise is right," Finn said quietly. "This is neutral ground, with no room for politics. And it's a party. Dance with me."

Juliet nodded and hoped agreeing wasn't the stupidest thing she'd ever done.

Elise slipped away, not even trying to hide the relief plastered all over her face.

Juliet's eyelids pricked with tears as something shuddery and optimistic filled her empty soul. She would wallow in her few precious hours with Finn, and maybe it would lead to more. Maybe time and distance had diluted their differences.

Maybe he'd finally understand what his support and strength meant to her. She'd lost so much more than a brother a year ago. She'd also lost the love of her life.

* * *

Finn led Juliet to the dance floor, a minor miracle since his knees had gone numb.

This whole thing was ridiculous. He'd known there was something off about a matchmaker approaching his father, but he never could have predicted Elise's actual motivation or the result of his trip to Dallas.

What would the king say when he realized what he'd inadvertently done? Finn had been matched with a woman who'd caused his family immeasurable misery and created a scandal that had spawned countless aftereffects.

Yet Finn and Juliet had met again, paired by a supposedly infallible computer program. Everybody he'd talked to raved about EA International's process. Raved about Elise and how much she truly cared about the people she helped. So yesterday, Finn had walked through Elise's extensive match profile, answered her questions as honestly as he could and hoped for the best.

Only to have Juliet dropped back into his life with no warning.

The smartest move would have been to turn around and leave without a backward glance. Staying was the surest method to end up insane by the end of the night.

He'd asked Juliet to dance only because manners had been bred into him since birth. This was Elise's party and they were business associates. It was only polite.

But now he wasn't so sure that was the only reason.

Seeing Juliet again had kicked up a push-pull of emotions he'd have sworn were buried. Not the least of which was the intense desire to have her head on a platter. After he had her body in his bed.

Fitting Juliet into his arms, they swayed together to the music. It took mere moments to find the rhythm they'd always shared. He stared down into her familiar face, into the green eyes he'd never forgotten, and felt something loosen inside.

It was *Juliet,* but in capital, sparkling letters with giant exclamation points.

She'd been transformed.

The alterations were external, and he'd liked her exactly the way she'd looked the last time he'd seen her. But what if more than her hair had changed?

Could he really fly back to Delamer without taking a few hours to find out what might be possible that hadn't been possible before?

Now that he had her in his arms, the anger he'd carried with him for the past year was hard to hang on to.

"You look different," he blurted out. *Smooth.* Juliet had never tied up his tongue before. "Amazing. So beautiful. You're wearing cosmetics."

She blinked sultry eyes and smiled with lips stained the color of deep sunset. Even her height was different. He glanced down. Sexy heels showcased her delicate feet and straps buckled around her ankles highlighted the shapely curve of her legs. He had the sudden mental image of unbuckling those straps with his teeth.

That was it. Dancing was officially a form of torture.

This was all so surreal. She was still the same girl who'd stabbed him in the back but not the same. Tension coiled in his gut, choking off his air supply.

"Thanks. Elise gave me a few tips on how to be a girl." Juliet extended a hand to show off long coral-tipped nails. "Don't expect me to hoist any sails with these babies."

Finn couldn't help but grin. If she was going to play it as if everything was cool, he could too. "I'll do all the hard work. Looking at you is reward enough for my effort."

Her brows rose as she repositioned her hand at his waist. "Like the new me, do you?"

He could feel those nails through his jacket. How was that possible?

"I liked the old you." Before she'd skewered his heart on

the stake of her stubbornness. "But this you is great too. You're gorgeous. What prompted all of this?"

Long nails, swept-up hair. A mouthwatering backless dress he easily recognized as high-end. She was double-take worthy and then some.

"It's part of Elise's deal. She has a lot of high-powered, influential male clients and they expect a certain refinement in their potential mates. She spends a couple of months enhancing each of us, though admittedly, she spent far more time with me than some of the others. *Voila.* I am a new creation. Cinderella, at your service." Juliet glanced at him with a sweeping once-over. "She didn't tell you how all that worked?"

"Not in those terms. It was more of a general guarantee that the woman she matched me with would be able to handle everything that comes with being a princess."

Which, in Juliet's case, had never been a factor. He couldn't have cared less if she flubbed royal protocol or never picked up mascara. Because he'd loved her, once upon a time.

But that was over with a capital *O* and in an arranged marriage, he might as well get what he paid for—a demure, non-scandal-inducing woman who could erase the public's memory of the past year.

"Are you disappointed you got me instead?"

His laugh came out of nowhere. "I honestly don't know what I am, but disappointed is definitely not it."

Juliet could have been a great princess. She'd always understood his need to escape from his position occasionally. Finn gave one hundred percent to his job protecting Delamer's citizens, gladly participated in charity events and didn't have a moment's guilt over taking time away from the public eye. A lot of women wouldn't support that, would insist on being treated to the finer things in life.

Juliet had been perfectly content with a beach date or

sailing. Or staying in, his own personal favorite. No, it wasn't a surprise the computer had matched them.

The surprise lay in how much he still wanted her despite the still-present burn of her betrayal.

"What about you?" he asked. "Has the jury reconvened on whether seeing me again is a pleasant surprise?"

"The jury is busy trying not to trip over your feet while wearing four-inch heels."

The wry twist of her lips pulled an answering grin out of him.

He relaxed. This was still neutral ground and as long as everyone kept a sense of humor, the night was young.

"Let's get some champagne. I'm dying to know how you ended up in Dallas in a matchmaker's computer system."

As they turned to leave the dance floor, light flashed from the crowd to the left and then again in rapid succession. Photographs. From a professional camera.

Finn sighed. With the time difference, his father's phone call would come around midnight unless the king's secretary somehow missed the story, which was unlikely.

Finn would ask Elise to match him with someone new. Later.

Juliet waited until he'd led her to the bar and handed her a flute of bubbly Veuve Clicquot before responding. "It's your fault I sought out Elise."

"Mine?" He dinged the rims of their glasses together and took a healthy swallow in a futile attempt to gain some clarity. "I didn't even know Elise existed until a few days ago."

"It was the engagement announcement. If you were moving on, I needed to, as well. I couldn't do that in Delamer, so here I am." She spread her hands, flashing coral tips that made him imagine what they'd feel like at his waist once he'd shed his jacket and shirt.

The temperature in the ballroom went sky high as internal ripples of need spread. He'd only *thought* he was uncomfortable before.

"Like I said, there's no engagement. Not yet. My father and I agreed it was time I thought about settling down and he went on the bride hunt. Here I am, as well."

It was a sobering reminder. They'd both been trying to move past the scandal and breakup by searching for someone new. Was that what she truly wanted?

The thought of Juliet with another man ripped a hole in his gut. A shock considering how angry he still was about what she'd done.

"As much as I've tried to avoid it, I've seen the pictorial evidence of why your dad thought you needed to settle down. You've become the Party Prince." She shot him a quizzical glance, her gaze flat and unreadable. "It seems so unlike you. Sure, we had some fun dancing at clubs and stuff, but we usually left after an hour or so. Did I miss the part where you wanted to stay?"

"I never wanted to stay. I was always thinking about getting you alone."

"Some of the pictures were really hard to take," she admitted quietly, and he didn't need her to elaborate.

Heat climbed up his neck and flushed across his ears.

He'd always known she'd probably see all the photographs of him with other women and hear about his exploits, but he'd honestly never considered a scenario where they'd have an actual conversation about them. There wasn't a lot about the past year that filled him with pride.

"As long as we're handing out blame, that was *your* fault."

To her credit, she simply glanced at him with a blank expression. "How so?"

She *had* changed. The Juliet of before would have blasted him over such a stupid statement. "Well, not your fault, per se, but I was trying to drown out the memories. Focus on the future. Moving on, like you said."

"Did it work?"

"Not in the slightest."

Their gazes crashed and his lips tingled. He wanted to pull her against him and dive in. Kiss her until neither of them could remember anything other than how good they felt together.

She tossed back the last of her champagne as if she hadn't noticed the heavily charged moment. He wished he could say the same as all the blood rushed from his head, draining southward into a spectacular hard-on.

"What do we do now?" she asked.

"Have dinner with me," he said hoarsely. "Tomorrow night. For old time's sake."

Neither of them thought this match was a good idea. He knew that. But he couldn't resist stealing a few more forbidden hours with Juliet. No matter what she'd done in the past, he couldn't walk out of this ballroom and never see her again.

"I should have my head examined. But okay."

Her acceptance was fortuitously timed. A svelte woman and her friend nearly bowled Juliet over in an enthusiastic attempt to get a photo with him.

It was a common-enough request and he normally didn't mind. But tonight he wanted to be selfish and spend as much time with Juliet as he could, before his father interfered. Before all the reasons they'd split in the first place surfaced.

She'd always be the woman who burned a Delamer flag at the palace gates. The people of his country had long memories for acts of disloyalty to the crown.

And so did he.

There was no way crossing an ocean could create a different dynamic between two people. Because Juliet would never see he couldn't go against his father, and never understand that as the second son, Finn had little to offer the crown besides unconditional support.

If she ever did finally get it, all her sins would be forgiven. By everyone, including him.

That would happen when it snowed in Delamer during July.

Until then, he'd indulge in Juliet, ignore the rest and then ask Elise to match him with someone else.

Three

Juliet stared in the mirror and tried to concentrate on applying eye shadow to her lids as Dannie and Elise had shown her. Multiple times. Her scrambled brain couldn't focus.

Dazed and breathless well described the state Finn had left her in last night, and it hadn't cleared up in the almost twenty-four hours since. Finn's clean scent lingered in her nose, evoking painfully crisp memories of being with him, loving him.

And suffering the agony of finally accepting that he cared nothing for her. Cared nothing for her pain at losing the brother she'd helped raise.

All Finn cared about was zipping himself into the uniform of Delamer's military and wearing it with nationalistic pride.

Madness. Why had she agreed to this date again?

Elise stuck her head in the door of Juliet's room.

"Almost ready? Oh. You're not even dressed yet. What are you wearing?"

A flak jacket if she was smart. And if they made one you could wear internally. But she'd come to America in hopes of finding a new direction. She'd stay open to the possibility that time had dulled Finn's zealous fervor.

One date. One night. What did she have to lose?

Her eyes narrowed. She'd stay open, but that didn't mean Finn didn't deserve to suffer for his sins.

"I want to wear something that will show Finn what I've endured in your makeover program because of him. The sexier and more painful for him, the better." Hours and hours of hot rollers, facials and balancing on four-inch heels were about to hit his royal highness where it hurt.

"Yellow dress, then. I brought you something." Elise held out a velvet jewelry box.

Mystified, Juliet opened the lid to reveal a silver heart charm dangling from a matching chain, and another heart dangled from the first, one clutching the other to keep it from falling. "It's beautiful. Thank you."

Simple but elegant, perfect for a tomboy who'd rather be doing something athletic than primping.

Elise clasped it around Juliet's throat. "I give all my makeover clients a necklace. I'm glad you like it."

When the hired car with dark windows rolled to a stop outside Elise's house, Juliet was slightly ashamed to realize she'd been haunting the window for nearly fifteen minutes waiting for its appearance. How pathetic.

She swung open Elise's front door, and the sheer heat in the pointed once-over Finn gave her swept everything else away.

"Hi."

"Wow," was all he said in response.

Little pinpricks worked their way across her cheeks in a stupid blush. "Yeah? It's okay? Elise picked out the dress."

And what was under it, but odds were slim this date would go well enough to model the silk lingerie.

In answer, he grasped her hand and led her out of the house. "I like what I see so far. Come with me so I can properly evaluate the rest."

Her arm tingled from his touch against her palm, warming her in places Finn had always affected quite expertly.

Whom was she kidding? Finn was nothing if not talented enough to get her out of the sunny yellow dress and ivory alligator sandals in less than five minutes if he so chose.

She let him hold her hand down the walk. Partially because she wanted to pretend things were somewhat normal. That this was a date with an exciting man who was whirling her off to a night of possibilities.

He tucked her into the backseat of the luxurious town car and settled in next to her, his heavy masculine presence overwhelming in such close confines. She almost jumped out of her skin when he leaned forward, brushing her arm and setting off a throng of iron-winged butterflies in her stomach. But he only pressed the button to raise the dividing panel between the driver and the back, lingering far too long for such a simple task.

The car slid smoothly away from the curb and flowed into traffic.

"Where are you taking me?" she croaked and cleared the awareness and heat from her throat. "Some place trendy and hip?"

"Not on your life. I'm not sharing you with hordes of paparazzi and gawkers."

Oh. "Are your bodyguards in another car? They're never far away unless you're working."

He squeezed the hand he was still holding. "Worried? I'll keep you safe."

Without a doubt. It was what he did. Most people ignored those in distress, but he reveled in protecting people. Always had.

They chatted about inane topics such as Dallas weather, but thankfully, he did not mention football. The only sport he'd ever followed was Formula 1 racing, but he respected her complete boredom with cars looping a track and seldom talked about it.

"We're here," Finn pronounced as the car stopped under a tree.

Juliet took in the scene through the window. Beyond the roadway lay a secluded private park, where a single table and chairs had been set out with a perfect view of the sunset. A man in a tall white chef's hat stood off to the side, chopping with a flashing knife on a temporary work surface.

"Nice," Juliet acknowledged with a nod and peeked up at Finn from under her lashes. "Out of curiosity, what would you have done if it was raining?"

"We'd get wet. Or we'd ride around and look for a drive-through with decent takeout and eat in the car."

She smiled at his pragmatism. He'd never let a little thing like a change of plans put a hitch in his stride. "Then I'm glad it's a clear night."

His answering grin warmed her neglected parts far past acceptability.

"After the obscene amount of money I paid to rent this park for the night, including an added fifteen percent to buy out the existing reservation, it wouldn't dare rain."

No, it wouldn't. Rain didn't fall on the head of the privileged. Once, he'd made her feel as if the evils of the world couldn't reach them, as if he'd always be the one person she could count on. Until he wasn't.

Finn jumped from the car and helped her rise from the low leather seat. The driver sped away after being told to return in two hours. They were alone.

Juliet started to walk up the path to the center of the park.

Finn tugged on her hand, swinging her around face-to-face. "Maybe we should get something out of the way."

"What's that?" The words were half out of her mouth when the sizzle between them and the glint of anticipation in his blue eyes answered that question.

He was going to kiss her.

Involuntarily, her tongue came out to wet suddenly dry lips and his eyes lingered on them before he met her gaze squarely.

"This."

Juliet froze as Finn's mouth descended.

A part of her screamed to break his hold, to run before it was too late. Her legs wouldn't move.

Then his lips claimed hers, taking her mouth powerfully, demanding a response. It was *Finn.* So familiar and hot and everything she'd been missing for a very long time. She moaned and leaned into it, desperate to taste the divine, to plunge into him.

Euphoria rushed through her veins, deluging her senses with sharp, slick desire. Pushing eager fingers through his short hair, she held his head in place as the kiss exploded with incandescent energy.

Their bodies melded, aligning just right, just as always. *Yes.* Oh, yes, she'd missed him.

Missed how he never held back, missed his intoxicating presence and missed how his strength enabled hers.

His hand slipped beneath a spaghetti strap at her shoulder and he skimmed silky fingertips down her back. If he kept this up, her lingerie would be making an appearance after all, very shortly.

He pulled away before she'd even begun to sate herself on the thrill of his touch. Breathing heavily, he rested his forehead on hers. "That didn't quite do what I hoped."

It had certainly done plenty for her. "What were you hoping for?"

"That it would allow me to eat in peace instead of thinking about whether you still taste the same. Now I'm pretty sure a repeat is all I'll be thinking about."

She hid a smile. "If dinner goes well, a repeat might be on the menu."

His eyelids dropped to a sexy, slumberous half-mast. "I'll keep that in mind. Shall we eat?"

"If you insist." He might be able to eat. The flip-flopping in her stomach didn't bode well for her.

There were still plenty of sparks between them. Not that she'd wondered. But that kiss had at least answered one lingering question—whether they could pick up where they'd left off.

The answer was a resounding yes.

As long as they could sort through the past. The scandal. The utter sense of betrayal he'd left her with.

Suddenly, she didn't want to think about it. There weren't any laws that said they had to immediately hash out how abandoned she'd felt.

Finn led her to a chair and helped her sit, then took his own seat. As the chef served a delicious first course of tomatoes drizzled with balsamic vinegar, Finn mentioned the queen's bout with appendicitis and Juliet murmured appropriate well-wishes. She then shared that her second-youngest sister was expecting a baby and nodded at Finn's hearty congratulations.

A very pleasant conversation all the way around. Thankfully, at least some of the social graces Elise had tirelessly drilled into Juliet's head had held.

Except she couldn't get that kiss out of her mind, and watching him talk wasn't helping. It had been a very long time since she'd been kissed. Since the scandal.

Finn hadn't let any grass grow under his feet in the female companionship department, but she'd taken the ostrich approach. If she stuck her head in the sand long enough, all those feminine urges would dry up and go away.

She'd been pretty successful thus far. Yet in two seconds, he'd done a spectacular job of reminding her sheer will couldn't stop the flood of longing for the tender affections of one very talented prince.

"Did you quit your job in Delamer?" Finn asked once the chef finished serving the main course of corvina sea bass and asparagus over quinoa.

"I did."

The short phrase communicated none of the grief she'd experienced over resigning her position teaching English to bright young minds. She loved the children she taught and had hoped to find a way to continue teaching in America.

Then she remembered.

She hadn't been matched with an American husband. If things worked out with Finn, she could go home, go back to her job, back to the sea. Back into his arms.

Was such a fairy tale actually possible?

With renewed interest, she swept her gaze over the man opposite her. "Are you still flying helicopters?"

"Of course. I'll do that until the day I die. Or until they ground me. Whichever comes first."

No shock. He'd always loved flying as much as he did the search and rescue part of his job. The source of contention wasn't *what* he did but whom he did it for.

"Hmm," she said noncommittally and forked up a bite of fish. "I wasn't going to jump right into this, but I'm on uncertain ground here. Tell me what you hoped to gain from Elise's match. Are you really looking for a wife?"

Finn set his wineglass down firmly and focused on her, the warmth in his expression all too easy to read. "I can't keep being the Party Prince. The best I thought I could do was an arranged marriage, like my parents. Means to an end, and I'm okay with that. What about you?"

That focus unleashed a shiver she couldn't quite control. "I was prepared to marry whomever Elise picked. I couldn't stay in Delamer. Not with the way things fell apart between us. Marriage was a means to an end for me, as well."

She'd like to stop there and just enjoy this date. But there were too many unanswered questions for that.

"What is this dinner all about? We aren't having a first date like we would with the matches we'd envisioned for ourselves. This is something else. We have history we're avoiding. Important history. History that has to be resolved."

Finn's gaze grew keen. "You want to throw down? Go for it."

"No, I don't." She shook her head, though he was certainly the only man who could take whatever she dished out. "We've fought enough in our relationship. I want to work things out like adults. Can we?"

With a smile, Finn picked up her hand and rubbed a knuckle with his smooth thumb. "Let's hold off on history with a capital *H*. Dinner is about me and you reconnecting. That's the part of our history I prefer to remember."

"Okay."

She'd waited this long. What were a few more hours? The time would be well spent working through what she'd realized she'd done wrong a year ago. Instead of fighting so hard to convince Finn to talk to his father, she should have gone about this a whole different way.

If Finn was truly looking for a wife, what was stopping her from marrying him in order to bring about change from inside the palace gates? Princess Juliet would have far more power to influence the king away from mandatory military service than plain old Juliet Villere.

And then maybe she could finally be rid of the crushing guilt she felt over Bernard's death.

Dinner forgotten, Finn nearly swallowed his tongue when Juliet pushed back her chair and waltzed to his side of the table wearing a sultry smile and sporting a very naughty glint in her eye. She extended a hand, which he took silently, and then he stood, allowing her to lead him up the path into a more heavily wooded section of the park.

"Interested in the native fauna and flora?" he asked when the silence stretched on.

"More interested in how well the flora conceals us." She backed him up against a tree and stepped into his torso deliberately, rubbing her firm breasts against his chest.

Oh, so *that's* what she had in mind. Obviously, she remembered how good it had been as well as he did. And apparently she had no problem rekindling that part of their relationship, impending matches to other people notwithstanding. Fantastic.

"That earlier kiss was good. Make this one better," she commanded.

Instantly, he complied, yanking her into his arms and exploring her back flat-handed. Their mouths met, aligning perfectly, and heat arced between them.

Juliet.

Desire thundered through his body, soaking him with a storm of need. She was in his arms, overpowering his senses as if he'd jumped from his helicopter without a parachute.

Thank God Elise had pulled her devious stunt to put them in each other's path again, if only for one night. Tomorrow, he and Juliet could both be matched with more suitable mates.

The kiss deepened and Juliet snuggled against him as if she'd never been away. Heat swept along his skin, craving the perfection of Juliet's beautiful body against it. He groaned and shifted a knee between her legs, and his thigh hit the sweet spot immediately.

That was some dress. The high-heeled and insanely sexy shoes helped too.

He lifted his lips a fraction and murmured, "I've missed you. Can we take this someplace more private?"

Her smile curved against his cheek and she nodded.

Grasping her hand, he pulled her in the direction of the newly returned town car, settled her in the backseat and nearly dived in after her.

He'd never been able to resist her, and now he didn't have to.

Somehow, Finn had been granted a reprieve. The king hadn't phoned him to demand an explanation for the photographs from last night. Now he had this one chance to recapture a small slice of heaven before submitting to an arranged marriage.

He'd hoped, against all logical reason, that the woman Elise matched him with could heal his broken heart. The odds of that happening with the woman who'd smashed it in the first place were zilch. Especially since he'd never in a million years give it to her again.

So he'd grant EA International another chance. Once he had a new bride by his side, the public would forget about the Party Prince and he could become known for something worthwhile.

The People's Prince. He liked the sound of that.

In the meantime, he could have Juliet…and all the good things about their relationship. Without getting into the painful past.

"So I take it you thought dinner went well?" he asked with a grin he couldn't have wiped off his face for anything. "You know, since you agreed to a repeat of the kiss."

Her hair was a little mussed from his fingers. He itched to pull out all the pins and let those silky locks tumble over him.

"I'm staying open to where the night leads. But it's been good so far." She studied him speculatively. "We're not fighting. We're connecting, like you said."

They weren't fighting because they'd thus far avoided the problem. And he was totally prepared to keep avoiding history with a capital *H* for as long as possible. "If this driver would step on it, we'd be connecting a whole lot more."

She laughed. "We have all night. But while we're on the subject, does connecting mean you're open to being on my side this time around?"

Apparently she did not subscribe to the same desire for avoidance of the past. "I've always been on your side."

"If that was true, you'd never have taken the stance you did." Her expression closed in. "You'd have supported me and my family when we tried to talk to your father."

That was the Juliet he'd last seen in Delamer. His stomach dipped. The connection part of the evening appeared to be over.

"You say that like I had no choice, like I had to agree with you or it equaled lack of support." But that's how he'd felt, as well. As if she couldn't see his side. Instantly, it all came roaring back. All the hurt and anger he'd been living with for a very long year. "You didn't support me either. And I never asked you to go against everything you believed in."

She yanked her hand from his. The heat in her expression reminded him she got just as passionate about taking his head off when they clashed.

So much for dinner going well.

"That's exactly what you wanted me to do." A lone tear tracked down Juliet's face and his gut clenched. It hurt to see someone as strong as Juliet crying. "Forget about Bernard and support you every day as you put on the uniform of the Delamer military. Every day, I'd be reminded Bernard died wearing the same uniform and I did nothing to avenge that. Every day, I'd be reminded you chose to stand with the crown instead of with me."

The car stopped at the private entrance to his hotel. It was positioned discreetly in the secluded rear section of the property, off to the side of the underground parking garage.

Finn didn't get out. This wasn't finished, not even close.

"Vengeance well describes it. You humiliated me. That protest garnered the attention of the entire world. Juliet—" Finn pinched the bridge of his nose. They should have recorded this conversation and played it back, saving them the trouble of having it again. "I'm a member of the House of Couronne. You burned the flag of the country my family rules *while we were dating.* How can you not see what that did to me?"

Not to mention the man she'd vilified was his *father.* He loved his father, loved his country. She'd wanted him to choose her over honor.

"My family is forever changed because of your father's policies. Bernard is gone and—" Her voice seized, choking off the rest. After a moment, she stared up at him through watery eyes laced with devastation. "A man who claimed to love me would have understood. He would have done anything to make that right."

But he wasn't just a man and never would be. He could no sooner remove the royal blood in his veins than he could fly blindfolded.

The tearing in his chest felt as if it was on repeat, as well. "A woman who claimed to love me would have realized I have an obligation to the crown, whether it's on my head or not. I don't get the choice to be someone other than Prince Alain Phineas of Montagne, Duke of Marechal, House of Couronne."

He belonged to one of the last royal houses of Europe and he owed it to his ancestors to preserve the country they'd left in his care. No matter how antiquated the notion became in an increasingly modern world.

Now he was ready to get out of the car. To be somewhere she wasn't. That was one thing that hadn't changed—Juliet causing him to feel a touch insane as he veered between extreme highs and lows very quickly. She followed him to the curb, clearly determined to continue twisting the spike through his heart.

"I never wanted you to be someone else. I loved *you*."

Past tense. It didn't escape his notice.

"You meant everything to me, Finn. But it's peacetime. The mandatory military service law is ridiculous. Why can't you see that your royal obligation is to stop being so stubborn and think about people's lives?"

"For the same reason you can't see that the military is mine," he said quietly.

He'd never wear the crown. Flying helicopters was the one thing he could do that Alexander, as the crown prince, couldn't. Juliet's refusal to get out from under her righteous indignation prevented *her* from taking *his* side.

She was the stubborn one.

Anger coated the back of his throat. Juliet was still the same crusader under the cosmetics and sexy dress. She was still determined to alter the heart of the institution to which he'd sworn loyalty.

Suddenly, it was all too easy to resist her. He didn't have the slightest interest in rehashing all of this for the rest of the night, regardless of the more tangible rewards. He'd never bowed to anyone before and he wasn't about to start now.

Arms crossed against her abdomen, Juliet stared dry-eyed at the unoccupied valet booth behind Finn. "I think it's safe to say the date was not a success."

"I'll have the driver take you back to Elise's house." Finn tapped on the passenger-side window.

The squeal of tires on cement reverberated through the quiet underground lot. A van sped down the ramp and wedged tight against the rear bumper of Finn's hired car. Four men with distinctly shaved heads, beefy physiques and dark clothing jumped out, trouble written all over them.

"Juliet, get in the car," Finn muttered, angling his body to shield her as the men advanced on them.

He never should have given his security guys the night off.

It was the last thing he registered as the world went black.

Four

Grit scraped at Juliet's eyeballs. She tried to lift a hand to rub them. And couldn't.

Heavy fog weighed down her brain. Something was wrong. She couldn't see and her hands weren't working. Or her arms.

Rapid blinking didn't improve her eyesight. It was so *dark*.

She never drank enough alcohol to be this fuzzy about her current whereabouts…and how she'd gotten there… and what had happened prior to.

"Juliet. Can you hear me?" Finn's voice. It washed over her, tripping a hodgepodge of memories, most of them X-rated.

Finn's voice in the dark equaled one activity and one activity only. Pleasure, the feel of his skin on hers, urgency of the highest order to fly into the heavens with him—

Wait. What was *Finn* doing here?

"Yeah," she mumbled thickly. "I hear you."

Pain split through her brain the moment her jaw moved, cutting off her speech, her thoughts, even her breath. Inhaling sharply, she rolled to shift positions—or tried to.

Her muscles refused to cooperate. "What's…going on?"

"Tranquilizer," Finn explained grimly and spit out a nasty curse in French. "I think they must have used the same dose on both of us."

The sinister-looking men. An unmarked van. The date with so much promise that ended badly. And then got worse.

Juliet groaned. "What? Why did they give us tranquilizers?"

"So they could snatch us without a fight," Finn growled. "And they should be thanking their lucky stars they did. Otherwise I would have removed their spleens with a tire iron."

Snippets of dinner with Finn flashed through her mind. Okay, good. So she hadn't lost her memory and she wasn't suffering from the effects of a hangover. "We were kidnapped? Stuff like that only happens in the movies."

"Welcome to reality." The heavy sarcasm meant he was frustrated. And maybe a little worried. That didn't bode well. Finn always knew what to do.

Shifting along her right side indicated his general vicinity. Not too far away. "Can you move? Are we tied up?"

It was hard for her to tell. Everything was numb. That's why she couldn't move. She'd been *drugged*. And blinded, maybe forever.

What sort of scheme had she stumbled into simply by being in the wrong place at the wrong time with the wrong companion?

A strong, masculine hand smoothed hair from her face, throwing her back to another time and place where that happened with frequency.

"Nah," Finn said. "They shot us up with enough narcotics that they didn't need to tie us up. I'm okay. The cocktail didn't affect me nearly as long as it did you."

Gray invaded her vision and got lighter and lighter with each passing moment. Thank goodness. "Where are we?"

"Not sure. In a house of some sort. I was afraid to leave you alone in case you needed CPR, or the welcoming committee showed up, so I didn't do more than look out the window."

A fuzzy Finn swam through her eyesight, along with a few background details. White walls. Bed.

Finn held her hand. She squeezed, gratified that her fingers had actually responded, and then licked dry lips. "Guards?"

"Not that I can tell. I haven't seen anyone since I regained consciousness." Finn nodded to a door. "As soon as you can walk, we'll see what's what."

"Help me sit up," she implored him.

Finn's arm came around her waist and she slumped against him. Two tries later, her legs swung off the bed and thumped to the floor.

Barefoot. Had they taken her shoes? She wasn't even completely over the sticker shock at the price of those ivory alligator sandals and now they were probably in a Dumpster somewhere. And she'd actually kind of liked them.

"Now help me stand," she said. Their captors might return at any moment and they both needed to be prepared. Sure Finn was stronger and better trained, but she was mad enough to take out at least one.

Finn shook his head. "There's no prize for Fastest Recovery After Being Tranquilized. Take your time."

"I want to get out of here. The faster we figure out what that's going to take, the better." Throbbing behind her eyes distracted her for a moment, but she ignored it as best she could. "How far do you think they took us from your hotel?"

Elise would be worried. Maybe she'd already called the

police and even now, SWAT teams were tearing apart Dallas in search of Prince Alain.

Or…Elise might be smugly certain she'd staged the match of the century and assume they'd gotten so wrapped up in each other, Juliet had forgotten to call. The matchmaker probably didn't realize they were missing yet.

"There's only one way to find out where we are. Come on." Finn took one step and her knees buckled.

Without missing a beat, he swept her up in his strong arms and she almost sighed at the shamefully romantic gesture.

Except he was still the Prince of Pigheadedness. Why had she ever thought she could marry him—even under the guise of changing Delamer policy from the inside?

Finn deposited her easily on the pale blue counterpane and kept a light but firm hand on her shoulder so she couldn't sit up. "It's early afternoon, if the daylight outside the window is any indication. We've probably been captives for about eighteen hours. The entire Delamer armed forces are likely already on their way to assist the local authorities. Stay here and I'll go figure out the lay of the land."

"You're not the boss just because you're a boy."

He scowled. "I'm not trying to be the boss. I'm trying to keep you from cracking your stubborn head open. If you think you can walk, be my guest."

With a flourish, he gestured toward the door.

Now she had to do it, if for no other reason than to prove His Highness wrong. Slowly, she wobbled upright and took excruciatingly slow steps, one in front of the other.

The door opened easily, despite her certainty that she'd find it locked. It swung open to reveal a bare hallway. "Let's go."

She'd almost taken an entire step across the threshold when Finn leaped in front like her own personal bulletproof vest.

She rolled her eyes. Of course. Bullets bounced off the perpetually arrogant all the time, right?

"Don't you have any sense?" he growled in her ear. "This is a dangerous situation."

If the kidnappers had wanted to harm them, they would have. Finn was more valuable alive than dead. "If anything dangerous is lurking in these halls, it's going to get you first. Then who will protect me?"

"What makes you so certain I'd lose?" he whispered over his shoulder as he flowed noiselessly away from the bedroom. He'd always moved with elegant flair, but this cloak-and-dagger-style grace was sexier than she'd like to admit.

She dogged his steps, tearing her gaze from his spectacular backside with difficulty. "A hunch. If the kidnappers had tranquilizers, they probably have guns. Unless you think they're in this for the opportunity to have afternoon tea with royalty."

"Shh." He halted where the hallway ended in a large room and poked his head out to scan the space with a double sweep. "All clear."

An inviting living area with a fireplace and high-end furniture opened up around her as she stepped out of the hall. "This is not what I would have envisioned as a place to keep captives."

A breathtaking panorama of sparkling sea unfolded beyond a wall of glass. The house perched on a low cliff overlooking the water. That particular shade of blue was etched on her heart, and her breath caught.

"We're not in Dallas anymore," Finn announced needlessly. "And those were some serious drugs the kidnappers used if they brought us clear across the Atlantic without me realizing it."

"We're on an island."

She was home. Back on the Mediterranean, close to everything she loved. She'd sailed these waters often enough to recognize the hills rising behind the city, the coastal landscape.

Home. She never thought she'd see it again. The small ripples in the surface of the water. The wheeling birds. The sky studded with puffy clouds. All of the poetic nuances of the sea bled into her chest, squeezing it, nearly wrenching loose a sob.

"Yeah." Finn skirted the large couch and squinted at the shoreline visible in the distance. "About two miles off the coast of Delamer. There are, I don't know, at least four or five different islands in this quadrant. It's hard to tell from the ground which one we're on."

"There can't be more than a handful of people who own houses on these islands. It would be pretty easy to figure out who kidnapped us." She shook her head. "We were taken by the dumbest kidnappers ever. They dumped us right in our own backyard."

"Dumb—or really smart. Who would think to look for us here? We're both supposed to be in Dallas."

"Well…good point."

So if all the search efforts were concentrated on the other side of the Atlantic, they were going to have to rescue themselves.

"And leaving us on an island means they don't have to stick around," she said. "Very difficult for us to escape. I assume they took both our cell phones."

He nodded. "And I'm sure the kidnappers did a full sweep to remove all devices with access to the outside world."

Gingerly, he gripped the handle of the sliding door and pulled. It slid open, and the swift Mediterranean breeze doused her with its unique marine-life-drenched tang.

Goodness how she'd missed it.

She followed Finn outside onto the covered flagstone patio, set with wicker outdoor furniture around a brick fire pit. The cry of gulls overhead was like hearing a favorite song for the first time in ages. There were worse places to be held captive than in a cliff-side villa in the south of France during early summer.

But they were still captives.

Finn gripped the wrought iron railing surrounding the patio and peered down the cliff to the rocky shore below. "The slip is empty."

Sure enough, the dock was boat-free. "Maybe there's a kayak or something in storage that the kidnappers forgot about."

"We should definitely check around. I'm still not convinced we're alone." Finn grimaced. "Why would they leave us unsupervised in what's essentially a vacation spot? None of this makes any sense."

"Kidnapping as a whole doesn't make any sense. How is kidnapping you, and by extension me, going to achieve changes in the king's policies?"

Even in the midst of her lowest point of grief over Bernard's death, she'd have never willingly put another human in harm's way to promote her political agenda.

"One would assume we're being held for ransom." Finn shot her a wry sideways glance. "Not everyone is a crusader, you know. Though I find it a bit endearing you immediately jumped to the conclusion that the motive here is political gain."

Her spine stiffened. Why didn't he call her naive too, while he was at it? "You don't have to make fun of me. I get that you don't agree with me."

"I'm not making fun of you. I was being dead serious. Your passion for your principles is one of my favorite things about you."

He tipped her chin up to force her gaze to his.

She let him and blamed it on her half-tranquilized brain. But no quantity of numbing agents could stop the flutter in her chest when he looked at her with his eyes all liquid and bottomless and beautiful. Worse, it was clear he was telling the truth.

She looked away without comment. Because really, what could she say to that? It was the perfect encapsulation of their relationship. He appreciated her passion but not what she was passionate about. She loved his sense of loyalty but not what he swore allegiance to.

His hand fell to his side and he stared out over the water as if engrossed by the view.

The endless vicious circle they'd been plunged into could never be broken, and the crushing sadness of it gripped her insides anew.

Maybe she should catch a clue from the kidnappers. They'd exhibited a ruthless determination to reach their goals—whatever those goals might be—and she could do the same.

Not everyone was a crusader, but it took only one to upset the status quo.

For Bernard.

If she eliminated her emotions from the equation, perhaps she could still figure out a way to get the reform she wanted. First, she had to figure out how to get off this island.

Finn laced his fingers at the back of his neck to keep from reaching for Juliet again. She obviously didn't welcome his touch. He understood why—the storm of last night's argument still lingered between them.

But he'd been forced to watch her ashen face for an eternity, praying she'd wake up soon. Praying their captors didn't return with unsavory appetites. He didn't have a problem doing others bodily harm to protect Juliet, but he liked it better when he didn't have to.

Now that she was awake, he had a nearly incontrollable urge to fold her into his embrace and assure himself she was really okay.

She cleared her throat. "We should split up and search the property for a boat."

Obviously she was on the road to recovery.

"Are you out of your mind? Why on earth would you think I'd let you out of my sight?"

She'd just made an excellent point about men with guns, and she thought splitting up was a good plan?

Scowling, she tied her hair up in messy knot, as if preparing to wade into a brawl. "Because we need to get off this island in a hurry and we'll search faster if we do it separately."

"We're not splitting up," he growled. "Walk fast and that'll achieve the same end."

With a withering glare, she took off down the stairs bolted to the cliff side, and her pace was a clear dare-you-to-keep-up. He scrambled after her, easily matching her long-legged stride until they hit sea level. Wordlessly, they tramped over the rocky shoreline and he clamped his mouth closed lest he accidentally show some concern for the sharp rocks digging into her bare feet.

If she'd slow down a minute, he might have volunteered the location of her shoes—in the closet of the room where she'd slept off the tranquilizer. Though the sexy spiked heels probably weren't the best choice for beach-tramping.

"There's nothing here," she said, hands on her hips. The breeze pulled stands of hair from the knot at her nape, wrapping them around her face and neck.

His blood pumped faster as he took in the sight.

Did she have any idea how beautiful she was? Especially framed by the homeland and sea he loved.

He still wanted to sweep her into his arms and forget everything else but pleasure.

He glanced away. "There's a lot of island left to cover. Don't give up yet."

"I wasn't giving up. I was reevaluating. We should be looking for some way to start a fire. Surely there are people out on the water, and someone is doing your job in your place, right? Smoke signals are a better bet than searching for a boat."

"That's a good idea," he lied.

It would never work. Everyone knew the dozens of small islands off the coast of Delamer were owned by wealthy, influential people. Who would dare intrude on someone's private domain to investigate what they'd assume was a bonfire on the beach?

But it was better than doing nothing.

They climbed the stairs to the patio. In the lavishly appointed kitchen, Finn slung open cabinets and drawers in search of matches or a lighter.

Juliet poked her head out of the walk-in pantry. "Well, if we aren't rescued soon, at least we won't starve. Come see this. There are enough provisions in here to feed all your coast guard buddies for a month."

It was the second time she'd mentioned his job in less than ten minutes, and derision laced her tone without apology. She didn't see anything wrong with disparaging a profession he loved.

He wanted to wring her neck as much as he wanted her naked. Push-pull. Seemed as if he'd never escape it.

He swallowed the frustration and joined her. True to her description, boxes and jars lined the shelves of the well-stocked pantry. Cereal, pasta, canned beans and fruits—nearly every variety of dry goods he could imagine.

Curious now, he exited to the kitchen and pulled open the double doors of the stainless steel refrigerator. "Same here. Our captors went to great lengths to ensure we'd have three square meals a day."

The refrigerator held steaks, chicken breasts, fresh vegetables and staples such as milk and butter, all unopened and unexpired.

Juliet brushed his arm as she came up beside him to

peer into the interior. "It makes me uneasy. How long are they expecting to keep us here?"

Worry lined her face, which was still a little white. Most of her makeup had worn off, allowing her true beauty to shine through. He hated seeing it marred by stress.

"Wish I knew." Frustration returned in a rush. With it came the "if-onlys": *If only I hadn't given Gomez and La-Salle the night off. If only I'd invited Juliet to dinner in my hotel room. If only I'd had five more seconds to react when the van pulled up.*

That was a sure way to get his temper in a knot and resolve exactly nothing.

"Why don't you check over near the fireplace for matches?"

The farther away she was, the less she could affect his senses.

As she left the kitchen, he shoved both hands in his pockets. Paper crinkled under his knuckles and he withdrew an envelope with the king's seal prominently displayed in the center. An envelope that hadn't been in his pocket last night.

A strange sense of foreboding slid along Finn's spine.

He slipped an index finger under the seal and withdrew the folded page, his mind already piecing together aspects of this odd kidnapping plot into a whole he didn't like.

Exactly as he suspected, the page bore a note written in his father's bold hand.

Sorry to inconvenience you, blah, blah, but unexpected events caused me to reevaluate blah, blah.

Finn's gaze zeroed in on the last paragraph:

The Villere family is gaining traction in turning public opinion against my rule. Use this time I'm giving you with Juliet well. Patch things up with her and use your relationship to influence both her and her family into dropping their inflammatory political campaign. Marry her and en-

sure it's clear the Villere family sides with the crown. It's the most advantageous match for everyone.

Now Finn knew why he'd never heard from his father about the photographs from Elise's party.

The king had orchestrated a kidnapping plot instead.

Finn's throat tightened. No wonder their captors had left them unsupervised in paradise. It was forced seclusion so Finn had the opportunity to seduce Juliet into siding with him instead of her family. Kidnapping allowed Finn to claim innocence in the deal, and furthermore allowed them to commiserate as they endured their circumstances.

It was fiendishly ingenious. And insane.

The paper crumbled in Finn's fist. His father had gone too far. Juliet had been drugged, not to mention frightened. For what? So Finn could perform a miracle and make Juliet an advocate of the crown? If that was possible, he'd have done it a year ago.

"Found the matches," she called with the most cheer she'd exhibited since coming out of unconsciousness.

Matches were totally unnecessary given this new development. No one was looking for them.

No one would take the slightest bit of notice of a plume of smoke coming from this island, which he now knew for certain was Île de Etienne, where Alexander and Portia owned the only house occupying the entire hunk of rock. This luxurious cage doubled as a lover's retreat for the crown prince and his wife, which was why Finn had never been invited to check it out.

Was his brother in on the plot too? Was everyone in the royal family waiting to see how Finn would handle this twist?

The best way to combat the king's underhanded tactics was to tell Juliet exactly what was going on.

"A fire isn't going to help. Listen, you need to—"

"No, you listen." She scowled. "You don't know everything because you're in the military. You can sit around here and wait for your buddies to show up, but I'm not going to. I want to go home."

Turning on her heel, she flounced from the kitchen, her gorgeous backside swinging under her crinkled but still very sexy yellow dress. The shush of the sliding door opening and then being shut—likely with Juliet on the outside—reverberated in the suddenly quiet house.

Finn sank onto a bar stool with a groan and put his aching head in his palms. What an obstinate, hardheaded woman. Those very qualities had caused him immeasurable pain a year ago, and only an idiot would step up for a repeat.

The last thing he wanted to do was chase after her, and the only silver lining in this situation was that he didn't have to. If nothing else, the king's note reassured Finn they weren't in any danger from zealous criminals who might return at any moment to start slicing off fingers.

What had the king been thinking? Well, that wasn't a mystery. It was all there in blue fountain pen. Finn had an opportunity to make an advantageous match, exactly as his father had discussed before sending Finn off to Dallas. It was merely the definition of "advantageous" that had changed.

If it hadn't been happening to him, Finn might have appreciated the brilliance of the move. With no access to the outside world, Juliet wouldn't realize her family was turning the tide in their quest to see someone pay for Bernard's death. Furthermore, the king surely knew he was playing to Finn's sense of honor and duty to the crown.

Hands flat on the bar, Finn shoved to his feet. He would not be an active party to deceiving Juliet, especially not to the point of marrying her and then influencing her to side against her family. *Influence* was code for *coerce*. Their differences could only be truly resolved if she chose him willingly.

And that wasn't happening. She was far too stubborn and she still made him far too angry.

Finn went outside, determined to tell Juliet what the king had done. Then, they could work together to escape this ridiculous plot.

Smoke plumed from the rocky shore. He peered over the cliff's edge. Juliet stood near a blazing wood patio chair, turned upside down on the ground. Apparently his brother would be short a piece or two of furniture the next time he was in residence, which was Alexander's due for lending the house to their father's scheme.

"Any luck?" Finn called as he descended the stairs.

"Yeah, can't you see the Delamer armed forces storming the beach?" she retorted, throwing his earlier words back at him. "You must not be as important as you think since no one's come to rescue us yet."

Actually, he was *more* important than he'd thought, which was why they were both in this situation. "I tried to tell you a fire wouldn't work."

"Feel free to come up with a plan that will work, Genius."

He opened his mouth to blurt out the truth. Something in her posture, or the wind, or something beating through his chest stopped him.

He was important.

More important than he'd realized.

The king wasn't pushing chess pieces across his royal board—this situation had been carefully constructed to allow Finn to shape the future of Delamer. His brother couldn't do this. Neither could his father. Only Finn had a prayer of swaying Juliet and her family away from their attacks on the king and the Delamer military.

Finn, the second son, wasn't useless after all.

The king possessed a sharper mind than Finn had credited. If Finn told Juliet about the king's involvement in the kidnapping, it would only fuel her ire. Who knew what she'd do to retaliate? The goal was to get her to stop disparaging his family, not make it worse.

Furthermore, if Finn *didn't* do as his father asked, the king might find another way to handle the problem of Juliet and her family, a way that could potentially destroy their lives.

Finn alone held all the winning cards.

If he did as his father asked, he'd save his country and have Juliet again. In his life, in his bed. But never in his heart. That part of their relationship was over.

Juliet stared out over the water, her face troubled.

"I'm racking my brain for a plan," he told her. Which was true enough…but it wasn't a rescue plan. It looked a lot more like a seduction plan. But could he really go through with it?

Glancing at Juliet, he fingered the crushed note out of his pocket and dropped it into the fire. The paper curled, turned black and then burst into flames.

If only his misgivings about the task before him were so easily destroyed.

Five

Finn coughed away a bit of smoke. "So, here's a plan. Let's go back to the house and eat. We'll talk about next steps once we've fueled up."

The reprieve would also give him time to think through what he wanted to do. Could he really seduce Juliet out of her position against the king's military policies?

He'd been convinced at dinner last night she hadn't changed, but in their year apart, she'd quit a job she loved, flew across the Atlantic and enrolled in a matchmaker program with the intent to marry an American.

Obviously *some* things had changed. But enough things? Things he hadn't begun to uncover during their short dinner last night?

Crossing her arms, Juliet met his gaze. "We should stay here, by the fire. If someone comes, they might put it out and leave, never realizing there are captives in the house."

He bit back a groan. Of course she would still be concerned about rescue, and unless he clued her in, she'd continue to be. But he couldn't tell her yet, not until he figured out what he wanted to do.

Such was the problem with deception. One small omission became many big lies.

"Fine, then I'll make us something and bring it down. We'll have a picnic on the beach."

She eyed him. "You can't cook."

"I'm not talking about a four-course meal complete with soup and appetizers. Will a sandwich work for your delicate palate?"

"Sure." With a small smile, she plopped down onto a large rock. "I'll be waiting."

Angry—and not entirely sure at whom—Finn slapped peanut butter and jelly on wheat bread and wrapped the sandwiches in napkins. This whole situation grated on him. Food was not going to soften the rock or the hard place he was smack in the middle of.

A quick search revealed a tray worthy of balancing a couple of water glasses down a steep flight of stairs, and he was back by the fire in ten minutes. With a less-than-perfect solution to his screaming conscience.

"Eat your sandwich, and then we'll start fires all around the perimeter of the island," he advised her. "I'm pretty sure this is Île de Etienne. If anyone with half a brain is paying attention, several fires will be cause for investigation."

He'd forgotten how Juliet constantly challenged him to be better, smarter, faster. In the past year, he'd floundered without her influence, something he'd only recently recognized. The blondes should have been a clue.

Eyebrows raised, Juliet gulped water from her glass and swallowed. "That's a great idea. Thanks for the sandwich."

Finn nodded and shoved his own sandwich in his mouth. The faster he finished, the faster they could get off this island—because no one said he had to wait around for his father to come get them. He could seek rescue on his own. Then he wouldn't be catering to the king's mad plan, but neither did he have to tell Juliet about it and risk damaging relations with her family further.

In the meantime, if they could find a way to spend time together without fighting, which was doubtful, marriage might seem like more of a possibility.

Finn and Juliet clambered up the stairs to the patio and threw as many wooden objects to the beach below as they could pick up. Alexander could bill their father for the damages as far as Finn was concerned.

The cliff went halfway around the island's perimeter and gradually sloped to sea level on the side facing south toward Africa, but they agreed their odds were best suited to fires along the shore closer to Delamer. Deep-water fishermen and cargo boats would pass by in the morning, and if the fires along the Delamer side didn't generate interest, they'd focus efforts to the south tomorrow.

The first patio chair burned a few yards from the stairs. Broken pieces of the rest of the patio set littered the shoreline beyond it. They rounded the fire and began spreading out piles of wood along the northern shore. The process was effortless. No speech required. She seemed to read his mind, leaning the boards into a cone shape, then stepping back so he could light it.

Finn had a strange sense of déjà vu or the feeling that the past year had been a horrible nightmare he'd woken from, sighing in relief because he and Juliet were together and still in love. Still happy.

At the same time, the pain of her betrayal rode in his chest, right where his heart was supposed to be. The protest had happened. They weren't together.

It was that push-pull paradox he didn't enjoy.

Juliet's hair had blown loose from the messy knot long ago and her cheeks had turned bright pink under the afternoon sun. She'd never say a word, but he'd bet her feet were cut and bloody too.

That was how she challenged him—with silent strength

he couldn't help but admire. Couldn't help but strive to match.

"Let me finish setting these fires. Why don't you go back to the house?" he suggested after they torched the third patio chair.

"What for?" She tossed a glance over her shoulder, already off to the next pile of wood—a side table.

"So you can rest. Take a long, hot bath. I'm sure you can find some jazz music to play in the bathroom." He followed her and cut to the chase. "You're getting sunburned and it doesn't take two people to set these small fires. Don't worry. If someone comes, I'll make sure they don't leave without you."

She halted in her tracks and they nearly collided. His arms came up to steady her, but she spun, eyes bright and searching. "You remember that I like to listen to music while I'm taking a bath?"

The sheer hopefulness in her tone uncoupled something in his chest, and the caustic scent of smoke sharpened a sudden memory of roasting marshmallows in the fireplace of his living room one evening when they'd opted not to brave the paparazzi.

"I remember everything about you."

The way she'd looked in the firelight that night. The way she'd felt in his arms when he'd made love to her right there on the floor. How he hadn't cared about anything but being with her; the obligations of his position, job, family—everything—eliminated for a blissful few hours.

He wanted that back. Wanted to forget all about the scandal for a while and indulge in the paradise around them. The paradise of neutral ground, no hurt, no past. The paradise of Juliet.

Marriage might be off the table, but maybe romance wasn't.

Her breathing changed, ever so slightly, and a hint of hunger bled into her expression. As if she'd read his thoughts. The throb of awareness spread, coiling through him.

As if she hated the separation between them as much as he did, she swayed into his space. Their lips played at meeting, hovering in hesitation. Then he closed the gap, taking her mouth firmly.

She flooded him, drenching him with need. Hands to her jaw, he angled her head, deepening the kiss, tasting the fire of her mouth. She moaned under him, building the pressure of sheer want in his system.

He slid a palm down her spine to cup her sweet rear, molding her body to his as he hiked that sexy yellow dress up so he could feel her bare skin. Like satin. He groaned and blindly went for the hem to remove the dress completely. Fingers ready to whip it off, he paused to give her a chance to stop him, seeking an answer to his unvoiced question.

With the scent of the sea, of fire and of Juliet engulfing his senses, he prayed the answer would be yes.

The weight and pressure of Finn's amazing lips on hers dissolved Juliet's knees. Never at a loss, he tightened his arms around her, supporting her against his body. *More, more, more.*

All the anxiety and fear she'd carried around since awakening in a strange bed in a strange place vanished. Finn was here, with her. Nothing mattered except losing herself in the sensations of a sea breeze and him. It was very welcome. Effortless, as it had always been between them.

No other man had ever made her feel as this one did, as if a tide of power had swept through her. Her body electrified as his energy zipped into her very blood.

Her dress bunched up at her waist and his fingers teased her flesh, brushing against her thighs, then her stomach. Yes. She wanted his hands everywhere.

As the kiss drew out, her heart soared.

And then plummeted.

She couldn't let him affect her this way. This wasn't an opportunity for a second chance. She'd tried at dinner last night and it hadn't worked.

No emotions. Ruthless determination.

Breaking loose—with incredible effort—she shook her head and pulled her dress back in place. "Um, we have to…"

What? The man scrambled her brains like a double heat-stroke. The cuts on her feet weren't even as painful after Finn's mouth had numbed all her extremities. No more kissing. Or other stuff. It was too mind-altering.

He let her go and jerked his head toward the house, his expression blank. "Go inside. I'll finish here."

How very Finn-like to turn bossy when she didn't respond to his original suggestion. "I'm not taking a bath when I could be putting effort toward rescue."

His huff of frustration nearly made her smile. "Then go back to the house and see if you can get on the internet through the TV. I'm pretty sure I saw a video game console too. Try both."

"Aye, aye, Lieutenant." She gave him a saucy salute to hide her relief at the perfect excuse to remove herself from his overwhelming presence. Before she kissed him again.

She had to keep her wits about her and keep focused on escape, not her humming girl parts and desperately lonely soul.

She left him on the beach and limped up the stairs to the house, her mind turning over the kiss.

One minute they were setting fires, and the next she couldn't have stepped away from him at gunpoint. They'd both agreed in the car after dinner that they didn't make sense together. Somehow, she'd given him the wrong signals. Or they'd both been caught up in the heat of the moment, like two survivors in a disaster movie, inexplicably drawn to each other over shared circumstances.

Either way, it didn't matter. If it hadn't been for the kidnapping, she'd never have seen Finn again. Being held captive together didn't change facts. She could never marry him solely to promote her agenda. It would be too painful, too difficult.

And when he kissed her, she forgot all that.

She had to get off this island and away from him. It was best for them both.

The TV wasn't the kind with an internet connection, but it did have satellite cable service, offering more than three hundred channels, including all the premium movie ones. Quickly, she cued up a news channel to see how much coverage their disappearance was receiving.

After fifteen minutes of zero mentions of the missing Prince of Delamer, Juliet gave up. No one realized they'd been kidnapped yet. What kind of kidnappers waited so long to make their demands?

The credenza did indeed house a Wii console on the bottom shelf, tucked way in the back. Only Finn's sharp helicopter-pilot eyesight could have spotted it.

She hit the power button, but despite many attempts, the console couldn't connect to the internet. No service, likely. The kidnappers had been quite thorough. Absently, she flipped through the hundred or so games lining the shelf next to the console, hard-pressed to think of a title not present and accounted for.

They certainly wouldn't suffer from boredom here in this gilded cage.

Heaving a sigh, she turned off the electronics and spent several minutes opening cabinets and drawers looking for a laptop or cell phone or *something* that could be used to contact help.

The sliding glass door to the patio opened and shut, announcing Finn's return.

"Shouldn't one of us stay on the beach in case someone comes?" she asked with raised eyebrows. "I'll go back down if you don't want to."

She definitely didn't need to be in the same room with him, not while he looked all deliciously windblown and wild from being out in the elements.

His jaw tightened as he pushed his rolled sleeves up over his elbows. "It's late. I doubt there are many boaters out on the water. If one of the guys is doing my rounds, he'll land on the south side of the island to investigate. The sound of a helicopter would be hard to miss. I think it's okay to be in the house."

There was no argument for that. Her feet could use a break anyway.

Gingerly, she crossed to the couch and plopped down to contemplate. "I guess we should think about dinner."

"A shower wouldn't be out of line either."

"Are you suggesting I need one?" she teased, and nearly bit her tongue.

It came so automatically to joke around with Finn, when really, there was nothing funny about being kidnapped. Nothing funny about being stuck on a small island with him when things were so impossible between them.

His smile did nothing to ease her consternation. "*I* need the shower. But if you want to join me, I'd be okay with that."

Accompanied by an exaggerated eyebrow waggle, the invitation was clearly not intended to be taken seriously, but of course now she was thinking about Finn's unclothed body, water sluicing down his sinewy muscles as he soaped himself.

"Uh…" She shut her eyes for a blink. It didn't help. Images danced across her mind's eye, growing increasingly erotic. "Thanks. I'm good."

He chuckled as if he'd guessed the direction of her thoughts. "I'm taking the bedroom at the end of the hall. You can have the one where you woke up. See you in a few."

Moments after he blew from the room, water hummed through the pipes in the walls. *I will not think about Finn naked. I will not think about Finn naked,* she chanted silently as she heaved off the couch to see about dinner.

Naked was actually better than thinking of him fully clothed and gazing at her with his heart in his eyes. She missed that far more than sex.

Listlessly, she rooted around in the refrigerator and then the pantry, but inspiration did not strike. She'd spent two months enduring hours upon hours of wife training under Elise's and Dannie's expert hands, including many sessions in the kitchen. Proper wives learned far more than how to cook, Elise had explained. They knew ingredients, how to pair food and wine, the true cost of a meal…even if they had professional chefs or the funds to eat out regularly. Otherwise, lack of knowledge gave caterers a license to rob you blind, or the charity fund-raiser you helmed ended up way over budget.

Surely some of the lessons had stuck. After all, the entire time, Juliet had assumed she'd be matched with an American businessman, as Dannie had been. She'd paid close attention, she really had.

Instead of trying to pull information from her brain that clearly wasn't there, she spent far too long searching for a cookbook. Zilch. The gourmet kitchen with its stainless steel appliances and stone countertops either typically accommodated a chef who knew what she was doing or it was strictly for show.

Chicken breast. That seemed easy enough to pop in the oven and cook at…some temperature. When in America, the conversion between Fahrenheit and Celsius had confused her, and now here she was cooking in Europe with an oven using Celsius after all. It was enough to drive her to drink.

Well, that sounded like a plan. She hunted for the wine cellar, and sure enough, it was off the kitchen and fully stocked with labels even she could tell were pricey and rare. The cool stone walls held the chill, promising perfectly temperate wine. With no small amount of glee, she plucked an aged Bordeaux from the rack and hoped the kidnappers had a stroke when they realized the thirty-year-old bottle was gone.

Back at the maddening stove, but fortified with a full glass of the deep red wine, she hummed as she plunked chicken into a dish with one hand and drank with the other.

"Now there's a sight. I do believe that's a happy tune you're humming."

She glanced over her shoulder. Finn lounged at the kitchen entrance, one shoulder against the wall, watching her. His dark hair was still damp and he wore a pair of jeans with a navy T-shirt, which fit as if they'd been custom made for his lanky frame.

"The kidnappers brought your luggage?" She perked up. Half a glass of wine had already gone a long way toward improving her mood, but clean clothes would be a very nice bonus indeed. "Did they bring mine?"

Her sunny yellow dress had become more the shade of ten-year-old linoleum, and a long brown streak of something she'd rather not identify marred the skirt.

His high-watt smile could have baked the chicken by itself. "Afraid not. I found these clothes in the closet of my bedroom. There were some girl outfits too, so I put one on your bed for you. What are you making?"

"Chicken."

After a long pause, his eyebrows rose. "And what else?"

"There has to be more? What's wrong with just chicken?"

"Nothing's wrong with just chicken, but I'm starving. What about some bread or..." He rummaged around in the refrigerator and held up a head of romaine. "A salad?"

"Feel free to contribute whatever you like to the meal. Have some wine," she offered magnanimously. "It's a Bordeaux. Might as well take advantage of our kidnappers' hospitality."

"Don't mind if I do. Alexander's always championing the merits of that label. Let's see what all the fuss is about." He poured himself a glass and bustled around the kitchen alongside her, throwing salad in bowls and slicing hunks from the baguette he'd pulled from the pantry.

Juliet pretended not to watch but *oh, my God,* what was it about a man in the kitchen that was so sexy? Or maybe it was just *this* man, with his fluid grace and his gorgeous, muscled butt that his borrowed jeans showcased as if they'd been stitched together deliberately to induce drool.

The oven timer dinged, startling her out of an X-rated fantasy starring the tabletop, her dress around her waist and Finn's jeans on the floor.

Gah, wasn't she supposed to be *not* thinking about him naked?

Quickly, before he noticed naughty guilt plastered all over her face, she plated everything and they sat at the breakfast nook overlooking the patio. A spectacular sunset splashed the sky to the west and nearly made dinner with the former love of her life bearable.

Finn chatted about nothing and earned major points for failing to mention the dry, tasteless lump of plain chicken on his plate. And she had the nagging thought that poultry and red wine weren't supposed to go together, which someone who regularly attended formal dinners with heads of major countries probably knew like the back of his hand. He didn't make another move or even flirt with her, and he'd helped her set the fires, despite originally hating the idea.

Maybe it wasn't so bad to be stuck here with Finn.

"This is the second night in a row we've had dinner together," she commented and wished she could take it back. Why had she brought that up? She didn't want him to think she approved of the idea.

"Yes." He gave her a long look, and the heat in it meant he'd definitely interpreted her observation the wrong way. "We used to eat together all the time."

"Well, hopefully this is the last time." She cringed. "I don't mean because you're such a horrible dinner companion. But because I hope we're rescued soon."

"I knew what you meant." He stuck a bite in his mouth and chewed thoughtfully. "Once we're home, are you planning to stick around?"

"I haven't really thought that far ahead."

"You could ask Elise for a different match." His smile flattened and he put his fork down in favor of drinking deeply from his wineglass. "If you still wanted to find an American husband."

"I don't."

It was a bit of a shock, but she recognized it as truth, despite not having consciously made any decision of the sort. Her flight from Delamer had been driven by Finn's false engagement announcement. Even if it hadn't been, she'd taken the coward's way out, and that didn't sit well with her anymore.

She rushed on lest he think *he* had something to do with her decision.

"Being back here…I can't leave Delamer again. But I don't have a job, or a place to live."

He shrugged. "That's easily rectified. The new school is short on qualified teachers, and I'm pretty sure I could lean on a few people to find you an apartment."

"Why would you do that?"

Because he thought she was on board with a second chance? That kiss on the beach had led him down the wrong path.

But it hadn't meant anything. The man was a good kisser. *That's* why she couldn't quite put it out of her mind.

"Don't sound so suspicious. I saw your face on the beach. I know what the water means to you. Frankly, I was shocked you'd leave in the first place." He stared out at the sunset for a long moment. "I talked my father into building that new school. For you."

Her wineglass bobbled, nearly spilling the contents, but she caught it with only a few splattered drops sacrificed to her clumsiness. "What? You did not. The existing school was overcrowded. Everyone knows that."

She'd had thirty students in her class last year and mourned letting them go on to the next grade without having given each of them more attention. The new school had been on everyone's mind. Tourism received the majority of the government's consideration at budget time, as it should, since foreign dollars filled the coffers.

"Yes, but it's been overcrowded for a long time with little action. How do you think the powers that be became convinced a new school was critical for the future of Delamer?"

The ribbon-cutting picture of Finn and the little girl sprang into her mind. Prince Alain had cut the ribbon because he'd made the school possible. When she stumbled over the picture, she'd always been too quick to click away the painful reminders to read any of the articles. "You never said anything. I've been complaining about the size of the classes since we first met."

His gaze captured hers, and she couldn't tear her heart away from the depths of his clear blue eyes.

"It was a surprise. I wanted to be sure it was a go before I mentioned it. They'd just broken ground when we split up."

"I don't...but that means..." Her brain and tongue seemed to be operating independently of each other, and a deep breath didn't help. "The king was opposed and you talked him into it?"

"Not opposed. You know how expensive it is to build in Delamer, when all the materials have to be imported. A school wasn't a top priority. I helped him see it should be.

With all the ammunition you gave me over our dozens of conversations about it, it was pretty easy to do."

"You did that for me?" she whispered.

"For you. And for my people. If I didn't think it was necessary, I wouldn't have supported the idea. But Delamer needs educated children who will grow up and become productive members of society. Who will help us compete in a global marketplace with ever-increasing opportunities. We have to start now if Delamer hopes to stay relevant."

She'd never said any of that. Her chief concern had been doing her job and ensuring the children had the best possible environment to learn. He'd drawn his own conclusions, creating a refined, big-picture angle that someone in her position wouldn't have considered.

But he had. Because of his role in the ruling family, he had a different perspective and a greater scope of concern than simply an overcrowded building.

Her head went a little fuzzy. Finn had conspired with the king to solve a problem she'd expressed.

But not the one she'd implored him to take to his father.

She braced for the familiar rush of anger—but it wasn't as harsh as normal.

How could she be mad at Finn? Together, they'd achieved something worthwhile. Of course, she hadn't been an active participant, but what if she was? How much more could they accomplish?

Clearly Finn had been listening to her and had no problem championing a cause once he bought into it. For some reason, he hadn't bought into her impassioned pleas for military reform. Why not?

But to ask might mean answers she didn't like. No reason he could give would make more sense than lifting the mandatory military service law. It couldn't. To believe in his reasons would be a betrayal of Bernard's memory, and that she could never do.

Deep down, she secretly wondered if her brother's death

was her fault. In a family of six children, it had fallen to Juliet, as the oldest, to help with the others. She'd spent so much time with her brother—but she obviously hadn't taught him well enough how to stay safe.

Her parents grieved the loss of their only son, probably more than she could ever imagine. They'd depended on her to ensure the same end didn't happen to another family.

The look on their faces when she told them Finn refused to budge…it had ravaged her. And after losing Bernard and then Finn, she'd have sworn she had nothing left to ravage.

Nothing could possibly fix that except taking this second chance to fulfill the quest her parents expected of her. Somehow, Finn must be persuaded to eliminate the mandatory service law in Bernard's honor. Finn's reasons for not doing so initially were completely irrelevant.

Not even if those reasons led her back into Finn's arms.

Six

The morning dawned with no more progress toward rescue or romance.

Not that Finn had expected much of either. But it was hard to tell his fully alert and female-starved body that yes, Juliet was sleeping in the same house, but Atlantis might rise from its watery grave before she visited his bedroom in the middle of the night.

Finn groaned and rolled over in the huge, lonely bed.

That kiss haunted his dreams. The feel of her flesh, the slide of her tongue.

Dinner last night had been torturous, especially after he'd told Juliet about building the school for her. The look on her face had affected him far more than he'd expected. More than he'd been prepared for.

He'd been about to suggest taking the rest of the wine out on the deck in hopes the evening might take a more passionate turn. But she'd closed off and excused herself for the evening.

"Good morning," Finn called cheerfully from his doorway as Juliet emerged from her bedroom. She had circles under her eyes and appeared to have slept as poorly as he had.

Because she'd been lying awake aching in kind but was too stubborn to admit she wanted him? Because she did want him, regardless of what had made her pull away. No one could kiss a man as she had and not mean it.

"It's morning. That's about all I can say about it," she grumbled before brightening slightly. "At least I got to take a hot shower. Thanks for the clothes."

The light sweater and pants were a little big, but she wore them with panache. Portia's taste ran to the conservative side, but then she was the crown princess and constantly under scrutiny.

"Let's eat breakfast," he said. "And then check out the south side of the island. I have an idea for another way to get someone's attention, but I have to see if it'll work."

"That sounds promising. And mysterious. I can't wait."

Juliet scored a couple of bagels from the pantry and spread them with jam. Finn brewed coffee, ignoring Alexander's lame Colombian brand for the dark roast Finnish label he'd found in the back of the pantry. They took their booty and some slices of cantaloupe outside to the patio, where a gentle breeze from the sea teased Juliet's hair and made him smile. Early-morning sunshine washed the view of Delamer in a silvery cloak and it was so achingly gorgeous, he hardly noticed the missing chairs, gladly sitting on the hard stone to eat.

Finn wanted his own island. Once they got home, he'd see about buying one. His future bride, whoever she was, might like a lover's retreat. Except he couldn't get the image of Juliet out of his mind, standing on the deck with hair falling out of a knot, melding with the background like a gorgeous sea creature too transcendent to catch.

The bite of bagel in his mouth wouldn't go down past the sudden lump in his throat.

Once he finally swallowed, he croaked, "Finished?"

He certainly was.

She held up her mug. "Yeah, if I can take the rest of this to go. I didn't realize how weak and boring American coffee is." She moaned a little in appreciation of the strong version in her cup. "What's the plan? More fires?"

That moan rippled through his still-alert lower half, which hadn't fully recovered from the night alone.

He shook his head. "Rocks. If we can find enough, we can spell out HELP or something that can be seen from the air. If the guys swing out to patrol the shipping lanes, someone will see it. The sooner we get it done, the better."

"Brilliant."

She disappeared into the house and reappeared with a travel mug. She'd also donned a pair of Portia's Timberlands, no doubt in anticipation of tramping along the south side of the island. "We still haven't made the news yet, by the way. Your HELP sign is a good plan since it doesn't even seem like anyone knows we're missing."

He should tell her the truth. But how could he without jeopardizing everything? If rescue came soon, he'd be off the hook.

They set off and soon had a pile of loose rocks from the perimeter of the island. As with the fires, they worked together seamlessly, but this time, Finn opted not to remain silent as they placed the stones in long lines.

"What if you didn't go back to teaching?" he threw out, picking up the threads of last night's conversation. "Could you be happy in some other job?"

Like Princess Juliet.

Where had that thought come from? He frowned. Still thinking about Juliet out on the deck, obviously, and how unhappy his father would be when Finn came home without having proposed to Juliet and without changing her mind.

"I'm sure I could find something I'd be good at besides that." She paused, a rock in each hand.

"What about something you'd like? As opposed to something you'd be good at." It was an interesting distinction, one he'd bet she hadn't consciously made.

With the "H" complete, he moved over to start laying the first branch of the "E." Juliet dropped her two rocks into place after his, clacking them together haphazardly.

"Ow!" She jerked her hand back and examined it.

"Are you okay?"

"Stupid fake fingernails." She frowned at the thin, bloody line splitting her index fingernail into two halves. "One got caught between the rocks and cracked down to the quick. I didn't even know that could happen. Usually I break them off."

"Why have them in the first place then?"

She shrugged and dropped her hand, the nail forgotten even though it had to hurt. "Such is the way of females, I'm told. We're supposed to be polished and put together."

"You don't have to have fingernails to be attractive, you know," he said.

"I know. You never cared about me being ladylike, which I always appreciated. That's why Elise's computer matched us, I suppose."

Actually, they'd been matched because they shared similar beliefs and moral compasses. Which was why he understood that she'd been upset and irrational when her brother died. If their positions were reversed and Alexander had been the one to walk into a live electrical field, Finn would be a wreck.

Polish mattered little in the grand scheme of things, but if he could convince her how wrong she'd been to take the position she had, they'd be dealing with a whole new set of dynamics.

Romance *and* marriage could be on the table.

Time healed wounds and afforded a different perspective. Maybe now she could see facts rationally. Could he really let go of the opportunity to feel her out?

Then he could truthfully tell his father he'd tried.

"You've never been out on the deck of the *Aurélien*," he said casually.

"No." She knelt carefully in the bare dirt where they were working, and placed the next rock with deliberate care, her back to Finn.

And that was the extent of her reaction to his abrupt subject change.

The stiffness of her spine and jerkiness of her movements told him she'd recognized the name of the ship where her brother had taken his last breath.

He almost backed off. His usual method of operation. Why should he have to spell out something she should already know?

But this was too important to stay in his comfort zone.

He sat down next to her and rearranged the already perfectly placed rocks. "It's an air defense frigate. I'm sure you've seen it from shore. Plenty of anti-aircraft guns and missile launchers and general busyness on deck. Extremely complicated equipment and lots of confusing levels."

"Yeah. I've seen it."

She wasn't going to make this easy, which was partly why he'd never talked about this before.

"They go over safety protocol all the time." He'd chosen his words carefully, but some things needed to be said without censor. "It's the responsibility of each private to understand the rules and follow them."

"Are you about to suggest that Bernard didn't?" she cut in, her tone strident.

"I wasn't there," he said as gently as possible. "But the reports were pretty conclusive. They interviewed all the shipmen aboard at the time. You can't go into the electrical rooms without proper protection."

Her head dropped as if too heavy for her neck to support.

"He shouldn't have been on that ship in the first place." She met Finn's gaze, and her ravaged expression tore through him. "He wanted to be in the coast guard. Like you. He worshipped you. Couldn't say enough about your flying skills or how heroically you rescued a swimmer."

That was a double spike to the gut. Finn wasn't a hero, or someone worthy of worshipping.

"The path to the coast guard is three years of mandatory military service," he said brusquely. "I did it too. I hated every second of being a shipman, but Juliet, half of Delamer borders the water. Our naval presence is paramount, and that's where we need men. Our population is so miniscule. How else would we get people on those boats?"

"Do you think the word *help* is enough or should we tack on an exclamation point?" She stood and gathered another pile of rocks with exaggerated movements.

He struggled with whether to drop it or not. Honestly, the subject was a little raw for him too. He'd liked Bernard. Finn could easily imagine having him around on a guy's fishing weekend or eventually becoming the boy's mentor, if he'd gone the coast guard route after serving his three years.

Juliet's broken half sob decided it for him.

Finn yanked her into his arms and snuggled her wet face against his neck. She snuffled for a moment, then her arms clasped him in turn. Her tears flowed unapologetically onto his shoulder, but he didn't care.

He held her, hurting along with her. "Bernard was a great kid. I miss him too."

"I just want to reverse time, you know?" she whispered. "Make it not have happened."

"I know." He breathed in the scent of her hair and the sea and lost a tear or two, as well. "It was a tragedy. But we have to move on, sweetheart."

She stepped out of his arms, and the rush of cool air

burned his Juliet-warmed skin. Obviously that had been the wrong thing to say.

"Move on. Good idea. This is done." She slid a finger under her wet lashes and then waved at the HELP sign stretching across the dirt before them. "You wait here for one of your buddies to make rounds. I'm going to the north side of the island to see if any boats are sailing from the marina to one of the other islands. Maybe I can flag one down."

This time, he let the matter drop. He watched her walk away and cursed.

Somehow, the dynamic between them had grown more complicated. And he had a feeling the longer they stayed on this island together, the worse it would become.

Juliet escaped and willed herself to stop crying. It wasn't working so far.

For brief odd moments, she'd experienced peace while placing stones with Finn, as if things had never become so mucked up. As if they were working together, teasing each other and laughing, then they'd look up and be finished without realizing any time had passed.

Then he'd ruined it.

Why did Finn have to pick at her wounds like that? And then be so understanding and comfortable to cry on? His shoulder was always on offer, always strong, and she'd missed it.

But then, she'd never really had it, not after Bernard died. The reminder was brutal.

The ache in her chest wouldn't ease, no matter how many deep breaths she took or how many times she counted to one hundred. Usually counting put her in a Zen-like state and cleared her mind. Not today.

She had to get away from Finn permanently. He was screwing with her sense of well-being.

"Come on, just one boat," she muttered.

A bright yellow catamaran skipped over the water about two hundred yards off the Delamer marina but no one on board would notice a lone woman waving at them from the shore of an island that was merely a smear on their horizon.

How long would she have to wait for a boat to come close enough to the island?

"I brought you an umbrella from the house."

She whirled. Finn stood behind her, umbrella opened and extended. Summer was typically the dry season in the Mediterranean. Only Finn would have thought to look for an umbrella. Only Finn would think of shielding her from the sun while she stood here waiting for a miracle rescue.

"I didn't hear you come down the stairs," she said.

"You seemed pretty intent on your self-appointed task. Sorry if I scared you."

She shook her head and took the offered shade. "Thanks."

Finn glanced out over the water. "It's a beautiful morning, isn—"

"I thought you were going to wait on the other side of the island."

They weren't doing this casual-conversation thing anymore. She couldn't take it. Not while it still felt as if an elephant was sitting on her chest.

If only he hadn't brought up Bernard. But he had and now it was alive again between them, hanging in that space where their love for each other used to be.

Surprise flitting through his gaze, Finn stared at her. "I can hear a helicopter on the north side as easily as I can hear one on the south. Thought I'd make sure you were okay."

"What, like I can't take care of myself?"

"No, like because you were crying," he corrected mildly. "I didn't mean to upset you."

"I'm fine." Since that clearly wasn't true, she offered the catch-all, noncommittal, leave-me-alone excuse. "Tired. Being kidnapped takes it out of me."

"Yeah, and the subject material too, apparently. Was it better to not talk about it?"

"I don't know."

Sometimes she *did* want to talk about it, and who better understood the anguish she'd endured than Finn? He knew her family, knew her history of helping raise Bernard, knew she was the oldest Villere child in a family of six and how her sense of responsibility had shaped her path.

He knew *her,* through and through. Which was why it hurt so much to be separated.

"What would talking about it solve?"

He shrugged. "Help ease the grief. It's something I didn't get a chance to do the first time. I want to be there for you. Let me."

The idea sprouted inside her, growing and twining through her frozen insides until she could hardly bite back the *yes.*

That had been the hardest part of the past year, that she couldn't turn to Finn during one of the worst periods of her life. She'd spent a lot of time with her parents, of course, but they had each other. Her sisters were understandably lost in their own grieving process, and none of them had helped raise Bernard. They'd lost a brother they loved, but it wasn't the same as losing a boy you'd helped shape and teach.

It wasn't the same as blaming yourself for not teaching him well enough. And then blaming yourself for exposing a sweet, impressionable kid to a man like Finn, worthy of hero-worship, worthy of inspiring Bernard to follow in his footsteps.

But then, no one could understand that. Not even Finn.

And still…the Finn-shaped hole inside yearned to be filled by the man within touching distance, to let him make good on that promise to be there for her. It had always been the two of them, together forever.

Two hearts being as one.

She stepped back, clutching the umbrella with both hands. Finn couldn't grant her absolution. He couldn't even give her the unconditional support she'd desperately hoped for. And then he'd tried to act as if Bernard was to blame for not following the rules.

Latching on to that as a shield against the firestorm of angst raging through her chest, she refused to fall into Finn's arms this time. "It's too late to be there for me. Just like it's too late for us. We're over and so is this conversation."

Finn's mouth clamped into a hard line. Finally, she'd gotten through to him.

If she could only get him to understand it was his stubbornness that stood in their way. All he had to do was lose it and then take her side against his father.

If he did, she was convinced that would be the key to healing. That one thing would allow her to stop blaming herself.

But that was never going to happen.

She sniffed and cleared her throat. "We're short a helicopter patrol and clearly we're too far out to be seen by any boats coming from the marina. The only way off this island is to swim. So that's what I'm doing."

His gaze cut to the sea lapping at the rocky coastline behind her. "Swim where?"

"To shore." She nodded toward the south bank of Saint Tropez. "It's not more than two miles if I head to the French side."

"You've never swam a stretch like that in your life. What makes you think you can do it now?" His tone was deceptively even, but she heard the condescension underneath. He thought she was too weak and too female.

"I can swim two miles. I've done it lots of times." She'd have that drive to succeed in her favor too, born of desperation to get out of this situation at all costs.

"There's a big difference between doing it in shallow

water where we sail and doing it from Île de Etienne to Saint Tropez." He gripped her shoulders earnestly. "Juliet, this is a rocky area. The boating lanes were cleared of submerged obstacles, so I could see you making the mistake of thinking the whole area's clear. It's not. You're talking about swimming in a straight line across open water."

The genuine concern on his face nearly had her second-guessing the plan. But what choice did they have? They were captives and people were undoubtedly worried about them by now.

"I'll be careful."

"It's not a matter of being careful." He shifted from foot to foot, and forked a restless hand through his dark hair. "I rescue people from these waters all the time. You know the number one reason they can't swim to shore on their own? Because they misjudged their strength against the current."

"You don't think I can make it."

She wanted to hear him admit flat out that his concern was about her abilities, not the water she'd been on or in for most of her life.

"This is not about you. It's about being safe and not taking chances. If nothing else, consider that you might get hit by a boat."

The eye roll might have come across a little exaggerated. But who could blame her? "The lack of boats is one of our current problems. At least if I got run over, the boat would notice me."

"You're being flip about this and it's not the kind of thing to be flip about. That's how people die."

The harsh, deep lines of his face hit her all of a sudden. He was worried about her dying.

And then it truly would be too late.

Her heart twisted painfully and she almost reached out to reassure him. Or maybe for another reason, one she could barely acknowledge.

She didn't want it to be too late.

She wanted to find a way to be with Finn again. To recapture the easiness of being in love, the shared smiles, the lazy afternoons, the comfort. To forget about what had happened and move forward.

Her pulse thumped erratically with the realization, scaring her. It was an impossible dream because she *couldn't* forget. They were like two battering rams, pushing each other with all their might but neither giving ground. Look what a disaster their date back in Dallas had become.

Even *thinking* about being with Finn again meant she had to get away from him before she did something she couldn't take back. Something she'd regret.

The umbrella dropped from her shaking fingers.

"Staying here isn't an option."

She jammed her hands down on her hips to hide her consternation. The fact that his concerns were valid was irrelevant.

"We've tried fires. We've tried your HELP sign. No one's come yet and the boats are too far away. We have to try something else."

She twisted her hair up in a knot and kicked off her shoes, but he grabbed her hand before she could flee into the water. "Wait. We're safe here. There's no danger from the kidnappers. They'd have come back by now if they were going to. We have plenty to eat. Why don't we pretend we're on holiday and relax for a few days?"

His earnest blue eyes bored into hers, pleading for her to reconsider. He was serious. "You're insane. We're prisoners. The luxuriousness of the cage doesn't change that. I can't stay here and pretend it's okay that we were kidnapped. I'll send someone for you as soon as I can."

"Juliet, there's something you need to know." Finn squeezed her hand, tight, preventing her from pulling away. "You don't have to swim anywhere because…my father is behind this."

"Behind what?" Her gaze flitted over his dark expression. Suddenly it all came together and she yanked her hand out of his grasp. "The *kidnapping?* Your father kidnapped us?"

Sighing, he laced his fingers together behind his neck, as if his head needed help staying upright. "Yeah."

Her stomach rolled. The king hired those men in the van, who had drugged both her and Finn, then left them here. "Wait a minute. You knew your father had us kidnapped? Since when?"

His jaw worked and then squared. "Since the first day. There was a note in my pocket."

He'd known the whole time and hadn't bothered to tell her. Where was this note anyway?

She cursed. "We've been running around trying to get rescued and setting fires and your father *knew* we were trapped here. He dumped us on this island on purpose. Why in the world would he do something so horrible to his own son? To me?"

"It's complicated." Finn paused and she nearly grabbed his shoulders to shake the rest out of him. "He saw the picture of us together at Elise's party and it snowballed from there."

"So this is an attempt to keep us out of the press." The *nerve* of King Laurent. Apparently a crown gave him license to do whatever he wanted. "Can't have any photos floating around of his precious son by the side of that extremist Villere girl."

"That's not the issue, Juliet. Be quiet for five seconds and listen."

That pushed her over the edge.

"Stop being so bossy! You've known about this all along. You had your chance to talk. Now it's my turn." For once, he clamped his mouth closed and crossed his arms, allowing her to vent every ounce of frustration. "How you sprang from the loins of such a coldblooded man as the king, I'll never understand. He put us in danger, just like he put Bernard in danger, and I'm tired of neither you nor your father seeing the problem. And I'm not going to sit around and wait for him to make the next move."

With that parting shot, she sprinted into the water.

The chill of it stole her breath. The summer was too young to have warmed the temperature, and she hated to admit it was an obstacle she hadn't even considered.

Well, it didn't matter. She could do it. She had to, if for no other reason than to prove to King Laurent that he didn't control her.

Stroking rhythmically, she pulled away from the island slowly, opting to conserve her energy for the middle stretch.

Breathe. Stroke. Breathe, stroke.

It was *so cold*.

She risked a glance around, and saw she'd hardly traveled more than three hundred yards. Checking her progress was a stupid thing to do. It was better not to know how far she still had to go and just swim. She'd hit the distant shore at some point. What did it matter how close she was?

A tingle in her fingers spread up her hands. Oh, no. They were going numb.

She stretched them as she stroked, hoping to increase the blood flow.

Then her side cramped.

And she sucked in a mouthful of seawater.

Coughing and holding her spasming waist, she treaded water mindlessly, frantically, praying the pain would ease as quickly as it had come on.

Water from her hair spilled into her eyes, stinging them. She backhanded the moisture away, but the second she moved her arm, the cramp in her side knifed through her anew, nearly sinking her under the surface.

The sea she loved had turned on her.

No, the sea was the same as always. Her time in America had taken its toll and she was woefully underconditioned for a swim like this. She should have been weight training and doing laps in the pool instead of learning how to balance a book on her head.

Her legs burned with the effort to keep her head above water. She wasn't going out like this, not by drowning in the Mediterranean. Any other body of water but this one, and she'd have considered giving in to the dizzying fatigue.

Gritting her teeth against the pain, she swam a couple of more yards, congratulating herself on each painstaking stroke and kick.

A wave rolled her and turned her head into the swell. Another unwelcome mouthful of seawater went down her throat.

Coughing impeded her progress once again. As soon as she started treading water, a vicious cramp lit up her abdomen, drawing her torso toward her knees involuntarily. Which were underwater.

She had to go back.

Relieved tears pricked at her stinging eyes. She could go back to the island. It didn't feel so much like giving up as survival, and that she could live with.

The decision made, she kicked in the direction of Île de Etienne and counted to five before the cramp in her side jerked her to a halt.

Water burned down her esophagus. When she coughed involuntarily, it shafted into her lungs. Death by drowning became a litany in her head, shouting its presence until she was nearly screaming *no, no, no.* But another mouthful of water contradicted that.

She wasn't going to make it.

This would be her watery grave, precisely as Finn had predicted.

Her tears of relief turned to tears of regret. So many regrets. She hadn't called her mom in a week. She'd never watch another child form his first words in English with her instruction as his guide. Her womb would never grow a child of her own.

Worst of all, she'd never have a chance to tell Finn she still loved him. Why had she clung to her anger for so long?

Just as she thought she'd black out for the last time, Finn was somehow there in the water with her, pulling her into a rescue headlock and towing her to shore.

She went limp and let herself float, desperately sucking air into her body and pushing water out. She wasn't going to die. It wasn't too late.

Seven

Finn tucked Juliet into the larger bed he'd slept in last night and put two blankets over her, cursing Alexander's inability to stock one tiny thermometer in this whole house.

Juliet's skin blazed, almost too hot to touch. She had a fever, no question. He would have liked the confirmation of how high. And whether it was climbing higher or dropping.

Stubborn woman.

Why had she tried to swim to Saint Tropez?

He knew why. She refused to believe he might be right, even about something as important as whether she could actually beat the sea he knew better than his own name. Even telling her about his father's role in the kidnapping hadn't convinced her they were safe and that escape wasn't necessary.

And that was a poor excuse designed to absolve his guilt. It didn't work.

He should have told her sooner about his father's involvement in the kidnapping. If he had, she might not have conceived of the idea of swimming across open water. If anything, his confession had pushed her into it.

No time to wallow in his mistakes. He shed his wet clothes in record time, then threw on some dry ones. Slipping beneath the sheets to lay on the other pillow, he watched her chest rise and fall, telling himself he wanted to be near in case she needed him.

It was a lie.

He couldn't physically separate himself from Juliet after nearly losing her in such a heart-stopping fashion. There on the rocky shore, he'd performed the sloppiest mouth-to-mouth resuscitation on record, but he hadn't been able to stop shaking.

Finally, she had convulsed and started breathing on her own. How he'd managed to haul her up the flight of stairs and into the house with legs the consistency of a wet noodle, he still didn't know.

He held her hand tightly underneath the covers. She was so weak, her fingers slipped from his if he let his grip go slack. Her tangled, still-wet hair draped over the pillow, and he wished he'd thought to grab a towel and dry it before settling in.

The ill-advised feelings stirred up by her unconscious state had to go. But she was so fragile and beautiful, and he couldn't stand the thought of losing her.

Time passed. An hour, then two. Juliet thrashed occasionally and then fell so still, it scared him into pressing his fingertips to a pulse point, just to be sure she hadn't taken her last breath right there in front of him.

Surely the king couldn't have envisioned his plan playing out in quite this way. Despite exhaustion, which ran deep into his bones, Finn found a bit of energy left over to be furious with his father.

Juliet was sick and they had no method of communicating with the outside world. No way of contacting a doctor, of shipping in medicine or shipping Juliet out to a hospital.

Sheer helplessness ran rampant, weighing him down more than the fatigue and concern. It hadn't been easy to swim through the island's natural eddies, then tow another person back to shore, all the while terrified Juliet had already succumbed to the hidden dangers of the sea.

Hunger forced him from the bed as the sun began to set. He dashed to the kitchen, shoved some crackers down his throat, drank two full glasses of water and dashed back to the bed to pick up his vigil where he left off.

A tug on his hand startled Finn into opening his eyes. Automatically, he glanced at the digital clock on the bedside table. Three a.m. Had he fallen asleep?

He glanced at Juliet. The dim light he'd left on in the bathroom spilled over her open eyes. She blinked at him owlishly.

"Hey," he whispered and cupped the side of her face. Still hot, but maybe not as hot as before. "How do you feel?"

She turned her cheek into his hand. Deliberately. As if she actually wanted to be closer to his touch. Then she licked her lips and swallowed a couple of times. "Like someone dropped me in a volcano."

"You have a fever. It was probably something you picked up back in America and it took this long to surface." His thumb trailed over her jaw and his lower half suddenly needed a stern lecture about Juliet's illness and the inappropriateness of being turned on by a woman too weak to respond in kind.

Too late. His body throbbed to life. Exhaustion and stress had lowered his defenses entirely too much for any sort of admonishment to be effective anyway. So now he'd suffer from unrequited sexual frustration in addition to everything else. Fantastic.

Hopefully she wouldn't notice.

"You saved me," she murmured, and the dim light perfectly showcased the tender gratitude beaming from her expression.

"Yeah. What else would I have done?"

"Let me drown. Like I deserved."

He made a face. "Right, that was going to happen."

"How...did you get there so fast? I was way offshore."

Of all the questions—of course she'd ask that one. She was the only swimmer he'd ever rescued who would have even realized the distance he'd traversed to get to her. He sighed and told her the truth, though she wasn't going to like it.

"I was following you. In the water. When you went in, I went in."

"Oh." Her eyes closed for a beat and she dragged them open with what looked like considerable effort. "You didn't think I could make it."

"No." He thought about apologizing. But he wasn't sorry he'd set off after her. Thank God he had.

"Why did you let me go?" she whispered, her voice raw.

"Because I'm not in the habit of forcing women to do things primarily," he said drily. "And also because you needed to try."

A trove of emotions traveled over her face. He couldn't begin to read them all. But he'd bet at least one of them was irritation at his lack of faith.

"That's...interesting," was all she said, and the break in her voice worried him.

"It's the middle of the night. You should be getting rest, not hashing this out. Sleep. I'll be here."

It was an unintentional echo of their earlier conversation, when he'd told her he wanted to be there for her during her grief.

"You don't have to take care of me," she muttered. "I'm the one who should be taking care of you."

"I'm not sick," he pointed out. "Next time I have a fever, I'll let you put me to bed, okay?"

Her hand squeezed his and went slack a few moments later as she drifted off.

Sleep eluded him and by dawn, Juliet hadn't moved so he risked leaving her long enough to take a much-needed shower.

Hot water flowed over his abused muscles, soothing them. He hadn't realized how much he needed a break from the uncomfortable position he'd elected to take in the bed, half hunched against the headboard. But it was the optimal spot for monitoring Juliet.

There in the confines of the enclosed shower stall, finally alone, the sheer terror he'd kept at bay loosened and bled from the center of his chest.

It nearly knocked him to his knees.

He could have lost Juliet. And only now did he realize how much he wanted this second chance his father had given him.

Somehow, he had to find a path to the other side of the huge wall between them. Not because of any advantageous marriage, but because he truly didn't think he could function for the rest of his life without her.

That was the king's ace in the hole. Finn hadn't fallen out of love with Juliet after all, and the kidnapping had brought those emotions to the surface.

What if he *could* find a way to change Juliet's heart? There was no better place or time on earth to try than while trapped together in paradise.

His own heart lurched sweetly at the thought of a future with the woman he loved by his side, all their differences resolved. Marriage. Family. A place where he could achieve some normalcy, away from the public eye.

Unfortunately, a path around that wall between them didn't exist, given that she'd seemed so eager to swim away from a perfectly good island with him on it. She hadn't even given him a chance to explain the rest of his father's plot.

That was the reality clutching his heart in its steely fingers—she didn't want him on her side of the wall. Reconciliation seemed quite impossible. No matter how badly he might now want it.

When he returned to the bedroom, she was propped up against several pillows watching TV. Some color had returned to her face, but not enough for his liking.

"Good morning," she rasped and scowled. "My throat hurts."

"I'll get you a drink, okay?"

She nodded and he fetched a glass of water from the bathroom, which she drank in two gulps. "Better."

"How do you feel?" He touched the back of his hand to her forehead. Still hot.

"Let's cut to the chase, shall we? I'm not getting out of bed for the foreseeable future. Will that make you stop hovering?"

Her bristly tone was back. "I'm not hovering."

She shot him a look and nodded to his side of the bed. "Unless you want to be known as Prince Mother Hen, sit down."

He did, gingerly. "I'm concerned about you. That's all."

"And I appreciate it, but I'm not going to break. I can't swim to Saint Tropez in my current physical condition, but I'm not so fragile that you have to be at my beck and call."

Ah, so this was about her dogged determination to prove she could do whatever she set her mind to. Admirable, but also the reason they weren't married with two kids right now.

She just couldn't admit when she was wrong.

He might have the capacity to love her, but not necessarily the fortitude.

She clicked the remote a few times and tossed it to the bed, then snuggled down into the blankets. Somehow, she'd scooted over the invisible center line, onto his side. "Did I say thank you earlier?"

TV forgotten, she blinked at him with a small smile.

Awareness rolled over him with the force of a powerful whitecap.

He waved it off, his mouth suddenly dry. "You can show your gratitude by getting well and making me a proper meal."

"I'm working on it." She lay back against the pillow. "So tired."

Her legs shifted under the covers, sliding along his until they were flush. She appeared not to notice, had probably even done it accidentally. No matter. Thick layers of fabric separated them, but his skin heated as if all the obstacles between them were gone.

Desperate to get off the bed before he did something foolish, like strip naked and slide under the covers with her, he blurted out, "Do you feel well enough for a bath?"

Her closed eyes fluttered open. "I'd like that. Will you help me?"

Bad idea, his conscience screamed, followed shortly by, *Shut up now.* "I thought you didn't want me hovering."

"It's not hovering if I ask you, silly." Her small, delicate smile blossomed into a larger one that hit him in all the right places. "My skin feels crusty. I don't think I can reach it all."

"I'll help you to the bathroom, but that's as far as I go."

She lifted a wan hand to her forehead. "I need you. Please?"

Coupled with the liquid depths of her pleading gaze, how could he say no?

He fled to the bathroom and ran warm water into the huge marble tub. For good measure, he dumped half a bottle of Portia's oriental bubble bath into the water, hoping the foam would cover enough of Juliet to allow him the possibility of getting through this with his dignity intact.

The exotic scent of sandalwood and jasmine filled the bathroom, and instantly transformed the space from utilitarian to seductive. So much for dignity. He could have plastered the walls with erotic pictures and not achieved such a sensual effect.

Because the torture wasn't already brutal enough, he flipped on the entertainment system mounted to the wall and found a jazz station on satellite radio. The heavy, sultry wail of a saxophone poured through the surround-sound system.

"Finn?" she called from the bedroom, and the sound of his name from her raspy throat spiraled the tension higher.

He shut his eyes for a beat, but it didn't fortify him nearly enough.

Clamping down on his imagination, he hustled to the bed and hustled Juliet out with nary a sidelong glance at the T-shirt he'd haphazardly pulled onto her naked body last night, in place of her drenched clothes.

The simple T-shirt hadn't seemed sexy last night. This morning, it pleaded for a man's hands to lift the hem, just a fraction, revealing all her secrets.

He groaned and turned his back. "Get in the tub. All the way in. Let me know when you're covered up by the suds."

Please take a long time.

"Ready."

"Trying to set the land speed record for bathing?" he muttered and peeked at the bathtub. Sure enough, she'd submerged neck-deep into the water, head thrown back against the tub's lip, eyes closed.

Worst nightmare and hottest fantasy rolled into one.

"Fever, fever, fever," he mumbled and tried to remember the quickest way to break one. He cursed. He should have drawn a *cold* bath—with ice cubes. Or maybe that was the cure for a raging erection. His could use an ice bath the size of Delamer.

Juliet's eyes drifted open. "I know I have a fever. I feel awful."

"I wasn't talk—never mind." Yanking the soap, shampoo and a washcloth from the cabinet beside the vanity, he parked on the edge of the tub. "Let me wash your hair, then you do the rest."

He poured out enough shampoo to wash at least four women's hair—because there was no way he'd have the stamina to do this over if he messed up—and lathered her hair as quickly as possible. "Okay, rinse."

With what looked like considerable effort, she ducked under the water and came up with her eyes closed. He put a towel into her questing fingers and was about to stand and escape when her hand covered his knee.

"Don't go," she murmured. "Scrub my back."

Dark, wet strands of hair covered the area in question, which he could not keep his eyes off of. "I thought we agreed you could do that."

"No, you issued a royal decree. Doesn't make it possible for me to lift my arms that high."

Scootching backward, she presented her bare form for his touching pleasure. Except this was supposed to be a utilitarian process, designed to wash dried seawater from her skin. Not foreplay.

He swallowed and soaped the washcloth. Maybe if he didn't actually touch her, it wouldn't be so bad.

The cloth skimmed down her spine, eliciting a small moan from deep in her throat. Heat spiraled tighter in his abdomen, traveling south whether he wanted it to or not. Body on full alert, he ached to drop the cloth and let his fingertips glide along the ridge of her shoulders instead.

A silver chain around her neck flashed in the low light, and he couldn't stop staring at the place where it met skin. The necklace was new. What did the combination of cool metal on hot flesh feel like?

One little touch. It had been so long. He could reacquaint his senses with the feel of her and wash the grit away at the same time. A practical solution and good for everyone.

But he didn't do it. And not because of the fever.

If they reconciled—*if*—he didn't want it to happen like

this, catering to his father's whims, with the possibility that Juliet might think he wanted to be with her because of her family's politics.

These extraordinary circumstances couldn't possibly create a connection that would translate into a lasting relationship. In his mind, the only real chance they had was to escape first and then see how things went back in Delamer.

If he recalled, the exact words she'd flung at him before trying for a gold medal in cross-country backstroke were, *We're over and so is this conversation.*

He swiped her back, lower, but she moaned again, crossing his eyes. Did she *have* to make that noise as if he'd palmed one of her breasts?

She whimpered and her head fell forward on her knees. "My skin is a little tender. Probably from the fever. Can you hurry?"

"Am I hurting you?" Horrified, he yanked the washcloth away, cursing under his breath.

While he'd been devolving into full-on guy mode, she'd been in pain. None of the names he called himself seemed enough.

"No, not too much. It's just…prickly."

"Do you want me to stop?"

Half of him hoped the answer was yes. The other half prayed it was no.

He missed the simple pleasure of being nothing more than a man touching a beautiful woman. Juliet gave him that. There wasn't a blonde on the planet who ever had or ever could.

She peered over her wet shoulder, eyelids lowered as if she had very naughty thoughts to shield from him. "It's okay. You can keep going."

Sure he could. No problem.

Sweat dribbled between his shoulder blades.

Why was he doing this to himself? The pain of the past year wasn't buried deep enough, the complications on top of that were rampant and she was so very, very naked. Masochism at its finest.

"Thanks," she whispered. "I'm glad you're here."

Warmth of the nonsexual, emotional variety spread through his chest. Yeah. That was why. He wanted to make her feel better, regardless of the cost to himself.

His outdated, inconvenient sense of honor really pissed him off sometimes.

"Me, too. You'd be shark bait otherwise." He swallowed all the squishy, girlie stuff and prayed her fever would break soon. So they could get off this island before he snapped.

After considerable effort, Juliet dressed in another borrowed outfit from the well-stocked closet and allowed Finn to help her to the sofa in the living room. She tucked her feet under the blanket and rested her aching head on Finn's shoulder. For all her grousing, she kind of liked letting Finn take care of her, though she'd deny it to her grave.

She made a face at the TV screen and winced at the stabbing pain through her temples. Everything hurt. Her chest. Her head. Her arms and legs—but that was probably residual muscle fatigue from her unsuccessful escape attempt.

"I'm sorry we're stuck watching this boring movie," she said.

But he couldn't be nearly as sorry as she was.

She hadn't made it to Saint Tropez. And now she was sick and Finn had been forced into caring for her after saving her life.

He'd rescued her. *After* he let her tear off into the water, knowing the odds of her actually making it to the other side were slim to none. He'd let her go anyway. Because he understood what drove her.

The wash of sheer gratitude almost soothed away the bitter taste of failure.

"It's okay. I hate that you feel so bad." His tender grin

looped through her stomach and came out a good bit lower, warming her insides. Okay, it wasn't *just* gratitude.

He'd unearthed something powerful and deep. And it cut through her in a terrible, wonderful way. Finn had been there, right when she needed him.

She hated needing anyone, let alone him. He hadn't been there before when she needed him. What if she let herself trust him and he let her down again?

But she still loved him, that much was clear. And she hated that too.

"I—" A coughing spell cut off the rest and she let it go. What could she possibly say?

I'm conflicted about how you make me feel. Thank you for rescuing me, but can you go to the other side of the island until I figure out how to not be in love with you?

Finn took her hand and held it in his lap, his attention on her, not the movie. Like old times. It kicked up a slow burn in some really delicious places. Places she'd rather he not affect, not when so many unwelcome, baffling things were swirling around in her heart.

"You don't have to talk."

His thumb smoothed over her knuckle, and the contact lit her up. Coupled with the emotional turmoil, watching a movie together sounded less and less like a good idea. But she couldn't face being alone in the bed, aching and wishing for something, or someone, to make her feel better. Someone like Finn.

He'd given her a bath, even though he clearly would have preferred not to. She didn't blame him. She'd been a little snippy on the beach and then he'd had to rescue her. She'd be mad at her too.

"I do feel like death warmed over, but I can still talk." More coughing made a complete liar out of her. Her eyes watered fiercely but not enough to hide Finn's told-you-so smirk.

Her arms were too heavy to lift, let alone smack him one. So she settled for glaring at him.

"Why don't you focus on resting instead of trying to prove me wrong?" he suggested and smoothed a strand of hair away from her face. "The sooner your fever breaks, the sooner we can regroup on the escape effort."

He sounded as exasperated about taking care of her as she felt about him having to. "Look at the bright side. We're stuck together in this beautiful house. There's no danger to worry about. We can hang out while I get better. It'll be fun."

Hang out had a much more superior ring to it than *nursing an invalid*.

His mouth quirked up charmingly. "Seems like that's what I suggested not too long before you waded out into the water."

"And here I am agreeing with you."

"If only that was the start of a long-term trend," he mumbled good-naturedly. "Since this movie is so boring, let's play something on the Wii."

That was why she'd always loved staying in when they'd been dating. Finn's creative streak never ran dry. Everything became fun or a precursor to making love. Usually both.

"Sure." She shoved all the unbidden images behind a blank wall in her mind. The last thing she needed to be thinking about was how much she missed Finn's particular brand of seduction. "As long as it's not too complicated or one of those war games with lots of blood and shooting. Oh, and no zombies. Or aliens."

"That pretty much eliminates..." He flipped through the titles. "All of them. Wait, here's *Super Mario Brothers*. That'll work."

In minutes, Finn set up the game and they began blipping through the levels, laughing as they battled over who got the power-ups. The colorful graphics and lively music infused a sense of peace over them. All their grievances faded away the further they journeyed into the fantastical world of plumbers, walking mushrooms and flying manta rays.

Though Finn and Juliet had never played this particular game together, they were a formidable team and the opposition stood no chance. When he went high, she instinctively went low. When she charged ahead into the thick of enemy territory, he followed, knocking out bad guys right and left, backing her up every step of the way.

As he had in the water yesterday.

Of course if he hadn't brought up Bernard, and then double-whammied her with his father's treachery, she might not have ever set foot in the sea. Yet, he'd been there when it counted, despite being told it was too late.

She couldn't stop thinking about it, about him and all the wonderful things that comprised his character.

It made her question everything.

"Piece of cake," she said after they'd defeated a particularly hard level.

She couldn't swim to France, but at least she could kick the pants off fictional villains. The cartoon monster on the screen fizzled as he died, and his expression made her giggle.

"I'm surprised you're enjoying this." Finn hit the icon to go to the next world. "Given that the object of the game is to rescue Princess Peach."

She scowled. "That's the object? I thought it was to get to the next level."

"The levels have to end sometime. On the last one, Mario rescues the princess from a birdcage."

"So you've played this before."

Disappointment walloped her.

Somehow, she'd built up a scenario where they were playing so well as a team because they were both focusing on the here and now instead of History. Because he really understood what lay beneath her surface.

Obviously their success was instead a product of his familiarity with the game.

"A few times with Portia." He looked away, likely feeling guilty over not having divulged this information before. "It's her favorite but I don't get asked to play very often. Only when Alexander is off doing crown prince duty."

"Figures she'd like it."

Portia was a princess through and through, as if she'd been born to the crown instead of marrying it. Juliet hadn't spent much time with the next queen of Delamer, but when she did, the gracious woman never failed to make Juliet feel gauche and as if they were lifelong friends simultaneously. It was a talent, no doubt.

"It's just a game," Finn said lightly and bumped her shoulder with his.

It was far from just a game. The whole concept encapsulated what was wrong with the world. And poked at her discomfort over the fact that she'd required rescue, as well. Because she hadn't been strong enough to save herself.

"It's sexist and stereotypical. How come Mario didn't get kidnapped?"

Finn glanced at her and did a double take at her expression. "Because Mario and Luigi are the stars. If you want to play something where a woman is the star, go get *Tomb Raider*."

"Why can't there be a setting or something that you flip that changes who gets kidnapped?" She warmed to the idea. "It wouldn't be that big of a deal to switch the characters around and put Mario in a cage."

The more women who believed in themselves and their own strength, the better. Portia could be a princess who liked ball gowns, afternoon tea with the queen and being rescued by her Prince Charming all she wanted.

Juliet didn't like any of that. And didn't that put a knot the size of the crown jewels in her stomach?

Juliet might not like being rescued by the prince, but he'd had to do it just the same. Did he look down on her for not doing what she set out to do? Of course, if she hadn't been coming down with a stupid cold, the swim to Saint Tropez would have been within reach. That was her story and she was sticking to it.

He grinned and put his controller down, settling back against the couch, looking as if he'd humor her until next week if need be. "I'm sure Nintendo would love to hear your thoughts on how to stop perpetuating the stereotype of princesses always needing to be rescued."

"*You're* not even taking me seriously. Let alone a Japanese conglomerate that probably doesn't have one single female executive."

He tucked a lock of hair behind her ear, and she couldn't quite suppress the shiver his touch evoked. She didn't want to. Her stomach clenched. In anticipation *and* fear. Finn's blend of sexiness, solidity and tenderness scared her. Excited her. How messed up was that?

"I'm taking you seriously. I love how passionate you get about…well, everything. Your unwavering opinions define your character."

"You don't like it when I have an opinion. Especially not wh—" She bit down hard on her lip, so hard, the salty taste of blood seeped across her tongue.

Especially not when it's about how you should have acted a year ago.

"I love everything about you, Juliet," he said, and the catch in his voice thrummed through her chest. "I love that as strong as you are, you let me rescue you. I love that despite your seemingly inexhaustible determination, you're willing to ask me to help you take a bath. That's why we're a good team. We each play to the other's strengths and recognize our own limits."

Goodness. If she'd ever wondered why in the world she'd fallen in love with such a draconian, he'd blasted that curiosity to pieces. Where did he come up with such poetry?

"You don't have any limits," she grumbled to hide the thrill his heartfelt words had unfurled.

"That's not true. You almost pushed me past them in the bathtub earlier." The pad of his thumb caressed her jaw, and it was impossible to misinterpret the heat in his gaze.

It was just as impossible to ignore the answering liquid tug in her core. Despite everything, or maybe because of it, she longed to lose herself in the feelings he clearly still had for her and she for him. To lose her inhibitions and fears in his arms, his body, his drugging kisses, so mindless with pleasure, nothing else mattered.

Why did their relationship have to be so complicated? Why couldn't they be together, with all the difficulties of the outside world and their places in it forgotten? Nothing but the two of them, feeding their starving souls with each other. Just for a little while, with no one the wiser, no reminders of their impasse, no public eye to record every nuance of their interaction.

Her pulse beat in her throat.

Wasn't that what was going on *right now?* They were hidden away, held captive on this island, with no hope of rescue anytime soon. She could conceivably be off her stride for several days. Why not take advantage of their time together to enjoy the good parts of their relationship?

No one said they had to kiss *and* make up. Maybe they could just kiss…among other activities. King Laurent didn't dictate the rules. She could be with Finn whether his father liked it or not.

With no future to concern themselves with, no family to disappoint, she didn't have to worry about trusting him. If she kept her heart tucked away, he couldn't break it again. *No emotions. Ruthless determination.*

All they had to do was stay away from the past and focus on now. Piece of cake.

Eight

Later that day, Finn took a short break from monitoring Juliet's condition—or hovering as she liked to call it—and took a cold shower. It went a long way toward easing the ache that had taken up residence in his lower half. But not nearly long enough. He suspected only a naked and willing Juliet could completely eliminate it. That or a coma.

When he emerged from his bedroom, Juliet wasn't ensconced on the couch watching a chick flick where he'd left her. Clanking from the kitchen piqued his curiosity and he wandered into the melee of Juliet attempting to wrangle a pan and some meat into submission.

He watched her struggle for a minute, thoroughly enjoying the backside view of Juliet's slender, barefoot form. Except she was still sick and now he was all hot and bothered again.

"Why aren't you resting?" he finally asked.

The pan clattered to the Italian marble, cracking one

square tile in half. Ouch. Portia was going to have the king's head.

She whirled. "Don't sneak up on me like that."

"Sorry." He stomped in place a few times, mimicking just having arrived. "I'm in the kitchen now. Okay?"

"Okay." She grinned and turned to her stove-top project. "I'm not resting because you asked me to make you dinner."

"I did?" Had he hit his head? Obviously so, if he'd deliberately asked for a repeat of the Chicken With No Taste.

"Earlier. When you said I could show my gratitude by making you dinner." Gingerly, she nodded toward the back of the house and winced.

Ah, yes, on the bed, when he'd been holding on to his sanity by the tips of his fingers. That would definitely explain why he'd done something so unwise as to ask Juliet to make him dinner. "You're nowhere near well enough to be off the couch. Come on."

Sliding his hand into hers, he tugged her toward the living room, ignoring the blistering awareness of skin on skin.

"But you need to eat," she protested and dragged him to a halt between the two rooms.

"I've been feeding myself for twelve years." They were still holding hands but she didn't seem to notice. Far be it from him to bring it to her attention. He liked the feel of her delicate fingers against his. "I'll manage. What about you? Are you hungry? I can heat up some soup."

"Not really, thanks. I ate some crackers. Did I leave the stove on?" Peering over his shoulder, she sank teeth into the plump curve of her bottom lip.

His mouth tingled. That sweet swell of flesh was delicious, as he well knew from personal experience, and he couldn't tear his gaze away from it. "If you did, I'll take care of it."

She made a face. "I'm sure you will. Is there anything you can't take care of?"

Oh, he could think of one thing. A cold shower hadn't

helped his raging hormones catch a clue that first of all, Juliet wasn't in reconciliation mode, and second…

She sighed, pushing her breasts out invitingly. Before he lost his mind, he backed up, inadvertently stretching their locked hands.

She glanced down and tightened her grip, then closed the gap between them. "Wait, don't go. If you won't let me cook dinner, sit with me on the deck and watch the sunset."

Pure desire quickened through his gut.

"I…you probably don't need to be outside." Watch the sunset? Like, together? It almost sounded as if she wanted to spend time with him, in what she probably hadn't even considered would be a romantic setting—a complication he did not need. "You're still sick."

Did he sound as much like a song stuck on repeat to her as he did to himself?

"I don't feel that bad," she muttered, but her face was rosy in all the wrong places and her head tilted listlessly.

Cursing, he picked her up and deposited her on the couch before she could voice another objection. "At least sit down before you fall down. If you're bound and determined to show me your gratitude, get better. That's an order."

"Yes, sir." Flipping him a smart-aleck salute, she burrowed into the cushions and flung the blanket over her body, shoulders to feet. "Happy?"

Not in the slightest. Every nerve in his body ached with unfulfilled need. "Thrilled. We have plenty of time to watch sunsets after you get better."

She blinked up from her nest of blankets, innocent and alluring at the same time. He longed to crawl in with her.

"Sit with me then." She patted the couch and shot him a small smile he couldn't refuse.

In desperate need of a distraction, he sank onto the cushion and hit the power button on the TV remote. A Formula 1 race in Singapore, one of his top five favorite circuits, filled the screen. Automatically, he flexed his thumb to change the channel, but Juliet's hand covered his.

"This is fine," she said, and removed the remote from his suddenly nerveless fingers. "I'd like to watch this with you."

The roar of engines and whine of tires reverberated around them as he glanced at her askance. "I'd ask if you're feeling all right, but I already know the answer to that. Your fever must be worse than I thought if you're willing to watch a Formula 1 race."

"I told you I don't feel that bad. Tell me something. I've always wondered how you know which car is in first when they're going around the same loop over and over." Her temple came to rest on his shoulder as she squinted at the screen.

"The standings are listed in the ribbon across the top." More information about how to gauge the driver's position instantly sprang to his lips, but he bit it back. Surely she didn't actually care.

"Oh. That's easier than I thought it would be. How come some of the cars are identical and some are different?"

"The participants are on teams." Interest in the race completely lost, he tilted his nose toward her hair, inhaling the fresh scent of Juliet and the shampoo he'd used to wash her hair. The memory of her wet and naked under all those bubbles kicked up a slow torture.

She glanced up, puzzled, but clearly engaged.

"The teams have more than one guy driving," he clarified. "Same car, same team."

And for the next fifteen minutes, she asked more questions, patiently listening to his answers and occasionally offering an insightful comment about the ins and outs of the process.

"Planning to apply for a job as a pit crew member?" he asked after her questions tapered off. "You know, instead of teaching? Monaco has a track. You could jet over and back in thirty minutes tops."

She laughed. "Not a chance. I'd be too afraid to touch a million-dollar car."

"Then why all the questions?" An old thorn worked its way loose and poked him. Sporting events bored her and she'd never hidden her contempt for his interests. As she'd never hidden her contempt for his job.

"It's something you like. I wanted to learn more about it." Shrugging, she laced fingers with his casually, as she'd done a hundred times before they split up.

It felt different. Coupled with her nonchalantly tossed-out words, the effect was potent.

Her eyelids drifted halfway closed and she peeked up from under them. "So, what if instead of dinner, I wanted to show my gratitude some other way?"

The question came coupled with Juliet's lazy index finger trailing over his pectoral muscle and left no possibility of misinterpreting "some other way."

What was she doing? First Formula 1 and now this. The fever must be curdling her brain. And the fingertip hold on his sanity was sliding away at an alarming rate.

"You have a fever," he reminded her needlessly since they'd already discussed it at least five times. Or was the reminder more for his well-stirred blood's benefit? "I shouldn't even be this close to you."

"I seem to recall you've kissed me in the last twenty-four hours. More than once and quite thoroughly." She watched avidly for his reaction and he struggled not to give her one.

But he was pretty sure the instant hardening below the belt hadn't escaped her notice. No fabric in existence could disguise it.

"Face it," she murmured and the space between them, what little there was of it, vanished as she threw off the blanket, snuggling up against his chest. "You're already contaminated with my cooties. What's one more little kiss? To show my gratitude."

His gaze snapped to the firm, rosy lips so close to his. "You said we were over. On the beach. Is your near-death experience hindering your decision-making abilities?"

It was certainly messing with his.

This wasn't the plan. Rescue first. Reconciliation later. Too much unsaid lay underneath the surface to go down this path now. How could he even approach the subject of telling Juliet she was his father's choice for Finn's bride? He needed a cooler head, among other things, for that conversation.

She smiled and cupped a hand along his jaw. "Clarifying. Not hindering."

"Clarifying it how?"

How he put actual syllables together to form cohesive words, he'd never know. But *something* had shifted after she almost drowned, and despite protests to the contrary, he suspected it had affected her in a way he didn't fully trust.

"I'm still a prince and y—"

"Shh." Her thumb skated across his lips, silencing him. "Prince Alain isn't here. I only see Finn."

Finn. Yes, here on Île de Etienne, he could forget the complexities of that dual-edged sword and be nothing but a man. That yearning constantly simmered below the surface, and it thundered to life. They could get back to reality after they were rescued. Right now, he could indulge.

Involuntarily, his hands sought her face, determined to touch, desperate to connect. Cool skin met his palms. *Finally.* "I think your fever's gone."

"Is this the part where I get to say I told you so?" She grinned and nuzzled his throat.

"Sure. I can take it."

"Can you take this?"

Drawing him closer, until their breaths mingled, she brushed his lips with hers. Just a whisper of sweet contact, and instantly his mind drained of everything but the sexy, gorgeous woman in his arms.

"Yeah," he murmured against her mouth. "I can take all you've got of that."

Threading his fingers through her hair, he dived into the kiss with every intention of burning off the raging need for Juliet. They could deal with all the implications later.

She moaned and leaned into him as if she couldn't get close enough, her bewitching fingertips sparking across his neck and gliding under his T-shirt to spread at the span of his waist.

Yes, there. And everywhere else. He wanted her hands on him, wanted to touch her in kind, then slake his thirst for the woman he'd missed so very much.

His palms rested lightly against her throat as he angled her head to take her deeper into the kiss. She felt amazing.

The essence of Juliet poured into his senses. She slung a knee across his lap and climbed aboard, breasts teasing his chest, still slaying him with her mouth. Tongues slicked together, twining and seeking. Pleasuring.

He couldn't wait to sink into her tight, wet heat and let all his passion for Juliet explo—

With considerable effort, he twisted his mouth from hers. "We have to slow down, sweetheart."

Slow down.

Two words he'd never uttered in Juliet's presence. He had a bad habit of losing all common sense when she was within touching distance, and that needed to change *tout de suite.*

She lifted her head slightly and wiggled deeper into his lap. "Slow down? Why?"

Her confusion mingled with his frustration, adding weight to the already impossible situation his father had created.

"Because…" Struggling to simply breathe around the sharp desire clogging his system, he raked a hand through his hair before it found its way back into place on her very tempting rear.

Why? *Advantageous marriage. History. Scandal.* All of the above.

And for what was both the best and very worst reason of all. He could never be Just Finn, not even for a few moments, and it had been foolish to pretend he could.

"There's not one single condom in this whole house."

Juliet froze, hands on Finn's chest, as the significance sank in and her mind wheeled off in a dozen directions. "No condoms?"

So much for her plan to seduce Finn out of his clothes and indulge in a short-lived, no-hearts-required reunion. And here she thought the past and future were the complications they should avoid. Now he'd dragged the present into the equation.

"Not one. I've looked. Are you on some form of birth control?" he asked hopefully.

"No. Why would I be on birth control?" She'd spent the past year pretending she had no sex drive.

"Because you'd gone to a matchmaker to find a husband." He shrugged. "It was worth a shot to ask."

In actuality, she'd gone to a matchmaker because she was running away. Intimacy hadn't been forefront in her mind. Thank goodness Elise had saved one of her clients from being matched with Juliet—it would have been patently unfair to some poor man who could never compare with the man sitting next to her.

"So that's it? We can't do *anything*?"

She accompanied the question with a slow finger-walk down Finn's torso and kept going. He sucked in a breath as her nails grazed his still-impressive erection.

"If I'd known those fake nails would feel like that, I'd have bought you some a long time ago." He lifted her hand from his lap and held it against his thundering heart. "So you have to slow down."

"We can be careful." She tilted her hips back and forth, rubbing shamelessly against his rigid length. Heat shafted through her core and she arched involuntarily, grazing his chest with her sensitive nipples.

Thighs quivering, he groaned and thrust upward to meet her hip rolls. "There's no such thing as being careful when I've got you naked, especially if you keep doing that. I've spent the last year at the mercy of tabloids. A surprise pregnancy would be icing on the cake."

A baby. *Finn's* baby.

Sheer longing twisted through her insides, intense and shocking. Where had that come from?

"Sorry, I'll stop." She started to shift but his iron grip held her in place.

"I said slow down, not stop." His sizzling blue eyes sought hers and held them as he slowly circled his hips, grinding his erection against her.

"So," she gasped as the friction lit her up. "If you make love to me really slowly, that's going to prevent conception?"

Slow wasn't going to be an option much longer. She wanted every stitch of clothing between them gone. *Now.*

The wolfish grin on his face shot her arousal up another notch. "I'm more concerned about the out-of-wedlock part, not the pregnancy part."

She shook her head but the ringing in her ears got worse, not better. "What are you saying? That if we were married, it wouldn't be an issue?"

"If you get pregnant, we'd have to get married." His hands slid up both sides of her torso, thumbs hovering near her breasts, almost but not quite circling the aching peaks. "It's non-negotiable."

Her brain couldn't keep up, especially not with Finn's really good parts flush against hers and her nipples strain-

ing toward his thumbs, begging to be touched. "Is this a...
marriage proposal?"

Marriage. Finn was talking about *marriage.* To her.
While mere molecules of damp fabric separated her sex
from his.

"Not precisely." He pursed his beautifully chiseled lips,
and she couldn't tear her gaze from them. "More like a
promise of one to come."

A litany of jumbled emotions swirled through her head.
Her heart. She wanted him to love her. In the physical
sense. In the emotional sense. She flat-out wanted *him* and
her body didn't seem to care how she got him.

This was a really bad moment to realize she'd done a
poor job of tucking away all her feelings. Why had she
thought she could?

"Why can't we talk about this later?" she murmured and
leaned into his thumbs until they brushed her taut nipples.
Pleasure fluttered her eyelids and flooded her senses. "I
just want to be with you. Without all the complications. Is
that even possible?"

"Not between us, no."

She almost laughed at the irony. "Because you're Prince
Alain. Always."

His gaze sought hers, hot with desire and a significant
glint. "Because I'm still in love with you. It messes up everything. If only there was a way to forget about capital *H*
history and live right here in this moment, I'd do it, come
what may."

She blinked away sudden tears as his confession bled
through her body, singing through her pleasure center,
heightening everything.

Finn still loved her.

Her heart threw its doors open wide, sucking in the sentiment with glee. Something sweet and wonderful coursed
through her.

The concept of an island fling had been a poorly contrived pretext to feel exactly like that—without having to do the hard work of reconciliation. Without having to compromise or deal with her own guilt or risk allowing him to hurt her all over again.

"I shouldn't have said that." He shook his head. "I—"

"It's okay," she whispered, shocked her throat had spit out that instead of the *I still love you too* fighting to work free.

With effort so difficult it drew sweat, she slammed the door on her feelings. She couldn't tell him she loved him. That was how she'd given him the power to hurt her before, by making herself vulnerable.

But this time, she didn't have to.

He'd offered the perfect solution. They didn't have to rehash History or even mention it at all. They could be in the moment, indulge in the pleasure of each other and sort out the future later. Much later—especially the part about their feelings.

Slowly, she lifted the hem of her shirt, watching as his expression darkened.

"Let's forget about what happened a year ago and just be together. If there are consequences, so be it. Right here, right now, be Finn with me, even if you can only do it for one night."

Nine

One night.

Finn watched Juliet reveal her bra-less breasts, pulse beating in his temple in an erratic pattern more closely resembling Morse code than a rhythm designed to keep him alive.

Too much coffee. Too much Juliet. Too much at stake.

The sharp awareness and desire coursing through her expression quickened his blood, drawing his own desire to a fine point. Her breasts were breathtaking, gorgeous, rosy-tipped, and he wanted to run his tongue over the peaks until she cried out.

"Are you sure?" he asked her, his voice thready with anticipation.

If she chose to be with him, it wouldn't matter that the king had thrown them together. It wouldn't matter if she got pregnant as long as she understood marriage would be the next step.

"I'm sure," she said immediately. Decisively. It was heady to know she wanted him that badly.

But she was female and he'd made a cardinal error. "You're not letting the fact that I said I love you cloud this decision, are you?"

The feelings had sort of spilled out in reaction to the moment, without any forethought.

I love you was there in his consciousness, ready to be voiced as if he'd said it to her the day before. He didn't question whether she still loved him too—it was in her touch, in her kiss. In her eyes.

As was the total conflict she felt over it.

Which was why he didn't press her about her feelings. Why the choice had to be hers. This would be a real reconciliation, not one fabricated to serve the king's mandate, or it wouldn't happen at all.

But he was very close to losing control.

"No." A smile played at the corners of her mouth, as if she couldn't quite decide whether to let it flash. "This is about me and you and what we want. Grab hold and don't let go."

He knew exactly what he wanted. Tonight, he wanted to simply be Finn, to experience that harbor Juliet had always offered, where it didn't matter if he was merely the spare heir.

"Can you really forget?" he asked.

She held up a finger. "There's no past. No tomorrow. Just you and me and tonight. That's the only rule."

That sounded like a fine rule. If there was no tomorrow, his father's plan wasn't a factor. Besides, her family would never side with the crown, regardless of what happened between them, so the whole point was moot.

Without missing a beat, she leaned forward and placed her lips on his in a searching, questioning kiss. The heavens opened and poured light into his weakened soul.

Or perhaps that was Juliet's strength infusing his.

He slung his arms around her and clung to the woman he loved, imprinting the moment on his memory, so he could take it out later and savor it. She was the only woman he'd ever held who felt substantial enough to withstand the pressures and difficulties of being with a prince. She'd never crumble.

Unable to hold back a moment longer, he firmed his mouth and kissed her with every ounce of pent-up passion.

She moaned and opened under his onslaught. Eager to taste, he twined their tongues. Eager to touch, he pushed her torso forward, pressing her magnificent breasts to his chest.

"Need this gone," she mumbled and lifted his shirt over his head. As soon as she dropped it to the floor, her hands were back in place at his waist, fumbling with the closure of his pants and nearly ripping them off in her haste.

Yes. Naked. Now.

He lifted her to her feet and slid his pants off and then watched as she did the same with hers. He drew her against his body, peaks and valleys settling into familiar grooves, and finally they were bare flesh to bare flesh. Groaning with the sheer pleasure of her skin heating his, he took her mouth again in a savage kiss, teeth clacking and tongues thrusting.

There was no more need to slow down. And he didn't intend to.

Backing her up against the wall, he slid a thigh between her legs and rubbed her core, up and down, thrilling at the slickness that meant she was hot and ready for him. He knew her body as he knew his own. Knew how to touch her, how hard she liked it, when to let up and when to take her higher.

It was familiar, but that made it only more exciting. No guesswork, no confusion.

"Hurry," she moaned, heightening his own sense of urgency. "It's been so long. I want to feel you."

And he wanted to give her that.

Boosting her up, spine to the wall, he spread her thighs wide and teased her with the tip of his length. Her heat sizzled against his flesh and his eyes slammed shut at the shaft of pure lust spiking through his gut. He couldn't stand it. He eased her hips downward and sheathed himself one maddening centimeter at a time, desperately trying to give her as much pleasure as possible before he exploded.

With no barrier in place, sensation swamped him, rolling over his skin in a heavy tsunami of pleasure and spreading with wicked, thick heat.

Her amazing legs wrapped tighter around his waist, heels digging into his butt, urging him on with matched fervor.

"Unbelievable," she whispered. "You feel unbelievable."

"Tell me about it."

She rolled her hips, driving him deeper, and his knees buckled with the strain of holding back.

"Juliet," he murmured mindlessly and gurgled some more nonsense, unable to hold it all in.

She grabbed his free hand and put it against her nub, lacing her fingers with his to guide him. *Yes,* he loved it when she took charge. When she took her own pleasure. It was powerful, beautiful. Passionate. And it drove him wild.

As he rubbed, she arched, flinging her head back and crying out. She came with powerful shocks that squeezed him so exquisitely, his own release followed.

Sinking to the floor, he gathered her up and held her, slick torsos heaving in tandem. He smoothed her hair back from her forehead and just breathed, his mind, body and soul in perfect peace.

That was what he'd missed the most.

"Maybe next time we'll make it to the couch," she muttered and heaved a contented sigh that he felt clear to his knees. Her head thunked forward to land on his shoulder.

"Maybe next time you'll give me a chance to get near the

couch." Hence his point about the impossibility of "being careful." As if he'd have the capacity to pull out early once Juliet invited him into her slick heat. He'd have a better shot at swallowing the entire Mediterranean.

His lips found her temple and rested in the hollow. For the first time in the history of their relationship, neither of them had anywhere to be. They could make love all day long if they wanted to.

And he wanted to.

Tomorrow, the lack of outside pressures might abruptly end, and what kind of fool passed up an all-you-can-eat buffet?

As long as they were naked, he'd be happy to find a few dozen ways to keep both their brains occupied. Then, the little circle of peace that was Île de Etienne would stay intact. The past didn't exist, and the future wasn't here yet.

Finn didn't have to think about either.

They made it to the bed. Barely.

Juliet flopped back against the pillow and moaned as Finn tongued his merry way up her thigh, leisurely, as if they had all the time in the world. They didn't. Their island paradise was short-lived and besides, she wanted him inside her *now*.

"How do you make that feel so good?" she murmured and then cried out as his lips nibbled her with exactly the right pressure to light her up.

The white-hot pleasure arched her back so fast, her spine cracked. But then he stopped right as a hot wave radiated from her center, the precursor to another amazing orgasm.

Before she could protest, he flipped her onto her stomach, sandwiched her against the mattress and drove in from behind. *Yes, perfect.* It wasn't just his favorite position. It was hers too.

Her eyelids fluttered in ecstasy as he angled her hips to take him deeper, his mouth on her shoulder, chafing her skin with his unshaven jaw. She rolled her shoulder, shoving it between his lips and he complied with her unspoken request, sucking with indelicate pressure.

He eased out and back in again, slowly. Way too slowly.

She locked her ankles together to increase the friction, the way they both liked it. Groaning, he increased the pace, as she needed, at exactly the tempo he knew would launch her into oblivion. She squeezed once and that was it. Stars burst behind her eyes, blinding her for a moment.

He groaned as he collapsed on her back, his climax pulsing inside her deliciously.

She'd lost count of the number of times he'd rendered her boneless. The first one, against the living room wall, had been a near out-of-body experience. The rest had been full-body experiences, a revel in the corporeal as only Finn could deliver.

She remembered that he was good. But reality far eclipsed the memory.

The man was incredible, tireless, physical. When he got excited, he wasn't gentle, but she liked it a little rough, especially because she'd evoked it in the first place. It made a girl feel sexy to have a man slightly out of control over her. Besides, she gave as good as she got, and that only boosted his passion. Which in turn, fed hers.

No wonder they'd been matched. They fit together, like the hearts on the necklace Elise had given her, entwined by passion.

Finally he rolled and they separated. Breathing heavily, he flung an arm over his head and shut his eyes, shamelessly splayed like a bad girl's fantasy across the bed, naked and gorgeous. She drank in the sight and just as shamelessly enjoyed every second of it.

His well-developed chest muscles flexed and relaxed as he breathed. He had a new line of hard, defined ripples across his lower stomach, the result of what must be a new workout routine. She heartily approved of the addition to the contours of his body.

At the same time, sadness crept into her bubble of bliss. He'd developed those muscles over the past year. While they'd been apart. He'd lived a whole year's worth of life that she knew nothing about because his stubborn refusal to open his mind had driven them apart.

Not going there, she reminded herself.

They'd agreed on one rule—forget the past—and already she was trying to break it.

"Let's go outside," she suggested, determined to slide back into a state of mindlessness.

One of Finn's eyes popped open to regard her warily. "It's dark. And I must be rusty at this if you want to go outside instead of staying naked in bed. With me."

She laughed. "I never said anything about getting dressed. One thing we have a distinct lack of is neighbors and paparazzi. It's June, with perfect weather. When else will we have such a unique set of circumstances?"

His brows lifted. "Sex under the stars. I like it."

He rolled from the bed and yanked the comforter along with him, waggling his brows over his shoulder as he dashed from the bedroom.

She followed him, and the view of his bare butt was nice indeed. She sighed. It would be so great if she could count on being able to see it whenever she wanted.

Whose bright idea was it again to be together without thinking about the future? Oh, yeah—*hers.*

She squared her shoulders and shut the sliding glass door to the deck behind her.

A sweeping panorama of stars blanketed the still night, breathtaking in its splendor. The quiet lap of water provided a melodic soundtrack. A bright moon hung in the sky to the west, lighting the way to Spain.

"Wow," she said. "I should get extra points for coming up with this idea."

Finn lay back on the comforter he'd spread on the deck and patted it in a nonverbal invitation to join him. "I was just thinking about all the ways I planned to thank you for it. It's amazing."

She scooted next to him and he curled her into his body, flesh on flesh. His arm lay heavy against her side, fingers stroking the curve of her waist, but it was oddly absent of any sizzle. It felt…comfortable, and tranquility stole over her.

It could be like this back home in Delamer. Surely it could. They were doing a fine job of ignoring the past. Why not keep it up? Maybe not forever, but for a little while at least, dipping back into their relationship slowly.

The stars shone, sending light to Earth that had left years and years ago, before she and Finn had split up. Before life had grown so complicated. If only there was a way to get back to that.

For a long time, she'd considered herself as star-crossed as her name implied. But did it have to be that way? If they loved each other, why couldn't that be enough?

Finn hadn't mentioned marriage or love again, but she knew it wasn't because he'd changed his mind. Finn was nothing if not constant, and she loved that about him. She never had to question whether he'd waffled on an issue or if he'd considered all the facts before forming an opinion. He meant what he said and said what he meant. It was an inexorable part of his character.

For the first time since Bernard died, it seemed like more of a positive than a negative. She'd never have to wonder if Finn would fall out of love with her one day. Never wonder if he'd cheat on her.

"What if I said you could call me?" she blurted out. "At home. After we get off this island."

They could try dinner again, have a civilized conversation and sit on their hands lest they rip each other's clothes off in the cab on the way back to his place, where they'd make love until dawn.

His mouth rested against her forehead, and she felt his lips turn up. "We're a little past that stage, don't you think? By the end of the month, we could be engaged."

An image of Finn on one knee, a diamond as bright as a star extended between his fingers, exploded in her head. Her lungs burned as she held her breath, hoping that would make the image go away.

He didn't want to marry her, but he would—out of duty.

Gee, *that* was romantic. How had this simple night together gotten so messed up? She didn't want Finn to propose to her because he felt obligated to. Neither did she want this idyll to be over.

She sat up and twisted to look at him. "What if I don't get pregnant? That's it? *Au revoir* and don't call me, I'll call you?"

"That's rich, Juliet." He squeezed the bridge of his nose. "You're the one who came on to me, which is like pouring wine down the throat of an alcoholic and daring him not to swallow."

She processed his backhanded compliment. If she'd decoded his analogy correctly, he couldn't resist her. That put a small smile on her face for some unknown reason.

"Should I apologize?"

Finn swore in French. "Is this really the conversation you want to have?"

"I don't know. Everything feels so backward and crazy."

He heaved a sigh that carried all the way into her stomach, rolling it over with its intensity. "Don't you think about being together? Long-term?"

"Yeah," she whispered. She'd be lying if she said no.

"Then let's make that happen—with or without a baby to force the issue. If that's what you want."

That's what I want.

Instantly, the idea took root and she accepted it as gospel truth. A deep, shuddery breath nearly wrenched a sob loose.

But she couldn't have it both ways. Either they'd split up again or they'd be together. He was right—there was no *call me and we'll see how it goes.* Their relationship was too deep for that. Always had been, always would be.

"You can't marry me. Speaking of coronaries, *both* our families would have one."

Her mother would probably have a breakdown right there on the floor. That's why Île de Etienne was so perfect—no one had to know she'd indulged in a little fling with Finn.

Besides, Juliet could never marry Finn, not with the fear she'd find herself capable of using him to her own end fresh on her mind.

She bit her lip. But if she did get pregnant, was she prepared to lie about whom the father was? That wasn't even remotely possible. Finn would never agree to stay silent about having fathered her child.

And honestly, he'd be a wonderful father. She didn't want to raise a child alone or deprive her kid of all the joys of having a nuclear family. Deprive Finn of being able to see his son or daughter every day.

Ice picks of pain stabbed at the backs of her eyes. All she'd sought was an uncomplicated island adventure with a mouthwatering specimen of manhood who made her blood sing. Was that too much to ask?

"That's not true," he countered. "They wouldn't bat an eye if you were carrying my baby. Besides, my father's opinion of you has softened."

"When did that happen?"

"When he saw the photo of us together. It was in the note. He realized there was still something between us."

"Of course." That picture must have captured some serious sizzle to elicit such a drastic ploy as kidnapping.

"That's why he dumped us here, so we couldn't hurt his image any further by being photographed together."

"That's not why. You never gave me a chance to explain. My father had us brought here so we could spend time together, away from everything. See if a relationship was still possible." Sagging a little, he stared at the stars and she caught a hint that something was very off.

"Why in the world would he do something like that?"

"It must have been obvious I didn't want an arranged marriage any longer. But he still wants me to settle down, though I never dreamed he'd…well, that's why I tried so hard to flag down rescue. Spelled out the HELP sign. I didn't want us to reconcile like this, playing right into his hands. I'm sorr—"

"Don't let your father have any more control in our relationship." None of this should be about accidental pregnancy, or Finn's interfering father, but about the future and what making love actually meant for their relationship. "Tonight is just about us. Tomorrow, we can deal with everything else. Including your father, the past and the future. Let it go for now."

She tried to do the same. She really did. But that blanket of peace wouldn't return, no matter what tricks she employed to clear her mind. Because she couldn't stop wondering what was going to make tomorrow different from the past year.

The fates couldn't have conspired to put her and Finn together only to cruelly rip them apart.

Maybe other women waited around for fate to step in, but other women didn't get so much as a first chance with a man like Finn. Juliet Villere didn't leave her future to the hands of fate. And she wasn't blowing her second chance.

Tomorrow, *she'd* be the difference. Somehow.

They had to work through their issues once and for all, create a level playing field and never bring up the past again. She wanted to have their relationship back, intact, exactly as it had been, where she could depend on Finn to put her first above everyone else in his life.

Then she'd know for sure he loved her, for real, for forever.

Ten

When Juliet woke in the morning, she'd hardly opened her eyes before Finn rolled her against his side, intent clear as day in the sizzle shooting from his deceptively sleepy gaze.

"Good morning," she murmured, and snuggled into his warm body for an enchanting moment of pure harmony that had nothing to do with sex. She'd missed the small things that made life so much sweeter—good-night kisses, falling asleep holding hands, waking up together.

A moment was all she got to enjoy it. He thoroughly compromised her in twenty minutes flat, and she had the whisker burn in eight very tender places to prove it. To be fair, she'd left behind a few souvenir teeth marks on him.

"Good morning," he finally responded when he'd caught his breath. Sated and clearly determined to be lazy this morning, he turned on the TV and slung an arm around her companionably as they settled in to watch nothing.

His dark hair was still sleep-and-finger tousled and his chest unashamedly bare, all hard muscle and delicious skin for her tasting pleasure. She could get used to waking up to *that*. She couldn't stop looking at his beautiful form long enough to even register what channel he landed on.

Until he sat up, eyes hard and riveted to the screen. She glanced at the TV. A cable news station flashed a picture of a sinister-looking warship with deadly weapons scattered across the deck.

Finn hit the volume button and the news anchor's deep baritone filled the bedroom.

"...gathering off the coast of Greece, within striking distance of the newly assembled army. World leaders are meeting in Geneva this afternoon to discuss a preemptive hit on the country's forces."

His body tense, Finn glanced at her and she did a double take at the harsh lines around his mouth.

Juliet's pulse slammed into her throat. "What is he talking about?"

"In other news..." The anchor went on to describe a peace rally in Athens protesting the aggression.

"Whatever it is, it's not good," Finn said grimly. "That warship is stationed in the Ionian Sea. I could practically throw a rock and hit it from here."

Her fingers flexed to grab the remote and throw it across the room in kind. Military aggression. Her least favorite hot button.

This was a watershed moment, where she could let the wounds of the past rule or forge a new future. This warship's presence in the Mediterranean was important to Finn, evident in the stiff set of his jaw and the severe tilt of his brows.

"Find another channel talking about it," Juliet suggested softly. "You need to know."

Nodding, he flipped through the channels until he found a news station describing how the government of Alhendra, a small but well-financed country sandwiched between Albania and Greece, had sent missiles into a civilian neighborhood in Preveza, a beautiful Greek coastal region. The casualties were high and world powers' thirst for retaliation was higher. It was an unprovoked act of antagonism that the United Nations couldn't ignore and didn't intend to.

She forced herself to listen alongside him, and when he slid his hand into hers, she stiffened her shaking fingers to keep him from knowing how deeply ingrained her body's response was to seeing warships on the news.

Bernard's death had been reported with similar shots of a ship at full cruising speed, cutting through the dark waters of the sea. Over and over, they'd played that clip, with a scripted spiel about the accident.

A noise of pure disgust growled from Finn's throat. "I can't believe this is happening and I'm stuck here. Delamer might be in jeopardy. Any coastal region could get caught in the crossfire. Our ships can be ready to deploy and stand with our allies immediately. At the very least, we should send someone to Geneva."

Stuck here. With her. He'd rather be back home, reveling in his armed-forces glory.

"Don't you think your father is already on top of it?" she asked with raised eyebrows. "This is his moment in the sun."

Finn's too. It was a golden opportunity to espouse the virtues of his father's military polices. To give her a big, fat I-told-you-so and laugh off her earlier argument that it was peacetime.

He shot her a withering glare. "Of course he's on top of it. But he needs help. He's probably got someone on the way to get me right now. I should be there."

She'd been wrong before. *This* was the watershed moment. She had to accept that his sense of honor would never allow him to side against his father, no matter what the man did. She had to find a way to live with the fact that Bernard's death would not be avenged through reform.

Or she had to not be with Finn.

Which wasn't going to be much of a choice if she was carrying his baby.

Bernard had died but Juliet was still alive, and her brother wouldn't want her to be miserable on principle. He'd loved Finn and would never begrudge Juliet trying to find a future with the prince. Her parents would learn to adjust—or they wouldn't—but her family wasn't the reason her relationship with Finn had fallen apart a year ago.

It was because there was no compromise.

"We should spend the day setting up more signals, just in case your father plans to leave us here a while longer." Her head dropped, suddenly too heavy to hold up. She'd expected the day to unfold with a naked romp in the shower and then another naked romp through a couple of other choice locales. The disappointment melded with the shock, cracking her voice. "If several countries are sending forces to the Ionian Sea, they have to pass right by here. Someone will surely see us this time."

Their island fling-slash-reconciliation-slash-precursor to a marriage proposal had screeched to a halt.

Gently, he tipped her head up to meet his gaze, and she blinked back the moisture she'd been trying to hide. He was watching her with dark intensity that unleashed a shiver.

"I love you," he murmured. "That's not going to change, no matter what happens."

Whether she'd conceived. Whether she hadn't. Whether their families intervened in their relationship or didn't. Whether the world stood at the brink of war or not.

"I know."

Because she loved him like that too. And it messed up everything because she still hated his fervor for the military. Hated that he might die like Bernard and abandon her again, but this time forever.

Recognizing there was no compromise wasn't the same as being okay with it. And she wasn't. She couldn't be. Could she?

Maybe this wasn't real love or else it wouldn't feel so much like one—or both—of them had to give up everything.

Or was this simply proof that love *wasn't* enough?

He shook his head. "No, I don't think you do. I don't think you could possibly understand how completely torn up I am at this moment."

Her laugh wasn't nearly as bitter as she'd have expected. "I have a pretty good idea."

"I know this is hard for you. I know what it cost you to bite back your opinion of my father and of my job. Don't give up your convictions. I don't ever want you to give up, especially not on something you truly believe in."

Her pulse hammered in her throat. He'd never said anything like that before. It almost sounded as if he admired her for taking a stance against his father.

Maybe she'd misjudged his reasons for not siding with her. As many times as they'd argued over the protest, they'd never really talked rationally. Shouted, accused, defended—yes. Well, mostly she did that. Diplomacy wasn't in her DNA.

Worse, when diplomacy wasn't one of her skill sets, how effective of a princess would she really be? If a marriage proposal could potentially be imminent, perhaps she should practice being diplomatic a whole heck of a lot more. What better place to start than with History?

If they could successfully navigate that, they could endure anything and still make it. She'd finally feel safe enough to confess she'd never fallen out of love with him.

Finn shoved food in his mouth, but he couldn't have said what it was for any price.

He kept waiting to hear the sound of rescue approaching. The whine of a boat engine. The drone of helicopter blades. The longer the silence stretched, the worse his muscles knotted with tension.

Surely the king wouldn't leave Finn here marooned on Île de Etienne while warships convened just across the Mediterranean. It was unthinkable.

At the same time, he'd rather keep the real world at bay and stay completely submersed in this new Juliet who watched Formula 1 and didn't slice him open with arguments against military force.

He glanced at her, and she was so gorgeous in a simple red sundress that set off fireworks in her brown hair. She smiled, and it yanked a long slice of warmth from his center. They were sitting at the table, eating breakfast like a normal couple.

Something had happened to get them here. Dare he hope it was enough?

Well, he obviously did dare because hope of the most dangerous kind had begun to live in the back of his mind. Dangerous because he wanted to sweep Juliet off her feet with an outrageously romantic marriage proposal—before she handed him a pregnancy test. Before he had to take up his uniform and rejoin the Delamer Navy in what might devolve into combat. Search and rescue was his day job, but he was still a lieutenant in the armed forces. And his country was worth defending, even with his dying breath.

Securing a "yes" from her before all that other stuff interfered would make everything else bearable. They'd be together, they'd be in love and nothing else could touch them.

But he couldn't propose as he envisioned because they'd done nothing to address capital *H* history, not that he was complaining. He'd rather they didn't talk about that at all, except if they got married, she'd have to understand the obligations that came with being his princess. No more protests.

And she hadn't actually told him she loved him yet.

The timing was wrong. He couldn't propose until all the issues were addressed. *All* of them.

Juliet lifted a lock of hair from her shoulder and twirled it absently as she contemplated him. "You gonna eat that or massacre it?"

He glanced at his hand, which was pulverizing what appeared to have once been a slice of bread. "Both."

Shoving it in his mouth, he chewed and swallowed the evidence, but he barely tasted it.

They *had* to talk. And he'd put it off too long already.

In addition to dealing with History, it was important that she find out about her family's renewed attacks against his father from Finn and not from whoever came to rescue them. The only way this reconciliation would work was if she understood he had no intention of using their relationship to influence her family. But if she loved him, she'd take care of it on his behalf.

"You're so tense, I could cut this butter with your clenched jaw alone," she commented mildly and nodded to his plate. "You done with that?"

"Yeah." If they were both finished eating, now would be the optimal time to get started on that long-overdue discussion. The sooner, the better.

"Good."

Standing so abruptly her chair crashed to the floor, she slid the plate to the other side of the table and nestled into his lap, front to front, fitting into the planes of his body. Instantly, he hardened against her soft core, which radiated heat through her panties.

Or they could talk later. Much later.

Relieved to descend into that place where they connected brilliantly, he snaked a hand under the bright swatch of skirt and palmed her backside, teasing her with light fingertip trails. Then he delved beneath the silky fabric to trace her feminine contours.

Her breath came faster, and desire bloomed across her expression. It thoroughly thrilled him. Hips thrusting and circling, she threw her head back and rode hard against his rigid length. Desperate to get to flesh, he thumbed beneath the scrap of cloth covering her and fused his lips to her throat as he plunged two fingers into her wet heat.

Hot, so hot. Her, the position, his skin.

He wanted to feel her on the inside, let his mind drain of everything but the sensation of loving her.

His spine tingled from holding back his own release. She rocked on his hand faster, then faster still, moaning her pleasure, arching back against the table and spreading her thighs wider.

"That's it," he murmured as her eyelids slammed shut in ecstasy and her core throbbed against his fingers. She came on a cry that shafted through his groin, both painful and erotic at the same time.

She collapsed against his chest and he caught her, binding her close. Her head landed on his shoulder, grinding her core against his inflamed erection.

She made him *insane.*

"Strip," she commanded in his ear without shifting her weight. Or offering to help. Or shedding her dress.

"Easy for you to say." But he lifted her one-handed and wiggled out of his clothes. Gracelessly, for sure, but who cared?

Since she appeared to have lost the ability to work a single muscle group, he hiked up her dress, yanked the panties aside and lowered her onto his shaft. The spiral of heat and light exploded in a whirlwind, sucking him into the oblivion of her body.

Finally, she came alive. Rolling her hips, she took him higher, deeper, faster, and the dual edges of the corporeal and the emotional crashed, culminating in a release of epic proportions that could be fully expressed only with the "*I love you*" that spilled from his mouth, rained from his consciousness, radiated from his soul.

At least he thought he said it out loud. But she didn't say it back.

He willed away the prickliness at the back of his neck. They were just words. Saying them or not saying them didn't make the fact any less true. She loved him. He knew that.

When he found the energy, he stood, easily picking her up along with the motion, and carried her to the bed they'd shared last night. There, he drove them both into the stratosphere again, but it was slightly bittersweet this time. He refused to examine why.

Later, as they lay draped across the mattress, he stroked her hair. "Hey, I'm not so tense anymore."

She turned her head to face him and rested a cheek on the sheets, a grin stretching her lips. "Mission accomplished."

Some perverse tendency compelled him to rock the boat. "You know this is all about to end, right?"

A wrinkle appeared between her brows. "Which part?"

"The island-seclusion part."

"Oh. Yeah, we were supposed to be setting up flares or something, weren't we?" She drew his palm to her lips and mouthed a wet kiss along the crease. "You distracted me."

"Ha. It was the other way around. I was about to bring up another topic entirely."

"We have to talk. I know." She sat up, taking his hand with her and clutching it to her heart. "I think I'm ready."

"You look like you're about to march up the steps to the guillotine."

"We've been putting this off for a reason. It's painful. And it sucks," she whispered. "We haven't dealt with Bernard. Or the protest. And we have to if we're going to be together. I just don't want to. I'm not very good at expressing myself without yelling."

The tension was back, tenfold, cramping his well-used muscles. "What is there to yell about? We agreed to forget about history and move forward."

Obviously that wasn't going to work, not that he'd really believed it would.

"Forget about it for how long? Until they bring you home in a body bag?" She dragged a pillow over her face, but it didn't muffle the heart-wrenching sob as much as she probably hoped.

"Hey." He ran a thumb over her one uncovered shoulder. "That's not yelling. I was promised yelling. Toss that pillow off and let me have it."

Actually, he liked it better when she yelled. That, he understood. They argued, they yelled, they made up. Except for that last epic fight a year ago...

Her laugh eased his tight gut more than he'd expected. They were going to get through this. They were stronger this time. Wiser. More determined.

She peeked out from beneath the pillow. "Rain check? I'd like to look back on this conversation and call it rational. I guess hiding doesn't exactly scream nice and sane." She heaved a sigh and flipped the pillow toward the headboard. "I grew up invisible. Too many kids in the house, I guess. You were the first person who saw *me*. Who loved me for who I was, not what I could do for you. When Bernard died...you refused to listen to me, refused to see I might have valid ideas about changes. It hurt. I felt abandoned and lost. I don't know how to get over that."

She'd told him variations of this before, but never with such brokenness. Never without shouting it, along with as many inventive slurs on his intelligence as she could come up with. He definitely liked the shouting better. It gave him permission to shout back and never deal with the emotions being stirred up.

With that sucker punch ringing in his ears, she twisted the dual-edged sword. "When I see warships on TV, it brings it all back. I want to be with you. But I need you to choose me as well or I can't."

Rational. It was a good goal. And suddenly he wasn't so sure he could comply with it.

"What does that look like, Juliet? How can I help you feel like I'm choosing you?" he said, picking his words carefully lest he lead the witness toward a conclusion neither of them could live with.

"I need to feel like you honor our relationship above all others. Like you're on my side. Especially when it's about an issue that destroyed my family."

There it was. He couldn't pretend to misunderstand. Not this time. But if she could do this without yelling, he could too.

Because he loved her and she was trying to do things differently.

He jackknifed to his knees and took her face between his palms. "I want you to understand something critically important. If I was a regular guy, Finn the helicopter pilot who digs this girl Juliet from down the road, I'd crawl over broken glass for a hundred miles to make you mine forever."

Something equal parts tender and shattered flashed in her eyes, gutting him instantly. Because she knew he wasn't finished.

And he wasn't. He couldn't bow to her demands just because she preferred it.

"But I'm not that guy. I don't want to be that guy because being Prince Alain Phineas of Montagne, Duke of Marechal, House of Couronne is a privilege. One I'm honored to live up to."

"So what are you saying?" she whispered, her gaze darting over his face. "*Au revoir* and don't call me, I'll call you?"

"No." He dropped his hands to his side. "That means I'm standing on the other side of a huge expanse of middle ground. I need you to meet me in the middle if we're going to work outside of Île de Etienne."

There. He'd said it as plainly as he could.

"Compromise." She nodded once. "If that's what it takes, that's something I can work with."

Relief jump-started his pulse. "Then you finally understand. You see how important the military is to me. It's part of me. Part of my identity."

Confusion marred her expression and she crossed her arms. "I thought your title was your identity. That you were honoring your blood. I don't see how the military is suddenly rearing its ugly head into this conversation. One has nothing to do with the other."

So she *didn't* get it. "They have everything to do with each other. Alexander's role is clearly defined. He's going to be king. What am I going to be? Prince Alain, the same thing I am now and always was. There's nothing special about me. Nothing I can do to make a contribution except provide defense for the country my father leads."

That, and marry advantageously. The thought added a ninety-stone weight to his shoulders.

"Oh, my darling." Her lips trembled and she clamped them shut. "You're the most special man I've ever known. Alexander was born to his role, but it's so narrow. You have the opportunity to make yours whatever you want it to be. You can be known as the prince who makes a difference in the lives of his people. By introducing reform to the mandatory service law. Get your recruits the right way, from those who choose it, instead of making it a requirement."

"The military is mine, Juliet," he bit out. "Reform isn't on the table."

Why were they having this conversation again? To prove History always repeated itself?

"I see." Her gaze hardened. "You're all for compromise as long as it's me who's doing the compromising."

"I'm all for both of us showing our respect and affection by honoring the other's position." This was the critical point, the one she had to get through her head. "If you love me, you can't only love part of me. You have to love the whole me, including the part that doesn't agree with you."

"Same goes." She took a deep breath, her bare breasts rising and falling in sync. "Have you ever considered that I am honoring my blood too? Bernard was my brother, and his memory deserves nothing less than my strongest convictions. You said I should never give them up. Are you going back on that now?"

Of course he'd considered that. Finn had a brother too. "No, I meant it. Integrity is important to me. I wouldn't love you if you didn't have those convictions."

"Integrity is important to me too. The fact that you stand so strongly in yours is partly why I'm here having this discussion instead of storming out."

That made two of them. But storming out was sounding better and better the longer they beat their heads against this wall between them. If they couldn't resolve things here without any outside pressures, how could they do it at home?

That was the reason he didn't storm out. Once they left Île de Etienne, it would be too late. They had to break down that wall here and now.

"Family is as important as integrity," he said. "To both of us. Honoring the other's position includes helping our families understand it, as well. You realize if we're together, your family can't continue opposing my father, right?"

From outside the house, the distinctive, unmistakable *thwack, thwack, thwack* of helicopter blades split the air. Juliet whirled toward the sound as if she'd been thrown a lifeline.

No. Not yet.

But willing away rescue didn't work any better than willing it here had. He'd run out of time.

Eleven

The drone of a helicopter cut off the last of Finn's sentence, but Juliet had heard enough of it to be simultaneously sorry and thrilled the king had finally sent someone for them.

Part of her wanted to hop on the helicopter and pretend they'd dealt with all their issues. The rest of her knew that wasn't going to work.

Slowly, she faced Finn, tamping down her rising temper with considerable effort. "My family can't oppose your father or I can't?"

"Neither. I can't take any more scandals. Or protests."

"Or what? Your father won't allow us to be together? This isn't the Dark Ages."

How long did they have until whomever was sent to retrieve them reached the door? They weren't even dressed, something she was happy to take care of. She needed something to do with her hands.

"My father isn't—" Finn thumped the bed in apparent frustration. "This is about you and me and our future. If we're married, you'll be a princess of a country that requires eighteen-year-old males to serve three years in the armed forces."

She paused in the process of slipping on the red dress she'd worn for a grand total of thirty minutes thus far today and glanced at him over her shoulder. "Yeah. That doesn't mean I have to agree with it."

"No, you don't. But you can't freely declare your disagreement. That's the point."

"Fine, then don't marry me." Her chest ached at the pronouncement. "We can be together without getting married. Couples do it all the time, and it solves every problem in one shot, right? It'll even make your father happy."

"It wouldn't make me happy. Besides, this—" his hand cut a zigzag line in the air, indicating the house at large "—was a chance for us to rekindle our relationship, remember? My father wants us to get married."

"What?" The king *wanted* them to get married?

Scooting to the edge of the bed, he pulled on his clothes without looking at her. "I told you that's what this was about."

Something seemed off. She couldn't put her finger on it. "Not the marriage part. I would have remembered that."

"Because it was irrelevant." He yanked his shirt over his head and then raised his eyebrows. "One night. No past, no future. That was your rule. It's tomorrow and we're talking about it."

"Yeah, because yesterday, I thought all we had to work through was the past. Your father wants us married. What don't I know?"

He shut his eyes for a beat, which didn't settle the sudden swirl in her stomach. "Let's just say you're my advantageous marriage."

Like a behind-schedule bullet train, her pulse rocketed into the triple digits. Being dressed didn't provide nearly the shield she'd have expected. "Oh, no, let's *not* just say that. Let's say a whole lot more."

"Your family renewed their attacks against my father." Finn locked gazes with her, his expression dark. Too dark. "If we're a couple, their position is neutralized. It looks like you're siding with the crown."

Dizziness rushed up out of nowhere, knocking her off balance.

This was a setup to get her family to back off. A sharp pain tore through her chest and kept going. Nausea churned up her stomach, and she swallowed against the burn rocketing up the back of her throat.

A *setup*. "And you went along with it."

"I didn't." He fairly bristled with the denial. "I would never use our relationship to influence your family. But if we're married, you see the trouble with continuing to protest Delamer's laws. Don't you?"

That had been the goal all along—get that Villere family to shut up. And she'd fallen for it without a peep of protest. "I slept with you. I was *intimate* with you. Because I thought you wanted to be with me. But it was all a lie. How could you do that?"

"I gave you a choice." His hands flew up in protest, palms out as if he intended to mime his way out of trouble. "I slowed it down even though I absolutely wanted to be with you. For exactly this reason, so you would know you made that choice, not me."

If you get pregnant, we'd have to get married.

A cloud of red stole over her vision and the most unladylike word she knew slipped out, verbalizing her rising distress.

There were no condoms in this house *by design*.

And she'd walked smack into it. This wasn't just his father's plan. Finn had bought into it, made it his own, twisting it into something so brilliantly diabolical, it nearly doubled her over.

"I made that choice without all the facts!" she shouted over the *snap* of her heart breaking.

Oh, God, without *any* of the facts. She'd been so worried about making sure her own motives were pure, that she wasn't using him for her own gain. It never occurred to her that he might not have the same compunction.

He'd been using her. All along.

Unforgivable.

She'd been trying so hard to figure out how to live with his refusal to compromise. Because she'd truly believed that the deficiency was hers. That she couldn't possibly understand the royal pressures he faced and if she wanted to be with him, she'd have to give more than he did.

She'd allowed herself to be vulnerable. To lay out her hurts and fears, trusting that he'd keep her feelings safe.

That might be the worst part of all.

"You had the important facts." His gaze sought hers as if he had a prayer of communicating something nonverbally. "Like that I love you."

Ha. That wasn't a fact. That was the purest fiction.

"*This* is your definition of love? Lying to me and using me?"

He'd used her body, but far worse, he'd used her feelings against her. In the end, it hadn't mattered if she'd told him she loved him or not. He still managed to eviscerate her anyway.

Bang, bang, bang. The helicopter pilot was at the front door.

Finn's forehead wrinkled but it was the only outward indicator that her words had any effect. "I didn't lie to you. I never saw you as my advantageous marriage. Actually, I wasn't even sure we'd work things out, especially not this way. But everything snowballed and I wanted you to hear about your family's renewed fervor from me. I didn't want you to find out from…"

"Finn?" The male voice called out from the living room.

"Alexander," Finn finished.

Crown Prince Alexander of Montagne filled the doorway of the bedroom, larger than life, and a grimace on his face. "What happened to my patio furniture?"

"This is *your* house?" Juliet truly thought she'd lost the capacity to be shocked. But apparently the deception went much deeper than she'd ever guessed. Finn had known that from the beginning too. No wonder the house was stocked with games and food that Alexander and Portia liked.

Alexander, to his credit, didn't flinch at Juliet's version of a royal address. But she wasn't too thrilled with any member of the House of Couronne at this point in time, thank you very much. Royalty earned fealty in her humble opinion, and being a party to kidnapping one of his subjects hadn't endeared Prince Alexander to Juliet in the slightest.

Finn threw up a hand in his brother's direction. "Can you give us a minute, please?"

"Only a minute." Alexander crossed his arms, and it was easy to imagine him piercing the members of Parliament with that same regal glare. Which he could jolly well go off and do. There was no room for another insufferable prince in this horrific situation.

He backed away and disappeared.

"Juliet. For what it's worth, I'm sorry. I could have done this differently." Finn approached her and reached out as if to touch her and then changed his mind at the last minute. Smart man. But not smart enough.

She gathered great gobs of red skirt in both fists before she decked him. "Why didn't you do it differently then? Why didn't you tell me?"

"I—" He sighed. "I honestly didn't think you'd take it like this."

"What, like if I got pregnant, you'd marry me and use that to force every Villere in Delamer to keep quiet?"

His head bowed. "That wasn't the plan. The plan was to get off this island. Then when we got home, I was going to

call you and see if we could start over. Things happened.
You started coming on to m—"

"I'm going to get in that helicopter with Alexander because I have to." There was *no way* he was pinning this
on her. "Once we hit Delamer, I'm going to get out and I
never want to see you again."

"Don't say that." His eyes glistened with vulnerability
she could hardly stomach. "This reconciliation was real.
Don't let the admittedly unusual circumstances take away
from that. We can make it work."

Her laugh shot out with surprising ease. "There was no
reconciliation. We might have been headed toward one,
but don't fool yourself. We still had a lot to work through,
and this last bit erased any progress. You still can't see that
you not only didn't take my side, you took your father's.
There's nothing you can say or do in a million years that
would make that okay, that would put us near the realm of
'making it work.' Nothing."

"There's still the possibility of pregnancy."

His trump card. The tips of her ears burned with the
mere mention of the word *pregnancy*. That was probably
the hardest part—that if she got pregnant, they wouldn't
be rejoicing over it together, as she'd stupidly let herself
envision.

"Maybe. But it won't involve a wedding or a happily-
ever-after. Stay away from me. I mean it."

He'd never know either way. If she'd conceived, she'd
never ask him for a single tiny diamond from the crown
jewels to support her or the baby.

For the rest of her life, she'd have to see Finn's eyes
in her baby's face. That was her punishment for trusting
him again.

"You can't mean that. You have the keys to my heart."
Finn slapped his chest in the spot where the organ in question was supposed to be—but wasn't—and his mouth softened. "It's not a throwaway cliché. You have the ability to

unlock it from the outside and come in without my permission. Rifle around and romp through me intimately. Use that power wisely."

He meant she could hurt him. And she fully intended to ensure he hurt every bit as much as she did.

Finn watched Juliet out of the corner of his burning eyes as she huddled against the helicopter seat without speaking to either him or Alexander.

Fragile and broken, she wore her bruised emotions like a cloak. She hurt and it was his fault.

How had this turned out so badly? They couldn't even talk over the whack of the blades and the rush of air as they flew toward the shore. But what else could he say? She'd made her point quite clearly—she wanted him to choose her, and in her mind, he hadn't.

As soon as Alexander touched down east of the palace, she launched from the helicopter and scurried toward the gatekeeper without a backward glance.

"I'm assuming that didn't go well," Alexander said wryly.

"Shut up. The kidnapping was a stupid idea from the beginning." Finn debated whether to follow Juliet and throw himself at her feet or keep what little of his pride remained and let the gatekeeper call her a taxi.

He turned toward the house, slashing the remainder of his heart from his chest. There wasn't anything else he could do but let her go. She wasn't in love with him. She'd probably never really loved him. After all, someone who loved him wouldn't have participated in the protest in the first place. If she loved him, she would have said so at least once, especially after he said it to her.

Her interest in Formula 1 had probably even been by design—to butter him up so she could get what she wanted.

"I told Father that," Alexander said in his typical matter-of-fact and annoyingly brief fashion.

That answered the question of whether his brother had been in on the king's plan too. Of course Alexander had been the one sent to fetch them. The fewer people who knew about what the king had done, the better, no doubt.

Not many people could fly a helicopter anyway. Alexander had fallen in love with piloting helicopters during his three years of mandatory service but now had to do it on the sidelines. He couldn't fly in combat. But Finn could. And when Finn served his three, he'd vowed to do that one thing better than his brother.

Thus far, he had. It was his calling, his first love. And maybe he tended to be a little protective of it. A long wave unsettled his stomach. Juliet might have recognized that well before he had.

"Why didn't you come get me earlier then if you realized it wasn't going to work?" Finn's fist doubled and he longed to take out his frustration on someone who matched him in strength and skill, who could take whatever he dished out and then some. Someone other than Juliet.

Alexander clapped Finn on the shoulder as they mounted the steps to the palace. "I said it was stupid, not that it wouldn't work. I actually thought you'd pull it off."

And didn't that rub salt in the wound? Not only had he not succeeded, but Alexander's glib comment devalued the emotional aspect of what had happened. As if Finn had merely been trying to land a large account or net a sizable income from an investment. "It was doomed to failure from the start because Juliet is too stubborn."

"Must have been like looking in a mirror then."

"What's that supposed to mean? You think I'm stubborn?"

"As a fish on a line that refuses to come out of the water." Alexander tilted his head. "We don't call you Finn solely for your ability to swim, my brother."

Smirking to hide the bloody trails Alexander had carved

through him, Finn flipped back, "Thanks for the pep talk. It's been hugely helpful."

Even his brother was against him.

Finn ached to take his wounded soul to the kitchen, where the palace cook would look the other way if he stole some leftovers from the refrigerator and a cabernet from the wine cellar. The refuge of his childhood called to him, but he swallowed it away.

Prince Alain didn't have the luxury of hiding or licking his wounds.

"Is Father in residence?" Finn asked instead. "I need to be briefed on the situation with Alhendra."

The crown prince nodded and jerked his head. "In his study."

Finn hadn't lived at the palace in twelve years, but it still welcomed him every time. Footmen called, "Prince Alexander. Prince Alain," as they passed, heads inclined. Maids smiled and bobbed. Finn gave each one a return nod or smile and prayed they didn't take offense if it wasn't entirely heartfelt.

The king glanced up as his sons entered his study. "Excellent timing, Alexander. Finn, good to see you, son."

Respectfully, both men waited for their father to continue speaking in deference to his station.

King Laurent stood and leaned a hip on the desk, as was his habit when doling out difficult news. "Tension is high with our friends in Greece, Italy and Turkey. We're going to send all four of our warships, and it's not going to be well received by the whole of Delamer's population. I trust you have good news for us in that regard?"

Finn shook his head as his stomach rolled. Alexander had excellent timing but Finn's was horrific—now would have been the opportune time to be announcing his engagement to Juliet Villere.

Yeah. He could see how Juliet had taken everything the wrong way.

"Juliet did not find the idea of marrying me to her liking." Finn laced his hands behind his back and spread his legs to brace for the full brunt of the disappointment to come.

His father's mouth flattened into a thin line. Because Finn had failed on every level to deliver to the king's expectations.

"That's unfortunate."

A tiny, inadequate word to describe what it truly was. "Yes, sir."

The king's gaze sliced through Finn and he was seventeen again, being called on the carpet to explain why he hadn't danced with the King of Spain's daughter at a charity ball. Or why he hadn't scored as high on his mathematics baccalaureate as Alexander. Why by age twenty-seven, he hadn't been promoted to captain. The past year had been full of such carpet-treading moments, especially when the photo surfaced of him twined with a leggy blonde on a pool table.

"The relationship is unrecoverable then?" his father asked, his forefinger tapping thoughtfully on his chin, as if they were discussing the budget for the country's infrastructure instead of his son's unhappily-ever-after.

"Yes, I'm fairly certain it's over forever this time."

The cramp in his chest blindsided him and he blinked away moisture from the corners of his eyes. Hopefully no one had noticed him being such a girl.

How was he supposed to get through this? Juliet had a bad habit of breaking his heart and he had a bad habit of letting her. But this time, it wasn't solely her fault. Despite his comment to Alexander, Juliet's stubborn nature wasn't fully to blame.

The die had been cast when the photographer snapped that picture at Elise's party back in the States. Once his father put the kidnapping in motion, things couldn't have played out differently. If his father hadn't kidnapped them,

Juliet never would have spoken to him again anyway—of that, he was certain.

And even if she had, clearly they lacked whatever was needed to finally resolve their history. Worse, she'd never side with the crown. What new disaster might Finn have invited into his life if he'd returned from Île de Etienne engaged, only to have Juliet create another scandal?

"Well, then." The king paused, nodding. "We need to find another way for you to be useful."

Useful. It was the only thing Finn had ever wanted from his father—to be told he wasn't the spare heir but someone with value and importance. Just like Alexander. "I'm happy to do whatever's required of me."

"You're hereby ordered to report to the bridge of the *Aurélien.*" The king's eyebrows drew together over his uncompromising and authoritative gaze. "If you can't inspire a girl to marry you, maybe you can inspire a country to back down."

A second chance. Finn latched on to it with gratitude. He could still make a difference.

"I can." He would, gladly. It was a place to vent his frustration and aggression, spending it all on the backs of Delamer's enemies.

"I wish I could be there." The slight wistfulness in Alexander's tone didn't escape Finn.

"The front line is not your place," Finn said as gently as he could, suddenly glad he had the freedom to take a few more risks.

Alexander was born to his role, but it's so narrow. Juliet's voice floated to him on a wisp of memory. *You have the opportunity to make yours whatever you want it to be.*

Uneasily, he shifted from foot to foot. He'd spent the bulk of his life feeling inferior to the crown prince. Perhaps he'd viewed his birth order with too limited a lens.

Had Juliet broadened his vision that much in a few short

days? They'd dated for nearly a year the first time without any such revelations. Seclusion had positives, too.

Instantly, he was back on Île de Etienne, lying with Juliet on a blanket with the heavens opened above them and talking about making it work long-term. He missed her so much, it weakened his knees for a moment.

"Yes, your brother is needed at home." The king's odd half smile had Finn doing a double take.

"Portia's pregnant," Alexander explained.

The word hit Finn square in the solar plexus. Pure jealousy warred with the joy his brother's announcement evoked. He was going to be an uncle.

But in that moment he wanted to be the one announcing his impending fatherhood, the one with that glint of pure awe and amazement shining from his eyes. At this very moment, Juliet might be pregnant—and Finn had ruined any chance of having a relationship with the mother of his child. Would she even tell him if she'd conceived?

"Congratulations," he choked out.

"Thanks. She's having…complications. It's been a little touch and go. The doctor has her on one hundred percent bed rest and there's still a possibility she could lose the baby." Concern for his wife added a weight to Alexander's voice that Finn didn't recall hearing before.

It never occurred to him that his brother might be walking such a difficult path while Finn had been off frolicking in Alexander's house and drinking his wine.

"Well, of course you can't ship out with the rest of us. Take care of Portia and your child. That's the most important thing you can be doing," Finn said firmly. "I'll take up the mantle of defense."

If that defense required him to lay down his life for his people, he would do that without a whimper. Juliet was one of them after all, and now, he had a whole lot more to defend. Portia was carrying the heir to the Delamer throne.

Finn's only regret was that he would go out with his relationship with Juliet so fractured.

Twelve

Home. Juliet threw her arms around her mom, and the smell of fresh bread and cinnamon in her mother's hair was enough to finally thaw Juliet's flash-frozen internal organs, which had seized up during the interminable helicopter ride with the Royal Duo.

"We've been worried." Her mom smoothed Juliet's hair, as she used to when Juliet was little. "We called your cell phone so many times without an answer. We finally tracked down Elise Arundel and she said you'd gone on an extended vacation with the prince. We were not expecting him to be your match."

Elise. The king must have contacted her and made up some story about Juliet and Finn jetting off to an exotic locale to reconnect, conveniently leaving out the part where they hadn't done so under their own volition.

At least Elise hadn't been left to worry. The king got a tiny minutia of a point for that.

"I wasn't expecting it either," Juliet muttered. "I'm sorry you were worried. But I'm okay."

A total and utter lie. Her insides felt as if she'd sanded them with sharp, grainy silt and then swallowed seawater. She longed for the hollowness she'd carried for the past year. Nothingness was vastly preferable to *this*.

Juliet needed to call Elise immediately and tell her EA International's computer program was fundamentally flawed. She and Finn were not a good match, they weren't meant to be together and if Juliet never saw him again, it would be too soon.

Her mother held Juliet at arm's length, peering over her reading glasses to do a sweeping once-over of her daughter. "Where've you been? Elise said we shouldn't worry, but it was like you dropped off the face of the earth. Did something happen with Prince Alain?"

Finn had insisted it was okay to tell the truth about what had happened, as if he could have stopped her from blabbing to everyone what he'd done, but the righteous burn of anger had so drained her, now that she had the chance to flay him alive to her parents, she couldn't open her mouth.

She just wanted to be here in the circle of her family, where no one had hidden motives and everyone loved her. She wanted to forget, not feed the flames.

"It's a long story. Nothing happened with Finn. Nothing is going to happen with him. I'll tell you the rest some other time."

Collette, her youngest sister and the only Villere sibling still living at home, clasped her hands together with bright anticipation. "Will you be going back to America then, or are you staying here?"

"I'm here for now. I have no idea what my plans are."

"Oh." Collette's face fell. "I got permission to visit you in America. I was hoping you were going back."

Maybe Juliet shouldn't have been so forthcoming with her family about her plans to marry an American. Of course, when she'd left Delamer, she hadn't expected to be back home, heart shredded again courtesy of the Triple Blade Finn Special.

"We're happy you're home, and you may stay as long as you like," her father said gruffly, with a warning glare at Collette, and gave Juliet a one-armed hug. "We have to move fast now that the king's announced he's sending forces to join the other countries standing up against Al-hendra."

That hadn't taken long. Finn had probably blown the "all hands on deck" horn the moment he hit the palace doors, firmly in his element.

Her father clapped his hands. "We're organizing a pro-test and you're our best strategist. It's a shame it didn't work with the prince. We could have used him on our side."

Juliet's legs weakened and she sank to the couch. She'd been home five minutes and they wanted to get started on another protest? Her parents were no better than Finn's.

"I'm pretty tired."

Did *everyone* want her around only for what she could do for them?

"Of course you are, dear. That's enough for now, Edu-ard." Her mother bustled Juliet into the kitchen to ply her with crepes stuffed with fruit and a steaming cup of Italian coffee. Their best. Because she was the prodigal daugh-ter, returning to the fold after running away to America.

Her family loved her. They weren't glad she'd come home so they could channel her passion against the king or hijack her strategic mind. Finn's betrayal colored every-thing, but not everyone was like him, using people for his or her own agenda.

No one mentioned Alhendra or protests for the rest of the day, and Juliet's spine slowly became less rigid. But when she stopped bracing for the next round of gleeful hand-rubbing over how to best foil King Laurent, her mind wandered to Finn, and she could still smell him on her skin.

Just a few hours ago, they'd twined their limbs together so tightly, it was a wonder the scent of his arousal and excitement hadn't infused her blood.

Leaping up in the middle of Collette's impassioned speech about why she should get to go to university in America, Juliet fled upstairs to her parents' one narrow bathroom and took a tepid shower, the best the water heater could do. She scrubbed and scrubbed but the scent of well-loved man wouldn't vacate her nose.

She dried off and buried herself in the spare bed, quilts up to her neck. And that's when the tears flowed. Crying. Over a cretin whom she never should have trusted in the first place. Who had systematically broken down her defenses in a plot to discredit her family's position against the king.

But in her mind's eye, she could relive only the absolute relief she'd experienced when he'd pulled her from the water. The care and concern in his expression as he watched over her while she burned with fever. The glint in his eye when he confessed he was still in love with her.

All lies and manipulation. Had to be.

By morning, she'd slept only a few hours and developed a raging need to do something—anything—to wash Prince Alain from her system once and for all. And if it hurt him, so much the better.

She cornered her father in the kitchen. "Let's talk about that protest."

Over the next few days, Juliet routed her energy into managing her sisters, cousins, aunts, uncles, their various spouses and offspring, as well as her parents, into a protest machine of the first order. Even the littlest ones could color fliers or staple pamphlets, and she corralled everyone with a fervor that earned her the nickname General Juliet.

The irony of the military-influenced moniker she could do without.

An organized protest was her first goal and the king's head on a platter her second. Figuratively, of course, but if it happened for real in her dreams, no one else had to know.

If King Laurent would simply call the warships home and show a commitment to staying out of foreign conflicts, that would work too. Then they'd have a shot at softening the remaining military mandates. Finally.

The Villere household buzzed with activity toward that end from dawn until midnight, which Juliet embraced wholeheartedly because she never had time to think. She didn't have the luxury of counting the days until a pregnancy test might yield accurate results, thus determining the course of her future.

At night, she shared her bed with a cousin, sister or niece—sometimes more than one—and the cramped quarters suited her well. If she wasn't alone, she couldn't cry, but the tears were there, waiting for the right tipping point to spill out.

One afternoon, as Juliet argued via phone with the local magistrate about a permit to assemble, Gertrude tugged on her skirt and held up a plain brown paper-wrapped package, proudly clutched tight in her five-year-old hands.

Please be the missing four-color mailers. They'd gotten only half the order from the printer and they had little time to go back to press. The protest was scheduled for tomorrow, at the palace gates.

"Thank you," Juliet mouthed to her cousin's daughter and set the package on the counter, sandwiching the phone between her shoulder and ear to slice the neatly taped lid with kitchen shears. "I'm aware the normal processing time is five days, Mr. Le Clercq," she said into the phone. "I'm asking for an exception."

She flipped the box open. The phone dropped from her shoulder and clattered to the floor.

Shoes. The box contained shoes—*her* shoes. Alligator sandals lay nestled in carefully arranged padding. The same ones she'd worn on her dinner date with Finn, back in Dallas, which she'd donned with a hesitant sense of hope. The same ones she thought she'd lost when she woke up barefooted in the dark, with Finn's voice as her only guide.

The cuts had healed where she'd tramped barefoot across the rocky shore of Île de Etienne. But the internal scars she'd developed there…those she could never be rid of.

"Are you ill?" Aunt Vivian eyed her from across the room, her warm brown eyes magnified by thick glasses.

Juliet waved at her, too numb and speechless to respond.

How in the world had these come back to her? Mystified, she glanced at the return label she hadn't bothered to read because she'd assumed the contents would be something far more innocuous.

Finn. Her heart squeezed. He'd sent them. Which meant he'd had them all along. Something sharp knifed through her chest. If only he could return the rest of what he'd taken from her. The possibility of a different match with EA International. Her ability to trust. Her ability to forget, especially if she ended up pregnant after all.

And now this. A physical reminder of what she'd gambled and lost.

Hands shaking, she smashed the lid closed, covering the sandals, and stuffed the box in the back of the pantry in a place no one would find it. Then she put a sack of potatoes on top.

Unable to quite catch her breath, Juliet fled to the living room, where Uncle Jean-Louis was dozing in front of the lone TV. The simple Villere house sported few of the luxuries she'd experienced while staying in Alexander's house, but she'd take it ten times out of ten over anything else. Especially a residence with a Montagne in it.

She just needed a couple of minutes to get the threat of tears a bit more under control. It wouldn't do for anyone to know she was upset or that a mere man had so negatively affected her. Mindless entertainment would fix her up in a jiffy.

Predictably, the remote was nowhere to be found and the news channel her uncle had tuned to was covering the conglomeration of warships in the Mediterranean off the coast of Greece. Because that was *all* the news stations discussed, as well as her family, she knew Finn was on one. Good. That meant he'd taken her request to stay away from her to heart.

And that was the tipping point. A single tear broke loose, tracking down her cheek. Then another, and suddenly the floodgates busted from their moorings.

This was clearly the wrong place to decompress.

As she was about to stand and flee, Aunt Vivian popped her head into the room and shoved Juliet's phone at her. "Weren't you talking to someone—oh, *cherie.* What's wrong?"

Mortified, Juliet shook her head and motioned the elder woman to go back to the kitchen. There was no way she could speak coherently. Neither did she want to, not even to her favorite aunt.

Vivian ignored the clear "go away" sign and shuffled to the couch to engulf Juliet in a warm hug. "It's not as bad as all that, is it?"

Juliet pressed her face into her aunt's midsection and nodded, too beyond any sense of control to care that she'd wet Vivian's dress through. She was still in love with Finn and apparently nothing he did, no matter how much he hurt her, could erase it.

"Your young man is a fool," Vivian clucked. "You'd think royal DNA would produce more sense."

Juliet's neck jerked involuntarily and she glanced up at her aunt. Had her mother spilled all her daughter's recent activities to her sister? "How did you know I was crying over Finn?"

She smiled and nodded at the TV. "He's a handsome devil but clearly addled in the head if he's given you up."

Finn's handsome face indeed filled the screen as he answered a reporter's questions. Clad in his finest dress uniform decorated with medals of honor, he was breathtaking. Literally. Her lungs hitched and she meant to look away. But couldn't.

Greedily, she searched his face for any clue, no matter how small, to his state of mind. Did he miss her? Was he sorry? She hoped he lay awake at night and suffered. As she did.

Absently, she gnawed on a fingernail. When he smiled at the reporter, it wasn't the same one he always gave Juliet. Fine lines around his mouth and eyes crinkled, aging him. He looked worn out.

When would the urge to soothe him and make sure he took care of himself go away?

Aunt Vivian settled next to Juliet on the sofa, careful not to disturb Uncle Jean-Louis, though a freight train at full speed probably wouldn't wake him. Juliet glanced at her aunt, who seemed content to quietly watch the clip with her.

"The first round of negotiations went well," Finn said into the microphone.

Negotiations?

Warships had assembled in the Ionian Sea to intimidate Alhendra into meekly laying down its arms. Might made right after all, in the minds of those with the might. At what point did anyone ever intend to negotiate?

Finn continued speaking smoothly in his rich public address voice. His royal DNA might have left out any sense, but it certainly afforded him authoritative command under pressure and the ability to look devastating while doing it.

He wrapped up with, "I'm gratified to be a member of the contingent invited into the interior of Alhendra. We hope to have a peaceful cease-fire and an end to this stand-off signed and delivered this afternoon."

Finn was a member of the diplomatic committee negotiating with Alhendra? Juliet shook her head, but the ban-
ner scrolling across the bottom of the screen reiterated
that point in capital letters. Not only was he a member of
the committee, but Finn had been instrumental in getting
through the ordeal with no discharge of weapons.

He wasn't a diplomat. He was far too pigheaded and
obstinate. Wasn't he?

"What was the key to the negotiations?" the reporter
asked.

"Meeting in the middle," Finn responded immediately,
and the words seared through Juliet's stomach. The same
thing he'd asked her to do, but then refused to budge from
his side even one little centimeter.

Yet he'd done it successfully with an entire country.
How?

The question stayed with her as she tossed fitfully that
night. Fortunately, she'd had the foresight to bar any cousins or siblings from her room, citing a need for alone-time.
Too much weighed on her mind to sleep. The protest was
in the morning, and they'd be doing it illegally since she'd
failed to secure the permit to assemble in time.

Juliet would probably be arrested again. At least this
time she wasn't publicly linked with Finn, thus saving him
the embarrassment of it.

And why would she care? He deserved everything she
had to throw at him.

The sentiment rang false in the darkened room.

Regardless of how much Bernard's death had hurt her
personally and hurt her family, Finn hadn't deserved the
fallout from Juliet's role in the first protest. It had been a
mistake. Born of highly charged emotions, sure, but handled very poorly, especially given that she'd claimed to be
in love with him.

For the first time, she thought about how he must have
felt. How he must have seen it as a betrayal and a clear di-

vision of sides. She'd chosen family over Finn. Kind of like what she'd accused him of doing back on Île de Etienne.

Her eyes burned with unshed tears. Finn had hurt her— but that didn't mean he didn't love her. Sometimes people messed up, and trying to forget about their mistakes wasn't the answer.

Her fingers felt for the knob of the bedside table, and she pulled open the drawer to extract the book inside, then snapped on the light. Each page contained a pressed flower, one from every bouquet Finn had given her. Why she'd kept it, tucked away here in her childhood home, escaped her.

Tonight, as she ran a fingertip over first one stalk, then the next, it comforted her. These blooms had once been alive, thriving, stretching toward the sun, and should by all rights have disintegrated into dust by now. It was the sad cycle of life for a flower. But she'd carefully preserved each one, pressing it dry until she had something that would last a very long time.

Was there something similar she should have done—but hadn't—to break the cycle she and Finn seemed destined to travel? All she knew was that she was miserable without him and wanted it to stop.

She clutched the book to her chest and held it until dawn. As the sun rose and light filtered through the curtains, warmth entered her body for the first time since she'd left Île de Etienne. And she was at peace with what came next.

They had to cancel the protest.

Finn had resolved the conflict by influencing everyone to compromise. She could compromise too. For real this time, by not leading a protest against the father of the man she loved. At least half—or maybe all—of her motivation in participating in the protest had more to do with their breakup. Not because she truly believed in the cause.

She'd started the cycle—it was up to her to end it. Her relationship with Finn might never recover from the stupid things they'd both done, but that could be dealt with later.

She had a protest to stop.

People milled through the kitchen, fired up and ready to see heads roll.

"The nerve," her father said, and stabbed a finger at the morning paper's headlines. "The palace is hosting a ball tonight to celebrate Delamer successfully throwing its weight around in Alhendra."

Her mother chimed in. "We're moving the protest to this evening. We'll stand arm to arm across the road by the gates and refuse to let anyone's limousine pass. It'll be very effective as all those wealthy, entitled people wait endlessly in their finery. They'll be forced to read our signs and hear our voices united against the king."

Juliet's sleep-deprived brain had difficulty keeping up with the rapid turn of the conversation. Those *wealthy, entitled people* were the friends and family of Finn, who had resolved what could have been a bloody mess without any loss of life.

"But the conflict is over. They said so on the news yesterday. What are you protesting?"

"It goes against everything we believe in." Her father thumped the table, rattling all the silverware and earning a murmured *here-here* from several of her relatives. "Romanticizing war and aggression with an expensive party and honoring those who traipsed off to perpetuate it is almost worse than forcing young boys into service."

"The king requires mandatory service because Delamer is such a small country," she blurted out. Her father stared at her as if she'd lost her mind, when in actuality, she'd just found it. "The armed forces would be a joke without it."

She'd heard Finn say it a dozen times. But never really listened. She touched the linked hearts fastened to the chain under her dress, one a mirror of the other. She and Finn were matched because they were exactly alike. Passionate. Stubborn. As often as she'd accused Finn of refusing to budge from his side, how many steps had she taken toward his?

He hadn't championed military reform to his father because he hadn't bought into it—and she'd completely discounted his reasons. He loved his people and loved his job. How much had she hurt him by refusing to see that was why he didn't take her side?

The hearts on her necklace clutched each other, one keeping the other from falling. But that worked only if the other reached back. Real love wasn't about what you had to give up but what you gained when you held on. That was Elise's message.

"Half the country borders water," Juliet continued. "Mandatory service leads to a strong naval presence. And maybe that's not the best way to staff the military, but we should be offering alternatives, not protests."

"Juliet!" Her mother's mouth pinched together, trembling. "Your brother died because of that philosophy."

"Bernard's death was an accident. We have to move on. Forgive ourselves and stop blaming the king. It's no one's fault. Which is the very definition of an accident."

The burden she'd carried for over a year lifted. Not completely, but enough. It wasn't her fault Bernard died. It wasn't the king's. It certainly wasn't Finn's, but she'd transferred some of her own guilt to him unconsciously. Guilt because she'd introduced Bernard and Finn. Guilt because she'd not better taught Bernard to listen when his superior officers listed safety regulations. That guilt had driven a lot of her decisions but no more.

She squared her shoulders. "The protest is illegal. We shouldn't do it for that reason alone. But maybe a protest isn't the best way to handle this in the first place. Let's try diplomacy for once."

"The way the king leads should be what's criminal, not a civilized protest. You had a chance to use diplomacy with the prince. That's why we're doing it this way." Her father swept her with his hard, cynical gaze, but she saw only a broken man who'd lost his son. It was easy to forgive him

"You go ahead with the protest, if that's your choice But you'll do it without me."

Juliet turned and left the room. She used Skype to contact Elise on the other side of the world, then realized i was still early morning in Dallas. Shockingly, the match maker answered almost immediately.

"Juliet. Is everything okay?" Elise had enabled video and Juliet could see her short, dark hair was slightly mussed as if she'd rolled from bed.

"I was about to disconnect. Sorry to wake you."

"You didn't."

Oh. Elise wasn't alone and worse, had been dragged away from something much more fun than a surprise call "*Really* sorry to disturb you then."

The matchmaker laughed, but the wistfulness in her ex pression wasn't hard to read. "I was neck-deep in my bud get. I only wish I had a better reason to be awake this early."

In the month Juliet had lived with Elise during her make over, the matchmaker hadn't dated at all. But she obviously wanted to meet someone and clearly loved a good happily ever-after. Why didn't Elise enter her own information in EA International's computer and find herself a match? I would only make sense.

"Well, since you're awake, I need your help." Juliet bi her lip and went for broke. It took her ten minutes, but she told Elise the whole horrible story, including the part about her own failings.

It wasn't so easy to forgive herself, but she'd taken the first step. Now she had to take several more, and there was only one place adequate enough, public enough, to do it.

"What can I do?" Elise asked. "Name it and it's yours."

Juliet didn't hesitate. "Wave your fairy godmother wand and make me look like someone worthy of a prince. I'm going to the ball."

Thirteen

Finn's head ached. The limo hadn't moved in ten minutes, but that was okay. The faster it moved, the sooner he'd get to the palace and honestly, he wasn't sure how much more back-clapping and accolades and festivity he could handle.

The conflict with Alhendra was over. But the tension Finn had carried for days wasn't.

With only Gomez and LaSalle for company, Finn had visited the neighborhood in Preveza. Alhendra's missile had decimated twelve blocks, killing four hundred people and leveling buildings. The city would never be the same. It haunted him.

The carnage propelled him to insist on being a part of the diplomatic committee working with Alhendra to put an end to the standoff. His father should have been the one, or Alexander at the very least, but it spoke of Delamer's standing in the United Nations that no one batted an eye when King Laurent announced Finn would be the delegate for his country.

His father's faith in him meant everything. Enough to forgive the king for his role in the kidnapping.

That vivid imagery of the devastated bombing site stayed with him through the cease-fire negotiations. It fueled him, energized him to the point of crystalline determination—Alhendra's leaders would not walk out of that room without agreeing to turn over their weapons. Period. But neither would he allow his ships or anyone else's to fire on Alhendra in retaliation.

Compromise.

It had worked.

He'd intended only to resolve the conflict—and in the process, he'd used the opportunity to expand his role, his usefulness to the crown. He'd made it what he wanted it to be instead of waiting for someone to define it for him. No longer did he feel boxed in by his birth order or as if the military was all he had or could hope to have. The sky was the limit.

The victory was bittersweet because Juliet wasn't there to share it with him.

Finn peered out the limo's front window. The tail lights of the town car in front of them flashed as the traffic screeched to a halt again. "What's going on, James?" Finn called to the driver.

"There are several people in the street," James said, eyes trained to the road ahead. "They appear to be blocking traffic."

That's what Finn got for going back to his modest house late last night after arriving in Delamer via plane, well ahead of the ships scheduled to return today. But he'd wanted to be alone and then his mother sprang this ball on him, insisting a party in his honor was the least she could do to show pride in her son. How could he say no?

"I'll walk from here, thanks." Finn reached for the door handle. "If you can get out of this snarl, go have a cup of coffee somewhere. I'll text you when I'm ready to leave."

He hit the pavement and Gomez and LaSalle followed. His bodyguards stayed glued to his side now that Finn had international celebrity for something other than the number of shots he could do in a row. Unfortunately, resolving a conflict with extremists solicited much more dangerous attention than that of paparazzi and socialites.

As Finn neared the palace gates, shouts from the people blocking traffic grew clearer.

Peace not war. No more warships.

The shouting people carried signs, holding them aloft and waving them at those trying to enter the palace gates.

It was a protest. Icy waves cut through Finn's stomach. Not this again, not now.

Almost against his will, he searched the faces, though it was almost unnecessary to confirm his suspicions about the identity of the protesters. But he had to know.

His eyes locked with Collette Villere. Juliet's sister.

The disappointment was sharp. But what had he expected? Of course Juliet was here with her family, standing on her side of the line with pride and stubborn determination. Nonetheless, something died inside, something he'd have sworn had been killed off long ago.

His gaze traveled down the row of Villere protesters but Juliet's brown hair and slight form wasn't among them. A ridiculous and fleeting bloom of hope unfurled. Ridiculous because she was probably perched halfway up one of the stone balustrades flanking the gates, bullhorn in hand, inciting the crowd verbally as her family held signs.

But she wasn't. Juliet was nowhere to be found.

Collette was too far away in the crush of people and vehicles to ask after Juliet's whereabouts. With one last puzzled glance over his shoulder, Finn walked the remaining five hundred yards up the paved entrance to the palace and mounted the steps.

Two footmen opened the wide oak doors, one to each side, and admitted him to the grand foyer. Finn paused at the head of the marble steps leading to the floor below, while another footman announced him, droning out his full title with pomp and ceremony. Necks craned as his name caught the attention of the crowd of partygoers below who had braved the walk to the palace from their boxed-in vehicles.

Applause broke out and Finn took it with a grin. What else could he do? These were his people and he'd walked into negotiations with Alhendra on their behalf. It was nice to know they appreciated his efforts.

Finn mingled with the crowd, accepting the hearty back-slaps and handshakes with as much cheer as he could muster, but his throat burned with each *bonsoir* and *how are you* he said. Unbelievably, no one wanted to discuss Alhendra, but the identity of the protesters outside was on everyone's lips. The sidelong glances and blatant comments about the year-old scandal from every knot of people Finn encountered grew tiresome.

Especially since both Alexander *and* his father got in on that action.

Thankfully, no one mentioned Juliet by name. Obviously she hadn't joined her family yet but the instant she did, placard in hand and shouts for justice raised above the noise of the street, he'd undoubtedly hear about it.

Alexander left to go home to the still-bedridden Portia, and King Laurent abandoned Finn to talk racehorses with his brother, the Duke of Carlier. As they'd competed against each other on the track for over forty years, Finn could have repeated their conversation verbatim without hearing a syllable of it. He was glad to be alone for a moment.

The queen worked her way over to Finn, and he bussed both cheeks. "You look stunning, Mother. This is a great party."

"Go on." She swiped at Finn with a gloved hand, but the tenderness she'd always held for her youngest shone from her eyes. "I'm glad you're home safe. I sent some of the grounds crew to the gates to deal with that…issue. Hopefully they won't disturb us further."

A shadow leached the pleasure from the queen's face.

When would this ever end? Juliet and her family were ruining his mother's party.

Finn excused himself as the Earl of Ghent struck up a conversation with his mother and scouted in vain for a passing tray of champagne. What kind of party was this where the hostess tortured her son with invisible waitstaff?

Finally, he caught up with a beleaguered waiter on the far side of the hall. The crush was stifling; more than a hundred and fifty people milled and laughed and celebrated. Normally Finn loved a good party, but this was overwhelming.

He raised the flute of champagne to his lips as a murmur broke out over the crowd, their gazes cutting toward the entrance. A footman called out, "Miss Juliet Villere."

The name echoed over and over and faded away until dead silence cloaked the room. Then, there she was.

Juliet paused at the head of the stairs, and the flute nearly slipped from Finn's suddenly numb fingers. She was resplendent in a shimmery gown, so light and airy, it looked as if it had been spun from a hundred silver spiders. Fit only for a princess. Hair swept up and pinned, face accented with a hint of color, she stole his breath.

What was she doing here?

She was pregnant. Joy flooded him so fast, his knees turned to jelly.

No, it was too soon to know that. There was only one reason she'd crashed the ball.

His stomach twisting with tension, Finn started toward her, fully intending to personally throw her out on her admittedly spectacular rear end. How dare she waltz in here? If she thought she was going to bring her rabble-rousing, anti-military rants into his mother's party, she had more nerve and less intelligence than he'd ever credited.

Juliet Villere was not going to embarrass or upset his mother.

The crowd parted as he marched through. More than a hundred feet separated him from Juliet, but their gazes locked and something gentle and shiny welled in hers.

"Stop!" she commanded, the word reverberating in the quiet hall.

Finn was so surprised, he did.

"Wait there." Juliet gathered her skirt in one hand and descended the stairs slowly, with a grace he'd never seen. She moved like an apparition, like a vision. Was that what was going on? He'd fallen asleep and dreamed up this scene?

Juliet reached the floor, flanked by wide-eyed guests in beaded gowns and black tie. She watched him as she approached, her gaze steady and unapologetic.

Everything broken inside ached that he couldn't greet her as a lover, with a passionate kiss. That they'd parted with insurmountable differences separating them.

"What do you want?" he called harshly.

Her smile was shaky but for him alone. "For you to stand there while I cross this huge expanse of middle ground."

His eyelids shut and he swallowed, but the tightness in his throat wouldn't ease. When he opened his eyes, she was still moving toward him, beautiful and real and exactly what he'd always wanted. She wasn't compromising—this was something far more profound.

She'd come here to try again, not to embarrass him or bring the protest inside. She wasn't even participating in the protest. She was siding with Finn, not her family. Publicly. It was an apology for participating in the first protest, the very antithesis of what she'd done a year ago.

Something massive welled up and broke over him in a wave, healing so many of his deep wounds instantly.

But then she stopped just past the halfway point. She

glanced down and then back up, her expression clouded.
The message was clear.

She wanted him to meet her in the middle.

After her brave entrance to this ball, uninvited and unwelcome, how could he not?

Yet he hesitated, the man and the prince at war, as always.

Juliet's dramatic and public move meant a lot to him.
But what had really changed between them? They would be
right back in the same boat next week—battling out their
opposite agendas and being stubborn and holding grudges.
Their families would always be a problem, always interfere
with their relationship.

He couldn't do this again, this back-and-forth dance between the duty and privilege of his title and the simple life
he wished for where he was just a man who loved a woman.

He couldn't walk across that middle ground.

So Finn sank to his knees and crawled to the woman
he loved.

Juliet nearly dissolved into a big puddle of sensations
as Finn crossed the remaining expanse of marble on his
hands and knees.

The murmurs of the crowd melted away as he reached
her and rose up on his knees to take her hand. His beautiful
eyes sought hers and out poured the contents of his soul.

"What are you doing?" she asked, emotion clogging
her throat.

"I didn't have any broken glass to crawl over. But I'm
here to tell you marble is a close second in the pain department," he said wryly with an endearing wince.

"But why are you crawling at all? Here, in front of everyone." The curious crowd pressed in, anxious to catch
every word of the drama unfolding around them in all its
titillating splendor.

"We can't keep going through the same endless loop,

arguing and hurting each other. It has to be different this time. You did your half, wanting me to meet you in the middle. So I did."

Oh, goodness. Her heart tripped once and settled back in her chest, content and peaceful for the first time in... forever.

He was coming to her as a man, not a prince.

It was symbolic—and so unnecessary. She shook her head. "I'm the one who needed to take those steps. You're who you are by blood, and I selfishly tried to stand in the way of that. Testing you to see if I was more important than your heritage, demanding proof of your devotion by asking you to be someone ordinary. I don't want that. Stand up. I want Prince Alain in all his glory."

Prince, lieutenant, helicopter pilot, lover, friend, rescuer and occasional video game partner—all rolled into one delicious package.

The crowd gasped and tittered and a couple of the women clapped. One was the queen. That seemed like a plus in Juliet's favor.

Still clasping her hand, Finn climbed to his feet, his expression solemn as he called out to the room at large. "Show's over, folks. Go back to the party and enjoy my mother's incredible hospitality."

Dispersing with glacial speed, the crowd drifted back to their conversations and champagne, shooed away largely by the queen herself. Juliet could really learn to like Finn's mother.

To Juliet, Finn simply said, "Dance with me."

Oh, no. Now she had to come clean.

"Is this the part where I should admit the buckle on my shoe broke?" Her mouth twitched and she tried really hard to keep the laugh from bubbling out. "I can't exactly walk."

She stuck her foot out from under the gossamer skirt to show him the offending alligator sandals that she'd rescued from beneath the potatoes. That had probably been the last straw for these poor shoes, which had followed her through thick and thin as she figured out the most important lessons of her life. There was no way she'd have worn any other pair tonight.

"*That's* why you stopped?" A hundred emotions vied for purchase on his face, and he finally picked self-deprecating amusement. "You were going to cross the entire length of the floor, weren't you?"

She nodded. "It was the least you deserved. I'm sorry I was so shortsighted over the last year. And I'm sorry for the protest. It was wrong and I shouldn't have done it. I love you. And did very little to show you how much."

A wealth of emotion swept over his face in a tide, transforming him from merely handsome to magnificent.

"I made mistakes too." He drew her hand to his mouth and pressed his lips to the back of her hand in a long kiss. "My blood may be blue but the organ pumping it belongs to you. Not my father, not Delamer. I love you too, more than I love anything. I'm sorry I didn't honor my relationship with you above them."

The words were sweet and the thrill in her chest even sweeter. That's what made it easy to refute his mixed-up declaration.

"But I'm saying I don't want you to choose me above them any longer. That was our problem all along. Too much pressure to make choices between absolutes. Love obviously isn't enough. Let's find the middle ground."

He grinned. "I take it you liked my speech. I had no idea it would produce all this." He motioned to her dress. "You're the most gorgeous woman here."

A blush that she hoped was becoming fired up in her cheeks.

"It was inspiring. But I think my fairy godmother had more to do with this look than anything. Elise," she clarified when he raised his brows. "You don't think I put this outfit together by myself, do you?"

The benefits of Skype and a webcam for the consummate tomboy could not be overstated. Elise deserved a bonus for working her magic across fiber-optic lines.

"I'm more interested in what's under it than how it came to be."

Heat zigzagged between them and her abdomen fluttered. "What's under it is a woman who's lousy at forgetting the past. Let's try forgiveness instead, shall we? Please, please forgive me for all the horrible hurt I've caused you."

So easy. The answer had been there all along. Forgiveness was the key, not forgetting.

Eyes shiny with tenderness, he smiled. "Already done. Will you do the same for me?"

"Done." She returned the smile and bumped his knee with hers. "That happened the moment you hit the marble. Are we going to make it this time, then?"

"Yes." He nodded decisively. "I couldn't possibly let you get away again. You're going to have to marry me. No pregnancy required, though I'd welcome one at some point in the future."

Princess Juliet. The thought shivered down her spine with equal parts trepidation and awe. "Is this a marriage proposal?"

He shook his head. "More of a promise of one to come, when I'm not so unprepared and dazzled by your sheer beauty." But then he paused and his expression turned earnest. "You'd be a princess for life. A card-carrying member of the House of Couronne. Princess Juliet of Montagne, Duchess of Marechal, along with a ton of other unwieldy titles. Can you do it?"

He didn't mean just the jumble of new names and royal protocol. She'd be choosing him over her family, over her commoner heritage, over Bernard's memory. She'd be far past that middle ground every day, forever. Thank goodness.

Best of all, Elise's efforts toward polishing Juliet's rough edges would actually pay off.

Her grip on his hand tightened. "The better question is, can you? I'm not diplomatic like you. I have opinions and I'll not be shy in giving them to you. The people may never forgive you for marrying me."

"They will. Because they'll see what I see. The People's Princess, who believes passionately in their best interests. You got that new school built. You care about their lives or you wouldn't have protested the mandatory service law."

In his eyes, all the qualities he'd listed reflected back at her. Elise's computer had matched them because they shared a bone-deep belief in their convictions. They were a passionate, stubborn, yet thoroughly formidable team, and together they could change the world.

"Besides," he continued, "when I came across the floor on my knees, it was as public of a declaration as yours. I'm on your side. Everyone will know that by the time the sun rises tomorrow."

"And I'm on your side." The best compromise—instead of giving a little, they'd both gained everything.

He drew her into his arms and said the sweetest words of all. "Let's get out of here."

She smiled, tipping her face up to bask in his potent, wonderful masculine strength. "That's the best royal decree I've ever heard."

She started to follow him and her alligator sandal fell off, broken buckle clattering to the marble. Before her Prince Charming could escape, she thumbed off the other one and left them both in the middle of the ball.

Where she hoped Finn was taking her—straight to heaven—shoes were optional.

Epilogue

Finn slid the patio door open with his hip and stepped out, champagne in one hand and flutes in the other. Île de Etienne spread out around him, its beauty unchanged in the month since he'd left it via helicopter, crushed and hopeless. Head tipped back, Juliet lay on the cushion lining the wooden patio chair they'd selected to replace the ones sacrificed to fire on the rocky shore below them.

She popped an eye open. "I thought you were taking a call. This looks like a celebration."

"It is." He poured her a glass and then filled his, dinging the rims together lightly. "Alexander just texted me. The papers are processed. Île de Etienne belongs to us."

"Well, technically just you," she corrected as he sat on the next chaise lounge. "Your father's horribly outdated laws don't allow us to own property jointly unless we're married."

"About that," he began casually and toyed with the stem of his flute to cover a sudden bout of the shakes.

Nerves? Really? He'd faced down an extremist government without blinking yet freaked out over a little overt display of affection for a woman who deserved the moon.

Their rocky relationship had finally smoothed out. The past could never be forgotten until it was forgiven, and once that happened, they both lost the desire to prove the other wrong or take sides. It made all the difference.

He cleared his throat and nodded toward the west. "You might want to glance in that direction."

She did and gasped. Written across the breathtaking blue expanse of sky were the words *MARRY ME JULIET* in white smoke. His version of an outrageously romantic proposal. Hopefully she'd think so too.

"A skywriter?" She shot him a glance full of her own brand of overt affection. "Is he on call to also post my response for the whole of Delamer to witness?"

Finn grinned. In one small sentence, she'd put them back on comfortable ground. "If you like. We're going to be in the public eye for a long time. Might as well give them their money's worth."

"Do you have to pay by the letter?" Tapping her chin, she pretended to contemplate. "Because a 'no' would certainly be cheaper."

"Not considering how much this set me back." He extended his hand to offer her his heart encased in gold. The ring was a simple band channel set with sapphires, but it was also one of the original Delamer crown jewels, circa the seventeenth century.

"Oh, Finn." Tears welled in her beautiful green eyes as she stared at the ring. "That's not expensive, it's priceless."

"You better believe it. I had to promise my mother you'd give her a grandchild within the year before she'd agree to let this out of the treasury." He held out his other hand, palm up, and she laid her hand in his without hesitation.

His Juliet was brave, bold and loved everything fiercely, especially him. He prayed he could spend the rest of his life returning it tenfold. "You're my calm in the storm and I need you. Will you marry me?"

She blinked back the still-present tears. "Are you sure? I'm not going to give up on convincing your father to pass the law giving kids a choice between mandatory military service and an internship for their eventual career."

The chuckle escaped before he could catch it. The next fifty years promised to be full of arguments and lots of really great makeup sex. "I don't want you to give up. How's this instead? Eighteen months of service and eighteen months of internship, if they want that instead of continued service."

The idea had come to him the instant she'd pleaded her case the night before. Internship allowed the next generation to begin learning their trade much faster, which in turn kept Delamer relevant and able to compete in the expanding global marketplace. The armed forces would continue to be staffed in the meantime.

"Compromise." Her smile lit her from within. "I like it."

He shrugged. "I've tried to tell you what a great team we are. Now, are you going to marry me or will I wither and die waiting around for you to decide?"

"I'll marry you." She squeezed his hand and he felt it clear to his toes. "But only if you promise I'll have the keys to your heart forever."

Something bright flared in his soul. "I'm afraid I don't have much choice in that. You've had them since the first moment I laid eyes on you right over there." He nodded at the shores of Delamer across the wide expanse of the Mediterranean. There, he was a prince. Here on Île de Etienne, with Juliet, he was just a man who loved a woman. The best of both worlds.

"Good. That means I can come in whenever I want and love you exactly as you deserve."

Finn slid the ring on her finger and kissed her to seal the start of their happily-ever-after.

* * * * *

MILLS & BOON

THE HEART OF ROMANCE

A ROMANCE FOR EVERY READER

MODERN

Prepare to be swept off your feet by sophisticated, sexy and seductive heroes, in some of the world's most glamourous and romantic locations, where power and passion collide.

HISTORICAL

Escape with historical heroes from time gone by. Whether your passion is for wicked Regency Rakes, muscled Vikings or rugged Highlanders, await the romance of the past.

MEDICAL

Set your pulse racing with dedicated, delectable doctors in the high-pressure world of medicine, where emotions run high and passion, comfort love are the best medicine.

True Love

Celebrate true love with tender stories of heartfelt romance, from the rush of falling in love to the joy a new baby can bring, and a focus on emotional heart of a relationship.

Desire

Indulge in secrets and scandal, intense drama and plenty of sizzling ho action with powerful and passionate heroes who have it all: wealth, sta good looks…everything but the right woman.

HEROES

Experience all the excitement of a gripping thriller, with an intense romance at its heart. Resourceful, true-to-life women and strong, fearless face danger and desire - a killer combination!

To see which titles are coming soon, please visit

millsandboon.co.uk/nextmonth

LET'S TALK
Romance

For exclusive extracts, competitions
and special offers, find us online: